To my dear friend

your
name
here
↓

Never forget the great
times we've shared;
I know I won't.
Best wishes

my
name
here
↓

Edited by Jennifer Lynn Baker
Cover illustration "executed" by Jennifer Lynn Baker

"Jennifer Lynn Baker" used by permission of Ian Baker and Nathalie Baker

Published by George D. Christie

Cover illustration by Jennifer Lynn Baker

Designed and produced by
Maine Authors Publishing
558 Main Street, Rockland, Maine 04841
www.maineauthorspublishing.com

I'm Just Sayin'

Or

Maine: The Way Life Should Be
And the way it really is...sort of.
And the way it really should be.

Or

"If you're going to own only one really,
really great book about Maine,
keep this one next to it."

George D. Christie

This book is dedicated to the countless pain-in-the-asses who are the bane of the miserable existence that is my life. Without your incessant intrusions upon my sanity this book would not have been possible. On the other hand, my beer tab would be considerably less and that would be a shame. In short, I thank you one and all for all your help. Now go away.
I'm Just Sayin'

Contents

Prologue

Maine is a one-of-a-kind state. Go ahead and check it out as I did when I carefully researched this entire book one morning during my coffee break. What I discovered was that there's only one Maine, this is it, and that's a fact. Another fact is that Maine is one of only a handful of states you'll never find yourself in unless you wanted to be there in the first place. Now, if you don't want to be here or if you want to avoid Maine, that's not hard to do; just carry on with your life. It's that easy. Go where you want to go. Do want you want to do. You're not going to run into us any time soon. We're not exactly what you might call "in the way." In fact, Maine's rather "out of the way," if you must know.

But let's say you wanted to come to Maine for one odd reason or another. I won't pry as to why; that's your business, not mine. You make your mistakes, I'll make mine. But just say you want to come visit us. While we're not easy to find, rest assured you can find us. Yes, you *can* get here from there, wherever "there" might be, but be forewarned: it's going to take you some effort. Some effort and some courage as well. The effort implies that you will have to make a special trip; Maine isn't on the way to somewhere else. The courage is needed because you'll have to pass through hell and high water to get to us. "Hell" is how I refer to New Hampshire. To get here, there's hell to pay. There's no way around that little inconvenience of a state, not if you want to get here and still remain in the good ole U.S. of A. along the way. As for the "high water," high water is, well, high water, but not to worry, there's a bridge at Kittery.

One way or another, if you're persistent, dedicated and courageous, you will, at the end of the day, arrive here from there. But remember, once you're here, getting back home is another matter altogether. You'll have a hard time getting back home because as the familiar saying goes, "You can't get there from here," and it makes no matter where "there" is once you're here. Besides, once you're here, there you are and there's nothing you can do about it.

As for those of us who live here, that's not a problem; we don't want to get away. In fact, you couldn't force us to leave, not without a notarized court order, that is. We're here for good, good or bad, and judging by my neighbors, most likely bad. *Why* we're here is another matter. Some of us were born here and chose to stay (or rather, and more likely, just never thought of moving). Others of us moved here from "away" to "live life as it should be." In other words, we were self-deluded and lacked good judgment. We chose to be here. We can't say that we were just passing through and decided to stay, because nobody just passes through Maine, and I mean nobody. To pass through Maine implies that you'd have to be going somewhere else and where would you be going? New Brunswick? Yeah, right! I don't think so.

So there you are. They—and by "they" I mean "we," and by "we" I mean "me and them" and by that I mean "us"—us are here for one of those two reasons. That is, it's either one or the other of the two. For me, I'm proud to say it was the latter.

And now here we are, over a million and a quarter of us. You know how we got here, but why, you might ask, do we stay? It's quite simple, really. We stay because we, unlike so many others who wake up each day and find themselves living those "lives of quiet desperation" of which Thoreau wrote, we Mainers actually love our state, our Maine, and its way of life. We are here and we choose to stay here for the best of all reasons: we love to live here.

Be honest: how many of you truly love where you live? Love your home *and* your state? Not many, I should think. How many of you love them so much that you felt the need to write a book? Really? Well, I don't believe you. I think you're lying. I've never seen your book and until I do, I'm saying you're a "no good, low-lyin' flatlander" and that's that.

As for me, I did write a book and you're holding the proof right there in your dirty, little, grubby hands. I wrote this book because I love Maine and I hope you will come to love her too. I also hope you don't decide to delude yourself, exercise poor judgment like I did, and move here. Now, don't take offense. I don't know you, and though I'm sure you're a nice person and all, even if you *are* a liar, I'd just as soon not get to know you. In fact, I hope I never meet you and I'm begging you not to move here. Does that bother you? Well, I'm sooooo sorry. Don't love where you live? No? Well too bad for you. You made your choice, now live with it, or in it. All I'm asking is please don't come here and live with me in Maine.

As for me, I love where I live and that's why I wrote this book. That and I was hoping to make a few bucks so I wouldn't have to go to work each day in quiet desperation like you, but that's another story for another day.

Anyway, welcome to my home, my love, my Maine. Kick back, relax and I hope you enjoy spending some time with us. I hope you learn something and maybe share a laugh or two along the way. And one more thing: if you do come to visit, while you're here I urge you to spend your money, preferably most, if not all, of it. I hope you buy a lot of our souvenirs—you know, the plastic lobsters, moose key chains, loon or puffin refrigerator magnets, light house calendars, and, oh yes, books, lots of books, books like this one.

Speaking of this one, thanks for buying my book and not stealing it. Stop by the house and I'll even autograph it for you for free if I'm in a good mood. Just do me a favor and don't plan on staying for more than a night or two. That puts me in a foul mood and pity the next guy who wants some scribble. As for the book, I hope you enjoy it and I hope you paid retail. Tell your friends about it, and tell them "No, you can't borrow it, it's mine. Buy your own damn book."

Thank you for doing your bit for a few of the "locals," even if this one's originally and (as far as the natives are concerned) will always be from "away." We appreciate it. And by "we" of course, I don't mean "us"; I mean me.

Disclaimer

You are now reading the small print disclaimer. The small print disclaimer enables writers to say what they want, and then cover their butts from lawsuits for the inaccurate, misleading, or libelous things they've said. You should always read the small print. For your reading pleasure, it should be noted that our small print is the same size as our regular-sized print, but smaller than our big-sized print. We used the regular print because it's cheaper for us and saved us the trouble of having to make it smaller. If you like your small print smaller, we recommend that you hold this page at arm's length from your body. You may have to squint some, but it's worth it if small print is what you prefer. The small print you are now reading is intended to qualify the small print you are about to read and thus should be considered a somewhat smaller print. You can therefore bring your arms closer to your body by a few inches when you finish reading this paragraph, making the ensuing small print still small, but bigger than the smaller, small print and thus, with less squinting, easier to read.

All materials in this book are of course, true and factual and can be researched and verified by anybody, anywhere, at anytime by using the same means that the author used. To learn of those means, simply send a check or money order to me, George D. Christie, for a large sum of money. We not only recommend, but actually *insist* that you do not include a self-addressed return envelope. We don't want anyone giving away his or her home address to a complete stranger. You don't want some weirdo stalking your neighborhood late at night, do you? What would the neighbors say? (Not that they're not a little weird themselves.) Besides, I don't want to have to travel that far, what with the bad weather forecast and all. So, just send the money and save us both a lot of unnecessary trouble and inconvenience. Besides, we don't need or want to get the police involved, do we? I know I don't.

Now, it should be noted that much of this book's factual material has been somewhat made up, twisted until it's unrecognizable or just simply totally fabricated by the author. As it is a well-known fact that not all facts are equally factual in their factuality, it is therefore up to the reader to determine which facts are true facts and which facts are not quite factual. That's part of the fun of this book and we include it at no extra charge. So enjoy yourself and don't blame me for what you've read; remember, I'm just the messenger and the facts are more or less what they are and probably less.

It is also quite important to note that this book should not be read by anyone either over the age of sixteen or under the age of sixteen. Possession of this book by a sixteen-year-old is a misdemeanor in most states and, unfortunately for you, you live in one of those states. Possession (and don't lie to me—if you're reading this book, technically you possess it, and possession is nine-tenths of the law, and we're talking about *law* here, so you and I both know you're guilty) will result in a fine of a considerable sum of money. Please send your considerable sums of money to me, George D. Christie. As noted above, please do not enclose a self-addressed return envelope.

Furthermore, any resemblance of any characters or things in this book to anyone or anything, either living or deceased, expected to be living, or even considering the prospect of living within the next six months, fictional or factual, extant or extinct, may or may not be intentional or purely coincidental. I'm just not sure.

Finally, this book is intended for purely entertainment purposes only. In other words, don't take it seriously, folks. Like authenticated scientific research results, five-day weather forecasts, the Bible, or statements of fact by our trusted elected leaders, this book is entirely true. (Sarcasm may be read into the above statement based upon your personal scientific, meteorological, religious, or political persuasions and/or beliefs.) It is therefore not recommended that you necessarily believe what you've read and live the remainder of your life based upon it. That may not be a good idea. Trust me on this one. However, if you want to pray to me, that's fine, I suppose. I think I'd like that well enough, and by the way, next Tuesday will be partly sunny with seasonable temperatures.

Last but not least, if you do not believe any of what you've just read in this small print disclaimer, please send a considerably large sum of money to me, George D. Christie, and I will demonstrate to you personally why you should not trust anyone with your thoughts, your beliefs, your money or your life, least of all me. As noted previously, solely for your own protection of course, please do not enclose a self-addressed envelope. Thank you, and I mean that sincerely.

Pre-Historic History

As Woody Allen once said, "In the beginning there was nothing and God said, 'Let there be light.' Of course there was still nothing, but at least now you could see it." Maine was kind of like that at one time. It was there, and there was light; only there was no one around to see and appreciate it. A lot has changed between then and now. That change took place over many eras called "-cenes" or "-zoics," by paleontologists and other experts in the field. These eras were known as the Pleistocene or Mesozoic eras, for example.

Now, not a lot was happening back then, but it still took a long time nonetheless. At first there was nothing but dirt, probably hot dirt, too hot for people to walk on, so it's a good thing there weren't any of us living back then. The world must have resembled a Florida beach in August except for the Canadians. In fact, there was no life at all—just dirt, some air, a lot of water and lightning. Again, imagine a place like Florida but without trailers or Canadians or Guatemalans. Suddenly the lightning struck from out of the blue (weather was different back then) hit the dirt, some of which had fallen into the water, and bingo: life began. Early life of course wasn't too smart, but it didn't have to be. I mean all it had to do was keep away from the lightning. There was a guy on the Late Show who got hit seven times by lightning, so I guess life in the beginning was a lot like him: basically someone to stay away from while playing golf near Orlando.

Anyway, from the first fairly stupid one- and two-celled organisms, life eventually joined together into complex creatures of three or more cells. These were called "goo." That goo, over time, evolved. "Evolution" is when a life form changes from stupid to not-as-stupid. It's like when your husband can't figure out how to wire a light switch and so he just sits in the dark and watches "The Three Stooges." Now, he can name all five of them (don't forget Shemp and Curly Joe), but he still can't wire a switch. Evolution is like that, only slower.

In time the not-as-stupid goo got the urge to travel and wanted to see the Tuscany region of Italy in fall so it eventually developed fins and later legs. In time, they either crawled, or were washed up, on land, which made traveling with their legs a whole lot easier as they could now "touch bottom." Once on land, they took a good look around, but not having eyes, they didn't recognize much of anything and, having never been there before, they went back beneath the salty waves and called it a day, or an era, or whatever. Not wanting to miss out on what their parents had told them they hadn't seen, some of the goo later developed primitive eyes so they might better focus and frame their souvenir photos of the charming countryside. In time, however, these inquisitive animals no doubt emerged from the waters for good and established themselves on the shoreline in small colonies where they sold postcards to the natives who would arrive later.

Curiously, a few of these zealot life forms likely climbed nearby trees from which they drew entertainment by dropping nuts at a passerby or two, or more likely, slower-climbing zealots. Either way, these creatures, though brainless, but with obviously well developed climbing abilities, later evolved into what we know as "squirrels." Some squirrels then devolved at an even later date, morphing into what we now call "cats."

(Incidentally, one of the great mysteries of all time, and of all modern science for that matter, remains unsolved to this day and that is this: how can a creature that lives in trees and does nothing but run around and collect nuts all day, not ever, not once, over the vast millennia of time, not ever, just once, come across the concept of actually throwing one of those nuts at another squirrel? Is that not a surefire survival-of-the-fittest mutation or what? As if the squirrel that develops a good right arm isn't going to have an advantage over the other non-nut-throwing squirrels. It makes no sense. It's too stupid to be true, and it has literally kept me up at night wondering. It is the one thing that makes me doubt the entire theory of evolution. Cro-Magnon man? Neanderthal man? The missing link? None of those things disturb my faith in evolution. But why I have never, not once, seen a nut-throwing squirrel really shakes my belief to no end. It haunts me to this very day. I can't get over it.)

As for the creatures that remained in the sea, these "goo-ites" as I call them, eventually turned into lobsters, kelp, clams, and Hawaiians. It's easy to see who got the better of that deal. Like if you were a clam you wouldn't want to live in Hawaii? Anyway, that's how life on Earth evolved. This evolution went on until eventually paleontologists ran out of names ending in "-cene" or "-zoic," which was a good thing, because the Ice Age was about to occur.

As it happened, about 12,000 years ago, the land mass that is Maine was covered with a giant sheet of ice: hence the name Ice Age. It was cold, as you might guess. Only animals that evolved warm, furry coats could survive. I'm sure that's why squirrels survived. You would think a snowball would have been thrown too, just once, but no, we have no record of such a thing. No fossilized remains of small creatures with large right arms and tiny little ball caps have been found. Nothing. I can't imagine it. It just seems impossible.

Anyway, as the ice retreated or as scientific lexicon denotes it, "melted," the glaciers left behind a pristine landscape. Once untidy, jagged mountain peaks covered with "crap" were polished off to more manageable rounded domes devoid of "crap." U-shaped valleys were scoured out and evened up around the edges, making them presentable, accessible, and most of all, ideal for yodeling. The whole environment was now pleasant to look at, spruced up and better than new. This is the landscape that greeted the first human inhabitants of Maine, this and some of the leftover cold crap and snow. It's still this way today.

And so it was, a land of wooly mammoths, musk oxen, and damn good sledding just waiting to be discovered. Still, it was not until some "native"

Americans crossed the land bridge from Asia onto the North American continent many thousands of years ago that anyone could enjoy the winter sports that awaited them.

Here I run into another conundrum. Would someone please explain to me how you get to be called a "native" when you come from someplace else? I've lived in Maine most of my life and I'm not a native and never will be. A native squirrel, yes, they crawled up out of the primordial swamp as we've just learned, but a "native" person? A native immigrant might be more apropos. You see my point? Does that bother you too? I just don't get it. And what is a land bridge? I looked it up and turns out it's just land. Nothing special, just land. You walk on it and over it. You can't walk under it, not really. It's not that kind of a bridge. Basically, it's dirt, dirt and rock, maybe some mud here and there where it touches water and might be slippery now and again, whatever. That's it. Nothing more. The point is, it's not really a bridge, just some dirt between some water.

Anyway, our ancestors just walked to Maine. Why? Who the hell knows? As if they knew. Maybe they were adventurous, bored, or more likely, they got lost going to the can. Maybe it was a Sunday, there were no churches then, and you could probably buy beer before 9:00 a.m. Maybe they were a little sloshed, they went for a picnic or a stroll looking for Tuscany, perhaps, and about 5,000 miles later, ended eating lobster or mammoth or whatever. When they got here they probably recognized a good thing when they saw it, kicked back and said that's it, we're home, pitched a tent or crawled under a rock and went to sleep. When they awoke, "Behold! The state of Maine!" That's just an educated guess, mind you (yes, I've been to college so I know all about educated), but I think it's gotta be fairly close to the truth. Be that as it may, the fact is that when the natives arrived for the first time, there were no doubt stupid, non-nut-throwing squirrels to greet them. True, there may have been saber-toothed squirrels, but you didn't need to wear a helmet in the woods. No squirrel was going to throw a nut at you. Rip your leg off at the knee? Yes. Toss a hickory nut to the head? No, not bloody likely. In fact, you were so safe from nuts, the natives could literally flaunt their disregard by wearing feathers on their heads with impunity, and they did so to beat the band.

So there you have it: a recently scoured landscape, some snow, squirrels, a smattering of wooly mammoths and other furry creatures, some newly arrived natives with feathers, and that's basically your Maine five or so thousand years ago and counting.

People being what they are (slobs), the new natives set about basically trashing the place. They ate their lobster and clams by the "ying-yang" or beach, and probably gnawed on a few cats as well, leaving piles of discarded shells, fur, and little bells and flea collars strewn randomly about. When one place became too filthy and cluttered to sit down in without having to constantly pick shell splinters out of one's butt, the natives moved on to what would soon become another dump, or as they referred to it, village. This establishment of permanency, however short lived, was the beginning of what we now call "civilization."

Settling down in villages, the natives soon learned to domesticate some of the wild animals they encountered, such as the wolf and the cat. Squirrels proved too independent to be tamed and besides, the little bastards can climb like the devil. Domesticated cats became pets. Non-domesticated cats became supper. "Here kitty, kitty, kitty," was originally a hunting or war cry, and was often followed by a muffled "whomp" sound followed by "good kitty" and no more purring. Later that night, the tale of the great hunt would be retold as legend by a very satiated native gently petting his new-found friend, Sylvester, who, though he loved his master, always slept with one eye open. Life was good, but as we said, the landscape was changing, becoming defiled and bespoiled. (Be-spoiled is like spoiled, only better and more formal. I like it, so I used it here. If you don't like it, don't read it, but I liked it.)

The weather warmed as the years passed slowly by, and the climate changed as well. The landscape in turn dried considerably and the natives could travel about without slipping or sliding. They could now run faster and jump farther, as they were no longer encumbered by the necessity of the half-rubber/half-leather shoe they had developed to keep their feet not only dry, but also fashionable. (L.L.Bean-types take note.) This simple, yet profound alteration would have huge repercussions regarding the development of native cultures as we know them today.

The natives, or "Indians" as they came to be more commonly known, learned to live ever more effectively off the land. They gathered fruits and nuts, some of which they threw at the stupid squirrels (whose lack of a good right arm they mocked unabashedly). Some of these natives would later become quite adept at throwing, such as the young Sockalexis who had the honor of the Cleveland Indians being named after him.

Those who gathered the fruits and nuts in time developed a means of preserving them by drying and shaping them into fruitcakes, which they created for the holidays, special occasions, and even rudimentary weaponry. One particularly insidious use was as a gift for relatives whom they especially did not like. Another was to drop the cakes given to them off high cliffs onto an unsuspecting prey, often those same relatives. There was no stopping civilization and its development soon began to steamroll.

As they became more civilized, the Indians began to organize and congregate in bunches with their chums in what they called "fraternal associations." Often these were named after the local animals of the region, such as the moose and the elk. However, as there was no such thing as recorded time, much less a "1:30 on the third Wednesday afternoon of every month," these associations quickly faded from the scene. They were eventually replaced by a more practical collection of Indians called a tribe.

Collectively, these tribes in Maine were called the Wabanaki. Individually, the tribes went by many names, and each had their own special meaning. There were the Malecites, (pronounced "Mala-seats," as in chairs) known for their habit of sitting on rough hewed, splintered stumps which accounted for their bad attitudes and penchant for standing at social functions. Theirs was an irritable clan and they were nicknamed the "malcontents."

There were also the Abanaki, or "have a knockies," a "knockie" being native slang for a type of trick candy given to guests made from clam shells and oak bark that would scar the gums and stain the teeth of the unsuspecting. There were the Micmacs, famous for their limericks beginning with "mic mac, paddy whack, give a dog a bone." There were the Penobscots, or the "five scots." A "scot" was a little chip or token, placed on a marked sheet of birch bark. Scots were used in a game that consisted of beads being drawn from a turning bowl, the object being to get five "scots" in a row, or four corners. Especially satisfying was the victory cry of the winner who shouted out in triumph while the other competitors moaned and cleared their barks for the next game. The games were attended by large numbers of older women, were often played for high stakes, and the prizes awarded included blankets, dinnerware, and felt paintings.

Another tribe was the Passamaquoddy, or the "pass me the quoddy" (or venison jerky, as "quoddy" was known during those days). And last but not least, the Watdahelwasat, a now extinct tribe of blundering idiots who, being sound sleepers, were easily surprised and set upon by other the tribes, at which time they were heard to utter in dismay the name by which they became known: "Watdahelwasat."

These many tribes learned to live off the bounty of the land and it was a bountiful land indeed. There were fish so thick in the streams that you could walk on them if you were so inclined. It was because of this, that the concept of building bridges was never fully developed by the natives, as bridges simply were not necessary. There were deer for meat and clothing, squirrels for mocking, and cats for eating and petting, in that order. There were also huge herds of wild game consisting of millions of moose and buffalo. Well, not in Maine maybe, and not moose, but you get the idea. In short, there was a lot of food that needed killing, but damn little else to do for entertainment (the Penobscots aside). Kids being kids, the natives became restless and turning to their wise ancestors and said, "I'm bored," to which came the reply, "It's not my job to entertain you. Go outside and find something to do." Some things never change.

Thus developed the popular form of entertainment that was the traditional turkey hunt of the plain, eastern Indians. Wild turkeys of prehistoric times were large, dark, cumbersome, and dull-witted birds, nothing like the domesticated birds we know today which are large, white, cumbersome, and dull-witted. They were not difficult to catch. Flying in large flocks, numerous quantities of the fowl would often land in trees to escape their pursuers, only to find the limbs of their perches bending under their combined weight until they sagged to the ground or snapped. Either way, the turkeys soon found themselves in the woods, on the ground, and running for their lives. No longer aloft in flocks, they scattered in large herds. At first, having learned from the plain, western Indians, the Indians of Maine tried herding these herds towards a tall precipice beneath which eagerly awaited the women and children of the tribe, armed with stuffing and yams, but wary of falling fruit cakes. Much to their dismay, however, the turkeys merely glided off to taller, sturdier trees and a feast of stuffing and yams, and thankfully no fruit cakes, capped off the great hunt. Eventually, the Indians, now wearing moccasins, learned to assume a steady gait that they could continue for hours on end and merely run down their feathered foes. Thus was born what was later referred to as the "turkey trot."

As I said or meant to say, these were the good ole days. Every day back then was basically Thanksgiving, but the natives didn't know it or appreciate it at the time, football not having been invented yet. However, there were unintended consequences. For instance, consuming turkey led to sleep, and, as there were no couches to sleep upon, sleep led to going to bed, going to bed led to some fun, and then bragging and storytelling. Storytelling led to having someone to tell the story to, someone who had to listen, which led to marriage, marriage and storytelling led to the wife rolling over and the husband to nudging her and asking, "Do you get it?" which led to the cold shoulder, which led to warming up the audience, which led to getting warm, which led to snuggling, which likely led to more fun, which led to babies, and that led to larger tribes and eventually neighbors.

Now, as Robert Frost once wrote, "Good fences make good neighbors." Native Americans, however, had no fences or even the precursor to fences—stone walls—and thus, they made for bad neighbors. They would rather throw rocks than stack them in neat rows one upon the other. All this rock throwing soon led to a glorious new pastime: fighting and warring with one another. This was fun and gave everyone another much needed form of entertainment. Besides, aside from getting killed now and then, it was a hell of lot better than building stone walls.

Warring Indians soon became wary and smart warring Indians. Those that didn't adapt became the stuff of legends, like that black falcon Bogart talked about. The brighter ones looked to see if another approaching Indian was carrying a rock and if they were, without those fashionable but slow boots they no longer needed to wear, they would simply run away before a stone came flying in their direction. Once all the dullard Indians were dismissed, warring became more difficult and inefficient. If warfare was to become productive, it was determined that warriors needed to better disguise their dark intentions; they needed to become what the early settlers would call "sneaky Indians."

Necessity being the mother of invention, to achieve this deception, they invented what they came to call "pockets." Pockets were great. Indians put pockets on all their loincloths, their T-shirts, everywhere. In these pockets they could carry their concealed rocks with enough room left over for their smokes too. Being now sneaky, they found they could also walk around whistling with their hands in their pockets, pretending to be cool and unconcerned. It wasn't until the French arrived centuries later that they were able to put a word to this new found behavior: they called it acting "nonchalant." By acting "nonchalant," they were able to trick another warrior into feeling safe until their victim wandered close enough to be bopped in the head with a well-aimed rock. But, as pockets came in only one size—small—if the warrior missed with his rock, and this was often the case, the warring parties were soon reduced to groveling for additional stones. This was deemed to be pathetic, and eventually it was agreed by all that throwing stones was simply not going to be productive in terms of respectable fighting and killing; thus stone throwing was banned byinter-tribal treaty in BC something '04.

No longer able to arm themselves with stones, Indians then set about developing the art of carrying no weapons at all. Hours of painstakingly doing nothing produced the desired results. Once properly not equipped, the warring parties would approach en masse, nonchalantly of course, hands in pockets, and kind of just push and jostle one another about a whole lot. Tiring of this "war dance" they gradually expanded upon the jostling part and began to include such clever new ideas such as taking their hands out of their pockets, forming them into fists, and hitting or striking one another until one or the other eventually tired of the sport and fell down. Once your opponent was down, you could step on him so he couldn't get up. This felt good and you could then "whoop it up," as Indians were known to do. Still, wearing moccasins, the effect was somewhat muted and as jackboots wouldn't be invented for centuries, warfare continued to lack that certain "je ne sais quoi."

Limited in their options, the Indians returned to the hitting, and began to perfect the art so that once hit properly their opponent wouldn't or preferably *couldn't* get back on his feet. This kind of hitting was facilitated by the invention of the war club. With the stone no longer thrown, but attached to a stick with leather sinews, once properly struck, the head of their opponent was called crushed or bashed in. The "bashers" could now step on their opponents to good effect as the "bashees" weren't going anywhere soon. They could then now step on their opponent to good effect, as he wasn't about to go anywhere soon. Ardent practitioners of the sport expanded upon their repertoire, moving from small clubs of stone, to large clubs of stone, slingshots, hatchets, knives, spears, and later, bows and arrows. Warfare had developed from a mere assertion of dominance and bragging rights, to a life and death struggle for survival. Warfare had at long last, finally become civilized.

This "art" soon was extended to the colorful painting of faces and bodies as well. Native American Indian warriors used the colors available to them, mostly the reds and yellows found in the surrounding soils on which their victims lay. In time these colors, especially the reds, permeated their skin to such a degree that they were passed on genetically, like the red in a lobster, although unlike lobsters the Indians didn't need to be cooked or steamed thoroughly to turn red. And unlike their victims, their color didn't squirt, ooze or run. Nonetheless, the "redskin" of the Indian evolved into a permanent and distinguishing trait, like braids.

Armed with their new, sharp and improved weapons, but being relatively scattered, thinned out and all, the natives had much time on their hands and very few neighbors upon which to practice their "art" upon. Bored, they thus began to carve upon what was available to them, mostly the trees and rocks of the forests, as opposed to one another. Needing something to carve the rocks and trees into, they developed a complex religious aspect to their daily lives, revealing gods, mythical creatures and folkloric legends. Unlike many other religions of the times, some of these actually existed in reality. This carving of religious images led to the development of totem poles. The higher on the pole, the more revered the image. Being man's best friend, the dog was often placed at the top of the totem. "Leading a dog's life" was as good then as it is now. Those at the top often literally had the "life of Riley," Riley being a popular dog's name at the time. The "top dogs," of the tribe thus assumed their envied position. "Being on top" was therefore good and the meaning of hierarchy was thus literally hewed into their lifestyle. We all know what the dogs used the bottom of the totem poles for.

The carving of rock into petroglyphs, was more difficult to accomplish. The rough hitting of one rock hard against another rock no doubt led to not only smaller rocks, but also the eventual discovery of what was commonly known as the gnarly knuckle. Various types of rock were employed, including flint. Struck adroitly, flint shattered into sharp shards, producing knives, spearheads, and arrowheads. Striking flint also produced sparks. The broken and singed gnarly knuckle was soon discovered and became a means of transporting fire. Life for the Indians would never be the same. As charred, broken knuckles became unfashionable, a safer means of producing fire evolved. Two pieces of flint strapped together over a birch container of straw and leaves became the equivalent of a modern day Zippo lighter and many have actually been unearthed bearing the names of their owners and crude pictures of early motorcycles.

The relative ease and ability to build fires soon led to cooking, rather than the predominant fashion of gnawing food, and also to the burning of enemies at the stake. On festive occasions, the two were often combined, and a merry time was had by all, with the possible exception of the actual enemy burning at the stake. This cooking led to cookouts, cook-ins, cooks, chefs, chiefs, chief chefs, and finally, the establishment of restaurants with catchy, fancy names, upright napkin displays, and busboys. Many restaurants were established, but sadly failed to endure due to the lack of one essential ingredient: a stable clientele who, rather than being served, were often clobbered senseless by those stones lashed to sticks. Such was the setting that greeted the first European explorers as prerecorded history passed into recorded time.

Not having had to stroll across a land bridge those many thousands of years ago on that fateful Sunday of yore, the Europeans had much more time to evolve into their own distinctive tribes. Stone walls (soon embellished upon and called castles) or not, Europeans developed into what historians now refer to as "really, really bad neighbors," each with their own distinctive customs and language. As such, each perfected the art of warfare through centuries of practice upon one another, pushing civilization to theretofore unimagined of heights. Passing from the Copper Age, through the Bronze Age, and into the iron and steel age, civilization shared an emerging transformation as culture destroyed culture with ever-increasing efficiency.

These were good times, and coupled with recurring plagues and scourges, were known as the Dark Ages and were not to be missed. And yet, something was indeed missing. After century upon century of the same old same old, the recipe for the very bread of life, the staple of progress and happiness was getting stale. Once thought to be impossible, ravaging and pillaging was indeed, "getting old." Something new needed to be added to spark the art of warfare lest its practitioners' interest wane and civilization suffer and decline as peace overtook the land.

To this end, the clever Europeans came up with two novel ideas: the Renaissance and the concept of a round world just waiting to be discovered. To prove their point, they soon began to wear frilly clothes and traveled to the ends of the known Earth and beyond, searching for new neighbors upon whom they could inflict their blossoming civilizations.

This travel led to lots and lots of walking. In time, having pretty much walked everywhere there was to walk, on all of the land bridges that existed, the intrepid explorers literally "fell" upon a new means of travel—a faster, more glorious means of conveyance and far more fun than merely putting one's foot "to the bricks" as it were.

Through sheer providence, the process had begun inauspiciously enough. A crude attempt at a bridge (fish being obviously less plentiful in Europe than in Maine), a local monarch had his engineer fell a tree to span a small stream. Filling the niche of the beaver, which didn't exist in Europe, and apparently equally as talented in directing the fall of the tree, the bridge "builder" failed miserably and the bridge fell into the flowing waters. Not overly impressed, the monarch ordered the engineer thrown into the stream as well, whereupon he landed on the tree, clung for dear life to it and thus the floating tree was discovered. It was also discovered that it was difficult to clamber aboard such a floating tree for even a joy ride, so the limbs were hacked off and—voila!—the floating log was invented. In short order, experimentation determined that if one floating log was a good idea, and it was, then many floating logs were an even better idea. Thus rafts came to be. Curiously, these rafts were found to often float downstream and out to sea, where they disappeared over the horizon. To avoid missing out on waving goodbye to their friends and family as they passed into oblivion, small shore-side villages soon sprang to life at the junction where the mighty rivers met the fathomless seas.

Once land was out of sight and all the festivities had died down, the rafts soon became waterlogged and began to sink. This led to the voyagers' clothing getting wet, which in turn led to the need for them to be dried. A stick was erected on the raft to attach a clothesline to, and thus were sails born. Blown shoreward by the prevailing winds, the presumably doomed raft dwellers would soon return to their villages, much to the chagrin of the townsfolk who were celebrating their loss with much mead and merriment. The return of their neighbors meant that the mead must now be shared by more, which meant less for everyone. The concept of "less is more" not having been developed, and being slightly inebriated, the villagers soon welcomed home their kin by occasionally slaughtering them in a drunken melee. Of course, as everyone was drunk, a few of the rafters would manage to escape and would raft off again, spurred on by the knowledge of their fate should they ever return.

In time, these rafters or "clothes driers" as they were known, became referred to as "sea tailors" and finally simply as "sailors." They could not only travel about faster than anyone had imagined, but were rather neat, clean, and presentable upon their arrival at a new, undiscovered place. These now rather nattily dressed and unexpected interlopers from away very much awed the native folk they encountered. To enhance the awe factor and to shock those who weren't in awe, the sailors drew their weapons and proceeded to slaughter and enslave their hosts en masse and then exchanged baubles with those left over. Thus was civilization being rapidly and neatly spread throughout the known world.

Now "the known world" was a very clever idea used by noted philosophers in their quest to understand the universe and the true meaning of life. The "known world" contained all they knew, plus God, and it was "right." The "unknown world" was what was left over, with no God, and it was "wrong." The "known" world was divided up. The "unknown" world was there for the taking. The "unknown world" could be discovered simply by seeing it and claiming it. It was a simple and easily completed process. One could claim a formerly "unknown" land, for "God and Country" simply by sticking one's stick of locally fashionable drying clothes, i.e. one's "flag," into the suddenly discovered soil and repeat the following phrase: "In the name of (insert claimant's name here), I do hereby claim this unknown land which will now be known as (insert new name here)." That was it. No dotted line to sign on, no deed search, no notarizing, no nothing. It was all legal and it was yours. That was that, no guilt attached. Now all you had to do was to kill anyone who objected or anyone else who tried to do the same thing. The age of exploration and colonial development was at hand. But we are getting well ahead of ourselves and must backtrack half a millennium or so.

The first Europeans to stumble upon the "New World," were known as the Vikings, or Norseman. Like everyone else, the early Vikings had to walk everywhere, and like everyone else, they didn't like it all that much. Their rafts would float out to sea and wherever they landed they would proceed to destroy the inhabitants (as was the custom of the day). It was difficult to direct these bulky logs tied to one another, so the Vikings filed a little here and shaved a little there and in no time at all, were sailing in ultra sleek vessels with a low coefficient of drag. These they referred to as their "long boats." Having large, fast, and sleek ships to carry them about, the Vikings combined these with a mixture of poor seamanship, fog, and a lack of maps to explore the far-flung shores of the unknown world, thus making it known and, of course, theirs.

Now the Vikings were large, red-haired, and burly men who protected themselves from the often-inclement weather by adorning their bodies with animal skins and pelts. This led to their sweating and smelling like, well, like a bunch of "stinking Vikings," as they were often referred to by their neighbors. This gave the Vikings a rather poor attitude towards non-Vikings that lingered and festered through the years. The Vikings, bad attitudes and all, were nonetheless only relative savages in the scheme of things. While their skins were often wrinkly and bunched up from time to time, they did have large furry hats with horns protruding from them that made them the envy of other relative savages with not nearly so neat looking hats.

As these "stinking Vikings" ravaged the coastline of northern Europe, they converted the other "savages" they encountered into burned and rotting corpses. Those they failed to kill, better known as "fast little bastards," began to drop stuff in their haste to flee and thus trade with the Vikings was begun. In time, trade became intentional, and bartering one item for an item of equal or greater value became the fashionable thing to do; thus commerce was born. Transactions often went as follows: "I'll trade you this really neat furry hat with horns for your sister there. If you say no, I'll kill you." The deal was then consummated in more ways than one. Trade began to flourish. Needless to say, the so-called "fast" soon found it incumbent upon themselves to become the so-called "smart" as well. As a result, the Viking hordes would, in the course of time, face a marketing dilemma.

Their hats, though useful in proving whose side they were on (as in "I'm one of you guys, really! See the hat?"), never truly caught on with the surviving plundered populations, and soon the plundered began to actually choose ravaging and death over exchanging their sister for simply "another damn, furry hat." The Norsemen, disappointed, tense, and restless (given their unsatisfied libidos), found themselves now also burdened with a growing overstock of unwanted horned hats. Something had to give, and so they bravely set sail for the horizon, new markets and whatever else lay beyond. Haggardly, haberdashers of hats, they cast their fears to the wind, and set off unafraid, to seek new lands and new opportunities. Along the way, while peddling their wares, they also learned to eat fish, drink mead, and sing merry songs. All in all, this was considered not a bad life, given the times.

Taking advantage of their legendary navigating skills and the often-impenetrable fogs of the North Atlantic, the Vikings leapfrogged across the vast salty expanse that lay before them as they journeyed ever onward. Setting ashore first upon a green land, they stuck their stick into its soil and proclaimed their discovery "Iceland." Venturing further into the unknown, they encountered a frigid, icy landscape that snapped their stick when they tried to stick it into the frozen turf and named this land "Greenland." This juxtaposition of naming and reality was what passed for humor among the Norsemen, and it became ever more evident that comedy was not their strong suit. They were great mead-makers though, and this was a good thing, as it took vast quantities of the honey brew to lighten up these vagabonds of the high seas to a point where they would sing their merry songs and chase the setting sun.

Having gotten as many laughs as they could from their inane humor, the Vikings pressed on in their long boats to discover new jokes. Modern long boats of the time were the creation of Sven Fordsen, a noted Viking entrepreneur. They came in any color, he was fond of saying, as long as it was "wood." The standard models were equipped with many rows of benches and a large clothes-drying pole in the center. The benches were for the crew who rowed the boats with long oars when the winds were nil and drying conditions poor. There were also nifty places to hang the crew's colorful wooden shields along the sides of the long boats. Long boats also had lifelike carvings of fearsome dragons rising from their keels and facing outward, away from the crew, so as not to frighten them. However, calling them long boats was a misnomer of sorts, as these were the only boats they had at the time or ever did have for all we have been able to learn. There were no longer boats or shorter boats. There were just boats. There was only one size and that was "long." "Take it or leave it," said Sven, just like the color. The good thing about the long boats was that you never had to turn them around to return from whence you came. Long boats came with two fronts, and no ends. You just turned yourself around on your bench and headed in the other direction. It was simple, it was neat, and it fit the times. They worked well and all in all, long boats were a definite hit with salty maritime types.

The Vikings eventually landed on the coast of Maine near present-day Blue Hill, on June 3, 1004 at about, oh, 2:30 or so in the afternoon, daylight savings. It was a Thursday. (The exact time is lost to history as Lars The Once Red-Headed But Now Gray And Bald's watch had stopped when he playfully splashed his friend Vulgar with some water, getting him back for raping someone's sister, but not joining in on the pillaging of the last settlement they had bartered hats with.) It was a nice day, warm and sunny. Many of the crew had been "slaking" (Norse for drinking) their thirst with something new, called a "brew." This "brew" was carefully crafted and distilled on these long ocean voyages. It was kept in an oaken bucket and concocted from pure, glacial ice waters and other choice ingredients such as spoiled, moldy, and lice-infested bread. It was the progenitor of what would later become Finlandia Vodka, minus the lice. It was distinguished by smell and taste from the excrement and dregs often stored in a more crude, oaken bucket and called "not brew." Given the Viking sense of humor, it is understandable that the two buckets were often swapped, especially on long voyages, leading to much merriment, and a few belly laughs at the expense of those who ended up slaking their thirst with the "not brew."

This having been a particularly long voyage, the Viking sailors were soon restless in their seats as they were much in need of relieving themselves. Though rapists and pillagers all (excepting Vulgar of course who, although often vilified, never really took to pillaging no matter how hard he tried), the Norsemen were notorious for being easily embarrassed. However, there was no privacy on a long boat and they therefore asked their leader, Eric Leif The Red, if they could go ashore. Eric Leif (who was also easily embarrassed and who blushed unabashedly at the first sound of a "tinkle," hence his name Eric Leif) giggled and quickly granted the request. Some suspect to this day that it was he who swapped the buckets while his crew was ashore just for revenge.

Having to wade to land, as there was no short boat on a long boat, the men quickly ran to the woods, seeking hiding places amongst the rocks and trees where they could tinkle or take a dump in relative privacy. But there was no privacy on that fateful day, as waiting for them, also hiding behind every available rock and tree, was a tribe of cash-hungry restaurateurs, Indians from the "Chez de Clam"! Business had been slow for the past fifty some years and tips had lagged. The Indians were in an ornery mood and had no time for small talk.

No match for their hosts, the Viking invaders were literally caught off guard and with their pants down. Easily embarrassed as we noted before, the Vikings ran from the harassing natives, red-faced back to their ship where they turned to the "not brew" to steady their nerves (much to Eric Leif's delight). Laughing heartily, Eric and his Viking horde sailed away in haste, leaving the natives behind, standing dumbfounded on the shore, clutching the cleverly designed menus they had so hoped to distribute. Legend has it, they were too depressed to even wave goodbye.

The actual site of this event was discovered centuries later when several copies of the Viking's "Lands End" catalog were discovered along with a rare Viking coin and a set of ox cart keys near a shallow hole, behind a rocky crag. The catalogs were largely intact except for a few pages, apparently torn from their bindings, smeared with a dark, foul smelling substance and deposited in and around the hole, as the Norsemen hurriedly made their escape.

The "Skraling" as the Vikings came to call the natives they had encountered, were apparently not much impressed with having been discovered. With non-nut-throwing squirrels, these Skraling had no need for the Vikings' vaunted hats and placed no orders from the catalogs left behind that day. Insulted, the Viking horde, all twenty-three of them, vowed not to return for another 600 years or so, and took the secret of their embarrassing defeat to their graves. Needless to say, upon returning home, they quickly got back in the swing of things, doing what they did best—raping and pillaging their old friends and neighbors—and soon forgot all about the Skraling. True to their word, these and other Europeans did not return for another six centuries. By then, the Vikings were of course all dead and forgotten, and the Indian restaurant they had failed to patronize had in turn failed and fallen into a state of much disrepair as the furniture was mostly wicker.

Having just missed out on not only being raped and pillaged, but also on getting to at least try on the Norsemen's really neat hats, the Indians of Maine returned to their quaint but inefficient massacring of one another in their traditional, primitive fashion. The Europeans meanwhile did the same, but in much larger numbers, making good use of their more civilized and effective means of destruction. Life and death were as they had been once more. God was in his heaven and hell was a tight pair of ill-fitting woolen underwear and a bad piece of goat's cheese washed down with "not beer."

But it got worse, much worse. I speak, of course, of the arrival of the French.

Mount Katahdin is the highest point in Maine at 5,268 feet above sea level. A recent literal translation from the original Penobscot dialect directly into modern English resulted in the following: "Hey, 'Ta,' I can see my wigwam from up here."

The Age of Colonization

The age of prehistory had nearly ended for the Indians of Maine with the Vikings' arrival upon their shores. Apparently the Norsemen, excellent sailors that they were, were also really good at keeping a secret too. Word of their discovery would never pass into the history books of the scholars and scribes of the day. Their near brush with immortality and fame would have to wait centuries more to be revealed. The true and accepted discovery of what would be known as the New World would have to await the coming of that greatest of all explorers, Christopher Columbus.

Christopher Columbus was an Italian sea captain who had a dream of sailing around a flat world to get to the other side. For centuries, scientists (who were known also as charlatans and heretics) had mixed feelings about the world and how it worked. Some of these scientists believed that the world was as flat as the map on which it was drawn and held to the belief that if you sailed "far enough," which was also known as sailing "too far," you would eventually fall off the kitchen table on which the map had been placed. Falling off was considered to be "not a good thing" and was to be avoided at all costs. Apparently no one ever had thought this through, however. After all, if the world was flat, just what held the waters of the oceans on that flat surface and kept them from falling off and draining the seas onto the linoleum floor? I mean if there was some kind of a lip or edge holding in the water, wouldn't that also prevent your ship from falling off as well? I don't think these early scientists were all that bright, if you know what I mean.

Anyway, the world was thought to be flat and to say otherwise was asking to be a stick in a large fire lit by the Pope himself on a slow Saturday night in Rome. Columbus was a smart man, however, and not wanting to be considered as kindling in the quest to light the fire of mankind's need to know, he left the Pontiff's domain and headed for the freethinking land of Spain. In Spain, Catholics ruled the roost, not the Pope, and it was safe to think, or so Columbus thought. Once there, he was inspired by rumors of a group of men, the protectors of mankind's search for knowledge, of man's need to inquire. And so, seeking their assistance, Columbus traveled forthwith, which is really fast, and headed straight for the much-heralded Spanish Inquisition.

Once facing the Inquisition, Columbus soon realized his mistake, and quickly adjusted the presentation of his views for their examination. He claimed he wanted to sail to the other side of the world, as in "the underside of the piece of paper on which the map was drawn," and not around the world, as in "the world is round and hand me that match over there, my good Cardinal." The Inquisitors were much impressed with his logic. He was also considered fearless as he never faltered in his thinking, even when it was pointed out that once on the "other side" everyone and everything in and on his boat would of course fall out as they would now be all upside down. The truth was, he hadn't had time to think of that as he was sailing by the seat of his pantaloons, and so smiling, he nodded in agreement with the inquisitors, said "at's a gooda one" and, laughing heartily, quickly backed out of the room and ran away. He took the first three boats out of town and the rest is history. "Better to light the world as a dumb hero than as a smart torch," he was fond of saying in his later years.

Hero or idiot, fearless or fool: take your pick. Columbus would nonetheless alter the course of history forever more. He would do the impossible: he would have a holiday named after him for no apparent reason whatsoever. (You have to admit, Columbus Day makes no sense at all, does it? Seriously, do we celebrate one explorer's not falling off the earth? A lot of other people didn't fall off either and we don't celebrate them. Likewise, we aren't celebrating that Columbus was Italian, are we? I mean, why not make St. Patrick's Day an official federal holiday if that's the case? At least everyone eats corned beef and cabbage on March 17. No one eats lasagna because it's Columbus Day, whatever day it is in October, do they? Of course they don't. The only reason we celebrate Columbus Day is the fact that for some stupid reason or other, and we truly do not care what that reason was or is, we don't have to go to work! That's why it's worth celebrating and that's why Columbus Day is the greatest of all holidays and why it is celebrated sometime or other in October in this, the greatest country of them all.)

Thus with the blessing of the King and Queen of Spain, Ferdinand and Isabella, who also liked a good joke, Columbus waved so long and headed out to sea, thanking his lucky stars that they too had fallen for his spiel. He had three good ships: the Nina, the Pinta and the Santa Whatever. Like he really cared what they called that other one. After all, he was on it and couldn't read the name written on the side. All Columbus cared about on that fateful day in 1492 was putting as much distance between himself, Spain, and the Inquisition as he could. If he fell off the earth and landed on the floor, so be it. At least he wasn't going to be toasted, literally, by some royal court or clergy looking to kill time and progress. He summed up his thoughts in those now infamous words he shouted once he and his ships were over the horizon or at least out of ear shot: "I'm a outta here, you all!"

It must be noted that Columbus was pleasantly surprised to learn that he and his crew, but mostly he, wouldn't fall off the earth, or out of his boat, or whatever, and land on the floor. He was more than a little happy to finally sight land, set ashore, and plant the flag of Spain in the name of God and Country in warm sand, even if it wasn't really his own country. God is God and after all is said and done, gold is gold. The Age of Colonization had begun. Let the good times roll.

Columbus was happy to have found a land of warm breezes, beautiful women, loose clothing and even looser morals. Not only that, but prices were more than reasonable, considering the exchange rate and all. Unlike the frightening encounter the Vikings had experienced before him, Columbus had a much nicer get-together with the local inhabitants. He called the natives "Indians" because India was where he had intended go. I suppose if he had been headed for Turkey he would have called the natives Turkeys. Just think of the repercussions *that* would have had. Indianapolis, Indiana, would be Turkeyapolis, Turkeyana and a Thanksgiving Day feast would be something akin to cannibalism in Terre Haute or South Bend. We'd be eating peanuts, swilling beer, and rooting for the Cleveland Turkeys. Our ancestors would have fought in the French and Turkey War. It's scary, and yet it's true. We came that close to being absurd, but fortunately for us we narrowly avoided our fate and none of this came to pass.

For Columbus, this first voyage was to culminate in a dream come (almost) true and end in disparagement, humiliation and poverty following future journeys. But the first was more than he could have ever hoped for. For the Indians, that same dream come true was to become their worst nightmare. Given the Spanish conquerors' quixotic inclinations to both share their faith with the locals while thanking the "Almighty for this slaughter we are about to inflict upon the heathen scourge," it could not have turned out worse for the natives. Dreaming of gold and glory, the conquistadors went to sleep in rapture while the Indians awoke to a nightmare of death, disease, and destruction. Fortunately for the Maine "Indians," the red-hot Spanish blood was not overly interested in the white-cold of the north. It was left to the French and English for the aborigines of the maritimes to one day thank for their ultimate "comeuppance."

As those in the know are fond of saying, the French and the Spanish are one and the same, only different. "Those in the know" being the English of course. In point of fact, the French and the Spanish are very different, only much the same. Their similarities separate them, while their differences unite them. So it was in the early 1600s, so it is now, and I suspect it will always be. Such are the French and so also the Spanish. The English are another matter altogether and are different from both the French and the Spanish, but in much the same way.

One way or another, once word of Columbus' and Spain's great triumph reached Paris and London and became known, suffice it to say, all hell broke loose and the race to colonize the New World was begun in earnest.

There were many early arrivals from Spain, Italy, and England, such as Amerigo (nicknamed U.S.) Vespucci, Giovanni da Verrazzano, and Sebastian Cabot. They came, they saw, they stuck in a flag or two, and then quickly floated away, bringing back to Europe tales of the great and bountiful land of Norumbega, just waiting to be rediscovered and settled at a later date by more hearty and foolhardy souls than they. These fanciful stories of untold wealth excited the wanderlust of many, including the French, who had many ships at their disposal, but nowhere to go—until now, "mon ami."

The French soon arrived in the New World, in the guise of a navigator who was named after a lake he would later one day discover. The lake was large and long, and would contain a mythical sea serpent by the name of Champ. This lake was situated between what would in a hundred and fifty years or so, become the states of New York and Vermont. The navigator's name was Lac de la Champlain and the lake he discovered was Lake George, or close to it.

Champlain, as he was called for short, was a very busy, exploring type of guy. He liked roaming about in his big boat (the sub-Scandinavians preferred calling their boats "big boats" as opposed to "long boats") and yelling "Mon Dieu!" as he discovered this and that and stuck his flag here and there. Setting his eyes upon never before seen sights (at least not seen by him), he was in his glory, transforming unknown lands into known lands, sticking attractive Fleur-de-Lis flags into the fertile soil, etc., etc. This Champlain, this was a man, a man consumed by his life's chosen work: discovering. He loved it, he reveled in it, and he was pretty damned good at it, too.

Having found some of those much sought after foolhardy souls, the French founded a settlement in the New World. The French, true to their nature of not wanting to offend anyone, least of all what was to become English-speaking Canada or the American-speaking United States, had the year before, just to be politically correct, established a colony on a tiny island between the two nations-to-be. It was a brilliant plan, except for the fact that it was a cold, miserable, desolate place surrounded by hostile natives, and there was no food to eat. In 1604, when Champlain returned the following spring to reap the colony's bounty, the ill-fated St. Croix survivors clambered aboard his ship and, at gunpoint, gently persuaded the good Captain that removing them to a more suitable location in which to die might be in his best interest as well as theirs. Not a dull-witted man (unlike the ill-fated settlers of St. Croix who had first disembarked a year earlier), Champlain promised the ill-fated throng that he would find them a more favorable location in which to be ill-fated. After all, when it comes to real estate, it's all about location, location, location. He left them, the ill-fated settlers that they were, with some meager supplies and set sail, leaving them, the ill-fated, to wonder among themselves what was up with that damn prefix, that damn "ill-fated," moniker that stuck to them like glue and to wonder if it would somehow come back to bite them in the ass.

Thus relieved of the ill-fated colonists, Champlain set about merrily doing his discovering thing, as he was so often apt to do, and quickly forgot the task at hand. His motivation lay in his insatiable quest to make the unknown the known. In no time at all he was in his full glory once again. He soon found and named Mount Desert Island. It is pronounced "dessert," and not "desert," even though it was named because of its barren and desolate appearance, which apparently resembled a dried hasty pudding left out in the windswept sun for a fortnight. The point is that it's either misspelled or mispronounced and as to why, I really don't care.

Champlain was much taken in by the natural beauty of area and especially the colorful Bar Harbor scene with its many eclectic shops and quaint, often rustic, New England homes. Fortunately for him, it was the off-season, so prices were greatly reduced and the crowds of summer tourists had not yet arrived. He had the island pretty much to himself, lucky man. He no doubt left with many trinkets, souvenir shot glasses, a lobster harmonica and comb set, and several T-shirts—seconds, no doubt—purchased at a more than reasonably discounted price.

He also discovered the Isle de Haut. Pronounced "eel day ho," either referring to its lofty granite mass rising from the sea, or the rather overly frisky, friendly native girl who, though without a visible means of support, nonetheless enjoyed a rather well-to-do lifestyle. Either way, again, I don't really care.

The island was a wonderful addition to Champlain's claims and he cheerfully stuck another stick into its rocky soil, though it took him several stabs and he once hit his own foot, which led to a lot of fancy French swearing. But not to worry; Champlain, like any self-respecting explorer, had an ample supply of sticks and flags in his ship's hold. He may have been a discovering fool, but eventually he remembered that he was also a man on a mission. After all, he had given his word to find a new home for the ill-fated compatriots he had left behind on St. Croix.

Judging his swift, promised return precisely to the day by calculating how long the meager rations he had left behind with the ill-fated settlers might possibly last, and then adding a few months give or take, Champlain returned to discover only their ragged, starved, skeletal remains. As luck or fate would have it, the ill-fated and unlucky St. Croix settlers had indeed been unlucky and ill fated after all. Having learned the bitter truth, Champlain stuck a flag in what was left of his discovery, claiming them and their little island once more in the name of France and set sail for King and Glory, though not necessarily in that order.

It should be noted that the English, not to be outdone by their French counterparts, established their own ill-fated colony at Popham that, true to its nomer, suffered the same dismal and ill-fated fate as those ill-fated souls of St. Croix.

Augusta, not Portland, is the state capital of Maine. It is pronounced "Augusta" by all, excepting, of course, native Mainers who actually reside there. They pronounce it "'Auguster,' not "Portland." By the way, it's also "Bang-gore," not "Banger." Or maybe "Bang-her." (Man, get your mind out of the gutter.)

Colonial Times

Time passed, the ill fated were once again forgotten, and the land of Maine gradually became populated here and there with "populators," or common folk type people as they came to be more commonly known. That name soon gave way to settlers or colonists and those "heres and theres" of colonists soon became villages and towns and in time, larger villages and larger towns.

The town of York, for example, eventually grew to become America's first chartered city in 1641. The inhabitants established a life for themselves growing subsistence crops, producing timber for ships, fishing for cod, whaling, and so on. They trapped for furs and traded with the Indians in such a manner that the friendship between the colonists and the natives soon blossomed into an all out war that lasted for the better part of a century. As it turns out, this event leads us to what I've found is the best way to chronicle the history of Maine, or any place for that matter, which is through the use of benchmarks, particularly benchmarks of war. Wars are pretty cool. They are distinct and divide up time in neat, tidy little packages. Besides, using peace as a demarcation for events is confusing. I mean, for instance, in 1848 it was noted that Sonia Smithington passed a rather pleasant birthday in her cottage and by the way, several Mainers died a glorious death before the fateful gates of Chapultepec fortress in Mexico City. See what I mean? Which are you going to remember? Me, too. We'll stick to the wars. Besides, I don't celebrate birthdays and I don't like to eat cake. This is my book, not yours. You want birthdays? Fine. Go write your own damn book. As for me, this is war!

The French, good Catholics all excepting for the Protestant Huguenots (damn their wicked souls!), soon married into the local Indian tribes, becoming "blood brother-in-laws" to many a brave, well, brave. This practice worked out well, as every other Frenchman in the New World was apparently a priest who paddled canoes, incited French patriotism among Indians leading them to war, and eventually married the chief's daughter. Along the way, many of the native savages were converted to Christianity as well, and those who did not convert were often summarily dismissed to their maker where supposedly he could work on their belief system more directly. Thus were the Indians saved, the French doomed, and late one Sunday afternoon, out on the ice there was always a hockey game or at least a fight breaking out.

The English preferred soccer, or football or futbol, and did not have near so many religious representatives of the Anglican Church in America. Not wanting to begin their married lives in sin (most couples tend to *end* it that way) they typically married first and then emigrated here. While they shared Thanksgiving with the Indians, or vice versa I guess, the English were far less likely to be invited over to the long lodge for Christmas, or Easter or birthday parties, or war parties than were the French. The French on the other hand knew most of the partygoers quite well to begin with (read Saturday night in Québec) and were likely related to them (read Sunday morning in Québec). Their ties were much closer. The implications would soon become apparent.

The French and Indian Wars took place from 1675 to 1760. They were called the French and Indian Wars because the English won. Had the English lost, they would have likely been known as the English Wars, only in French (Les Guerres d'Anglais). History has its way with words and the victors usually do the writing. In truth (and that is what this book is all about, is it not?) there were many little wars during this time. Wars such as King Phillip's War (pretty cool to be both an Indian chief and a king, *and* have a war named after you, isn't it?), King William's War (he was a regular kind of king and not Indian), Queen Anne's War (she was a regular kind of queen and also not an Indian), Dummer's War (who and what the hell was a Dummer?), King George's War (I like to call it the "I, Me, Mine's War") and for the grand finale, the French and Indian War as mentioned previously.

As you can see, there was a whole lot of fightin' going on, and eventually everyone who wanted to kill someone did just that; those who needed to be killed were, and the remaining survivors agreed to call it a bloody epoch and hit the sack. The end result was that the French lost, which is why our stop signs say "STOP" and not "Arrêt." It was sort of similar to modern politics, what with "bleu" states (the French) and red states (the British). The main difference being that when the red states won, the bleu state people basically had to pack their bags and vacate the premises. This led to the plight of the Acadians, the birth of Cajun music, good Creole cooking, hot sauces, Huey Long, and alligator wrestling in Louisiana. War can be hell, but on the other hand there are often such unforeseen benefits as these to be had if you're willing to wait long enough.

With the wars all settled, peace reigned supreme and Maine prospered. This land was a happy, patriotic place in the mid-1760s. Summers were always a blast, as they are now. Beginning on Memorial Day, the festivities of the season broke into full swing. The Fourth of July, then as now, was a day of great celebrations, family gatherings, potato salad, hot dogs, parades, and fireworks. Unfortunately, there is such a thing as too much of a good thing, and the times quickly took a turn for the worse. The British, haughty rulers that they were, didn't like their Colonies celebrating their independence without there actually having been a bloody war to earn it, so they decided to crack down on these upstarts and put an end to their shenanigans. By sheer coincidence, they decided to go to Lexington and Concord on, of all days, the third Monday of April, which, as we all know, is Patriot's Day, and the "shot heard round the world," was fired. The joy and merriment that had settled upon the land faded in the blink of a minuteman's eye. There was little doubt where Mainers stood when word of the brewing revolt against the Crown reached her wooded shores. All of Maine's many brave minions rallied to the call of freedom and then chose which side to support.

A company of men was formed, but not a ragged company of men as we often read about; they would come later. This was a rather nattily dressed group of perky lads, armed with muskets and wearing those jaunty tri-cornered hats that were just the rage at the time. Three-sided hats were "de rigor" in the English colonial world as well as in French circles. Square, pentagon and even hexagon hats were developed, but these proved to be cumbersome, even dangerous in the wind, and though equipped with chinstraps, resulted in numerous neck injuries and countless lawsuits.

Heroes to be, tri-cornered hats and all, the rebels marched south in answer to Paul Revere's warning, heeding the call of history, fame and fortune. To Boston they trod in their hobnailed boots and buckskin moccasins to the coming clash that would signal the beginnings of the Revolutionary War and the bloody birth of a nation. (Actually, they chose one type of footwear or the other, but not both. And by the by, hobnailed moccasins simply didn't work out at all.)

This company of men marched down the coast, passing the Yorks and Kennebunks, and the Smiths and the Joneses, too. Perhaps they stopped to play a little skeeball along the boardwalk, history doesn't denote, but even if they did, what of it? They didn't linger for long anyway, for they were on a mission; theirs was a quest of destiny and no mere arcade would deter them from their vaunted goal. No doubt they paid the toll in New Hampshire. Even then there was no doubt a guinea or a pence to be made; war or no war, the bills had to be paid. They likely bought some cheap booze as well, and fireworks to celebrate what was certain to be a victory. They were headed for Bunker Hill and immortality.

For the Mainers, skilled hunters and backwoodsmen that they were, Bunker Hill was not difficult to find and they quickly spotted the huge granite spire that afforded a great view of nearby Boston Harbor and its environs. Elevators had yet to be invented so the climb to the top was tiring to say the least, but most of the men were game and went up for a look see. And what a view it was! The harbor was filled with sailing ships of every description from the world over. There across the way was the spire of the South Church, on the south side of the North Church that rose on the eastern shore of the west side of Boston Bay, into which emptied the Charles River. There was the Fleet Center, home of the Celtics and the Bruins, Faneuil Hall and its many curious shops and food courts, and Fenway Park, bastion of our beloved Red Sox. But this was no time to take in the sights, or to even enjoy a ball game. History was waiting on that hot and dusty day.

The actual battle of Boston's Bunker Hill took place not in Boston, but in Charleston, and not on Bunker Hill but on Breed's Hill. It was initially to be fought not by the British and the colonists, but rather these dueling enemies had called into play their "seconds," and hired them to engage in a pre-reenactment of what had yet to occur. The colonists had hired Guatemalans, well known for their landscaping skills, who built beautifully graded ramparts along the crest of the hill, with little pathways, strategically placed shrubs, flower-beds, firing pits and cannons. The British pre-reenactors, in their bright red rented overcoats, were of course intrigued by the ornate gardens across the river and curious as they were, were ordered by their officers to march up the hill in straight lines, and slaughter the pretend colonists who awaited them and who in turn would attempt to slaughter them as well. The tension was unbearable on that fateful day as each side waited for the other to flinch. And then, suddenly, it happened. The "seconds" realized they had all been duped and they ran away. The British had no choice but to take up the challenge. After all, the red coats had already been paid for, and the rent for the battlefield was non-refundable. The colonists weren't going anywhere soon and most had made plans to spend the day, so what the hell? If there was to be war, let there be war and let it begin here!

To make a long war short, the redcoats that day marched up the hill in nice, neatly formed lines, while being shot and killed by the colonists who, when they saw how mad this made the dead British guys and their friends, then ran away, lost the battle, but lived to run away another day. That was basically the scenario that played out over the next eight long years of turmoil. All of that running away left little time for personal hygiene and the necessary mending and upkeep of clothing, which led directly to that rag-tag thing the colonists were famous for. In the end, the rag-tag beat the red-tag and the British finally decided that constantly winning the war was, overall, a losing proposition. They packed up their teacups, decided not to return the red coats after all, and high-tailed it for London and merry ole England.

Maine's role in the war was quite important; at least to the Mainers who participated and particularly to those who gave their lives, which having done so, would never be the same again. As with the general war itself, Mainers actually lost far more than they ever won, and then won the war. Go figure.

As for Maine's role in the war, in 1775, Benedict Arnold and Raymond Burr organized an expedition to capture the former French fortress of Québec City. They gathered over a thousand hardy souls and nearly as many men and headed north in small wooden boats called bateaux. We don't know why they called them bateaux—after all, these were Englishmen—but they did. They traveled from Massachusetts to Augusta, where they rested at Fort Western, which is the oldest and easternmost wooden fort in the U.S. today.

Setting out once more, they struggled mightily against the rugged terrain, disease, the cold, starvation, and the elements (particularly heinous were Iridium and Manganese). Losing (read: dead) over half their force, they pressed onward towards their ultimate goal: the Citadel atop the bluffs of the hills that bordered the fields of the Plains of Abraham. Judiciously choosing at random perhaps the worst night of the winter, on which to stage an attack, the remaining sturdy souls entered the city only to become lost in a swirling snowstorm. Not only that, but their devious enemy had left all the street signs in French. If you don't believe me, go there and see for yourself. They are still in French to this day. The befuddled attackers became quickly confused, disoriented, and disheartened. They had not expected their exploits to come to such an end. Theirs was not known as the "ill-fated" expedition to Québec. What had gone wrong? They came to rue the Rue de St. Louis in more ways than one! Those who were not lucky enough to be killed outright were captured. Benedict Arnold managed to escape, turn traitor to his country, lose a leg, and found a tasty and profitable bread company known as Pepperidge Farms. Raymond Burr was wounded and confined to a wheelchair. Gradually regaining his strength and moral integrity, he lived to kill Alexander Hamilton in a duel to see who would have their image on the twenty-dollar bill. Go figure again.

Maine is also famous for one other exploit during the war that resulted in the greatest naval disaster in our nation's history until World War II. Over forty American ships and 2,000 soldiers lay siege to a small British force at the coastal town of Castine. When faced by a fleet of seven—count 'em seven—British ships coming to their countrymen's rescue, the Americans scuttled their fleet and walked back to Boston. Paul Revere was court marshaled as a result of his heroics in the fiasco when he was discovered returning, carrying only the one if by land lantern, having hocked the two if by sea.

The only solace in the disasters that were attributed to our fair state during the entire war was that our failures were not those of Maine's, but of Massachusetts—for Maine was not as yet a state. Neither was Massachusetts either, I suppose, if you want to get technical, but that's not the point. The point is that "we" were "them" back then and since "we" don't particularly like "them" now, it was "they" who failed so miserably then and not "we" or "us." I know it wasn't me.

The English language is spoken by a majority of all Maine residents. It is understood by slightly less, given the French influence upon the state. The French language is spoken by a majority of the French speaking population. It is understood by slightly less, given the French influence upon the state.

Post-Colonial Times

As we all know, George Washington, by virtue of having lost more battles than any other general in the Revolutionary War, was without a doubt the most famous and beloved hero of the nation and, as such, was duly elected President of "these United States." Jefferson, Franklin, Adams, Madison, and the other "founding fathers" founded the foundations of our foundling nation's new-found existence. The principles of one man (women need not apply), one vote, freedom for all (slaves not included), and separation of church and state (in God we trust, put your right hand on the Bible, etc.), and so many others were chiseled into our eternal heritage, never to be altered until the end of time—except by a two-thirds vote of all the state legislatures or some random appellate judge's opinion. Aside from a few scattered complaints by the women, the slaves, and the poor and "unlanded" non-gentry, this system seemed to work for everyone and our nation happily prospered. That is, until once again those lousy limeys, those red-coated dudes with the stiff upper lips and all that posh, posh stuff, decided that they didn't really want to sail their ships and conquer the world; they just wanted to sail *on* their ships and conquer the world, and so they impounded the few, the brave, the unfortunate soon-to-be mariner types, to become sailors in her or his (pick one) Royal Navy.

The War of 1812 was so named to make it easier for history majors to remember when it happened. Besides, all the really good names like the War of the Roses, The Thirty Years War (we all know how long it was, but not when it was; what were they thinking?), the French and Indian Wars, and the Revolutionary War had already been used. The War of 1812 it was, by default if nothing else.

As a new nation and now having a history of how to fight a war, we took up where we had left off with the British thirty years or so earlier. The British continued to win the battles, burned the White House, etc. and then, having gone undefeated, decided to give up again and signed a peace treaty in Paris. It was only after the war was officially over that we finally won a big battle in New Orleans, so it didn't count and everybody who was killed died for nothing since it was too late to call for a "do-over." Life went on, except for, well, you know.

In Maine, the war for us ended too quickly. We had begun to build great forts to thwart the British invaders who rudely never bothered to come and attack them. The forts proved useless for war, but to this day make for really neat, scenic picnic spots. The British, still smarting and mad about losing again after winning, decided to take Calais, Maine, just for spite, and kept it for four years. In the end, however, they decided winning wasn't all that great either, and packed up and went across the river to St. Stephen, where they self-medicated by eating large amounts of delicious Ganong and Cadbury chocolates, and drinking Killian's Red Ale and Moosehead lager. Americans were stuck with Old Milwaukee Light and Mary Janes, so I ask you, who really won? Really?

Following the War of 1812, the United States began to inexorably grow westward. They had tried moving eastward, but all that got them was wet. This was a thrilling period in which to be alive and the word "ho!" was used a lot, which kept spirits up during trying times. Those were the days of the Louisiana Purchase and Manifest Destiny. Actually, the Louisiana Purchase came in 1804, so that's not "technically" correct and Manifest Destiny didn't really take off until later, but you get the idea. Ho!

Anyway, the nation began to re-invent itself, look toward the future, and industrialize in the north. All the while in the south, it un-invented itself, looked toward the past, and agriculturalized. This led to the emergence of an ever-widening and fundamental rift among the states. The first glowing embers of the raging conflagration that burst into the fiery conflict over the heated subject of slavery that was to burn into our nations' historical soul was ignited when the tinder-dry words of debate were sparked into flame by the flinty sharp tongues of politicians debating in the House and Senate chambers of Washington, D.C. Men such as Calhoun, Clay, and Webster brought oratory soaring to unheralded heights. The game was afoot and both sides looked to enlist more players for their respective teams.

For its part, Massachusetts was still deeply in debt from the last two wars they had lost and won. They had all this land in what they called the District of Maine, but no money to vacation there, and besides, there were those damned tolls to be paid in New Hampshire if they did venture Down East. Therefore, the wise and dirt poor legislators of the nearly destitute Commonwealth, decided it was in the best interests of everyone to sell off their wooded parcels to the north and make a quick buck.

Having done just that, they paid off their credit cards and outstanding debts, refinanced their fiduciary house, and invested in some stock market futures. Maine, having literally bought its independence, now wanted to be a player in the big game that called itself the United States of America. Signing a declaration on March 15, 1820, Maine became the 23rd state of the United States. It was admitted as a free state; that is, as a non-slave state. Missouri became a new state on that date as well, but it was admitted as a slave state. This came to pass because of what was called the Great Missouri Compromise. Why it wasn't called the Great Maine Compromise, or at least the Great Maine and Missouri Compromise, why they couldn't compromise on that, we just don't know. What we do know is that it's just not fair and it wasn't the right thing to do.

Right or wrong, Maine was now a full-fledged state, a free state. Its capital was Portland. There was no slavery in Maine for two primary reasons: slavery had been banned in 1788, and there were very few black people to play the part of the slaves. Slavery had no doubt been attempted earlier here as elsewhere when Maine was the District, but picking cotton must have been preferred to picking through hard rocks for softer rocks known as "potatoes." The work was tedious, as the potato gin had not yet been invented. The entire experimental enterprise completely fell through in early 1814, when the only remaining black family turned in the towel, raised the white flag, packed their belongings into a long, black wagon and headed due south towards the sunshine and the warmth. Apparently the enticing allure of potentially playing hockey from September to May couldn't overcome their preference for 80 degree days in February. Whatever were they thinking?

Later attempts at reviving the plantation's economic model were doomed when the concept of stuffing potatoes into the top of pill bottles failed miserably as the potatoes were either too big, or the pill bottles too small. Either way, the two could never be reconciled. Maine's economic future was sealed for the next hundred years. The ideas of hard work, poverty, and hopeless despair would have to be carried forth by Caucasians alone until the French migrated later in the next century from Canada to find work in the mills.

Now officially a state, Maine began to flex its muscles towards the North and the dominion of what would one day become the independent nation of Canada. My preference would have been for a little muscle flexing towards the west and New Hampshire, but such was not to be. In any event, the border between Maine and Canada had remained undefined since the Revolution had ended and it was now up for grabs. In the past, the moose hadn't cared whether they were American moose or Canadian moose, just as long as they were *alive* moose. But citizens of nations are not moose, at least not most of them. Some may be tall and ungainly and covered with flies, but they're still mostly not moose. They're proud citizens and, as such, have a problem not knowing to whom they belong, and whose country they're going to defend. Besides, they need to know exactly which flag to fly outside the post office and whether to deliver a liter of petrol into their lorry or pump a gallon of gas into their pickup truck.

To answer these and other pressing questions of the day, an army was assembled in 1839 and placed under the able command of General Winfield Scott, or "Old Fuss and Feathers" as he was affectionately known to his men. In any event, The Great Aroostook War turned out to be a really good war, as wars go. There was some necessary campaigning, some marching and camping, but damn little, if any, actual fighting. Like I said, it was a good war and it came to a peaceful conclusion with the signing of the Webster-Ashburton Treaty, but not until a great deal of liquor was consumed by the warring parties. If shots are going to fly, those are best shots of all: shots of Kentucky Bourbon and Canadian Whiskey. You've got to admire Maine and Canada; we know how to put on a war don't we? It's sad to say, but warfare just ain't what it used to be. Let's lift a cold one to war and take a vow to fight the next one like the Great Aroostook War was fought. Here's to "War, the way it should be."

By this time, Maine's capital had been moved to the more centrally located town of Augusta. Standing above the mighty Kennebec River, the new State House, designed by Mr. Bullfinch (who also designed the nation's capitol building) was an inspiration to all who bothered to look up at its golden Indian. In its hallowed chambers rose the voice of the people in active debate over oncoming the issues of the day. In 1848, that issue was the Mexican War and it divided the Nation into two groups: those who wanted desperately to go to war and those who didn't hardly care all that much at all. In the end it was war, but not the way it should be.

It really wasn't much of a war, actually. The U.S. and Mexico locked horns over Texas and that "let freedom ring" thing. Basically, the U.S. did most of the fighting and the poor Mexicans did most of the dying. This was a shame. The U.S. still had its bourbon, but the Mexicans apparently didn't know how to use tequila to their best advantage. In the end, blood flowed instead of booze. Like I said, there are better ways to fight wars.

We here in Maine had little to argue about with either the Texans or the Mexicans back then, so we pretty much kept to ourselves. Today, what with George Bush and Taco Bells everywhere, I think we'd have something to fight about, but it's too late. We stayed out of the last one and it's just too late to get another one rolling.

By 1860, however, Maine could no longer remain on the sidelines of history. The teams had been drawing up sides over the years and the titanic clash of civil war was about to begin. The North dressed in blue and filled their grandstands to overflowing on the side of Union and freedom, while in the South it was another story altogether. Dressed in chestnut and gray, the South had more limited seating but a better exposure, and cheered for states' rights and slavery. Captain Abraham Lincoln was president of the North squad and Hannibal Hamlin of South Paris, Maine, was his vice president. Jefferson Davis captained the Southern team. No one except really good Jeopardy players can recall the name of the Confederate's vice president. Anyway, following Lincoln's inauguration, the referee's whistle blew early on in 1861 at Fort Sumter, and the game was on.

This Civil War would rage savagely for five long years across our beloved homeland. The fighting was fierce and deadly; casualties were great. Family fought family, brother fought brother and uncles fought uncles. Those who were not related to anyone had to draw lots. In Maine, brothers had always fought brothers, uncles had fought uncles and everyone fought with their grandmother during the holidays. (If you knew her, you'd know why. She was ornery, dressed only in black, had her hair pulled straight back in a bun, and never smiled. You're probably familiar with the daguerreotype hanging in the parlor.) Anyhow, when the Civil War came, Mainers had to stop fighting each other for the common good and they took up arms against the South. They took up guns too, and swords, and pointy, sharp things with which to nick, cut, and slash one another to death. This was not a pretty war by any means. It was war to the bitter end—you know, that kind of war. War "really not at all the way it should be."

Maine was and is a small state and it suffered more than its share of the death and destruction incurred over those five long years of strife. The fighting between the states was cruel and inhumane, but the infighting between and among the political parties of the day was even worse. Hannibal Hamlin fell by the wayside, dumped unceremoniously into the ditch of history, a casualty of politics, to make room for Andrew Johnson and his political pull. Andrew Johnson who would tragically, in more ways than one, assume the Presidency as a result of Lincoln's assassination on that fateful April day in April of April, 1865. But amid the sadness and horrors, there were successes and heroes as well, and none more fabled than the dashing, noble Joshua Chamberlain of Brunswick, Maine.

Chamberlain had been an erudite professor of philosophy at Bowdoin College before the hostilities commenced. He was an astute man, mild of manner, with a strength of conviction and character beyond his years and station in life. He answered duty's call willingly and enlisted as an officer, a colonel, in an all-volunteer unit. Leaving friends and family behind, he set off with his men in 1861 towards his and their destinies.

That destiny would be found on a hot July day near a little junction town in Pennsylvania by the name of Gettysburg. Chamberlain and the 20th Maine were sitting high on a hill, Little Round Top it was called, at the far end of the Union Army's defenses on that sultry summer's day. They were the eye of the fish hook-shaped Federal lines that stretched out before them, its shank aligned with the low slope of Cemetery Ridge as it arched towards town and ended with the wooded barb of Culp's rugged Hill. Sitting comfortably high above the Devil's rocky Den from which Confederate sharpshooters exchanged lead with their Union counterparts above, Joshua Chamberlain and his men surveyed the changing scene below, secure in their elevated position. That is until they saw the flashing of bayonets in the woods below and to their left, and heard the first chilling hoots of the vaunted and much feared "rebel yell" approaching at the quick.

Chamberlain was a master strategist. He had studied military tactics to prepare himself and his men for whatever might come their way. No doubt, that was why when the 75,000 men of George McClellan's Army of the Potomac faced off against Robert E. Lee's much-heralded Army of Northern Virginia, Chamberlain did what any wise leader would do. He headed for the high ground, away from the center of what would surely be one hell of a bloody battle.

Chamberlain was no fool: "I'm up high. I got a lot of guys with guns all dressed in blue around me. We got a lot of rocks to hide behind. I got me a good telescope, and a great view of the doin's down below. I'm all set," he must have thought to himself. That is, until the glint of the bayonets of the Texans, North Carolinians, and Floridians marching towards him caught his attention. I don't know for certain, but I suspect he must have thought something else at that point, something along the lines of "Oh shit!"

Chamberlain steadied his men as they silently awaited the onslaught that scurried deftly from tree to tree below their defensive position. Everything was hushed, save for the continuous, deafening and ever-rising rancor of the rebel yells echoing off the maple and oak forest with which they were intermingled. He and his men must have thought they were watching a Saturday afternoon matinee at the movies, a harmless film of shadow and images only, playing out before them for their entertainment alone, when suddenly that raucous cacophony was broken, shattered as the wooded hillsides erupted with the bellowing of volley after volley of deadly musket fire. The pitched screams of the wounded and the soon-to-be-dying punctuated the orange-red flashes of fire and acrid billows of spent powder now clinging to the greenery. Somehow the scenery seemed ethereal and unreal in the filtered sunlight pierced the wooded canopy here and there amidst the boiling chaos of the scene. On and on the bloody carnage carried forth, exposing the bloodied meat of its mayhem before the exhausted eyes of the 20th Maine, until suddenly, as if without warning, the men in blue unexpectedly ran out of ammunition.

Chamberlain was stunned by the deafening silence. What to do? He ordered his men to continue firing lest the rebels realize the predicament he and his cohorts faced. How long before the Confederates would realize the ragged, staggered blue line before them were only clapping and clasping their hands before their faces and yelling "Bang! Bang!"? How long before their charade was discovered and all would be lost?

Chamberlain decided then and there to make use of the only option at his disposal: to do the unexpected. He ordered his men to stop yelling and clapping foolishly, to fix their bayonets, and charge. They looked at one another, incredulous at the command. Was he serious? Could he truly mean what he said? Fix bayonets, and without powder or round, charge downhill into the waiting guns of their enemies? They stood in disbelief. Chamberlain raised his Colt revolver and pointed it at his Captain's head and quietly spoke. "Don't make me have to shout 'bang' at you," he said solemnly. The men saw the fanatic desperation in his eyes. He wasn't just pulling their legs and trying to get a cheap laugh. He was serious, deadly serious.

The troops responded as they were trained to do. With a mighty "huzzah" (which, while it was no rebel yell, had worked pretty well for them in the past), off they went, helter skelter, charging down that hill into the jaws of almost certain death and into the everlasting accolades of history as they saved the day, the Grand Army of the Potomac and perhaps, ultimately, the very Nation itself.

Just one short day later, Robert E. Lee would pull the biggest, boneheaded blunder of the war as he ordered George Picket and his valiant men to charge into the heat of a summer's day and eternal infamy. With that brilliant, though idiotic and stupid move, the deal was done and the die was cast: defeated, Lee retreated south and the Union was ultimately preserved for the ages.

Chamberlain would later be wounded in battle, receive the medal of honor, and would accept Lee's own sword at the final surrender ceremonies at Appomattox Court House just a short, but deadly year-and-a-half later. Chamberlain would also become President of Bowdoin College as well as a distinguished four-term governor of Maine. A great man whose courage under fire shall forever be remembered in the annals of Maine's honored past, Joshua Chamberlain was just a really cool guy. By the way, Joshua Chamberlain Pale Ale is really cool too, especially if you're a history buff like me. I recommend you charge into one yourself on a sultry summer's day.

The Boring Years: 1865 to 1898

I don't know what you think, but in my opinion these were the most boring thirty-three years in the entire history of the world and by that I mean, of course, in the entire history of Maine. Help me out here, but what exactly happened that was exciting and stirred the blood Down East during this time? I'll tell you what: nothing, absolutely nothing. People lived, and people died, but not in a really cool way, at least not here in Maine and that's what this book is all about. No one was drafted and sent to die in an unpopular national war, no giant meteors struck in the dark of night and obliterated so much as a single outhouse, and no frozen prehistoric beast somehow thawed out and ate a town ... nothing! Oh sure, someone, somewhere fell off a horse here or there or someone ate some not-quite-pickled-enough something or other and somehow got poisoned, but really, does vomit and diarrhea count for history? I think not. So what happened over these thirty-three years? I'll sum it up for you: NOTHING.

Out West on the plains, however, life was vibrant and things were very different. Out West, the hearty pioneers, caught red-handed stealing Indian land, were being attacked by red-blooded (is there any other kind?) redskins who rode their war ponies around them and their wagons in ever-tightening circles. Around and around they would go until either they were all shot and dragged from one foot by their horses, or as more commonly occurred, everyone involved got really dizzy and a time-out had to be called before they all just fell down and looked silly. Meanwhile, stagecoaches were raising dust and rupturing kidneys, railroads were being built by lots of Chinese guys, black hats were flying off the racks in ever-increasing numbers, and buffalo were being exterminated by the millions, often by "dudes" shooting them from trains for mere sport (there was no NFL, remember) which today would translate to "just for the hell of it." Either way, the buffalo were not pleased by the results. Now all that stuff is pretty cool, you've got to admit, and makes for great history.

By the way, as regards stagecoaches, they were required by law to carry the following cast of characters: one clean-shaven driver good at yelling "whoa," a bearded, scraggly cohort who wore a rumpled hat with a beaded chin strap and carried a shotgun that was used solely for throwing down on cue when the bad guys surrounded them; one locked chest of money with no key that had to be shot open; one nattily dressed banker from the East wearing glasses and reading a newspaper; one old gunfighter (preferably alcoholic); one stranger sleeping; one decent, good-looking male with a penchant for glaring stoically when bad guys shoot bullets at his feet; and one spiffy woman in her late twenties dressed to the nines who was headed West to be either a mail-order bride or a whore. It was a good law and made for decades of fine TV and movies.

But back here in Maine, people were just living out their lives in happiness and ever-increasing prosperity. "Nice but boring" soon led to "very nice but very boring." This, in turn, led to very thin eastern history books, which led to a lack of self-esteem for millions and a general feeling of lethargy, malaise, and woe. I researched history book sales to verify my assumptions and yes, sales plummeted during this time due to what was called "a severe lack of current events." This was truly a sad time but in all honesty, there were some significant things that *almost* happened in Maine that should be noted. The foremost of these was that John Blaine was almost elected President of the United States, key word being "almost." Okay, that's pretty much it. It was obvious something had to be done and to the joy of everyone (except maybe the Spanish), we'll move along to 1898 and the advent of the Spanish American War.

As everyone knows, Maine is forever associated closely with the Spanish American War simply because a U.S. battleship of the same name sunk in Havana's harbor, setting off a chain of events that led to Puerto Rico continually holding referendums on possible statehood—a sad and tragic end to what was called a "splendid little war." To this day, historians continue to quibble over whether the Maine was deliberately sabotaged by the Spanish, or simply exploded from within due to a coal gas or gunpowder accident. Either way, controversy such as this makes for fine TV to the benefit of the History Channel, but I wish to suggest another theory and another motive for the incident that has not received its proper due: self-destruction due to boredom.

I suspect that the Mainers on the Maine were, in the main, mainly tired of being on the periphery of history (as we've noted) and simply took matters into their own hands. I suspect that they somewhat inadvertently blew themselves onto the front pages of the world in an act of stupidity. I suspect that one dark and not-so-stormy night, several Mainers were above decks smoking those large cigars Havana was and is famous for. I suspect that some of these Mainers placed those long cigars upright in the bowls of their trusty corncob pipes to enjoy. I suspect that others present thought this looked stupid. I know for a fact that this looks stupid because I drew myself a picture and thought, "That looks stupid." I suspect that this led to teasing, taunting, and eventually the following tragic chain of events.

I suspect that these sailors pondered their predicament as they puffed slowly on their lengthy stogies. I suspect that this discussion included a significant number of "ayuhs" and nodding of heads, and that, in time, led them to the idea that if a ship blew up in Havana harbor, the nation would rally to their salvation and through such a seemingly justified war against a weak and pathetically ill-equipped adversary, the United States would achieve its deserved share of unheralded glory and national vindication. What I don't suspect is that they thought this through.

Here's what I think happened. I think the sailors on the Maine decided that blowing up a ship to start a war was a good idea. You may think otherwise, but let's face it, education wasn't then what it is now, and besides you have the luxury of not sitting on a ship in Havana in 1898, having been bored out of your gourd for the past thirty-three years. Desperate times lead to desperate acts. I think that these sailors thought it was a good idea. I also think that they never intended to blow up the Maine, but intended instead to blow up the U.S.S. New Hampshire, another battleship bobbing tax-free nearby. I think they thought it might be enough to just start a war and kill the boredom, but, even if it didn't, it would be good sport none the less. So, just for the hell of it, they went ahead with their little scheme and even if it did not result in war, they thought sinking the New Hampshire would be just the kind of a funny joke people back home would appreciate. It was a win-win situation.

What I don't think happened was that these sailors thought that the boat they would actually sink would be their own, the U.S.S. Maine, and that they would all die in the ensuing aftermath, missing out on the glory part, not to mention the funny joke part of their plan. I think that what transpired was, in fact, all a tragic mistake, brought about by those foolishly long Havana cigars they were smoking. But this is not just what I think. This is not pure conjecture on my part, not at all. I have proof. I have "veritae." You see, in the course of my research, I have stumbled across a transcript of what I believe was a telephone conversation that would have been recorded had telephones, walkie-talkies, or radios been invented and existed at the time. The words were somewhat garbled and difficult to make out, but I managed to decipher them by holding them up to a really bright light or something.

The scene was set upon the glassy waters of Havana's harbor. It was a moonless night, dark and quiet. The air was still. There was not a sound to be heard save for the lapping of water gently against an iron hull—or was that the rhythmic chop of oars from a dingy that was slowly, stealthily approaching through the gloom? As you read this, you'll have to add your own Maine accent, as I don't feel up to it. "Uriah? Have you the powder?" Something garbled that sounded like an affirmative. "Uriah, you look stupid with that cigar sticking out of your pipe like that." Something garbled that sounded like 1890s swearing followed by "so do you." "Uriah, you look to be a foot taller than you are, what with that cigar poking up there over your head like that." Something garbled, some swearing, some laughing, some pushing followed by some jostling of places in the boat. The tape is difficult to discern at this point and there appears to be a significant gap as though someone tried to erase a segment of history to cover up or cause confusion. When the words are decipherable once more, it appears that following much laughter and mayhem, the dingy has been moving about erratically for some time in the dark but is now on course once more, very close now and alongside the large, looming, majestic shell of a warship towering above. Just then, another voice pierces the recording: "What's that smell, and what are all those red, glowing lights out there? Who goes there?"

followed by this telltale remark: "Whoa boy, Uriah! Ditch the cigars in that open port hole, boys, and row for your lives." This is followed by a moment's silence, some pathetic rowing sounds, a large explosion, and a longer silence.

The Maine was sunk and the rest is history. A head count of the surviving crewmembers indicated the absence and assumed death of four local boys from Harpswell, Maine, who had enlisted together several years earlier. One of their names was Uriah Holbrooke. Further inquiry back in Maine at the Harpswell Library archives led to the discovery that this Uriah Holbrooke, his twin brother Uriah Jr., their cousin Uriah Heath, and a friend, Uriah Menot, had all dropped out of school where they had been history majors, citing boredom as the reason for their leaving. In an interesting side note, in the classifieds of the Havana Newspaper-Rio dated the following day, this damning notice was discovered: "Found: several slightly charred corncob pipes and half smoked cigars. Many funny possibilities. Any reasonable offer accepted ... NO TAX!"

Thus, the Spanish American War began and the United States of America burst forth upon the stage of world events to a chorus of the now-familiar battle cry, "Remember the Maine."

But as for Maine, what were the lasting effects of this war? In point of fact, they were very few. Aside from some new marchers in the Fourth of July and Memorial Day parades (the Civil War veterans were getting quite old by this time and needed replacing), the Spanish influence in Maine is negligible. Why? Perhaps it's because sombreros never caught on up here in the north. They don't kill winter's chill, and in a strong wind they only serve to lengthen one's neck. I don't know for sure. But if you doubt me, I do know this. If you ask a Mainer if he's ever seen or been in a "bodega," he'll likely respond by saying, "No, not in person, but I sure would love to. The '32 models with the heavy chrome bumpers, the four hundred horse V8's and the ragtops were prime. Now that was one hell of a Bodega!"

What happened after the war until the present day is what I call current events for the most part or at the very least, recent history. I'm not going to recount it here and now, but perhaps in the future, when I'm bored, I just may give the juicy meat of Maine history another stab. You see, I relish a good chew of what's come before, but I seldom swallow all I read and neither should you. That sort of intellectual gluttony only leads to neuritis, neuralgia, an unsettled stomach and a case of the "vapors." And oh yes, be forewarned, history does have a history of repeating itself in the historical sense, so carry a napkin just in case.

New Hampshire:
"The Way Life Should Not Be"

Before we can further discuss Maine in the present and you can experience our current understanding of "the way life should be," I need to prepare you for the journey here. As I said in the Prologue, you are going to have to pass through New Hampshire to get to Maine. Yes, you'll have hell to pay. This is not all bad, however. Having been to hell and back myself, I can tell you that once having been there you'll appreciate heavenly Maine all the more.

New Hampshire. New Hampshire is the fifth-smallest state in the Union, but it is big enough to completely separate Maine from the rest of the United States. Therefore, simply put, while New Hampshire may be small, it's still way too big for those of us here in Maine. While it is not a very large state (Did I mention it was the third smallest state? Good, because it's not. It's the fifth smallest.), its very existence causes discomfort to many (if not most) Mainers. New Hampshire is what geographers refer to as "in the way." Its position, geographically speaking, is similar to a blockage of the colon. It's a constipating obstruction to the fluid flow of interstate commerce, and the strain this imposes upon Maine's economic system is unsettling to say the least.

Being what it is, New Hampshire, therefore, has resulted in the geographical, political, and economic equivalent of a hemispherical hemorrhoid. It's true; New England suffers from a case of the dreaded "piles." In other words, and please excuse my language, New Hampshire is a pain in the ass.

Being a pain in the ass, New Hampshire doesn't sit well with me and I despise it. I have often thought that if the gods ever inserted a giant tube of Preparation H (It would have to be a pretty big tube, even though I believe New Hampshire is the fifth-smallest state in the Union.) into the gaping orifice of the Piscataqua River and squeezed really hard, the entire state would quickly pucker, shrivel, shrink, and die. At least, I would hope so. I hate it that much.

Now, some of you might think that hate is a rather extreme emotion to harbor towards the fifth-smallest state. Well, some of you might be wrong! I hate New Hampshire and I'm not the only one. There are other perceptive and discerning folk besides myself that feel the same way. I know this is so because I have met them. They despise New Hampshire almost as much as I do, so I know I'm not alone in this. For instance, if you were to randomly select any family, say mine for the sake of argument, you'd find that the children and their father all hate New Hampshire with a passion, and the wife and matron of the home doesn't really like it all that much either. Surprised? You shouldn't be. Let me tell you why.

You see, New Hampshire is a decrepit little icon of what it calls "rugged individualism." Now, don't misunderstand me; I like a little rugged individualism as much as the next guy and probably more, but I like it as a trait in individuals, not in states. Like Thoreau, I admire a man who can march to the beat of a different drummer, but New Hampshire doesn't crawl, much less march. New Hampshire slithers. And it certainly can't carry a tune, at least not the same tune that the rest of New England is whistling as we all traipse hand in hand into the twenty-first century.

No, you see, New Hampshire likes to be different just to be different for difference's sake. It's not different to be good, not to be better, and certainly not to be the best—just different to be different. And as far as that goes, I give them credit: they've succeeded. New Hampshire is definitely different. Unfortunately for the rest of us it's different in a bad way.

Take a gander at a map of New England, if you will, and there you'll find your first clue that something is amiss. Use your imagination and you'll see that Vermont and New Hampshire resemble two splinters lying side by side. Vermont points down, like a harmless splinter should. New Hampshire points up, like it shouldn't. Now, to get to Maine you have to pass through, and by "through" I mean "over", and by "over" I mean "on," New Hampshire. What do you think is going to happen when you step on an up-pointing splinter? Right! The old revolutionary era flag read, "Don't tread on me" for a reason. But it's too late! Too late New England! You now have a splinter driven deep within you: a festering, infecting little intruder from hell.

Yes, it is an aberration. Look at it. There's just something about it that doesn't sit well, isn't there? Picture it and immediately it's obvious; something just isn't right with this picture. But what is it that's not right? I'll give you a hint and tell you what it is. It's a little something we call EVERYTHING, that's what it is. Every little thing about New Hampshire is not right. In fact, every little thing about New Hampshire is just plain wrong.

New Hampshire is a beautiful land mass, with rugged mountains, clear rivers and streams, and a glorious seacoast—all fifteen miles of it. Why does New Hampshire have a seacoast? Sure beats me! Who thought giving New Hampshire waterfront property was a good idea? I wouldn't have done it. What was the point? Didn't the founding fathers realize New Hampshire wouldn't be able to handle a coastline? They should have had a little foresight. I mean they got the constitution and the "pursuit of happiness" thing right, so why not this? Asked by some early New Hampshire settlers for a little beachfront property, they should have simply responded, "You want a little coast? You can't handle a little coast," and sent those malcontents packing back to their rugged, granite hills and clear mountain streams. But no, for some unknown reason, somebody in a three-pointed hat must have thought, "What the hell, they're only asking for a few miles of sand. It's only sand. What harm can come of that?" Well, my friends, let me tell you.

In retrospect, those fifteen miles of beach turned out to be about fifteen miles of beach too many. Fifteen stinking, lousy miles of sandy beach and what did New Hampshire do with it a mere 250 years or so later? They did what any aberration of a state would do—why, they built a nuclear power plant on it! They only have fifteen miles of precious sand and saltwater for their citizens to cherish and enjoy and they see it not as an endowment from the founding fathers to be preserved for perpetuity, but instead view it as a means to a quick buck, a moneymaking opportunity falling right into their greedy little, money-grubbing hands. They put a huge gray wart of a nuclear power plant smack dab in the middle of the forehead of what pitiful little coast they have. This could have happened only in New Hampshire. The only surprise I have is that it took them 250 years to do it! I suppose they were just waiting for the worst possible choice and weren't willing to compromise on something like a steel mill or a coal mine.

Think of it. Maine has over three thousand miles of pristine coastline. Three thousand! And how many nuclear power plants are there on three thousand miles? None. Zilch. Nada. Not a one. (Okay, knowledge boy, we had one, but it was a small one. We realized our mistake and corrected it. Maine Yankee is no more, so let's drop it already.) But New Hampshire, they have only fifteen miles of saltwater-sipping sand and they have a nuclear power plant bolted to the very granite base of the state, as if someone might come in the night and try to steal it out from under them. As if, perish the thought, there could ever be two New Hampshires. Not only that, but they actually tried to make this "honeypot" of power into a duplex of sorts, a two-plants-for-the-price-of-one scam, but things got so screwed up building the first one that ... well, enough said. Suffice it to say that, fortunately for the rest of us, things don't always work out as planned.

So, you say you don't buy my argument. You don't see the harm. Well, let me extrapolate on this concept if you will. Imagine that New Hampshire has Maine's coastline, all three thousand miles of it. Imagine also that New Hampshire doesn't have Maine's intrinsic values, judgment and conscience. Now imagine well over 200 nuclear power plants! If fifteen equals one, then 3000 translates into 200. That's right, 200, with a capital 2. Can you capitalize a number? Anyway, you'd have 200 nuclear targets available for potential terrorists to drool over. As in, 200 sources of possible radioactive leaks and contamination, and as in 200 concrete eyesores blighting the majestic scenery.

But surely, New Hampshire wouldn't be—couldn't be—so crass, so money grubbing, so insensitive and callous? Oh no? You don't know New Hampshire very well, do you? If there's a way to maybe not make but keep a nickel, New Hampshire will do it, but we'll get to the bottle bill later. Still, why be so negative?

Negative is where New Hampshire has it all over her simple neighbors. Here's where she leaves them all choking in her dust, drowning in her wake—her dusty wake if that's possible, which I don't think it is. New Hampshire excels in what we shall generously call "creative thinking." And by "creative thinking," I mean "creative," as in making something out of nothing. And by "something," I mean in New Hampshire's case, MONEY! For in the end, as far as New Hampshire is concerned, that's what it and everything else comes down to: MONEY and only MONEY. Is there anything else? No, in their eyes, there isn't. That's it in a nutshell or a nutcase state's shell, as it were. I repeat for clarification sake: if asked, the answer to all questions regarding New Hampshire is MONEY. Remember this because there will be a quiz at the end of the chapter.

Now, the name New Hampshire comes from the Latin, and as I see it, it translates literally as "We may be small but we can hurt you, do unto others, save a nickel make a dime, whatever you do, don't dare tax us, pay your toll and wave goodbye, first in the nation by law, most greedy on high, unencumbered by social conscience, land of the free to do what we want, to you, at your expense, hellhole of a stinking, lousy, no good, wretched, self-centered, self-important, egotistical, gloating non-entity." Now, it's been a few years since my last Latin lesson (believe it or not, I never actually studied Latin), but I think that translation is as the English often say, fairly "spot on" or at least close.

In actuality, of course, it's not the name that matters when it comes to understanding what a state stands for. A name is, after all, made up of only words, or letters actually. But a motto, that's something else altogether. A motto has both letters and words. It's usually really cool and, regarding states, it's their motto that tells you all you need to know. Maine's motto is Dirigo, or "I Lead." It embodies a culture of independence, self-confidence, accomplishment and direction. New Hampshire's state motto, on the other hand, can't be the well known and widely proclaimed "Live Free or Die," as they would have you believe. Don't be duped. "Live Free or Die" is a front. It's there for show only, to deceive the gullible, to pique your historical and patriotic interest. If you don't believe me, read the small print on their license plates. It's got to be there if you look close enough. I haven't found it myself, but I'm sure it's there. No, the actual "State Motto of New Hampshire" can't be "Live Free or Die," but rather must be "Live *Tax* Free or Die," and that my friends, *that* you can take to the bank!

Look, I respect "New Hampshirites." In point of fact, "New Hampshirites" have historically been known to toil twenty-five hours a day, eight days a week, on a failed sugar-free rutabaga plantation located in a salt mine, in the dark, living on Jujubes and Nutella sandwiches as indentured servants to Santa's evil twin brother, Harley, and the almighty dollar and never once even murmuring a hint of discontent. They may be lowlifes, but they are tough lowlifes, I'll give them that. But that same rutabaga miner, the one wiping salt off his brow in stoic grace, can be reduced to the likes of a child rolling on the ground, kicking and screaming, and crying his eyes out in mere milliseconds simply by suggesting he pay 5% in sales tax to support the needy and indigent like himself. That's all it would take: a simple, generous good deed. Imagine, a whole state of people like that and you have something approaching New Hampshire. That's them. And their motto, truncated, reduced, translated and condensed, can be summed up as follows: the "*Ka-Ching*" state. End of story.

Therefore, if, as the saying goes, "money is the root of all evil," then it follows that New Hampshire itself is the living, breathing embodiment of the phrase. No truer words were ever muttered (or uttered for that matter) and so utterly (but not "mutterly") transformed into reality. New Hampshire's evil dyed-in-the-wool. It permeates its being through and through, right to its gnarly roots clawing tight to the bony core of its very being, those granite rocks that form its spine.

Could it be otherwise? I don't think so, and that's why here in New England its evil nature is taken as a widely accepted and commonly known fact. It's not an opinion. Like dandruff, my second cousin Flo, and phlegm, it may not be pretty, but it simply is. How else can you explain that one day when I tuned in the Canadian Broadcasting Corporation's radio signal up Houlton way, there came the casual remark of a commentator referring offhandedly to New Hampshire's dyed-in-the-wool evil twin? I'm not making this up. This really happened. And remember, this is coming from Canada; they don't litter and they don't lie. Make no mistake: New Hampshire is evil.

How evil can that be, you might ask? Pretty darned evil, I say. Just listen to this conversation between two natives that I recently overheard in my head while walking alone on a "secluded" fifteen-mile stretch of nondescript seashore, in an unnamed state situated in the north Atlantic at, oh, let's say 42 degrees Longitude, 45 degrees North Latitude.

Lackey #1: Aren't you worried that the power plant might cause some natural disaster?

Lackey #2: What could go wrong with a nuclear power plant?

Lackey #1: I don't know. Something like Chernobyl, Fukajima or Three Mile Island?

Lackey #2: What? You believe those liberal press stories? That's just propaganda I tell you. Look, that stuff never happened and if it did, there's an up side no one talks about. Just think of the creative enhancement opportunities we'd benefit from. Think of the progress, my good man. No more tedious evolution. No, this will be rapid, genetic revolution with endless possibilities. Think of it: lobsters with six claws, all crushers by the way, thriving in the rosy glow of the newly energized and briny sea! And not far down the road, maybe within a week or so, certainly no more than a month, tops, those very same crustaceans emerging onto dry land, free to range in small lobsters herds. They'll be only two inches high you know. Think of the money we'd save on fencing alone! And that's just the start, just some random thoughts off the top of my head. The opportunities are endless. It'll be magic, pure magic. And remember, we live in New Hampshire, so it's all tax-free my friend, all tax-free.

Still think New Hampshire's not evil? Let's consider travel for the average Mainer. If we want to travel to the west, to the rest of New England, or anywhere else in the United States of America for that matter, we have to go through New Hampshire, and don't think they don't know it! They know and they're lying in wait for us. They know I-95 is the only interstate from Maine to anywhere. They may be rugged lowlifes, but surprisingly, some of them have learned how to read. They can also read maps and they're capable of spelling AAA if you give them a couple of tries. Some of them have even been to Maine and they know you can't get there from here, at least the vast majority of us, without getting there by way of I-95.

Yes, I-95. Fifteen miles of coast and they not only have a nuclear power plant, they have something even more insidious awaiting us. They have TOLL-BOOTHS! In fact they have many tollbooths. How many? I heard one of their minions cloaked in black whisper to another, "As many as it takes my friend. As many as it takes."

Now, you'd think a toll is a toll, but not in New Hampshire. These guys are tricky—tricky and cheap. These Granite Staters had figured out that by doubling and collecting the toll in only one direction, they could cut their costs in half, but not their revenue. Not only that, at one time the clever bastards let you leave Maine for free. They'd found that we Mainers, having seen what little the rest of what the country has to offer and realizing what we had left behind, we Mainers would gladly pay any price to get back home and as far as New Hampshire's concerned, that price was two dollars American, thank you very much. It's like a giant, evil lobster trap in reverse, sporting a tollgate. Want to go home? Fine, that's your choice, Mainers. That's what freedom is all about; New Hampshire's financial freedom, that is. That's the cost of freedom. You see, in New Hampshire, the price of freedom always has a dollar sign attached to it. The entire state is like a giant troll, a giant, rugged, ugly troll, sitting under a huge bridge, near a nuclear power plant, just waiting to pounce. I have never in my life seen another place like it, and I hope to God to never ever say otherwise.

Now, as a Mainer, you've been gouged at what substitutes for taxes in New Hampshire (the tollbooths) and you are but a few miles from the safe haven of Maine. But it's a long few miles and many dangers await before you can breathe freely. It's still some time before you can release that white-knuckled death grip you wisely have on your wallet. New Hampshire, on the other hand, will not easily let you go.

New Hampshire is like a leech and she has contrived many ways to suck from "out of staters" the green life blood she craves. We foolishly think we've run the gauntlet, paid our ransom and are home free. We unwittingly choose to exit I-95 before the bridge for a short break and a much-needed rest. But suddenly, we are spinning about, circling like the reverse of a vulture, just outside Portsmouth, literally circling, around and around until at last dizzy, confused, feeling light-headed and faint, we pull over. (Is this a mere happenstance of proper road design? I think not.) We exit stage right and before we know what's hit us, we're in a parking lot on the side of the rotary. The traffic circle has worked its magic once again. We have found what we weren't looking for.

We get out of our vehicle, steady our stance, clear our heads and gaze upon the neon lights beckoning us in: STATE of NEW HAMPSHIRE, *TAX FREE LIQUOR STORE.*

I don't buy much liquor at the New Hampshire State Liquor stores. I certainly don't buy any beer there, but that's for two very different reasons. First of all, for some reason New Hampshire doesn't sell beer at its liquor stores. But even if they did, I wouldn't buy any because unlike Maine, Connecticut, Vermont, Massachusetts, Rhode Island, New York, and every other socially conscious state in New England, New Hampshire doesn't charge a deposit on its bottles. Why? "Ka-Ching," that's why. You see it's human nature and that nickel bottle TAX working in reverse. That nickel is what keeps you from throwing your empties out the window. The same nickel that encourages a kid to pick it up if you happened to be feeling particularly rich that day, or if you're just a slob and you just didn't care, or if it was your turn to see if you could hit the next sign, or whatever. The point is, it's not a great burden or price to pay to keep the countryside clean, is it? Hell, no! After all, it's just a freakin' nickel—one measly nickel. But, if you are a reprehensible, reprobate of a state capable of adding one and one together, you work the numbers and realize you can parlay that "a nickel here, a nickel there and pretty soon you're talking a dime" mentality into some pretty big bucks.

New Hampshire is just that state. It has that mentality, and it is quite open to parlaying, no doubt about it. Why, they've practically built their entire economy on the principle. Remember, these are the same folks who offer you the chance to bet on disillusioned, worn out dogs chasing mechanical rabbits they can never catch. "Ka-Ching." Without them, where would our humane societies find a continuous supply of discarded tools also known to some as man's best friend? But I digress. As I said, New Hampshire can parlay. I'll give them that. And it is blessed by its close proximity to another Maine problem: Massachusetts.

Now most folk up here in Maine are reluctant to tell you what they really think about the land of "Mass-holes," but I'm not. They're afraid because those Massachusetts guys have guns, lots of guns, and they drive big, shiny SUVs. It's fall and they're heading to their shack just south of nowhere, which is where most of us Mainers live by the way, and the twelve of them—cousins, uncles, coworkers, whatever—are off to assert their manhood as they have been doing for generations. They are heading for their ancestral hunting grounds. They are heading to Maine to KILL! Kill what you ask? Who cares? Just to kill something, anything. Usually it's their thirst for rowdiness and liquor that dies first. Sometimes, though less frequently, it's a deer or a beer, I mean a *bear*, that stumbles across their path only to meet its fate.

Now understand, this is not a minor undertaking, this annual hunting expedition. You can't just set out willy-nilly. You have to plan just like the Allies did for D-Day back in '44. You see, if you're heading to Maine to hunt, then every penny counts. For one thing, one member of the group will even have to buy a hunting license in case someone gets lucky. The basic reasoning goes like this: You're going to Maine, and your wife is not. Translation: You're getting drunk with your buddies. You're also going to hunt. Translation: There's a good chance you're going to hunt drunk and that means there is going to be a whole lot of shootin' goin' on. You're gonna need to bring with you a fair supply of bullets. You're gonna need every penny you've got, and were not talking pennies here. We're talking nickels, my friend. So, like a true blue blue blood from Bean Town, you head off to the wilderness and your camp fully stocked with TAX FREE beer, wine and liquor and a whole lot of pennics. Your plan and New Hampshire's have worked. "A nickel saved," you know. You are loaded and on your way to being loaded. "Ka-Ching. Ka-Ching."

Of course, little did you know that the Maine State Police stake out the Portsmouth Liquor Store and if you take too much of those spirits into Maine, they will kindly relieve you of having to later relieve yourself, and will confiscate the overage. It's a good law. It makes sense to us up here. It makes you sober up to reality real fast, too. Now you'll have to buy some of your liquor here in Maine and you'll pay your tax like every other civilized person in New England. By the way, I think the police donate the confiscated booze to the poor who can't afford to drive to Portsmouth themselves. It's like government surplus cheese, only a whole lot better. That may not be true, but if there's a God and he's heard our prayers, then thy will be done, I say.

Now, I don't buy much liquor in New Hampshire. I do go into the liquor store, however. I look at it as a museum of sorts—a bottle museum. The best selection to peruse is the vodka collection. Vodka comes in all sorts of bottles, in all shapes, sizes and colors. See-through bottles with scenes of glaciers, cherries, lemons, geese, and whatnot. Fascinating stuff it is. Almost makes me wish I were a hunter from "away" myself, but I'm not. So I do some looking, use the restroom, and head on out.

Are you starting to get the hang of how things work in New Hampshire? It's a place that subsists in large part by way of relieving (read "stealing") folks of their money without actually having a sales tax, which is the generally accepted means of stealing money used by other states. New Hampshire somehow chanced upon the idea of not having a sales tax and they dug the idea. In fact, they've turned it into a veritable gold mine and they continue to dig it to this day. Every other New England state has one—a sales tax, that is. New Hampshire's scheme would collapse, of course, if the other states in New England did the same as they do. The idea works because New Hampshire is the only one doing it. It's just the same with their not having a bottle bill. One other plus for the state is that having no sales tax makes tallying up what to charge real simple; there's just adding the price. No need to complicate matters with multiplying and percentages. That saves money on math education and leaves "complicated" to the other states. The end result is that New Hampshire's goods and services are now officially cheaper, which of course is considered good by most of us. This encourages the kind of person who would like to move to New

Hampshire but can't afford to, to at least visit the state, do a little shopping on the side and save a few bucks.

To this end, New Hampshire has shamelessly built shopping centers that stand like sentry posts along its borders. No one may pass without spending some money. No one. It's almost a law and almost everyone obeys. New Hampshire has erected what amounts to "the great wall of commerce." It's a sieve of sorts, with portholes called "malls," that lure in the unsuspecting and almost painlessly separate them from their money. It's ingenious. You build a mall, throw in a quaint, rustic covered bridge or two just for effect, add a white steepled church and you're good to go. It's a Ponzi scheme of sorts, based on living off the civility of your neighbors. It's a vampire state's dream scheme come true, sucking dry its neighbors of the very lifeblood of commerce they need to survive. That sucking sound Ross Perot was speaking of way back when? It wasn't Mexico after all. You know what it was, and it still is.

And to think, we all go home, complaining about our taxes. Why are they so high? Why can't we be like New Hampshire? The simple answer is, we can't. The truth is that there's room for only one. If all of New England was like New Hampshire, New Hampshire simply couldn't exist. A parasite can only live off a healthy host. A parasite living off another parasite would soon die a bitter death, sucked dry. No, New Hampshire wouldn't be the shining star of capitalism and free enterprise it is made out to be by the conservative right if it didn't have those other healthy, socially liberal states on which it feeds. I think I said it before, perhaps in slightly different terms, but New Hampshire is a bloodsucking leech, and yes, I despise it.

My opinion aside, is this idea of New Hamphire's a success? You bet it is! And why not? It's a great place to shop! It's so successful that, to paraphrase Yogi Berra, it's almost gotten to the point that "No one shops there anymore because it's too crowded." It's only when the cost of travel in both time and money exceeds the savings from paying no taxes that life returns to normal, "the way life should be." I'm not sure exactly how far that is in miles. I live too far from the border to ever really know, but I do know it's too close for comfort, especially around the holidays.

These are just some of the examples of why I hate New Hampshire. There are many more. For one, you can actually purchase fireworks there, tax-free of course. You can't do this anywhere else in New England, and they are illegal to even possess in most places as well. (Okay, Governor LePage has changed that, but I didn't vote for him.) But you can, or at least could, to the best of my knowledge, purchase them in the Granite State. However, there was one caveat, I believe. New Hampshire knows that fireworks are inherently dangerous, so I think you have to take them out of state within three hours of your buying them, and of course you couldn't shoot them off in-state either; safety first! Anyway, stock up on liquor and explosives. It makes sense to me. "Ka-ching."

Am I surprised by anything concerning New Hampshire and money, you may ask? Well, yes I am, and it's this: I don't know why they stop at bottles, booze and boomers. I don't know why they don't carry the principle to its full potential and sell street drugs too. You know, there's a lot of money to be made on heroin, cocaine, crystal meth, crack, pot, and such. Just ask Colombia and the cartels. There's a never-ending demand for the product, so why not meet it? It would all be TAX FREE of course. Just don't shoot up until you cross the border; remember, safety, safety, safety. New Hampshire has *some* standards you know.

And what standards they have! For instance, they believe in the righteousness of the death sentence. They, and CT of all the New England states, have the death penalty. But not just any death penalty, mind you, NH's can be death by hanging, of all things. It's the twenty-first century for crying out loud, and New Hampshire still feels the need to protect the common good by stringing up the bad guys. They haven't hung anyone for a long time, it's true, but all the same, they won't get rid of the law that allows them to. Why not? Are they waiting for just the right set of circumstances? Don't they have enough heinous murderers to choose from like everyone else? Of course they do. But maybe they're waiting for a prominent Liberal to commit that special crime (that warrants death by hanging)—something like passing a sales tax or maybe jaywalking? Just one more thing. Do you know what the last name of New Hampshire's governor was when this was being written? It was Lynch. You can't make this stuff up.

But why be restricted to hanging, I ask? In the case of a Liberal, I'm sure that most of New Hampshire would agree that hanging is too good for them "thar" scurvy types. There must be a more suitable punishment for those guys. Why not use death by pressing, as Massachusetts' pious brethren used to do in Salem and thereabouts lo those many years ago. It's a simple enough concept and God knows they have the rocks for it. I mean it is the Granite State, right? Maybe they could reassemble the Old Man of the Mountain and lower him onto the chest of a deserving victim. How symbolic would that be?

And if they didn't want to use stones (I know they can be heavy and difficult to transport) they could use one of the many apple cider presses scattered throughout the state. It would save money (not a little matter in New Hampshire, as you now well know) in not having to go to the expense of hauling rock, building a set of gallows, or whatnot. Maybe they could have a two-for-one special. Maybe even sell it on "pay-per-view" like some heavyweight fight. They could use random prisoners (a lottery system comes to mind) to clean out their nuclear power plant's reactor core: you know, kill two jail birds with one radioactive stone so to speak. I wouldn't put anything past them. And best of all, it would all be TAX FREE of course!

Changing lanes, New Hampshire also has the distinction of being the only state in the Union not to have a mandatory seat belt law for adults. Imagine! They are the only state. They so want to be special and protect the rights of the rugged individual that they are willing not to enact a law that every other state and most countries (I'm not sure about Somalia) have seen fit to enforce, a law that without question saves lives. Rather than be inconvenienced by wearing a seat belt, New Hampshire sees fit to allow its citizens to suffer possible death or permanent impairment rather than be encumbered by a stinkin' shoulder harness. "Live Free or Die" should now be read as "Ride Free *and* Die." Also, in New Hampshire you can begin to learn to drive at the ripe old age of ... thirteen! You thought I was going to say twelve? Don't be ridiculous. A twelve-year-old is not mature enough to responsibly manage a ton or two of hardened steel barreling towards oncoming traffic at sixty or seventy miles an hour. What were you thinking?

They don't have a mandatory helmet law for motorcyclists either. What did you expect? I guess they feel that having brain-damaged citizens supported by the collective society is somehow beneficial to both the individual and the whole. I can understand how brain damaged "New Hampshirites" would blend in with the population in general, making them feel less conspicuous than they might otherwise. Not only that, but there's security in knowing that, as a general rule, the state population will remain more or less stable, as paraplegics are, statistically speaking, less likely to get up and leave the state in a fit of rugged individualism.

Moving right along, at this time I'd like to take this time to comment on New Hampshire's "first in the Union" primary. As you probably are all too painfully aware, New Hampshire has dibs on the first political primary held in the United States to select our next President. The election of our President begins here, which, come to think of it, might explain a few things about the quality of presidents we've had of late, but that's another subject altogether. Be that as it may, New Hampshire knows a good thing when it stumbles over it. They recognize and value the sound that a voting machine makes: it's the sound of "Ka-Ching" too! Like Pavlov's best friends, when New Hampshire hears that sound, it salivates, it drools, and it attacks.

"Do I sense money here? Of course I do—drip, slurp, drip—money and national exposure, free money and free national exposure. Free! Drip! Money! Slurp!"

You'd be best advised to wear hip waders during primary time; the drool and the political bull$#!% runs deep and you'll need the protection.

Yes, New Hampshire recognized what it had in that primary, and they locked it up tight, passing legislation declaring that its primary must, by law, be the first in the Union by at least one full week. They don't care when it is; it just has to be first. I would love to see another lowlife state (and I'm not in the habit of naming names or defaming regions, "y'all") get into a bidding war of sorts and have the election moved so far up the line that it takes place one year after the actual election itself and is exposed for the meaningless exercise that it is. Columnist Mike Ryoko was quoted in *The Boston Globe* once as saying New Hampshire should "move its primary back into the pack where it will receive the attention it really deserves, which is none." You can't argue with the truth.

Speaking of New Hampshire and looking back (the two go hand in hand),

Edmond Muskie wasn't crying in the snow of New Hampshire because of dirty tricks and tactics involving his wife; not at all. I've shed those same tears myself. He was crying for one reason and one reason only: he was stuck in the snow in New Hampshire and had to spend the night. That's all that was and that's enough for me to get my salty effluents flowing freely, too.

Speaking of crying in New Hampshire, didn't your state symbol fall down, oh mighty "Granite State"? Have you gotten over that yet? I know I have. You can only laugh for so long without hurting yourself. But as a reader, are you aware that the New Hamsphire state symbol really did collapse? It's true. The "Old Man of the Mountain" actually now more resembles a pile of rubble than the rugged individual he once pretended to be. You should have taken better care of it, New Hampshire. But no, that might have cost money. I don't know about you, but I think it's now a more fitting symbol than it ever was before. But don't despair; maybe you can make lemonade out of lemons. Maybe you could start selling bags of broken rock fragments, gravel if you will, and call them "Old Man of the Mountain" 3-D puzzles. The Old Man is gone. Long live the Old Man. May he rest in peace, or is it pieces? One way or another, it's about time to move on and select a new state symbol isn't it? May I suggest a tollbooth?

Now that we know what we're dealing with when it comes to New Hampshire, what comes next? What should we do with this thorn in our side? I have a suggestion. It's more of a plan, really. Well, it's actually a scheme of sorts, if you want to know the truth. With my little ingenious plot, I would resolve the matter of New Hampshire once and for the betterment of all, or at the least the rest of us in this world who don't live there. This is what I'm thinking: I would simply divide New Hampshire up among its neighbors, eliminating the state entirely. That's it—simple, sweet and effective.

The lower third of what is now New Hampshire, nuclear coastline included, would become a part of Massachusetts, provided that state agrees to remove those blasted tollbooths on I-95. Not a bad deal, if you ask me. That area of New Hampshire is practically identical to Massachusetts to begin with, except for the taxes, of course. Just think of it: "Taxachusetts" would assume control of the area and all its residents. The population is largely made up of emigrants and their descendants from Massachusetts in the first place, those who fled there just to avoid taxes. It would be poetic justice, to be sure. The nuclear power plant would now be in Massachusetts. If there's going to be a radioactive debacle, why not have it happen there? I mean, Massachusetts is a natural to take over as a lightening rod for hate, anger, and rage. Mainers already have a disinclination to begin with regarding the state. The thought of more "Massholes" simply increases our pleasure in despising them all the more. Besides, most of the rest of the nation doesn't like the state either. After all, Massachusetts has provided Democrats with two of their most bitter political failings of the last twenty years hasn't it? Can you say Dukakis and Kerry? And as for Republicans, consider this: Papa John, Rosemary, little Johnnie, Bobby, Teddy and the rest of the Kennedy clan all lived and thrived there. Need I say more?

As for the upper two-thirds of New Hampshire, it is far more rural and rustic in nature and has much more in common with Maine and Vermont than with Mass. Its beautiful, soaring, glacier carved mountains and scenic, pristine lakes should rightly be shared by these two sister states. The half-sister/step-child that formerly separated these siblings would be no more. This area would be jointly ruled as a kind of unorganized territory, kind of a "central" rather than "West Bank," if you will. The residents would be allowed to remain in their homes, of course, as long as they swear allegiance to their new masters, and take an oath to nevermore practice their evil ways. Of course, we'd continue with one evil way, the "first in the Union," primary. No one can pass up that kind of attention, although we'd blame it on the ornery, recalcitrant though rugged, individualist citizens we'd allow to remain in the region.

Having revised the region for the better, but not wanting to force the rest of the United States to alter their flags, we would make one additional change. Puerto Rico—"Buenos dias" and congratulations. You are now the fiftieth state! You finally get to vote in our national elections and have a say in your future. By the way, let me introduce you to a part of that future: Here's your federal income tax form.

If Puerto Rico balks and refuses to cooperate, then maybe Israel or Palestine will volunteer to step up to the plate. Hell, we might as well combine the two erstwhile foes, eliminate a nagging hotbed of conflict, and take them all in as one. I mean we couldn't have *two* new states. That wouldn't work. That's one star too many. It would cost too much to change all of our flags and these are times of austerity. Besides, we could use the Nobel Peace Prize money we'd receive to build higher walls in the area just to ensure the residents would continue to be good neighbors.

Speaking of walls and summing up, I will only say that Robert Frost was born in the vicinity of New Hampshire and he lived there for most of his life. By all reports he was a miserable, miserly, taciturn man of distasteful character. He was also a wise, insightful man, and he lived where he deserved to live and I thank him for that. He was a great poet, of that there is no doubt. He was right, of course, more right than he'll ever know when he wrote of the "road less traveled." You see, there's a reason that road is less traveled. For one thing, that road leads to New Hampshire. For another, it's a toll road and unless you're staying, it costs a a buck, maybe two to escape.

He was also correct when he spoke of fences and stone walls, strong and sure, making for good neighbors. Given who he was, he no doubt heard such comments emanating from his own neighbor's lips, from their side of the property line, from the other side of the wall. Well, I live in Maine, and I want Maine to be a good neighbor to its lone, bordering, Granite State. I truly do wish this from the bottom of my heart, and with thoughts of good will and benevolence alone, I suggest we begin bettering our relationship immediately by building a tall, thick, impenetrable stone wall across the middle of the bridge at Kittery, just for starters. Let he who casts the first stone be praised. Hallelujah!

Addendum: It should be noted that when this was written some, most, but certainly not all of the above was true. Times have changed and while it's not easy to get someone with a granite skull to change, it is possible that New Hampshire has. It's not probable, but it's possible.

Why I Want to Live in Canada, Why I Can't, and How I Can

My family has always had a connection to Canada, one that I have always cherished. My grandfather and his brother immigrated to Montreal from southwestern England in the early 1920s, leaving behind an entrenched and static society for one that was youthful and vibrant, full of hope and promise. They expanded upon their equine training as grooms and established a livery service, offering horse and carriage rides to the top of Mount Royal, looming above the city. They offered rides back to the bottom of Mount Royal, as well. If, however, you declined to ride and opted to leisurely stroll back down with your loved one, arm in arm, enraptured by the quaint ambiance of the city, they would not be pleased with your decision. They would ride slowly behind you, mocking you every step of the way and telling the passerby, or anyone else who'd listen or didn't have their windows tightly shut, that you were a cheap so-and-so. Eventually, my grandfather, John Towne, got so good at mocking and arguing with his fares that he emigrated to New York City where he fit right in, opened a taxi business, and prospered. His brother, my uncle Ernie, remained in Canada, in Québec, marrying a native beauty, my aunt Vic. They settled in the small village of St. Adele, nestled along a pristine lake in the Laurentian Mountains. It was there, visiting as a young child, that I began my lifelong love affair with our friendly neighbors to the north and with Canada.

As a young boy filled with dreams of adventure, journeying to the mountains, woods and lakes of the Northland was far preferable to descending into the regimented concrete confines of Franklin Square, Long Island, where my grandfather eventually made his home. In short order, I learned to love and worship Canada and Québec, and conversely, to hate and despise New York and "the city." In Canada, I was free to be myself. In New York, I had to be what was expected of me. In Canada, I ran wild. In Long Island, I sat in a drab, smoke-filled house and learned to swear under my breath. I'm not complaining. That part was good, the learning to swear, but Canada was better. Canada was freedom and a breath of fresh air while New York was confinement, and choking smog. In Canada I could be. In New York I could only dream of being … dream of being in Canada.

I don't know why, but I've always felt a kinship with the folk from above. No, not angels, but come to think of it, Canada was heaven to me. Even as a young child, I felt more at home up there, away from my home, than I ever did in my own back yard. Maybe it's simply my nature, but I have always chosen the path apart, the "road less traveled." When everyone else turns to the right, I turn to the left. I always have. I grew up with Dwight Eisenhower as President, and that's why I'm a Democrat, or was, until I bucked them too and became an Independent. It's also probably why I'm famous in my own family for driving the wrong way down countless one-way streets. For others that's a mistake; for me it's called instinct and I'm very instinctual by nature. Just ask my wife.

As an emerging teen, Henry David Thoreau was my guiding light. Yes, he lived in a cabin way before electricity and his was a flickering light at best, but still I was drawn to it. Thoreau's real name was David Henry, but like me, he liked things the other way 'round and I think that pretty much explains who I am in a nutshell. I got life backwards or "bassackwards" as they in the know are fond of saying. Either way, I emerged from my shell not to tower as an oak of a man, but to grow back into a nut. Go figure.

Now, it's not that I don't follow others because I think of myself as being better than anyone else; I don't. I'm not stupid and I know myself far too well to think that. It's just that I want to be me, me alone, and special to me, not like everyone else, or anyone else. I am comfortable being different and alone. The two tend to go hand in hand. I am uncomfortable and anxious and most of all lonely in the crowds of sameness that I often see surrounding me. I need to feel special, if only to myself. So, in the end, maybe it was that need more than anything else that attracted me to Canada: the freedom to be different and the need to be me.

Speaking of being different, I could never understand the benefits of being a melting pot of humanity. What's with that? Why does America pride itself on this misguided concept? Why take all that is unique and special in the world and its peoples—their languages, cultures and history—and then blend and coagulate it into an amorphous lump of "Americanese"? Why not celebrate and share the differences? Canada does it. And by celebrating those differences, it has learned to not only accept those differences, but to embrace them as well. In simple terms, it's called "tolerance." Canada has it and we should too.

Maybe this one simple concept of accepting differences is what makes America in its own way so very different from the rest of the world. Americans like who they are; they want everyone to not only like them but to be like them. If you don't want to be like they are, they're suspicious of you and ultimately won't like you. If you really want to be an American, essentially you need to give up being different. It's that type of thinking that baffles me to no end. And what I find really extraordinary is that many of the citizens of this mongrel mutt of a big, bad dog called the United States of America now consider themselves superior to the very ingredients that they're composed of. How has this sameness somehow become a virtue? Do we really want only one color of M&Ms? Do we really want only one really big M&M to a bag? I don't think so. Why do we dye our Easter eggs if we really think white alone is not only fine, but in fact the very best?

To my way of thinking, America is a restaurant advertising its cuisine as "home style cooking," and I don't get it. Who wants to pay top dollar for meatloaf and mashed potatoes with a side of green beans and a glass of milk? Not me. I want something I can't cook myself. I want something different, something special. That's why I go out to eat, because I can't get the real thing at home. Otherwise, I'd just stay at home every night and eat hot dogs and baked beans from a can while watching TV—just like I did last night.

For some reason, Americans tend to have a hard time with "different." Why are you coming here if you don't want to be like us, they ask? Here we offer you the freedom to be one of us, to be just like us. If you don't want to exercise that freedom properly and use it to give up who you are for what we think you should be, then stay right to home, stay right where you are, thank you very much. Stay home, or go to Canada. Go ahead, go to Canada and be different if that's who you are. As for America, love it or leave it, or better yet, don't even come here in the first place.

You see, that's where I'm having a hard time digesting America's home cooking. If I love something, it's because I admire what it stands for and what it is. I have a hard time loving something that demands that my only choice is actually no choice: that I have to love it or I have to leave it. When a country or a meal says that, I get indigestion. I have a hard time loving it, but when at the same time it's my home, and I can't leave it either. Do you see the problem and *my* dilemma?

Of course, Canada was never and isn't now perfect, either. Being a child (and therefore, as I like to define the word, an "ignorant, but cute, little bastard"), I didn't always fully appreciate the events that were transpiring about me. I was simply an American kid spending a few weeks away in a really fun place where everyone talked funny. It was as though they put Disneyland in North Carolina. I was unaware at the time that the Québecois were beginning their struggle against the cultural inundation and suffocation of the Anglo world surrounding them. I didn't know that they were fighting to be different too, just like me.

I always wondered why my uncle picked up his mail in town and never went to the mailbox. I should have picked up on the fact that something was amiss, as his mailbox was blackened, shredded, peppered with holes and smelled of gunpowder and explosives. But I didn't. I just thought my uncle had a really cool looking mailbox.

In Canada, in Québec, Canada, my uncle was just a little different than his neighbors. It was a subtle, but definitive difference. He was English and they were French. They didn't try to make him change to fit in like Americans would have done, not at all. They accepted his being different from them. I like to think they respected him for his differences as well. They just tried to blow him up from time to time. It was their way of saying, "Bonjour, mon ami."

But back to my dilemma. I have a hard time loving and not leaving America now and again. I want to love her unequivocally, but I struggle with doing so. If to love her means that I have to turn a blind eye to her faults, then I can't love her, I won't. I want her to be what she claims to be, not what some right-wing hothead wants her to be. I don't want her to be a melting pot. I want her to be alphabet vegetable soup, not some pureed, cream of vegetable slop. And I want to be not only able to criticize her, but to be respected for criticizing her. That's what I want to love about her. I want her to recognize and celebrate dissent and differences of view. I want to love my home, and so, I want her to change. I want her to be something different, something more like, well, more like Canada. But I don't see that happening anytime soon. What am I to do? Should I have to leave my home then and move to Canada? I don't think so. I don't want to leave my home. I love my home. I love Maine. I truly do. So again, what am I to do? What would you do?

I don't know what you'd do, but as for me, I have given this a great deal of thought, and I have settled upon what I consider a most reasonable and doable solution. Take a deep breath. Sit back and get ready for what's coming. Try to keep an open mind. This may be a little different way of thinking than what you've been used to.

Lewiston is home to a large number of Somali immigrants, making it the "Addis Abbaba of the Androscoggin." At least it would be known as this if Addis Ababa were in Somalia and not actually in Ethiopia. The Somali influence upon Maine culture extends from beyond the third floor or higher in some of the more remote areas of Lewiston, down to the very street.

Le State Il De La Province Des Maine

People are always asking me, living way out here in Maine as I do, if we here feel like we're a part of the United States. I can't speak for everyone, of course, though I'd like to, but speaking for myself, I'd have to say no, no we don't. I don't feel like we're a part of the United States. And it's not solely the geography I'm talking about either, although that no doubt plays no small part in the mix. It's more the attitude of the people who live there, in the "States"—their lifestyle, culture and political stances that make me feel set apart from the lower 47. Personally, as I've said, I feel more akin to Canada than to the U.S. in a host of ways. Speaking with others who agree with me, I find my feelings are becoming increasingly ever more common, especially since the election of 2000 and the American incursions into Iraq and Afghanistan. So, where is this "different" thinking taking me? Pull up a comfortable chair; this may take a while, and I'll tell you.

I am a Civil War buff, or at least was when I was growing up. I admired those who, for principles they held dear to their hearts, often fought within their own families, brother pitted against brother, cousin against cousin, and uncle against uncle. I never read of a brother fighting an uncle or a cousin's uncle, so I think there were some restrictions in place, though I can't prove it. Personally, more than once I've found myself thinking of declaring war on my own brother and some of my cousins as well, but I'm digressing.

As an idealist, I admired men like Robert E. Lee who forsook Lincoln's offer to command the Grand Army of the Potomac, and instead chose to swear allegiance to his native state of Virginia. In my idealistic moments I like to think of myself as a modern day counterpart to Bobby, but without the gray uniform; all those shiny buttons; his gray, felt fedora; Traveler, his horse; and a host of slaves. Did I mention that I also don't have an Army of Northern Virginia in my back pocket? Well, regretfully, I don't because that makes it a tad more difficult to get my point across to others. Still, I am more than willing to try.

Now, while I haven't been asked, I would accept leadership of the Maine National Guard because I truly feel a love and allegiance towards Maine. I always have. From before I read of Joshua Chamberlain's heroics at Gettysburg, I felt an affinity to this place, of all places among the states. You see, I had a childhood connection to the Maine woods and grew up reading and dreaming of the state. Then I married, became a father and head of a young family. When the time came to settle down, build a home and establish a life, I could not abide living in New York, Connecticut or God forbid, New Jersey. Somehow, I just can't look upon shopping as a really fulfilling hobby. There has got to be more to life than trying to outspend your neighbors. I also didn't want to toil fifty weeks a year working to pay for a two-week vacation someplace I'd rather be living in, in the first place. I decided that I would have to live where I would vacation and what better place to do that than "Vacationland" itself?

I set off with a little money, and a whole lot of naiveté, and drove north until I found a nice piece of open bottomland we couldn't afford and, as usual, without thinking, I followed my instincts and bought it. Soon afterwards, we moved to Maine. I built our home myself and we settled in. We didn't have much, but it was ours. We were hardly set, but we were hardy settlers, at least in our own minds.

Now, I'm a kid at heart and hopefully always will be. Coming to live in Maine with my family was like going back in time to when I was a youngster of say twelve or thereabouts. I believe those were truly the happiest of my years. However, being in Maine, feeling like a twelve-year-old, and having access to a woman were a close second. Living in the Farmington area, and New Vineyard in particular, was just like going back in time to when I was growing up more than a decade earlier only now I had to shave occasionally. My relatives were dumbstruck (no explanation needed) and would ask me about the culture shock and challenges we encountered. What could I tell them? There were none. Somehow, different as we were, we just fit in. Moving to Maine was like slipping on an old pair of shoes; they might look worn and torn and not long for this world, but they're some kind of comfortable. I was comfortable. I was home. We were home.

During the past thirty years, I have noticed a decided change in the political climate of both the U.S. and the state of Maine. The country at large, the United States of America, feels more divided than at any time I can recall with the possible exception of the Vietnam years. We're divided now into Red States and Blue States. Maine, however, is neither. It's more of a Plaid State. You see, Maine is a freethinking state. We don't like to be categorized one way or the other. We have two red senators (not "commies," far from it, but Republicans). And they're not your currently fashionable, neoconservative Republicans. They're remnants from our nation's distant past called "moderates." They're independent thinkers, and they also just happen to be women. Our two congress*men*, however, are just that, men. That is all of them, with the exception of Chellie Pingree. She's a woman. They are also Democrats. Our Governor is currently a Democrat, but that changes periodically, shifting from time to time to a Republican or, even more likely, an Independent as well. As luck would have it, we now have a Republican about to be sworn in soon. As you can see, Maine is different. Maine is special.

Maine is also compassionate. It is a state of social responsibility. Yes, we are taxed more than any other state, but there's a reason for that: we care about one another. We have a social conscience. We didn't move here (as in my case) or stay here (if you're a native) because of the love of money. You don't live in Maine to get rich. You work here to make a living so that you can live here; it's that simple.

Where is this heading, you might ask? Well, it's heading to this: Maine is different, different from any other state. We are out here on the fringes of the United States, and always have been, isolated and alone. We read for ourselves, we listen to what others have to say, we think about it, and then we come to our own conclusions. It's my conclusion that Maine simply doesn't belong with the rest of the country anymore. We don't fit in with the United States as a whole any longer. We don't reflect the sentiments and thoughts of the rest of the country. We're not like Texas or Florida or, God forbid, New Hampshire. We respect other cultures. We respect others' rights. We don't tell our citizens how to live, what to do, what to think and we don't like being told by others how to live, do, or think ourselves. We want to be left alone to be who we are and we're not uncomfortable in letting you be who you are. We are, in short, at least in this respect, more like Canadians than Americans!

How can this be? What have we come to? If we're honest, we've come to the truth, to our senses. Oh, it might seem painful at first, but really, it's not. Read on and I'll make my case. Throw away your preconceived assumptions and worn out parameters and open your mind to the possibilities I offer. You may be surprised where your thinking may take you. I know I was.

Now, Maine is the only state in the Union that borders on only one other state. That's just wrong. It's especially wrong since that other state happens to be New Hampshire, but that's another chapter altogether, as you already know. On the other hand, we border on two provinces of Canada: Québec and New Brunswick. You do the math; two provinces vs. one hideous little (it's the fifth smallest) state. Is it any wonder we in Maine think differently than the rest of the U.S.? I don't think so.

Still not quite sure? Go back and reread the earlier chapter on New Hampshire and then return. Take your time. I'll wait for you. I'll shovel off the deck 'til you're done.

Good, you're back. Just give me a second here to tidy up and knock the snow off my boots. There, I'm all set. So, you've refreshed your memory regarding the little horror sitting to our left, on our west? Let's turn our backs on that thought for a second, we're not of that ilk, and let's face towards the east. What do we see? A rising sun, that's what we see. Now turn to the west. What do we see? A setting sun, that's what we see. To the east we see new and up, and to the west we see old and down. Take off your shades, fellow citizens. Are you beginning to see the coming light of a new day or are you hiding in the shadows of the setting sun of our past? You have a decision to make.

As for me, I've decided. So here I am, still stuck with this dilemma: I want to live in Canada, but I don't want to move from Maine. So what am I to do? Well, I have given this a great deal of thought, and I have settled upon a solution. It's simple, it's rational, and I think it will work. At least it will work for me. As for everyone else, well, that's not my problem, that's your problem. My problem is getting my idea off the drawing board and onto the map.

The answer to the conundrum? I would simply have Maine secede from the U.S. and become a part of Canada: The State of the Province of Maine.

Pretty simple, is it not? Of course, if Maine secedes, I will have to honor her with my allegiance. After all, I started this thing. But besides that, like Robert E. Lee, my heart lies with my native, well, *adopted* native state. I'm a "states' rights" kinda guy, I guess, which is not a provincial thought, is it? Well, it should be.

The province of Maine is a great idea! I already fly three flags: the Maine state flag, the Stars and Bars, and the Maple Leaf. I've simply got to reposition them slightly and I'm willing to make that effort. I'm willing to be flexible with my thinking and with my flagpole. If I have to go to all the trouble of placing the Maple Leaf in the center position and the Stars and Bars to left or right of it in my triad of allegiance, well then, I'm going to go the distance and make that sacrifice. It's the least I can do, really.

Could you imagine Maine changing her national affiliation and me not having to do anything more than move a flag or two? I can't either and that's why I love this idea. But the ease of transition is not the only reason I like this province of Maine idea, not by a long shot. As you may have suspected, I have a whole lot of reasons and here are just a few.

First, consider all of the gasoline that we'd save if Maine were a province. Given our looming energy crisis and the ever-rising cost of fuel, this is no small matter. No longer would we Mainers have to drive "all the way" to Québec or New Brunswick just to visit Canada so we can say "oot" instead of out, or to buy some Ganong chocolates instead of a Hershey bar. There would be no traveling; we'd already be there or "there aboot!" Want to go to Canada? Just open your back door and there you are. For me, it would be one small step rather than eighty-five miles or so of scenic driving. Hell, it wouldn't even have to be a step; I could shuffle or even limp off to Canada if I wanted to. I'd have that freedom.

Of course, there would be a downside. Mass produced imported beer would now suck dust! My drinking selection wouldn't make me feel special any longer. But if having to drink a local beer like Molson, Labatts, or Moosehead is the price I'd have to pay for not being special, that's okay, as long as we also had our microbrews like Shipyard or Gritty's.

Still, there would be some getting used to the changes in my daily life. For instance, six packs would be now be .6 ten packs, what with the decimal system and all. Twelve packs would become 1.2 ten packs and a case of beer would be undrinkable while you're thinking about it. Fortunately, thinking becomes a non-issue after .5 of a .6 ten pack.

Where will this all lead? I'm not certain, but I suspect the U.S. might have something to say about the entire affair. I realize the U.S. has invaded several nations over the past few years as they have helped impose freedom and democracy upon the oppressed, and I'm fairly certain that they would try to do the same to us. Still, the bottom line is this: George Bush is no Abraham Lincoln. For instance, he's not that tall, he doesn't dress in black and doesn't wear a stovepipe hat. Besides, even if you managed to somehow disguise Bush as Lincoln, once his mouth opened and he spit out the silver spoon and shoe that nearly hit him upside the head, the jig would be up. No, Bush is not Lincoln.

Bush aside, all of the U.S.'s battle-ready troops are already overseas, and the New Hampshire National Guard is probably in no mood for another "overseas," or "over river" as it were, mission. Oh sure, they might manage to sneak a few border-crossing guards onto Fort Gorges in Portland Harbor, but like Fort Sumter, I don't think they could hold out for long. Remember, the city wouldn't allow DeMillo's to build a restaurant on the island, so they'd have to ferry in supplies and the only ferry available is slow and yellow: an easy target. Like I said, I don't think they could hold out for long.

And if they attempt to cross the stone wall on the bridge in Kittery, well, they had better bring a lot of quarters with them because the Maine Turnpike will be lying in wait, and we just might up the fares! We can get nasty if we have to, especially if we're at war. No, all in all, I think we'll survive intact. We might face a hostile frontier for a time, but hell, we already have to live with New Hampshire, what more could they do? Raise their tolls in retaliation? I believe reason will prevail. The U.S. will come to see the light and accept our secession. Here's why.

To the north we see Québec, a different kind of place and not unlike Maine in many respects. For instance, Québec is a francophone province, the only such place in Canada. French is spoken there and somewhat understood, but not necessarily by the French. This isn't France's French we're speaking, speaking of, and speaking "aboot." No, this is a unique French, a Canadian French. Like those who speak it, it's more than just a little "different."

Here in Maine, we speak English. But not the King's English, and certainly not George Bush's English. We have a hard time understanding his English; our English is different. Ours makes sense. No, this is a unique English, a Maine lingo all its own. But if you have a New York clip, or a Bostonian yammer, we'll tolerate you nonetheless. We won't mock you, at least not to your face. If you have a Texas drawl, however—well, that's another matter. You're on your own there. My point is, that for the most part, we Mainers are tolerant and respectful of differences in language, just like the province of New Brunswick.

New Brunswick is the only Canadian province that is officially bilingual. French and English are spoken there. So, you see, Maine is strongly influenced by its neighbors to the north and east, sharing their differences and their tolerance for differences. Being a part of Canada, we Mainers can be both bi- and married. That didn't come out right, but it's still true.

Let's examine the benefits of becoming a province of Canada, and there are many. First of all, we will be Canadians. I like that. I always wanted to be a Canadian. I just never wanted to move. If Maine is a province, then I'm a

Canadian and I can still live in my own home. That's pretty good right there. I can live with that.

Next, we can begin to lose our guilt complex. You know those guilty feelings we share about pushing our noses into everyone else's business simply because we have an enormous military/industrial complex and can do it. In fact, if we're Canadians, we'll lose both those complexes. I like that too.

Geographically speaking, we are now where we belong on a map. We are no longer the sore thumb of America, but rather, the natural extension of Canadian stability. Take a good look at that map once more. What do you see? Right you are. We would be in fact, the southern most of all the provinces of the Great White North. Think of what that would mean: we would become the "Florida of Canada."

No longer would we have to journey 1500 miles just to go to Disney World, Epcot, Sea World, and Universal Studios. Canada would build them for us, build them right here, right in Old Orchard! And why not? We already have the beach. And the Québecois, they don't care that the water is a little "on the stiff side," as I like to say. So what if it's bone-numbingly cold? It's still wet, isn't it? They already come here to swim until they turn blue, are numb as a clam, and sink to the bottom, so that's not going to be a problem for them. As for the ambiance, we'll build concrete and plastic palm trees bordering Old Orchard Beach and Saco, and no one will know the difference. Of course, there might be licensing problems, so it wouldn't be exactly like Disney World, but it would be close enough. It would be similar, but different. Disney World, "sans le mouse," as we'd say. Maybe we'd have Stanley the Squirrel or Bucky the Beaver instead. Better still, we might choose Mickey Moose! Whatever, it would be great, and great for our economy.

Speaking of the economy, being the southernmost province, we would be to Canada what the Gulf Coast region was to the U.S. before Katrina and the oil spill struck. We'd be a must-see, warm weather destination. No more would we have to listen to people "from away" expressing their pity for us as they ask, "Just how low do the temperatures drop in the dead of winter?" Instead, we'd be the envy of a continental giant! When we say it's only twenty below, they won't be able to hide their jealousy. Think how wonderful that would be.

Just think of the benefits of not having to check the box on all those government forms as to whether or not you are of Hispanic origin! You're not! You're Canadian. Get it? Besides, Mexicans haven't pushed any farther north than those infamous killer bees, so what are the chances you'll ever be asked? No, you're a Gringo and always will be.

Additionally, Maine would act as a filter for Canadians traveling to the U.S. We would buffer the harsh transition from French-speaking Québec to the totally English-speaking, or should I say "American"-speaking, New Hampshire. Culture shock would be radically lessened if not entirely eradicated. We'd be a sort of halfway house for Canadian "homies." Emergency rooms could go back to treating automobile accident victims rather than raising the feet higher than the heads of French tourists trying to figure out what the hell a hoagie is and whether or not eating hot mayonnaise is a good thing.

Getting back to Maine as the southernmost province, it would be a natural for Portland to become Canada's leading port, wouldn't it? Imagine, a harbor that doesn't freeze over, or at least not all that often. Why, our economy would positively boom. We could supply Canada with fuel imports. We already have a pipeline to Montreal, pumping oil to the frozen North so the connecting infrastructure is already partially in existence.

Speaking of connections, we once had the Scotia Prince cruise ship leaving daily for Yarmouth, Nova Scotia, and may still someday have the hydrofoil Cat again, so travel connections to the Maritimes, although done, would already be a done deal. There's also the Cat's sailing out of Bar Harbor, as well. This is making all too much sense, don't you agree?

Being "southern," like Bobby E. Lee (remember him a few pages back?), we would be expected by the rest of our new nation to be a little special, a little quirky, and we could do that easily. We already speak differently than the rest of English-speaking Canada, so our native "drawl" would be a natural drawl. We won't be saying "eh" after every thought like our brothers to the north, but our "eh-yah" (or more traditionally spelled, "ayuh") is both pretty damn close and yet still unique in its own right. It's quaint, it's different, it's a winner in my book, and this is my book, so I win on all counts.

We'll keep our cuisine as it is, however. I can't see us dishing out cheese grits smothered in onions and topped with jalapenos anytime soon. There will be no Waffle Houses on our side of the border. Doughboys will remain "de rigor," however, and will continue to be the solid foundation upon which our food pyramid is built.

Consider for a moment, if you will, the social benefits of our proposed "move" to the north. Maine is already far ahead of most of the rest of the U.S. when it comes to socializing medical care, for instance. We now have Maine Care for our children and Dirigo Health, so a single payer, universal care system wouldn't be a giant step for mankind, but something more akin to a slight shuffle of our feet. We also already enjoy government-sanctioned travel to Canada to get our pharmaceutical medications at a much more reasonable cost, so what's to change? Anyway, the logic is irrefutably sound overall and the move appears to be the right prescription for what ails us as a state. It makes sense for both Maine and Canada. It's a two way street. After all, Canadians already have had to travel to Maine for radiation treatments they can't get at home. It makes sense for us all and all too much sense.

Speaking of healthcare, unlike most every other state in the U.S., we use our tobacco settlement money to discourage tobacco use, not to patch holes in our budgets or highways, while the U.S. Federal government subsidizes its tobacco farmers. We know for a fact that cigarettes lead to unnecessary medical costs and possible death. They should cost more than they now do and in the future, they will. Cigarettes would become very expensive once Maine becomes a province and Mainers would have to adjust to not being able to carry them in their turned up t-shirt sleeves since the traditional Canadian boxes (like Players brand, for instance) are too long and wide for that—unless you're a weightlifter and what weightlifter would smoke? The boon to Canada would be great in that the smoking Québécois and New Brunswickeritanarianites (is that right? God, I hope not) wouldn't be able to scoot across the border and pick up cheap smokes in the States. That in and of itself would thereby reduce the smoking rate in those bordering provinces, again save gasoline, and help lower the costs of socialized medicine for everyone here in Canada. Provincial Mainers could, of course, cross over to the U.S. and New Hampshire but really—travel to New Hampshire just for lower prices? I think we've sufficiently covered that subject already. We won't cross that bridge again, either literally or figuratively.

There's also the idea of Molson "Canadian" and Labatts, Moosehead, Keith's, et al., not being expensive imports any longer. That's an idea I can go for. Of course, natives having to get used to Old Milwaukee Light becoming an expensive import will take them some time, perhaps forever, to get accustomed to, but I'm willing to turn a deaf ear to their whining for the benefits to be gained by the rest of us.

Are you with me yet? Not quite? Do you still need some convincing? All right, let's move along and consider our societal stances on the issues of our day and where that places us. Do we sit closer on the bench of public opinion to Canada or are we snuggled tight next to the U.S. of A.? I'm thinking we're rubbing shoulders with Canada. If you don't agree with me, no great whoop, that's okay. We're Canadian, remember. We'll tolerate you even if you're wrong. Just slide your butt on over and make room for my ever-increasing number of friends.

We think Maine's view of the world, politically speaking, is far closer to Ottawa's than it is to that of Austin's. I'm thinking we're more north and left and the U.S. is more south and right. We're Vancouver and Gas Town, they're Miami and Little Havana. We're becoming a world and a culture apart. They're speaking Spanish, while I understand only English, and the rest is Greek to me, even the French. I don't understand it. I try to figure out what Democrats and Republicans stand for today but it's no use. Left and right, I get; donkeys and elephants, I don't. It's too confusing. Let's just call them what they are, or should be—the Liberals and Conservatives—just like they do in Canada. Yes, there are Tories, DNP's, and the Québécois block, but I choose to ignore them for the sake of making my point.

As for what we stand for, well, we in Maine don't stand for a death penalty, for one thing. It's alien to our nature. We kill ourselves by overeating, reckless driving, and domestic violence. We live in the twenty-first century, not in some time-warped hellhole like New Hampshire. We don't agree with government-sanctioned death. We like to think we can be both human and humane.

What's our belief regarding security? Sure, we like to feel safe, but do we really believe we need such huge and sophisticated armed forces? I don't think we do, not if we're not going to be imposing freedom and democracy upon other countries. Do you feel safer because of the giant military presence we have overseas? Be honest. Do you think you'd feel more secure walking the world in general with "Old Glory" tacked to your back or a Maple Leaf? You know the answer. I'm not saying America is bad; I'm just saying that Maine's way of thinking is simply and basically different in a lot of significant ways from that of the U.S. of A.'s.

As we can see, while Maine is no longer feeling a part of the U.S., we have to be honest and admit that we are also different from a good deal of Canadian thinking as well. There is no denying it. We are being objective and honest here, and we just will have to accept the truth for what it is. Therefore, upon further thought, I take back everything I said. I'm admitting I made a mistake. Hey, I'm a big guy. Here's what I'm thinking now. I am proposing that Maine not secede from the U.S. and join Canada. I'm sure that makes a goodly number of you happy to say the least. Well, not so fast. Don't get too comfortable. I'm not done.

What I am now suggesting is this: that Maine becomes a nonaligned, semi-autonomous nation, cooling our heels in the shade of both the U.S. and Canadian military umbrellas. This makes much more sense to me. Since we can't get there from here, and we don't truly fit in anywhere else, I'm thinking, "What the hell! We should stand alone." Well, not completely alone, but sort of a bit apart, somewhat to the side, but with our feet straddling both borders, east, west, and north. We should be an end point and an entity in and of ourselves. We should be a destination to get to, not just a distance to pass through, like say Iowa or Indiana.

We should become "The Republic of Maine"!

As a new nation, we will need a new flag. I have a number of thoughts on this and will share them with you in the next chapter. Suffice it to say that our flag will be a dazzler. What an awe-inspiring sight it will be! Blind people will actually wish they could see when they hear of its beauty. Deaf folk will wish they could hear what the blind people have to say about what they see. And dumb people just won't get what all the fuss is about, so to hell with them; you can't please everyone, can you? Besides, they're dumb.

In a later chapter, I will write about changing Maine's monetary system to reflect her uniqueness. Canada's money is a little unique itself, what with the funny animals, the colors, the hockey, and the loons, but I believe it would be to Maine's benefit to go forward with her own currency. After all, never forget, if we go this route we are Mainers, first and foremost.

So there you have it. There you have my thoughts on the Maine, The Way Life Should Be. I hope I've brought you to a new way of thinking about our home, our heartland, our harbor, our haven, and our Maine. I hope you are with me on this, with *us* on this. We, the movement, want you with us. We want you to be one of us. But if you're not, that's okay too. We won't hate you. We won't speak ill of you to your face, just behind your backs as we do with

Texans. You won't have to love us or leave us. We're tolerant. Just be careful what you say and do, and to be on the safe side, I suggest you open your mailbox with a long pole, if you know what I mean.

P.S. As a postscript to this chapter, I have two more things to say. First, the Maine legislature has actually considered legislation that would place Maine within the Atlantic Time Zone, effectively making us one with the Maritimes as far as our clocks go, one step closer to Canada and one step farther from the U.S. Had the bill passed, we would have been separated by one hour from the rest of our country. Heck, we're centuries ahead of the South as it is in terms of our culture, so what's another hour going to do? Sadly, the legislation didn't pass, this time. But the move is on. The push has begun. It's subtle, but it's there. As one of our governors once proclaimed, "Maine is on the move." Come with us and get on board the Polar Express ... Believe!

Finally—and this is a very remote possibility—when and if we do secede from the Union and they allow us to do so, Canada may very well consider invading! It's unlikely, but we have to be prepared for the possibility. I've heard on the sly, that they already have, that they came across the border just last week and gassed up their Hummers, Pontiac Fireflies, and Ladas. I hear they're ready to roll. I have only one thing to say to Canada: "If you're really thinking of trying to take over Maine, Lordy, no! Please don't throw me into the briar patch! Whatever you do, don't throw me into the briar patch, *eh!*"

'Nuf said.

Portland is the largest city in Maine. It is not the capital. The population is composed of the working class (12%), shoppers (38%), the non-working class (43%), immigrants from "away" (54%), and Yuppies (74%). Non-working Yuppies from "away" who shop and live in condos were excluded from this survey.**

Our State and/or Republic Symbols: The Way They are and The Way They Should Be

Maine, as with every other state, has its own unique and well thought-out state symbols. Over the years, the dedicated legislators of our great land have spent countless hours in harried debate arguing the merits of a certain beetle over a particular bug, or a type of rock as opposed to a particular piece of soil. It's time consuming and arduous work, but that's what we pay them to do—that and something to do with budgets, taxes, the civic good, civil rights, and whatnot. The end result of all this effort is that we are not only the most highly taxed state in the Union, but the range and breadth of our state symbols is just plain ridiculous and our finances are in ruin. Luckily, although Maine is hurting, you yourself can't be hurting too badly. You found the money to waste on this book you're reading, didn't you? As for the symbols, we'll begin with the Maine state flag.

The Maine flag is majestic and inspiring to observe as it snaps to and fro in a brisk breeze, provided you don't look too closely. Actually, it's pretty neat up close too, but saying that just wouldn't serve the purposes of this book, now, would it? At a distance, the background is your basic dark cloth with a smidgen of other stuff sequestered somewhere in the middle. The blue background represents the sky or the sea or perhaps something blue. Maybe it's a blueberry, but I doubt it. Anyway, it's blue, or as the French would write it, "bleu." I don't get that, do you? Just by reversing a couple of letters, do you think that somehow you now have yourself a whole other language and culture? It makes no sense. It's dumb, or as the French might spell it, "dubm," which really is dumb. But back to the flag.

That smidgen in the center of our flag is quite different from other state smidgens. New Hampshire's smidgen has a toll taker with his left hand held out as if demanding your money and his right holding what appears to be a loaded .357 Magnum pointed at your head, or at least that's what I assume it would be if it were at all reflective of the state and what it actually stands for. Still, there's a small chance it might not be as I've suggested. Either way, I don't trust the Granite State.

Our flag's smidgen, like I said, is different. We have a farmer to the left of center and a sailor to the right. These figures represent our proud heritage on the one hand and the foundational basis of our historical economy on the other. The farmer is resting on a scythe (the same tool that that the Death guy wielded to great effect during the Bubonic Plague during the Dark Ages) while the sailor is resting on an anchor. In the middle, beneath the North Star, is a large shield embossed with a moose resting beneath a tall pine tree. That strikes me as a lot of resting for one flag. I live here in Maine and I don't get to rest like that even though this is Vacationland. If all that resting were truly accurate of our past, nothing ever would have gotten done here in Maine, and there's a lot of stuff here that suggests someone must have been busy, so at the least I'm suspicious. Resting aside, overall, the flag's attractive, quaint, stately (that's important in a state flag), and was probably mostly factual in its day—resting aside, as I've said. Unfortunately or not, however, that day has passed and to paraphrase a once somewhat popular pop song of the 60s, "our day has come." And with that day, I think our flag's time is up. It's time for a "flagualistic" update. Times have changed, and so have we. It's high time we revise our state flag.

To my way of thinking, just as the old folks did with their flag in their day, we should do with ours: reflect the current economy of our state, as it exists today. The flag we fly may have been appropriate in the 1800s, but not now. (Actually, our state flag was officially adopted in 1909 but that's neither here nor there. It's more like when.) I'm fairly certain that if we went back a century or two before our current flag, we would discover that another banner of some sort was being hoisted up the local post office flagpole. That flag might have had a Native American on the left clubbing a beaver in the head with a rock lashed to a stick and, to his right, perhaps another Indian clubbing a settler, or vice versa. The point is, a flag should be kept current if it is to remain meaningful. That's why there are fifty, and not thirteen, stars on the U.S. flag, right? Agreed? Good.

Now, our new flag has no reason to be all blue. That blue background I'm told is a traditional military background. Maine's not that militant a state unless you count the conservative, far right wing of your local neo-Nazi faction, or an angry Methodist for that matter. Though we're peace-loving folk by and large, we do have a lot of forts, but most were never used as such. These forts, as far as I can tell, were constructed primarily as tourist attractions for future generations. Except for Fort Knox, which has a really spectacular "spookarama" thing going for Halloween, our forts really didn't scare anyone away. In hindsight, you've got to give our ancestors credit for having had 20/20 foresight, don't you?

As for the "defending the collective peace" concept, the last time we got into a serious spat here in Maine was with Canada somewhere in the mid 1850s. The only fighting that took place back then was between a few idle soldiers from the two warring factions who were just sitting around, snacking on chips, drinking beer, and watching TV to pass the time away. I believe they only had one channel back then and I think it was the Home Shopping Network, 24/7. War really was and still is hell, you know.

Being Americans, our side made fun of the "oot" word, you know, as in "get oot of my country, you hoser, you." The Canadians, who weren't Canadians back then because there was no Canada, must have taken offense at being made fun of, eh? They retaliated by asking the Mainers to say "hoss" as in "why don't you get on your hoss and go home, Yankee?" over and over again. Needless to say, this being a part of Red Sox Nation, fisticuffs ensued, but that's as far as the actual fighting ever got. It seems both sides were more upset that the cable company was screwing them once again, so they shook hands and went back to their respective homes to settle their score with the real enemy. Judging from my TV programming, it's obvious who won that skirmish.

As for the flag, I think ours should have a background of green, not blue, representing the fact that ours is now the most wooded state in the Union. That's a fact. You see, I did a lot of research for this book. I'm not just making this stuff up as I go along, you know. But getting back to our flag, to be more realistic, perhaps it should be green on top and brown on the bottom—you know, more like a real tree. I also figured we'd go with this green background all year long to better represent the overwhelming conifer tree population and to avoid the issues involved with deciduous leaves. We have a lot of pine, spruce, cedar, and hemlock, and fall presents a real problem if we were to go with the alternative. It was a difficult choice and I actually debated it, Oxford style. It made no sense having one flag with a green tree four months of the year, another more resplendent, colorful flag for the month of September and the first two weeks of October, and yet another bearing a barren skeleton of a tree for the remaining seven months of the year. That would be too much. And then there's the fact that we're also called the Pine Tree State to deal with.

So, I talked it out, convinced myself that I was right, and now it's settled. I'm in agreement with me. The background will be green on top and brown on the bottom. Okay, we need the blue above too, blue above, as well as below. Maine is more than just a coastline, but does have a coastline, so yes, we'll put some more blue on the bottom of the flag. (It should be noted that since we now have a Republican Governor, Governor LePage, the Gov is rumored to be considering swapping the blue background for one of red, better reflecting its new political affiliation.)

So there we have it, from top to bottom, bands of blue, green, and brown, and yes, another sliver of blue. It works, but now what about that smidgen thing every state flag must have if it's going to be old and authentic, even if it's new?

First of all, it's not a "smidgen," and I'm tired of writing the word. It's a "thingie" or a "sealie" and every state has one except the ones that don't, though not every state puts it on its flag. Still, I think we should have one, and I've included a "sealie" on our standard. While I like to change with the times, I also like to maintain a modicum of tradition for tradition's sake. I'm pretty firm on that, I think. We need a "sealie" sitting up there for its eye-catching appeal; otherwise, we're like a poor imitation of Portugal or something. Here's my idea for the "sealie/thingie."

Farmers are pretty much a thing of the past aren't they? Yes, they were once as numerous as black flies in May, but no more. Now we're just annoyed by black flies. You drive around Maine and you're not going to run across all that many farmers standing out in their fields. In fact, unless you frequent the Farmer's Union on a Thursday morning, you may not encounter any. I don't understand why that is, but for some reason farmers, and former farmers, come into town on Thursday mornings in their pick-ups, if they're working, and their Buicks, if they're retired, and stop at the "Union" where they talk about the way things were. It's just the way things are now. It's what they do in these times, these times being what they are.

Be that as it may, though the farmers are, sadly, fast disappearing, their farms remain. Well, maybe not the actual farms, but I've seen some of the barns. The barns and their silos remain scattered about the countryside, left to slowly deteriorate and provide a weathered, rustic and inspirational centerpiece for countless watercolor paintings that will later be sold to tourists. I guess they serve the same purpose that lighthouses now serve artists along the coast. I think the farmers get a percentage on the paintings sold, which they in turn invest in keeping those barns in a well-maintained state of weathered disrepair. This income helps supplement the social security checks they don't get, having been wealthy, independent businessmen who carelessly vacated their inherited vocation when they couldn't afford to work at it any longer. Suffice it to sadly say, farmers are fast becoming passé.

I believe a much more realistic and representative depiction of the "new" Maine must reflect the most common current means of making a living in our state. Therefore, the first symbol on our new flag, the one on the left, would be a store clerk/cashier wearing one of those little colored vests that identify them as an employee and not a customer just wandering about from aisle to aisle. We could add a lighted number above the "sealie/thingie" we'll create as well, indicating they're ready to check you out and not just standing around talking about how cheap the company they work for is, or how many hours short of forty they worked last week, not to mention the poor health benefits.

So, it's settled. The store clerk has to be on the flag, that's a given. He or she also needs to be resting, if we're to be historically correct. To represent this, I suggest we turn to modern technology and use a hologram of a clerk. Using a hologram, as the flag blows and waves in the wind, and depending on your perspective, the clerk will be there one moment, and "on break" (or resting) the next. There one second, and then nowhere to be seen. Just like in reality. Pretty cool!

Now, we have the right side of the "sealie/thingie" to decide upon. This is a more difficult decision because we have one less something to choose from, now the clerk has been used. I've narrowed the choice to three options, and I suggest you fly with the one that suits you best. I think it is a tossup between a school administrator, a teacher or Ed. Tech., a call center trainee, and a state worker. I mean as far as "industries" go, these have got to be right up there at the top, at least for now. We do have a new governor, you know. But maybe having a "state guy" on a state "sealie/thingie" seems a little too much like communism, so I'll opt for the school person. I don't like call center people. They don't tend to "habla" English and if they do, they have such an accent from "habla-ing" their native language that I can't understand them anyway. They are out.

As for the resting part, we could fly special flags for spring break, winter break, mid-winter break, fall break, the "holidays," personal days, teacher workshop days, I-think-if-I-went-to-work-I-might-possibly-catch-a-cold days, my-dog-is-acting-antsy days, and so on and so forth. These flags could show a sick teacher recuperating in Cancun, Paris or Orlando, or on a cruise ship, if they could afford it. Which of course, being paid worse than teachers in 45 other states, they can't. In the summer, the resting thing is a given, however. (The previous statement about pay was inserted for my benefit by my daughter who edited this book and who is a dedicated teacher. She also included the following as a personal note. Guess I got "schooled." ["This really upsets me. Do you know how many sick days we actually take? Almost none! We can't afford to, because our jobs are so damn demanding. I'm not going to support more teacher bashing. Please change it."] Well, here you go, Jen.) Then there would also be the opportunity to get the "state guy" represented and involved if only for a short time. We could depict, oh, I don't know, maybe a guy, or better yet a group of guys with a foreman, of course, leaning on rakes, wearing hard hats to protect themselves from the rakes, standing around a sign that reads "Vacationland: Go slow, your tax dollars almost at work, bridge freezes before road, fines doubled." There's room for thought here and I'm open to other suggestions.

In the center of our flag we'll still have to have a shield to pay homage to the original. I like the pine tree, but in place of a moose, or better yet, next to and beneath the moose, why not have a tourist in shorts and sandals resting in a colorful Adirondack chair? That works for me. We'll place a Moxie or a microbrew ale in their hand for authenticity. We'll still have to keep the word "Maine" in block print under the shield just in case other states decide to update their flags as well and they all start to look the same.

So that's our new flag's symbols, revised and updated. I like it, don't you?

Those symbols completed, we now need to take a look at the state motto. Our motto used to be, well, technically I guess it still is "Dirigo." "Dirigo" is Latin for "I lead." I used to like that motto until it became clear that the one thing Maine leads the nation in is taxes. Now, I don't like that slogan so much anymore and judging by the election of a Republican governor, I'm not alone. We need to change it. Here's a suggestion. Our new state motto should be should be revised to "Welcome to Walmart." If you think that's a tad too sarcastic and crass, and I do, here's my personal selection: "Ayuh—it's what we used to say." I prefer that one. It represents both who we once were and what we now are, "ayuh." If you agree, don't say anything. If you're opposed, keep it to yourself. Let's see. It was close, but I, I mean we, have selected to go with "ayuh." Good choice.

Now that we have a flag with a motto that we can all salute, let's tackle the other designated "major" state symbols that every self-respecting jurisdiction feels compelled to have. We'll begin with the state animal.

Maine's creature is currently the moose, the majestic and mighty lord of the northeastern woodlands. The moose is not a bad choice at all. After all, Maine has more moose than any other state in the lower 48, and we've got the death toll statistics from highway crashes to prove it. Each year, roughly a certain number of people collide with a moose and one or the other or both die. Why? Because moose are what scientists refer to as "really big mothers." In Maine there are a lot of moose and a lot of cars. Can you see the problem? Every so often, you even read about a motorcyclist meeting his maker head-on while seated on a Harley. Not a pretty picture. German Nazi WWII helmet or not, that's just gotta hurt!

Why do so many people die in collisions with moose? Okay, the motorcycle guy is pretty obvious, but why do so many perish in cars? Again, it's simple if you think about it. Moose are not only "really big mothers," they are "really big, tall mothers" as well. When you take out a moose with a Mazda, Mercedes, or Mini, you are quite likely taking out only his legs. His body stays on up where it was, up there in the air, and what goes up eventually comes down, down onto your hood, and ultimately lands (you see where this is headed don't you?) on you. If you are quick enough to duck, you're one of the lucky ones, and you're crushed to death. If not, if you panicked and lost your head in the moment, you get to lose your head again a moment later. I'm not kidding. You will likely, literally, lose your head. It's not a pretty picture, even if you are better looking than your typical Harley dude. So be careful, drive slowly, watch out for large, tall furry "mother" type objects standing in or by the road. And by the way, you might want to think about investing in a St. Christopher dashboard ornament or two while you're at it. You can believe what you want, but you'll never know, not until it's too late, so I suggest you err on the side of caution and cover all your bases.

Incidentally, a little known fact that I uncovered through my research indicates that moose are highly adaptable creatures. Centuries ago, before the introduction of the automobile, moose were still large "mothers," but not at all considered to be tall. Any collisions with an errant running North American aboriginal native would likely result in some minor bruising, but nothing warranting a trip to the vet's. It was only after the emergence of the auto that moose began to suffer significant losses to their population. According to Sir Arthur Conan Hoyle, the father of modern evolutionary theory wrote in his treatise "The More Things Change, The Less Likely They Are To Remain The Same," the moose quickly evolved into a tall "mother," and began to exact its revenge upon its aggressor. According to Hoyle, the moose evolved from an herbivore, to a "car'nivore" in a matter of only a very few model years. Given evolution and judging by the Ford Excursion and other similar SUVs, the moose may soon evolve to the hideous stature of a giraffe-like, wooly mammoth-like mammal with a nasty set of antlers. It's a scary thought, but as someone once sagely said, "Only the strong survive."

The Maine state animal will remain the moose. This is my story, and I'm sticking to it.

The state berry is the wild blueberry. It's not a "bleuberry," you "francophone" types, you. It's a blueberry, and it's a keeper. I've got no argument there, either.

The state insect is the honeybee. Now, I do have a problem with that and here's why. I like the honeybee; don't get me wrong. It's certainly industrious and productive and does a lot of good, I'm told. But it should not be our state insect. For one thing, there's a parasite or something out there that's ravaging the honeybee's ranks and if you're a gardener you can testify to the fact that most of our pollinating is now done by the dreaded bumblebee, not the honeybee. Incidentally, for your information, the bumblebee looks like the singer Sting, only younger. Besides, every state has honeybees and we're supposed to be choosing something special, something much more unique and representative of what makes our state of Maine so special. No, I would drop the honeybee and choose, instead, the black fly.

The black fly, or "flyus biteus darkus" in Latin, is my hands down choice for state insect for many valid reasons. First of all, the damn things are everywhere and they're nearly impossible to kill, much less damage for that matter. They're as common as tourists, but somewhat, though only marginally, uglier and less rude. They only breed in clear, pristine mountain waters, so you know they're healthy little buggers too. No pesky parasite's gonna put them down. In fact, they're so ornery, they'll probably feed off the damn parasite. They're nasty SOB's, that they are, but they're *our* nasty SOB's.

Black flies don't sting. They don't sting, but man, can they bite. They're the pit bulls of the insect world. But they are not all bad. While yes, they can be literally a pain in the neck, and they do inflict large, itching welts, they also serve a very beneficial service: they keep down the numbers of tourists, or at least the numbers who seriously consider moving to Maine. For that alone we should bestow upon them the honor of "State Insect Emeritus" and enshrine them in the state symbol Hall of Fame. That is when and if we ever build one.

One more thought about the black fly. How many insects do you know of that a have a festival each year? The black fly does, so that's pretty special in and of itself. Go to Rangeley and check it out. I think they still hold it every summer and I think it's still in the IGA parking lot. In point of fact, the festival is so popular they had to build a new and bigger IGA up to Rangeley just to accommodate the fans. And, oh yeah, when you visit you'd best bring some bug repellant while you're at it. Something with DEET to the tenth power should do it. I hear the mosquitoes are killers up there and as big as black-capped chickadees.

Speaking of which, the Maine state bird just happens to be the black-capped chickadee. Okay, it may not be perched on the highest branch of the ornithological food tree, but which would you rather have on a snowy winter's day, a chickadee feeding out of your hand, or a raptor feeding on it? I'll take the chickadee, thank you very much. I've gotten used to having fingers. Chickadees are also very cute, I can sound somewhat like one, they are everywhere, and they won't hurt you except when you shell out for sunflower seeds at the Union or Agway. Maine's former and future choice for state bird shall remain the black-capped chickadee.

The Maine state fish is a no-brainer, which is not to say it's stupid. It's the land-locked salmon and as far as I can tell, they're as smart as most other fish and probably smarter than, say, a guppy. It's ours, it's special, and no one else has it. It's a fine selection. There's nothing more to say about it, so I won't.

There is something to say about the Maine state herb, however. Presently it's the wintergreen plant. It's a pleasant enough sprout, I suppose, but really, should it qualify as the state herb? Do you swoon over the benefits of the wintergreen leaf? Do you grow it, use it, or even know how to use it? Have you ever even seen one? I think not. I know I haven't come across it at Hannaford's, so how important can it be? My nominee is an herb that the majority of Mainers are quite familiar with, from children to adults. It's grown by more people than you'd suspect and, as for me, I suspect you. It's used by countless others to spice up many a boring meal. It's versatile. In fact, it's been known to turn a simple snack of chips and dip into a full-fledged culinary orgy. It's lush and green, fast-growing, rugged, and able to winter over in our harsh climate. It's distinctive in its leaf shape and mellow in its aroma. Yes, I'm talking about perhaps the largest cash crop in Maine. No, not the potato, but "weed," cannabis, marijuana, or Mary Jane. And it's my selection for our state herb.

The state flower is the white pine cone and tassel. I don't know about you, but that's unimaginative and, to be honest, stretching the concept of a flower a bit too far for my taste. The white pine as the state tree is fine. It's everywhere and you can't really object too awful much now, can you, but its tassel as the state flower? I don't think so. Have you ever seen a grove of white pine trees with blooming white pine cone tassels resting in a vase on someone's windowsill? I didn't think so and neither have I. I want a real flower, you know, with petals and other flower-type stuff. I don't want any half-morphed piece of furniture "wanna be" jammed down my throat by some lame, know-nothing legislator I voted for over that other idiot. I want a real flower, but not any pansy of a flower such as, well, a pansy, either. I want something with a little heft, something with a stalk or a stem. It has to be pretty, and yet tough—like my wife says Paul Newman used to be before he died.

My choice (and I think you'll like it) is the ubiquitous lupine. It's distinctive and though common here, is yet fairly unique to Maine. It comes in assorted colors too so most folk can find one to their liking. The only problem I can foresee might be if and when we become a semi-autonomous region of Canada. If that's the case, we might want to rethink the lupine and select something else, perhaps the white pine cone tassel, for instance, but for now, the lupine will do fine and I endorse it as our choice for state flower. I'd ask you to vote on this, but quite frankly, I don't care what you think, though I'm not stupid enough to actually say it. I just assume you'll agree.

Moving right along, you won't believe we even have one of these as a state symbol, but we do. Maine actually has a state fossil! Really. It's the Pertica Quadrifaria. It lived—thrived in fact—390,000,000 years ago during the Devonian Period (in case you're interested, and I sincerely hope for your sake you're not). We have a state fossil. It's amazing isn't it? I just told you what our legislators have selected as their choice, but do you really have a clue as to what it is, or was, or does, or did look like? Could you pick out the Pertica from a petunia? Well, yes, maybe the thick rubbery hide and its sharp fang-like incisors might give it away, or that it's now a petrified rock, but in the dark or from a distance, could you tell them apart? I don't think so. I think the choice is a silly one. I suggest we claim a fossil not from the Devonian Era, but from a more recent time and yet one that's just as scary, at least to me. I suggest we select from the McCarthian Era and I choose as our state fossil, with of course your assumed consent, the honorable lady senator from the great state of Maine, Ms. Margaret Chase Smith!

Talk about unique Maine fossils! She was a one-of-a-kind find, at least until Olympia and Susan came along. Still, if you're talking fossils, and we are, Margaret has got to win in a landslide. No need for a secret ballot or even a show of hands. It's done; Margaret it is. She is now the one and only official Maine state fossil. We thank you and as you leave be sure to pick up your complimentary fossilized rose, Margaret's very own signature symbol as you might well know.

The state fossil was silly, but what would you call having a Maine state soil? I'm not kidding. I guess even geologists and earth scientists must have a sense of humor too. It's obviously an odd sense of humor perhaps, and one not widely shared, but a sense of humor it is nonetheless. What is our silly soil? Why it's the infamous Chesuncook Soil Series of course. Did you really need to ask? I'm sorry, but I have to stop. I can't go on. I'm stunned. We actually have a state soil—unbelievable!

We also have a state gemstone. That's fine with me. It's the tourmaline and overall, a good choice. Watermelon tourmaline is beautiful and unique to Maine, unless you count those other places where you can find it. We won't because it's that uniqueness that makes us feel so special. Still, I feel fairly secure in its appropriateness and acquiesce to the judgment already exercised by our wise and trusted elected officials. Obviously this was decided long ago. Some might say Margaret Chase Smith was a gem as well, but that's pushing it. Tourmaline it is, Maine's state gemstone.

Wrapping up and concluding this short foray into our state symbols, we end with our last and final category, the state cat. Yes, Maine has a state cat and yes, it is the Maine Coon Cat. Again, it is a logical and good choice, solid in its merits. I plead no contest. I have no bone to pick with that cat. What I do question is why we don't have a Maine state dog? Now, *there's* a bone to haggle over. You have the state cat, you have the state bird, so why not the state dog? Here's my thought. We have raccoons—big ones, rabid ones. Dogs hunt them, so why not a Maine Coon Dog? We also have birds, and dogs hunt them too; why not a Maine Bird Dog? You say there is no such thing. You may have a point there. But think of this: there are actual, authenticated photos of a Sasquatch, for crying out loud, and we all know that it doesn't exist. The same goes for the Loch Ness monster, "Nessie." Why can't we have a Maine Coon Dog? Think of the interest that will create among the canine crowd. Even though it may not really exist, there's no reason why we can't have a photograph of one, is there? We have the technology; it can be done. It should be done. And by gum, if I have anything to say about it, and I don't, it will be done. As Yule Brenner quipped thousands of years ago while wearing only a loin cloth and a dish towel as he slaved over slaves slaving slavishly to build the pyramids, "So let it be written, so let it be done." If it worked for a freakin' pyramid, it'll work for a dog. Trust me.

That's it. We're done. Let me congratulate you on a fine job. On a final note, I've got to believe that our updated and revised list of Maine's flag and state symbols is now much more relevant and appealing to those who think about such things, whoever that person might be. And on a final, final note, I would only add that the Maine state song is, in fact, don't tell me you guessed it, that's right, "The State of Maine Song." Really, it is. You can't make this stuff up, and I know. I try all the time.

P.S. When this was being written, the Maine legislature was considering adding an official state beverage to the list. Nominated was Moxie, and only Moxie. It's a Maine original. Moxie is best described as an "acquired" taste, as in "I bet you can't drink the whole thing, Rasputin." Its tangy bite is best described as somewhat of a mishmash of cola, root beer, sarsaparilla, birch beer, tar, arsenic, and medicinal herbs. It's "wicked good," too. It's sold in six-packs and two-liter bottles, but I think you have to be over forty and they'll card you. No one I know or associate with buys it by the six-pack, just one judicious can at a time. By the way, it's a carbonated soft drink, just in case you couldn't tell, and it gets my vote for the Maine state beverage, which in fact it now is.

Money

If Maine is to become unique, or "uniquer" as it were, she will need to rethink her monetary system. American money is boring, to say the least. Green and only green, and a sickly green to boot—how mundane, how pedestrian, and how unimaginative. It's a downright embarrassment to a nation that prides itself upon its ingenuity and invention. Canadian money, on the other hand, is colorful and has beaver and hockey players on it. Now that's cool. But it's already been done. Mainers could and should come up with something different, better than the hand we've been dealt and, to this end, I have given the matter a little (very little, if the truth be told) thought.

First of all, no dead guys on the face of the bills. If we wanted a history lesson we'd have paid attention when we could have at least gotten credit for knowing who those guys were. Making citizens on a daily basis stare dumfounded at dead, old guys we don't know is insulting and demeaning to our lack of intelligence. We should be able to recognize what we're looking at, right? So we're agreed: no dead, old guys for Maine.

Next, we need to brighten up the currency slightly more than a tad. I mean blue threads? Really! I'm thinking the basic Crayola crayon colors would be an excellent beginning. ROYGBIV to the max. Think of it, coloring would become educational too. A mom watching her son coloring a rainbow could take pride in his artistic talents while his dad could stand proudly aback and proclaim, "Look at my boy there! Someday he's going to be a banker!" Educational and fun, like Sesame Street for the wallet. There now, we have our parameters defined: no dead, old guys and lots of color, so let's move on to the actual money.

Our most basic denomination should reflect a commonality among Mainers. With so many choices to choose from—which is what makes them choices in the first place, I suppose—that's a hard one. But, honestly, no matter what you do in life, if you're living it (and remember, no dead, old guys) we all get dirty (dead, old guys get dusty, and there is a difference). It's the nature of life, the basis of life. It's dirt. Everyone gets dirty somehow, so let's start with brown: a dirty, nondescript, brownish, dirty dirt, Crayola brown. Now, continuing to rail upon this train of thought, what is common, brown, and totally Maineish? Why, dirt and the potato, of course. Now, we can't eat dirt, so we select the potato. Therefore the basis of our new currency should be a big, fat golden potato on a field both brown and barren, a background just like any typical Aroostook County vista in November. Naturally, we would affectionately refer to our new basic currency as "the spuddah," as in "That's gonna cost yah two spuddahs, mistah." Sounds good to me.

Now that we have a canvas upon which to paint, we need a logo or motto to guide us. "In God We Trust," which was fine in its day 250 years ago, before evolution and all, will not do. Our "spuddah" should reflect a real Mainer's quest for the truth and will simply read as follows: "You're so smart, prove it." I think that says it all. Finishing off the front of our bill and replacing the dated pyramid (and no, I don't care how they were built) would be a brown pine tree (spruce budworm, no doubt). The shining eye would become a guiding lighthouse beacon. And, finally, no vicious bald eagle for us, at least not on every bill, and surely not on this one. We'll place a friendly black-capped chickadee on the "spuddah," thank you very much, and go upon our way.

Rounding out our bill, and not to confuse the new "spuddah" with any other, a large number one would reside in the upper left-hand corner and nowhere else. We don't need to put large and small number ones all over the place like American money; ours is brown, there's a one on it, it's a "spuddah," we're not stupid, we get it.

The back of the note would be the back of the front, literally the back of the front. The potato would still resemble a potato—well, duh. The pine tree would now provide a background for the lighthouse that was behind it. It makes sense. And a profile of a chickadee is a profile of a chickadee. Left to right, right to left, it's still a chickadee. So there you have it, the "spuddah," our basic unit of currency.

Once you have your fundamental "spuddah," we would move onto the larger denominations. A five "spuddah" note could be red, with a green lobster gracing its surface just to show we know a live lobster from the dead insect once selected by third graders for our license plates. In the lobster's mighty right crusher claw, would be five golden French fries providing a logical progression from the ubiquitous "spuddah" to the five "spuddah" note. There would be a number five in the upper left corner because, besides the number, it's red, and yes, we still get it.

The back of the note is where we take the less traveled road of numismatists. The back of the note could be changed every year or every other year reflecting current trends and events. In 2004, for instance, a picture of George Bush in a red circle with a line across it would be a true collector's item in a Blue State like Maine. Likewise, John Kerry's image in a slashed red circle (we could use a holograph so it could change its position constantly, just like the candidate) would be a big seller in the Red States. Think of it. By changing the back of the bill, we'd create a natural collector's edition, kind of like the U.S. mint quarters, only all from one state and far more rare and therefore valuable. People would actually buy this money. It's brilliant. We could actually sell our money for more money! It's pure genius and pure profit!

And, once demand dropped below a certain point, we could create a new five "spuddah" note with perhaps New Hampshire's Old Man in the Mountain in a red circle with a line slashed across it. Who wouldn't want that one? I know I would. I'd take two. Of course the "Old Man" would now be a pile of nondescript rubble, but we'd still get the message. Going a step further, we could create a note with each state's symbol in a circle with a line slashed across. It's a no-brainer. It's simple human nature. Everyone has a need to feel superior to someone else, so why not take advantage of it? Everyone who lives next to another state hates that other state. That's just life. New Yorkers hate New Jersey. They also hate Connecticut. Connecticutters, or is it Connecticutites, hate New York with a passion. New Jersey hates both Pennsylvania and New York. Oregon hates California. Vermont hates Massachusetts. (Well, what would you expect?) And let's not even start with Texas! The whole world hates Texas. Let's just simply say there's a lot of money to be made here if we play our cards right. If Monaco can do it with stamps, we can do it with money. Maine, the Monaco of the New World! Let the presses begin to roll and the money to flow, filling our coffers with joy and abundance for all.

Moving right along, the ten "spud" note could be a blue sky over a blue ocean with a blue lobster, blue heron, blue whale, and the "Blue Nose" schooner, all awash across the bill. The bill would be blue. Yes, and the lobster would be holding ten golden French fries in its claws, five on the crusher side, five on the pincher side; neat, simple and logical, all.

Having a ten "spuddah," one would think we would move straight away to a twenty "spuddah" bill, but that makes no sense at all, so it's right out, replaced by the more rational 25 "spuddah" note. The 25 "spuddah" could be indigo and violet, "lupinated," as it were, throughout. This would be our veggie note with assorted fruits, vegetables, and flowers planted in abundance. We could print new ones for each season of the year, as it were, again creating a demand for collectibles. Instead of wearing out, the 25 "spuddah" would be made of natural plant fibers and would wilt and crumble if not spent in a season. Thus, we have our currency, which also provides us with a ready means of continuously enriching and stimulating the economy. Isn't this fun?

Carrying on to the 50 "spud" note, this would come in two colors, yellow and blue, both being translucent. This bill's little twist on the ingenious would work like so. Everyone knows that $100 bills are the drug runners' and counterfeiters' denomination of choice. Why? Because they are large enough in value to be profitable to forge, but not so large as to draw too much attention to themselves. Our notes would confound the counterfeiters on two counts. First, the bills would come in the two aforementioned colors causing the prospective perpetrators of deceit to double their efforts, thus halving their profit margin. Secondly, each new note would allow for a unique profile such that when combined by placing one atop the other, back to front, together they would produce the new 100 "spuddah" note offspring, uniquely different from either of its parents. It would be economic and genetics combined. It would be like a MAD Magazine centerpiece that when folded in the middle, produces a new picture altogether. Added to this, not only would the newly conceived note promote an entirely distinctive motif, but behold! With the combination of the yellow and blue, the note is now green! You can't beat that by dressing up some dead, old guy in new threads, no matter how obscure and forgotten he might be. You just can't do it.

Beyond the 100 "spuddah" note, we Mainers would have no further paper currency. There's no need for it. If you carry any larger denomination bills, you're just flaunting your wealth and that's not in keeping with the Maine way. Besides, you're setting yourself up to be robbed and we don't want that, even if everyone has a right to earn a living. No, beyond the 100 "spuddah," Mainers would use their credit cards or write a check. Understated, reserved and dignified—just like Maine.

So there you have Maine's new paper currency en totale. Now, we move on to coinage, and a whole new rethinking of our ways.

Coins are as old as, well, really old coins. They've been around since the very first cash registers and vending machines, if not earlier than even that. And why are they so popular? Because they last! They last and you can jingle them in your pocket while you decide whether to buy something or not. Add to this the fact that you can look at your stash and still not know how much you're worth until you actually put it down and count it, and you have all the ingredients for a successful currency: you can hold it, can jingle, toss and flip it, you can count it, and when you're done, you can spend it, exchanging it for something else altogether. All that in one tight little package. How can you not like it? I'll tell you how. When your wallet contains less than a "spud" and it's an inch and a half thick and weighs two pounds, that's how.

Our coins are stupid. That's all there is to it. And we're too dumb to change the system. It's like Fahrenheit and Celsius. Pick one, for God's sake and go with it. But no, that makes too much sense and besides, it's not democratic; it's un-American. Let's try to persuade or, yes, trick ourselves into using the Celsius system by putting it on our time and temperature clocks. That way, literally "over time," we'll slowly get used to the change. But how will we know what the temperature is in the meantime? We might risk freezing and not even know it. Right! We'll put the temps up in Fahrenheit, as well. That will do the trick. That will makes sense, surely! No, of course it won't. It doesn't make any sense at all, which is why it's stupid. We just wait for the stupid Celsius numbers to go away and the stupid Fahrenheit numbers to appear. It hasn't taught us how to gauge temperature with the rest of the world at all; it's only taught us to be patient, and we already have the DMV for that.

It's as stupid as the one dollar Sacagawea coin, or the Susan B. Anthony coin before it. They're all stupid. But, you say, Canadians have a one-dollar coin, called the "loonie." Yes, they have a coin that sounds stupid and yet it works, so why not us? It's a good question, but I'll go you one better. Canadians even have a two-dollar coin called a "toonie." Now that's really dumb, and yet it too works. Why? Because Canadians aren't Americans. We're Americans and we're stupid and we might as well accept it now and be done with it. We're Americans and we don't want our government or anyone else telling us what to do. It's un-American. We don't mind our government telling everyone else in the world what to do; we rather like that. Just don't tell us what to do. We want to choose for ourselves. After all, that's what freedom is all about.

Canadians, on the other hand, are easygoing slackers who in our eyes don't stand for much of anything. They just kinda go with the flow. "A one-dollar coin, now, is it? Cool. No paper ones anymore you say? Sure. Makes sense to me. Two-dollar coin too. Fine. Why not? They jingle. Hey, they work in a vending machine too, just like in the old days with real money! None of that paper in, paper out, paper in, paper out. Cool. Sure glad we're Canadians, eh? You betcha!"

But we're American. We vote, we choose; it's our way. "A dollar coin. What the hell is this? It looks just like a quarter. I don't want this friggin' thing. What do I want with a coin when I've got this here ole greenback in my wallet? I'll keep a couple for the grandchildren, but that's about all I can tolerate. Nobody, not even Walmart, is gonna make me use that stupid thing. Nobody, I tell ya. I'm an American. I'll pay for my Pepsi just like my dad did and his dad before him. Now take this frickin' dollar you stupid ass, SOB machine. You spit that out one more time and I'll kick the livin' $#!% out of you."

Well, we're Mainers and we live somewhere between America and Canada, somewhere between stupid and slacker. And I call that smart. So we'll make up our own money. And the first thing we're going to do is rid ourselves of the infamous penny!

The penny, now that's just a dumb anachronism. It's been a useless burden, a chore, but we can't just throw it away, because after all, it's still money. Even if it's worth practically nothing, that's still something. And so, we put it in a pickle jar and save it for, well, for forever. Pickle jars and coffee cans are just the wrong answer to the question of the penny and what to do about it. The right answer is this: we'll collect pennies in a pickle jar because the copper is valuable and besides, they don't make the damn things anymore. Up here they're a collectible. That's going to be the right answer, at least in Maine.

If you bring a penny into Maine, you best plan on leaving with it, too. We don't want it. We don't want your penny ante problems. We've got our own problems, but a penny won't be among them. And just who is that dead, old guy on it anyways? We don't do money like that up here. We think for ourselves up here. Yes sir! Have you seen the "spuddah?"

In Maine we have a Lincoln town, a Lincoln county and a Lincolnville. What do they all have in common? Right. None of them were named after Abraham Lincoln. They were named after three other Lincolns, so don't come round about confusing us with another one.

We in Maine will have no use for the penny. It will be outlawed and done away with. We will move straight up to the dime. We'll have a dime, a quarter, a "spuddah" piece, and a two "spuddah," if we like, but that is all. No penny, no nickel, no fifty-cent piece, none of that. And our coins will work in both stupid and slacker vending machines so no one will be "stuck" with a tin "spuddah." On the contrary, the "spuddah" will be the coin of choice.

Our coins will have a heads and a tails like the rest of the world, but we'll have a true head-or-tail coin. Don't insult me with flipping a useless penny. Make your flip count, man! Hand me that "spuddah" and make your call. No unidentifiable dead, old guy on one side and a lame, unidentifiable building on the other. What's with that? There's too much not to know there. No, we'll have a moose with a huge rack on the head side of a "spuddah" and a big, old, hairy moose butt on the other. Just like in reality, our coins will have a front side and a real "back side," so to speak. And they'll be colored as well. A silver "spuddah" coin will have a brown moose. A silver quarter will likewise have a black bear's head and a black bear's butt. A dime will have a ten point white tailed buck with a white tail on the tail side no less. And a two "spuddah," if we so choose to go that route, will have a blue whale spouting on the front and a tail of a whale following behind. That's a fact, no whale of a tale, just the tail of a whale. Our money will be colorful, useful, and factual. Like one and one is two, it will make sense and yet will have no cents at all. And how can this be you ask? Allow me to explain.

In Maine, as sadly is the case most everywhere, we wait on lines at stores while little old ladies count out the "correct change." They've got that penny hidden away somewhere. But no, this cannot be. Where is it? "Hand me back that ten note, dearie, and I'll write you out a check. I know I have that checkbook in here ... somewhere ... or did I leave it home by the mantel? Oh, that's where my keys were, Mildred. Now I remember." What you just read won't be the case in Maine for two reasons.

First, we won't be burdened with the penny because we won't need it. In Maine, all our purchases over ten "spuddahs" will be rounded off the nearest "spuddah." Whole numbers will abound. $10.38 becomes simply $10.00, while $10.78 becomes $11.00. The government takes 5% in taxes and the beauty of the system is that, in the end, everything of course balances out. Lines will move faster and there will always be that sense of adventure, of waiting out the final tally. Will I make off with some money, or will I be taken to the cleaners? Who knows? That's life! Life in Maine, it's an adventure just like Reny's, so come join in the fun! For purchases under ten "spuddahs" you'll have to pay the difference, up to the closet coin. Sorry! Even fun has its price.

And so there you have it: Maine money. It will be beautiful, colorful, useful and sensible. What's not to like? Maine will become what the rest of the world could only dream of becoming. Maine will be that unique and charming glimpse of what life should be if only the rest of the world had the gumption to try to live it, if only they were "Mainers."

One more note. We're thinking of "Seinfelding" the gas pumps in Maine. Think of what that would mean. Gas will pump at only one speed—fast, of course—and if you stop the cost counter exactly on a whole number, you win a "spuddah." If you're under, you owe the difference. If you go over, well, you pumped it, so pay for it. Just don't forget to round off. It's simple, it's fun, and hey, you were going to buy it anyway. You all come back now, "ya heah, ayuh, eh?"

One more *one more* note. What we can do with our money we can do with our stamps, too!

The Kennebec River is not the longest river in Maine. After careful research I found that, in fact, over forty percent of the rivers in Maine are not the longest either. The Kennebec flows all the way from its humble beginnings to its majestic end, which ironically is referred to as its mouth. If it were a politician, that would explain a lot, but it's not; it's a river, the Kennebec River. My point is this: If all the toilets in Maine were to flush at precisely and exactly the same moment, that would be a really unusual coincidence, but it would not, I repeat, it would *not* affect the length of the Kennebec River, which, by the way, is not the longest river in Maine.**

Maine License Plates

I have several very old Maine license plates. They are plain, they are simple and, as such, they represented Maine well. To look at one of these plates, you are not impressed, but you get all the information you need, plain and simple: i.e., this vehicle is from Maine. Times have changed, however, and so have our license plates. Let's take a moment and explore how our new, colorful, and expensive plates came to be and where they might be going.

In the olden days, before the discovery of metal smelting, license plates were carved out of wood. It was a painstaking process, but that was fine, for back then there weren't nearly as many cars as there are today. With the passing of the centuries, more and more vehicles began to appear on our blacktopped highways. Times had changed and so had Maine, only a little more slowly. Something had to be done.

As costs for producing the hand carved plates went up what with inflation and all, Maine found that it needed to somehow pare down the expense. One idea put forth was having inmates in our prisons produce the plates. At first this didn't work out well, as giving the inmates knives to carve with turned out to be "not such a good idea." The phrase "didn't see that one coming" was quite popular for a while with the press until, as a remedy, it was decided to make the plates out of metal instead of pine. The metal tended to dull the inmates' knives as they carved, and in a matter of just a few decades, the prisons became a safe haven once more where murderers could reside in peace. Of course, more time passed with more inflation, and costs went up again. Prisoners demanded higher wages to keep up with the rising cost of living and their pay escalated from, say, six cents a week to, say, eight cents an hour. Obviously the economics were out of control. Once again, something had to be done.

The legislature set to work and quickly arrived at a nifty solution: they came up with the idea that maybe, just maybe, they could pass a law and make it mandatory that Mainers affix a plate to their vehicles. Up until now it had been optional. They also thought that they could then actually charge Mainers money for the privilege. It was a win-win situation, except for your basic Mainer, who turned out to be the big loser in the deal.

To make the bitter taste of coughing up a few bucks for something you didn't really want in the first place palatable, it wasn't long before some inspired trendsetter came up with the idea that we should attach a slogan to the plates and then the simple Maine folk would think they were actually getting something more for their hard-earned money. At first they tried to be cute and put "I paid the state a bunch of money that I had to pay 'cause they said so and all I got was this stupid license plate" on the plates. But that didn't fit. Changes were made, but then the print was small and it was too hard to read unless you were tailgating. So finally, someone suggested they could put the word "Vacationland" on the bottom of the plate and that was that. It was a resounding success. The slogan made those of us who live here think we were having fun all the time. And when Mainers traveled out of the state to really have fun, it also intrigued "out-of-staters" into following them back to Maine to see what the hubbub was all about. This approach worked well for a while, and then the cost of the plates went up again. What to do?

Cars having wheels and people having eyes, someone high up in Maine state government soon realized that other states were not only providing the usual necessary information on their plates like Maine, but were also bragging up those states and decorating their plates to catch the motoring public's eye. Even states like New Jersey and Connecticut were getting into the act and, as we know, they don't have anything to brag about. Yet there they were with neat looking decorator plates gracing their vehicles instead of their former cream and blue obscenities. The plates created an interest and a buzz. This was "free" advertising and Maine was missing the proverbial boat when it came to the automobile. Something had to be done and done fast. As a state, Maine had to put the pedal to the metal, and not only catch up, but pass everyone else on the advertising highway just as soon as we could.

And did we ever! We determined to change our plates once more, but how, and to what? The brain trust that is state government in Augusta got together and came up with a novel, if stupid, idea. They decided to form a committee to come up with another novel and hopefully not as stupid idea. That novel idea could be anything the committee decided as long as it included a design for a new license plate, this time with not only a slogan, but also a symbol to represent Maine. Being highly educated and therefore not representative, our representative legislators in their infinite wisdom then decided a second grade or some such elementary school class of typical Maine students could do as fine a job as college-educated, professional artists and graphic designers. So, they sent out their request far and wide and what I call the "ignorant little bastards," my children and yours, set to work on a new Maine license plate and logo.

What was the end result of this massive Manhattan Project of miniature minds? It was the now infamous "red and dead, insect-like, lobster critter plate." The plate was a disaster. Surprise, surprise! But who was to blame? The kids were, of course, just that: kids. They may have been professional kids and really good at being kids, but they were still just kids. They thought, "Gee, let's put a lobster on the plate," which actually is a real good place for a lobster, but on a dinner plate, not on a license plate. The space for the lobster was small, so they decided to make it eye catching and therefore red, which also meant it was dead. It resembled a dead, red cricket or scorpion-like insect, an eye-catching critter if you could see it, but not exactly attractive and not exactly representative of our state. As I said, it was a disaster. The committee had done its job well. Maybe not well, but well, like a committee.

It was such an ugly plate that there was soon a huge uproar among the citizenry, the driving public, or anyone with eyes for that matter. People who didn't live on the coast, like myself, resented Maine being depicted as merely a rocky coastline with apparently some dirt and a few trees behind it that just happened to stretch a hundred miles and more, all the way to Canada. We wanted some of that dirt on the plate. We wanted to be represented too. Maybe a mountain, a pine cone, a tree, a moose, or a potato would do the trick. If you had a cooked lobster, the least the second graders could have done was put some French fries next to it on the plate. They could have gotten the necessary eye-catching red from the ketchup and we all know coleslaw is a most colorful side dish as well, not to mention a bright yellow ear of corn on the cob. But no, the dead crustacean was the beginning and the end-all of their inspiration. The bottom line is this: they don't stop education at the second grade because second graders are stupid.

To their credit, and as a result of their lack of foresight, the state legislature had inadvertently stumbled across a lucrative way out their dilemma. Having made the new license plate so ugly and such a huge disappointment, they had created a pool of Maine people who were now desperate for almost anything else to bolt to their bumpers. They were willing to pay real money, whatever the cost, to avoid the "creature," "critter," or "bastard beastie." I myself believe this was no accident, but was carefully planned, because in no time at all, the DMV came up with the idea that for twenty dollars more, you could have a nice looking loon plate as opposed to a dead, red, radioactive perhaps, scorpion-like insect lobster critter plate. It goes without saying that the loon plate was a big seller, and its popularity rose in direct relationship to the "creature's" abysmal hideousness.

In short order, having served its purpose and served up "mucho dinero" for the Conservation Department to consume, the lobster plate passed mercifully into history and is now a collector's item, sort of.

We Mainers now have a chickadee on our vehicles' plates, our state bird, resting on a white pine cone tassel, our state flower. For us simple folk, it's nice and pleasant, not divisive or obscene, and represents us all quite well. We are satisfied. We are happy again. The loon plate and other suitable renditions are now available and all are well conceived, and executed works of functional advertising art. Maine license plates are "the way license plates should be," and we can be proud Mainers once more.

That is, until someone in Augusta decides that they need to make another quick buck. Until they form another committee and that committee decides that maybe, just maybe, the error made in the past process was in using such highly talented, gifted and educated second graders. Maybe, just maybe, the answer lies with Head Start. Maybe we need a "See Dick, See Jane, See Maine" plate! And then again, maybe not.

The Portland harbor area contains an actual working dairy. It is comprised of a few real live fisherman, DeMillo's Floating Restaurant, several other restaurants that would sink if you pushed them into the harbor, and roughly ten thousand small eclectic shops owned by "farmers" dedicated to the milking of the proverbial tourist from "away."

Demographics

Maine's population is primarily of Caucasian heritage. That is to say, it is white, as white as the new fallen snow. In fact, Maine is so purely white, that if it were soap, it would float. I get incensed when someone asks me what race I am. I get incensed for two reasons. First of all, it's no one's damned business including yours. This country has been too racially divided since I can remember and that's saying something. It's time we started practicing what we preach and forgot about race and ethnicity altogether. We're supposed to be a melting pot America, so melt already!

The second reason I get peeved is that, "Hello! I'm from Maine!" You want to know my heritage? You take a guess. The state is 99 point something percent white! I'm not going to spell it out for you, take a chance and go out on a limb. I'm Caucasian? You think? Hey, listen up, DNA testing would have you declared the father of a child with less accuracy than you would have taking a stab in the dark about race in Maine, pun intended. Men have been sent to their deaths on less. I am begging you, America, let it go; let the race thing go. Everyone, join in and sing along now with a heartfelt, gospel beat: "Let my people go."

Barring the U.S. Census Bureau's passing away in its sleep or waking up to actually doing what's right, I suggest you do what I do. In fact, I would encourage everyone who feels the same as me to do what I do. What is it that I do? It's simply this: I do what is right, honest, and true to my beliefs: I lie about my so-called race and ethnicity whenever I'm asked. You should do the same. But why lie? you ask. Because, for one thing it's fun to lie, as we all know, and besides, it's proving a point to the pointless.

When the census people check their figures and notice that there's a cluster of several hundred Aleuts named Smith, all living in a small, central Maine town, they're going to begin to doubt their figures. When I say I live at a certain address and I'm from Mauritius or Fiji and ten years later, I'm the same person I was before, only now I'm Norwegian or Turkish and my kids are native Swazi-landers, maybe they'll spot the anomaly and begin to wonder. When everyone starts to lie to them, maybe, just maybe, those census people will give up the whole damn scheme and the government will begin to treat all its people the same, just like the constitution says we should.

Should it matter what heritage or race you are? No! This is America. Even the Government will tell you that; it has to, it's the law. So, until America actually becomes what it claims to be, go ahead and have some fun and play with the system like I do. As for me, for the next census, I'm planning on being Ecuadorian. My wife is going to be Tibetan. We will have four wonderful children, an Eskimo and a Hawaiian (they're twins, you see), a Bahamian and a Cossack. You see how much fun this is? Try it yourself and maybe, just maybe, we can stop pretending we're "Americans" and actually become Americans at last.

The only people in this nation who deserve to be treated differently from the rest of us are the Native Americans, and that is by treaty. All others are equal, end of story. I wish.

The Scotia Prince is, or more accurately *was*, a ferry/casino ship traveling to and from Portland, Maine, and Yarmouth, Nova Scotia, on a daily basis during the summer. The ship contained many small rooms, some containing closets, and many large closets, some containing rooms. The most diverse ethnic population to be found anywhere in the state of Maine while the Scotia Prince was operating was not actually in the state, just docked *next* to the state beneath the "Million Dollar Bridge."**

Great Mainers

The following is a short, and surely not inclusive, listing of significant contributors to the heritage of our great state of Maine. The comments are my own and do not represent those of the management. In fact, there is no management, and besides, they may not even represent my own views for that matter. I'm not sure, but I wrote them down just in case I might be right. You be the judge. If I'm wrong, they're not my views. If you think I'm "spot on," well then, I'm back to not being sure. I mean, if you knew what was right and what wasn't, you would have written your own book, wouldn't you? The hell with it all then; just read on and let it go.

George Mitchell. George Mitchell was a senator and also Secretary of State of the United States. He got the Irish Catholics and the Irish Protestants to stop killing one another, to sit down, and to finally begin talking once again. The problem is that the only thing they could agree on was that the English totally sucked big time. Now he's trying to get the Israelis and Palestinians to sit down and hate the British too. In case he fails, the U.N. has sent Tony Blair over to the Middle East to support and hasten the effort of hating the British.

Edmond Muskie. Muskie too was Secretary of State of the United States. He cleaned up our rivers so we can swim and catch fish and not pulp logs or a rash. He cried in New Hampshire, but then again who hasn't or wouldn't (aside from someone who's not been there)?

Margaret Chase Smith. She was the first and only woman senator in the United States during her lifetime, which oddly enough coincides with the time period in which she lived. She was nice. She got along with people by sporting a rose on her blouse instead of a chip on her shoulder. A lot of things are named after her here in Maine, such as schools, bridges, and the Margaret Chase Smith House, which is where she lived when she was alive. Go figure.

John Blaine. He was a distinguished senator from Maine who, like Margaret Chase Smith, lived during his lifetime. He had the presidency of the United States all wrapped up, only to have his inauguration preparations cruelly interrupted by the actual election results. His house was named after him as well and it's now the governor's residence in Augusta.

Mr. Lobster. He is the stupidest invertebrate on earth, but still smart enough not to evolve to the point of living on land. He has no backbone when it comes to ethics or politics. Fishing for lobster is an oxymoron. Mr. Lobster is stupid for tasting so good, especially with butter, corn, coleslaw, and rolls.

William Cohen. Bill was an independent-minded Republican. He later served in Bill Clinton's Democratic administration as a cabinet member where he was the token independent-minded Republican. He is married to a non-Caucasian, which only served to emphasize his independent stature. He should have been a Democrat, but for all his liberal persuasions, was too narrow-minded. He played basketball in Bangor.

Angus King. He was a well-liked former Independent governor who didn't blow with the political winds. He initially supported George Bush, #43, for president, but then, being smart as well, actually thought about it and changed his mind. He retired and rode in a bus around the country. He's back home, thinks blowing with the wind is a good idea for energy, and he's now in favor of it.

Tony Shalub. Tony is, or was, Mr. Monk. Either way, I like or liked him. He needs or needed medication too, just like me. He graduated from U.S.M. I didn't. That's why Mr. Monk and Tony Shalub, are so smart and I'm not.

George Bush (#42). He is the former President of the United States who owns a large, prestigious, stone mansion situated upon the rocky Maine coastline. He also had a motel room in Houston (can you say thirty-five electoral votes vs. Maine's four?) and is therefore obviously a Texan. He likes to race about in a large cigarette boat and hold up striped bass for photographers. He likes to golf on a golf course. He stayed the course in Iraq. He never jumped ship, but nowadays he jumps out of planes. He's a good Joe for a George.

Barbara Bush (#1). She is the former President's wife. She is white, very white, from her white skin, to her white hair to her pearly white teeth to her pearly white pearls. She can read real good too. She wants everyone to read and talk good, gooder or even gooderer, than they do. Her son, George W., the President (#43), him don't talk too gooder at times, but don't tell his mom, her gets mad, 'cause she readed to him, but he no listen good.

Santa Claus. Santa is a good guy and great independent thinker. He does only good things and spreads joy and happiness wherever he goes. He has an environmentally sound transportation system. He doesn't allow himself to be pinned down on his Palestinian position, which keeps him popular in certain Hashamite circles.

Hannibal Hamlin. Hannibal Hamlin was Abraham Lincoln's vice president. He came from Paris, Maine. He spoke with an accent, but even though he was from Paris, it wasn't a French one. Hannibal was well known for being famous.

Olympia Snowe. How could she not be from Maine with a name like Snowe? It's a great name, but the "e" on the end is a little much don't you think? She is an independent-thinking Republican, like Bill Cohen, the senator she replaced. I may be wrong on that last comment, but I think I'm not sure. She's married to a jock by the name of Jock McKernan, a former Maine governor.

John Baldacci. He was the last governor of Maine before the next one who is LePage. If   you've seen a photo of him—Baldacci, that is—his name is obviously not an oxymoron, at least not the first syllable. A lot of people think he is or was, however, a moron. These people are called Republicans. As for me, I'm not sure. I think he might have been a Democrat, but I'm not sure, just like a lot of other people.

Hiram Maxim. Hiram Maxim was an inventor who killed time by killing things with his Maxim machine gun. If Hiram hadn't invented the machine gun, someone else would have, but that would have made celebrating the birth of the machine gun in Maine just stupid. He also invented the mousetrap and the silencer. It's because of Hiram that millions of poor souls perished quickly on the fields of Flanders and elsewhere in WWI from gunfire rather than suffering the indescribable pain of stepping on mousetraps strewn indiscriminately about the battlefield.

Stephen King. Steve is a scary guy. Have you seen him? He's married to Tabitha. He should have married Morticia. He should have been Gomez on the Addam's Family TV show. He writes really great books that somehow almost always make really bad movies. I think he uses a lot of words to say not a lot of stuff. I'm glad I'm not his typewriter or editor or him for that matter. He scares me.

Susan Collins. Susan is the U.S. Senator from Maine's 2nd District, where I live. She talks like a really old Katharine Hepburn; painfully slow with something like an echo somehow involved. I don't think she's married because Henry Fonda is dead now. So is Katharine Hepburn for that matter.

Paul LePage. Paul is the new governor of Maine and he likes to swear, which is what I like about him. He managed Marden's discount stores where they sell stuff cheap. Cheap people shop at Marden's. I shop at Marden's, but you'd better take my advice and check it out before you've "bought it, when you saw it, at Marden's." Check out what Paul's selling before you buy it too. I'm worried that I'm going to run across stuff I've seen in the Blaine House in Marden's someday. If it's cheap enough, I might buy it. I don't think Paul is really married to that Marden's lady, the one you see on TV, but you never know for sure. As they say, politics makes for strange bedfellows.

Chester Greenwood. Chester invented the earmuff. He also invented the nose muff and the far less successful eye muff. Strangely, although he was a great inventor, he didn't invent the muffler. He muffed that one.

Crime in Maine

Maine is one of the safest states in all the United States. You are far more likely to be hurt skiing than you are to be robbed of your ski equipment. Oh sure, after you've collided with a tree and broken your leg, neck or whatever, and you've been dragged off cold and stiff on a toboggan, someone might, by "accident," take the bloody mittens you left lying there in the snow, but really, we're talking a pair of mittens here, not murder. Besides, that's hardly a crime in my book. You weren't going to miss those mittens anyway. It probably took you a week just to remember your name, so get over the mittens already. If it makes you feel any better, they didn't really fit all that well so I put them in the lost and found at a church for some poor kid, okay? Sheesh! Anyway, when I talk crime, I talk murder, and murder doesn't happen very often here in Maine. Like I said, Maine is a safe state.

In fact, if you're going to die in Maine, you are far more likely to die from complications from obesity than anything else. Try killing a fat person, and I'm talking really fat now, with a knife. They have so much blubber unless your knife is called a sword, you won't even begin to penetrate their outer shell much less hit a vital organ. They're more likely to die from a heart attack trying to run away than be killed by your little knife. And if they try to diet, that's highly likely to kill them as well, what with all those crazy diets going around. I mean it's criminal what these diets are doing to us.

No, if you want to talk death, let's talk mass murder. Let's talk of supersizing our fries. McGruff the Crime Dog should be standing in his trench coat and L.L.Bean boots, holding a Pepsi to his head with one hand, and a doughboy to his mouth with the other. Beneath would be the familiar caption: "Only you can take a bite out of crime." That's what we should talk and write about, but then again, let's not. Let's watch the movie. Reading is hard.

The point is that Maine is a safe place to live, unless you know someone, that is. Now I realize that last little caveat would lead one to believe that many, if not most of us, are at risk. Fortunately that's not the case, but I'll explain. You see most crimes in Maine as elsewhere, are committed by someone (the perpetrator) who knows someone else (the victim). Therefore, if you know someone personally, it stands to reason that the more people you know, the greater your chances, at least statistically speaking, of becoming a victim and vice versa. Incidentally, vice versa is a crime term from the Latin base. Vice, meaning immoral or illegal behaviors of one kind or another (use your night-time imagination and try not to smile) and versa, meaning against. Thus vice versa, or "crimes against."

Research has shown that most crimes are in fact committed against someone else. After all, it would be pretty stupid to sneak up behind yourself in a parking lot late at night, bludgeon yourself over the head with your own hand gun when you weren't looking, rifle through your own wallet when you come to, rummaging for a couple of bucks you know you don't have, which is why you decided to rob someone in the first place, and then stagger away into the darkness, unable to satisfy your craving for a Big Mac and fries, wouldn't it? No, it doesn't happen like that. Crimes tend to be committed by someone else and that someone else is most likely an acquaintance. Therefore, it stands to reason that the more people you know, the riskier is your lifestyle, and the greater your chances of being killed.

To my way of thinking, then, the safest people I don't know are hermits I haven't met who live alone and don't know me or anyone else. Meanwhile, the most at-risk person I can think of would be, oh, let's say a "greeter" at Walmart. I know I've been tempted on occasion when approached by a "greeter" to have some of those vice versa thoughts. Statistics should prove this to be true, but anecdotal evidence to the contrary would argue otherwise, or vice versa.

How many times have we read something along these lines? "John Doe, a hermit, living unbeknownst to anyone at 134, Apt. B on Main Street, Anytown, Maine, was found dead from multiple gunshot wounds to the head. Police, who said that John was poor and could not afford to buy multiple bullets, are calling the death suspicious and are not ruling out foul play." How many times? Too many times for me, thank you very much, which is why my trailer door is locked tight and I don't care if I am out of mascara, you and your pink Cadillac are not getting in so stop honking the horn and go away. On the other hand, how many times have we read that a Walmart greeter was attacked with a baseball bat and robbed of his happy face stickers? You see my logic here? Statistics (and I too for that matter) can and do lie, which brings me to my next point.

My problem with researching crime in Maine is that crime is tracked through the use of those very same, lying statistics. Now, statistics are merely numbers and as we've noted, numbers can lie. My wife refers to me as a "number one liar," but I'm not alone. Our entire economy and stock market is based on this principle (remember Enron, the Savings and Loan scandal, Wall Street?) and who am I to question its validity? However, I believe a more accurate measure of community malfeasance may be obtained through the measured use of anecdotal evidence as provided by real people. I trust people. I value what my fellow citizens have to say, even if I have to make it up. People don't lie, at least not when talking about something as serious as crime and that's a value you can't put a number on. Just refer to the hermit versus the Walmart greeter and my point is proven beyond a reasonable doubt or at least by a preponderance of evidence of a clear and convincing nature. Okay, I have a hunch.

The first anecdotal evidence of crime in an historical vein was discovered several years ago by a rock hound searching for tourmaline in Maine's Oxford County. An apparently petrified piece of birch bark protruding from an outcropping of schist caught the geologist's eye. On this bark, deciphered by somebody of some note, were written some symbols or etchings that have been determined to be without a doubt, although with some room for question, a crude form of ticket for a minor traffic violation: proof irrefutable of law and crime, thousands of years before recorded history. Even then, our ancestors (well technically not ours and surely not mine, maybe yours, but somebody's, no doubt) felt the need for the structure and oppression of everyday law.

I'm certain that even the so-called "savages" of the day recognized a basic need for law and order in their society. No doubt, there must have been a time when one warrior plucked from an unsuspecting other warrior's hat that warrior's coveted "big feather." Such a heinous act wouldn't go unnoticed for long and was likely pointed out at the next big shindig at the local long lodge. The conversation must have gone something like this:

RatsOnOthers: "Grumbling Belly, isn't that your missing 'big feather' over there on You Calling Me a Liar?'s hat?"

Grumbling Belly: "I do believe you're right, RatsOnOthers, my trusted compadre. Here's a shell. Don't spend all it on the first pretty face you see.
(storming across the lodge) Hey, You Calling Me a Liar? I do believe that's my big feather on your hat there."

You Calling Me a Liar: "You calling me a liar?" (Whomp!)

It's easy to see that the need for a less radical, hands-on means of resolution to such matters was called for. In an effort to meet those needs, over the years the Native Americans developed a primitive concept of justice and ownership, which evolved into more appropriate and acceptable consequences for anti-social behaviors such as stealing than the traditional, though admittedly fun, "whomping." Spanking about the face and head with a stone war club became discouraged and frowned upon among the more civilized of tribes. In fact, "time outs" were commonly used, although the lack of corners in wigwams hampered the broad acceptance of the practice, especially among the plains tribes.

By the time of the first settlers' arrival in the New World, the concept of law and order was generally commonplace and widely accepted among the native tribes. When the early colonists arrived in Maine, tall black hats and buckles were all the rage, not big feathers, and relations with the natives were relatively tranquil for a time. However, there soon arose some quibbling among the new neighbors over such minor points such as just whose land was whose and who would have to vacate or die.

The Indians took offense at being robbed of their ancestral homelands by the settlers, while the settlers objected to having their homes burned to the ground and their families dragged off as captives by the Indians. Both sides had a point. Both sides bickered incessantly about what they saw as the "injustice" inflicted by the other before agreeing that something must be done to resolve the matter once and for all. As the Indians' and the settlers' law codes varied a tad—especially regarding handicap parking, bottle returns, and plundering—they called together one another's greatest intellects and agreed to settle matters amicably through intermittent warfare. This arrangement worked well for a hundred years or so.

However, during sporadic periods of peace, those relatively boring times, the settlers felt the compulsion to combine law and order with the need for community entertainment. To this end, they decided upon the concept of putting the kibosh on certain trivial behaviors that earlier had gone unattended such as heresy and witchcraft. Thus we were treated to spectacular burnings at the stake, multiple hangings of the wicked, and unmerciful teasing of those burdened with a lisp or other speech impediment. Cheating in marriage was scorned and, as Hawthorne noted, it was a "red letter day" in town when an adulterer was discovered.

To their credit, the Indians were not to be left out of the fun and had their own long-running battles among their various tribes to indulge in. And let us not forget, there were also the French, as well as the occasional Jesuit priest, wandering around to be picked on, affording a ready source of merriment to all (with the possible exception of the Jesuit priests). Times were good, but all good things come to an end, as they say, and so it was with the halcyon days of peaceful, intermittent warfare and random persecution. The settlers, as we all know, eventually won over the Indians to their way of thinking by persuading them with well-reasoned arguments not to mention their overwhelming numbers and superior, technologically advanced for the day, firepower.

Once peace reigned supreme and everyone except the loser were happy and content, the settlers had the time to sit down at their whale oil lamps and write laws governing their society's most basic interactions. These essential laws of community, laws such as no killing for the most part, no stealing, and no dancing or wearing of colorful beachwear after dark, were quickly established. But what exactly constituted "colorful" beachwear?

In no time at all, the need for solicitors to clarify and argue the finer points of these edicts quickly arose. "My client wasn't dancing, she has, perchance, the palsy. And are there not degrees of colorful, not to mention what's with Bermuda shorts? Is mauve inherently less evil than, say, magenta? Where does paisley fit in the mix, and are Hawaiian prints right out?" Clearly, the need for courts, juries, and judges was recognized by all, even those most die-hard of all organized anarchists, the private label designers.

In a matter of a few short years, the numbers of laws grew in a proportion roughly equivalent to the increase in the number of attorneys. Coincidence? I think not. Lawsuits rose similarly. The impact of this rapid expansion of the law catapulted a once rustic, common sense society to new and complicated heights, as it became evermore common for the "full weight of the law" to be used in determining exactly what constituted "justice." In the New England colonies, for instance, where death by pressing was implemented, laws were passed until the guilty were simply crushed and eliminated by the sheer weight of the preponderance of evidence against them. That and the tons of stone placed on their torsos, God willing, of course.

This was all well and good with the settlers as long as they were in charge of the "pressing" and were not the "oppressed," so to speak, which is to say, not long. When England realized the settlers had done with the dirty work of the actual "settling," the mother country changed their nomenclature without any input from settlers, who were no longer settlers, but colonists. Suddenly the heavy-handed shoe of legality didn't fit so quite so snugly on the right foot of democracy as it took its first stumbling steps towards freedom, justice and the American way. Jolly Old England no doubt had a good chuckle over that one, however.

When King George ordered stipends to be paid on the import of tea, his ever-loyal colonists revolted. Had the King hit them right between the eyes with a rifle butt instead of in their wallets, he might still be King to this very day. That and had he eaten nutritiously, and exercised moderately but regularly. But no, he blundered and so he's dead. The King is dead; long live the dead King. The King had made the same mistake that George Herbert Walker Bush would make two hundred years later when he uttered, "no new taxes" and failed to follow through on his promise. Of course *he* exercises regularly and plays golf, so he's still alive, or was when this was written.

Having witnessed the benefits of past conflict resolution with the Indians first-hand, the colonists decided to employ the same tactics anew and declared war on the British. Of course, they were all British, so to speak, so this was confusing to everyone. To end the confusion, the British wore red, while the other British, those in revolt, didn't. Eight short years, and a lot of dead guys later, the United States of America was born. The tyranny of the King was ended, and the tyranny of the almighty dollar began.

Beginning with a few simple rights and laws as written in our Constitution and Bill of Rights, the need for additional laws was gradually recognized until today, you can't even set fire to your neighbor's annoying cat without someone raising a fuss and threatening to do something or call someone. Whatever! It was a cat for God's sake. If God didn't mean for them to burn he wouldn't have made them flammable, now would he? Sheesh! Get over it. I'll get you another one. It's not like they're hard to come by. They breed like rabbits, or vice versa. Anyway, that brings us to the present day state of affairs here in Maine.

Maine is a very civilized state. So much so, that crime in Maine is now illegal. Not only that, but Maine has gone so far as to pass laws against crime. These laws are called "crime laws." Crime laws make certain things you do or have, illegal. Without crime laws, we wouldn't know what was bad for us. Crime laws, however, can change with the times. Drinking beer was once a crime. Then the government found it could make money by taxing the drinking of beer. Drinking beer was no longer a crime. This is an example of change that is called "good change."

The bad crime laws that we still have are enforced by bad crime law enforcers, also known as the police, the "cops" or "the fuzz" for short. People who break the law are technically called criminals, but are more commonly referred to by the "bulls'" as "reprobates" or "scum." All bad crime lawbreakers are scum to the bulls, but not all scum are bad crime lawbreakers. This may seem confusing at first, but if you've ever been to a family reunion you'll understand the not-so-subtle point being made.

These scum are also known amongst the knowledgeable few who are in the know of such knowledge, as common scofflaws. Scofflaws know that what they're doing is a crime and is therefore bad, but they don't care; they just do it anyway. They scoff at the law, hence "scofflaws." All scofflaws are also scum, but not all scum are scofflaws. For instance, the dark, impenetrable ring around my tub, that is scum, but it is not a scofflaw. Unlike your common bathtub scum, a neighborhood of scummy scofflaw types can be cleaned up by the police without the use of expensive Scrubbing Bubbles and other modern crime fighting technologies. In wiping up these scofflaws, the cleansing process is completed by flushing the scum down the proverbial toilet, or in other words, sending them to rehabilitation centers called jails, or to use the vernacular, "the hoosegow." Incidentally, common scofflaws are the preferred kind of scofflaw. Just thought you might want to know.

"The hoosegow" got its name from a certain Wilber Muttonchomper, a local eccentric shepherd who in the late 1850s would frequent courthouses in north central Maine near the village of Palmyra. Whenever a defendant was convicted and sentenced, Muttonchomper would shout out, "throw 'em in the hoosegow, Judge, throw 'em in the hoosegow" as the guilty party was being escorted off to jail. Years later a bystander asked Wilber where the phrase "hoosegow" had come from. Wilber confessed he didn't know; he'd just made it up one afternoon, thought it had a certain ring to it and liked to shout it out. That's all there was and is to it. Somehow, the name stuck.

The term "hoosegow" has come to be used in reference to a brief one or two night incarceration at most. If you are bad and confined for more than that, though it's the same place you're sent to, you're heading for jail. In Maine, most county seats have a county court, and every county court has a county jail. It's not often when a plan comes together like that. These jails are scattered among the sixteen counties of Maine. The jails have to be scattered about because lowlife criminal types will not cooperate by congregating in central locations, although they've been asked nicely to do so on more than one occasion, and sections of Lewiston have been known to come close. What can you expect from lowlife scum?

Now, if you are a really bad scummy lowlife type, you may be sentenced to more than a year in jail, in which case you don't go to jail, but to a detention center. Maine has two of these: one on a big windswept hill in Charleston and the other in Windham. These are nice and relatively new. They look just like colleges, Ivy League Colleges, Ivy League Colleges with razor wire. And they're easier to get into than Harvard or Yale, but it's a lot harder to get out.

If you are really, really bad, and are deemed a total "nogoodnik," you get to visit Maine's newest facility now located in Warren. Originally the maximum-security prison was in nearby Thomaston, or "Tommy Town," as the locals call it, on the coast near Rockland. Although "stone walls do not a prison make," Mainer's figured out early on that they are a damned good place to start and will do in a pinch. This massive granite complex was your stereotypical huge brick and stone, guard towers on the corners, huge iron bar gate, "that's where you're headed son unless you shape up damn fast," totally badass prison. They even had a real quarry inside to supply the big rocks the inmates broke into the little rocks just like in the movies. They also had an inmate shop where you could buy handcrafted furniture, wooden carvings, and so forth. It was a great place to visit, but it's all gone now, torn down and just a memory. If you want to see the new prison, the best way in is to rob a bank or a Big Apple with a baseball bat, I'm told. If you rob unsuspecting citizens of their life savings to the tune of millions, you'll only be fined thousands and won't get in.

Just a personal observation, and a true one, not that everything you've read here isn't true, but when I first moved to Maine almost thirty years ago, life was more simple than it is today. Farmington was the county seat, had a county court, and a county jail, both of which were next to the local Sampson's super-market and just down the street from the then only traffic light in Franklin County. That was one long run on sentence so take a second to catch your breath.

Okay? It was that kind of time, in that sort of town where those kind peo-ple would come from thirty or forty miles away just to run the red light on that kind of a slow Saturday night. Many of them, well some of them, okay, more like a few of them (I'll vouch for at least one of them) were sent to the "hoose-gow." Along with this person I knew, there were those who were passing time in jail for more serious transgressions like jaywalking, hunting out of season, or attempted murder. Times were more informal then and the prisoners would get to go outside in the afternoon and toss around a Frisbee while they shot the breeze. There was an actual line painted on the parking lot next to the Samp-son's that the inmates couldn't cross and if their Frisbee did, a shopper would have to get it and toss it back to the criminals. That's the way it really was back then. Those were the good old days. I'd like to think we could do that still, but I doubt it. Frisbees cost a lot more than they used to, you know. They might not be tossed back.

Just a personal observation worth remembering, but one I'll never forget and one I thought you ought to be aware of: If you are ever sent to the "hoose-gow" or even jail for that matter, you'll be glad to know that we have here in Maine some very nice ones. Most unfortunately are overcrowded, especially in winter. Go figure. It's warm in jail, it's cold outside, there's food in jail, it's cold outside, there's TV in jail, cable TV, and yes, it's still cold outside. There's got to be a connection somewhere there, but I'll be damned if I can figure it out.

If you are sent to jail or even if you go willingly because it's cold outside, you will have to wear an orange jumpsuit. It is not without coincidence that most jailbreaks occur during hunting season in Maine. It may appear logical, but this does not constitute what I would call a well thought-out plan. Ten men running through the woods wearing orange, not one with a valid hunting license ... oh no, that won't draw any attention. They're probably just another hunting party from Massachusetts driving deer.

Listen up—it doesn't work, you criminal types. You are not going to get a deer that way. Besides, you criminals are just going to be re-apprehended and are going to be sentenced to an even longer jail term now that you've been caught both hunting without a license and impersonating an out-of-stater. It would make more sense to simply escape around Halloween towards the end of hunting season. At least then if you guys knocked on a lonely farmhouse door, someone might actually let you in, or at the very least you would stand a 50/50 chance of coming back with some candy treats in your pockets. Candy's hard to come by in jail and those jumpsuits have pockets, don't they? If they don't, just ignore this entire paragraph because without pockets there's just no point to escaping in the first place.

If you should ever find yourself in jail in Maine, there's a good chance it was because you did something while driving a vehicle. It could be speeding, or an OUI, or smuggling dope, or kidnapping someone, or robbing a bank or actually just stealing the car for that matter. The point is, beware: Maine has strict driving laws that are enforced in an evenhanded and uniformly random manner, so pay attention.

Enforcement of motor vehicle laws is entirely contingent upon the numerous factors that come into play during the actual violation. Taken into consideration by the arresting officer, for instance, may be the nature of the violation itself, the name of the state on your license plate (it is not good to be from Massachusetts, not good at all) and the mood of the arresting officer. Also to be considered is the immediate financial health of the local police department in question. Now, don't get me wrong; we don't allow speed traps in Maine like they do, or did, or do, down south. We just don't enforce the laws most of the time. We let bygones be bygones and lull you into thinking everything is just hunky dory and then suddenly, without warning, we decide to pull a few officers together and strictly enforce that 25 mile per hour zone there just around the corner from that 50 mile per hour sign. It's technically not a speed trap, but it might as well be; the fine costs the same.

As a general rule regarding speeding, the likelihood of actually being issued a ticket instead of a warning increases proportionally in relation to the shortness of the officer's hair, inversely to his age, conversely proportionally to the miles per hour over the posted speed limit you were traveling at the time of your arrest, inversely to your skirt length, and exponentially out of all proportion to your bust size, with marital status thrown in as a tie breaker should one become necessary. If you're a married, bearded man wearing a calf or ankle length skirt or longer and a small, low cut sequined halter top showing off your minimal cleavage and affording a glimpse of your hairy chest, speaking from experience, you are, to quote a lawyer friend, "oh so screwed." Take my advice: don't argue, don't contact a lawyer, and don't get your picture taken for the paper. Just pay the fine, say you're sorry, and move on with your life, if that is at all possible. You may want to consider just moving to another town altogether, come to think of it; people are so judgmental and oh, do they ever gossip.

Unlike speeding, some traffic laws in Maine are non-negotiable. For instance, it is illegal to drink and drive in Maine unless you are driving a pickup full of gun-toting, hooligan bird hunters on a logging road near Patten, or are ramming around in a gravel pit on a Tuesday night in your father's four wheel drive with some of your underage drinking buddies instead of doing your algebra homework like your probation officer told you to do. Aside from those two exceptions, .08% or more blood alcohol is going to land you in the "hoosegow" if you're lucky, and in jail if you're from "away." Fight it in court and lose? You might want to apply for Maine residency as well. You're going to be with us for a while.

As for other moving violations in Maine, it is apparently legal to run a red light if it has not been red for at least five or ten seconds minimum. In Portland, you can double the time frames. I've personally sweated out heading under a red light more than once, searching frantically to see if a cop was watching, only to look in my rear view mirror and find that five other cars behind me did the same thing! You can't stop if the light's changing; they won't let you. I found this out while being pushed halfway across downtown harbor town one day last summer. You stop while the light's yellow and you better know a good chiropractor.

I also discovered on that same day that all traffic laws in Portland are discretionary. They're to be observed at the whim and whimsy of the individual driver's judgment or folly as the case may be. Don't want to stop? Then don't stop. Want to speed up to forty in a twenty-five when the light up ahead has already turned red? Hell, go for it. No one's going to say anything. And why not, you ask? For the simple reason that they're all doing the same thing. It's as if Bean Town has moved en mass, from Mass., to Maine. It can't be wrong if everyone's doing it, can it? Well, yes, it can be and it is wrong.

But fellow law-abiding citizens, take heart. There is reason for hope, slim reason and slim hope, but hope nonetheless, that this insanity won't spread to your hometown. So far as I can tell, the NIH (National Institute of Health) has managed to confine the spread of the disease to greater Portland and areas to the south. You can protect yourself from contracting the illness, but it won't be easy to do. Still, we have to try. You may have to drive with your windows up, even in summer, and wear gloves while in town, but it's worth it. Be careful and take care, lest you become infected. Don't be a carrier and infest the rest of the state. And for God's sake, note the warning signs. If however, you feel the urge to run a red light even though a half dozen or so cars are stopped in front of you, then sadly it's too late. You've got the disease. Do yourself and me a favor: just kill yourself. Put yourself out of my misery, will you? You know it's the right thing to do. I'm begging you.

There are other peculiarities of driving in Maine that should be noted. One is the law that says you must throw your hands up in disgust if the car in front of you actually stops at a stop sign when no other cars are coming. Obviously, like I said, there is no oncoming traffic, but highways have to flow now, people, and we can't slow everyone down by stopping just because some silly red sign says to. As for yield signs, these simply cause problems for everyone. They're debatable, aren't they? To yield means something like to kind of/sort of/maybe give way sometimes, doesn't it? But that's too much leeway when you're driving. Yield signs are just an invitation to play "chicken," another way of saying, "Go for it my automotive friend. We'll see who's gonna yield to who." It's fun, yes, but I say get rid of them anyway.

Maine has one very special driving experience in store for everyone—in fact, there are several of these—but the two I am thinking of are in Augusta. These are the traffic circles or rotaries on either side of the main bridge crossing the Kennebec. That's the bridge you can't jump off anymore because they put up a cage-like safety enclosure over the handrails. What kind of nut thought that was a good idea? Now you have to walk all the way to the I-95/Route 3 bridge and who's going to do that? But enough of that. I'd like to shake the hand of the nut who came up with the rotary idea. He's probably confined just down the road at AMHI, the Augusta Mental Health Institute facility, laughing from behind a barred window for the criminally insane. Either that or he's in the witness protection program.

Who in their right mind could have thought up something so stupid? If you want to get in an accident in Maine, head for Augusta and the high bridge; you'll never find a better opportunity for a collision. And what is really dumb, and dumb doesn't begin to describe it, is that they didn't just set up the opportunity for accidents to happen naturally; no, they actually have gone out of their way to ensure that the accidents actually happen. How? Simple. By law, when exiting these two lane traffic circles, you are required to exit from the inside lane! Can you imagine? It's true. I read this in the paper. It was a safety tip. The police had felt the need to clarify the driving regimen on the rotaries apparently because accidents were down. It seems too many people were doing the right thing, the logical thing: exiting from the outside lane. Well, duh! Who in their right mind would cut across traffic when you don't have to? No one. That's why we have the law. You are ordered to cut in front of the cars in the outside lane while you exit. And why not? How else are you going to get broadsided by a fast moving truck? How could we have the most accidents in the state if we allowed people to exit from the outside lane where they couldn't be hit?

It makes no sense. If someone cuts you off in traffic, any sane person is going to scream and holler, swear up one side of the idiot and down the other, while giving him the finger and threatening to ring his neck. But in Augusta, it's the law! You are required to cut the other guy off. In fact, you could get a ticket for driving like a sane, levelheaded and courteous person. This could only happen in Augusta, only in Augusta, Maine. Well, almost only there.

New Hampshire has a similar rotary in Portsmouth and Maine has a smaller version in Kittery, as well, but neither one is nearly as productive as their cousins up the pike in Augusta when it comes to producing car wrecks. Is it any wonder there are so many lawyers in the Capital City? Makes you think, doesn't it? Maybe that nut who came up with the idea wasn't so crazy after all. Maybe he was just a lawyer trying to drum up business.

Anyway, motoring on, in Maine it is illegal to go more than one hundred, or less than twenty, miles over the speed limit on the interstate. If you do, you'll either be stopped for speeding or run off the highway. This rule is strictly enforced by radar and/or airplane surveillance and by large tractor-trailers driven by really sleepy guys who—take it from the clerks at the Irving's in Newport—need a shower in a bad way. The only exception to this law is people from New Brunswick who, while driving huge, oversized pickups or SUV's and hauling ass with a thirty or forty foot travel camper to or from Frederickton or St. John, can't and shouldn't be bothered by the rest of us. Those folk can do whatever they damn well please, especially if they're on the Airline Road, and there's nothing you can do about it except get the hell out of their way. They're oblivious to us anyway, so what's the use of risking life and limb? You couldn't get their attention if you stripped naked and danced on their hood. Their eyes are fixed. They're in another world altogether, and they're headed for a better place, so unless you want to get there just ahead of them and by that I mean riding on their front bumper, just pull over and like I said, get the hell out of their way.

I think that covers traffic for now. There are other things to be discussed but we'll encounter them elsewhere. We need to get back to real crime and not just the misdemeanors and mass mayhem and murder of the highways.

In Maine, we don't have many murders, or at least not the grizzly ones I used to read about as a child in the old *National Enquirer* or today's *Boston Herald* or *New York Post*. We have had a few deaths like that, here and there over the years, but nothing really approaching the caliber of a Mafia slaying or a true gang war. If we do get a few of these, they're usually out-of-staters just doing their thing up here in the boonies or the back alleys of Portland.

Some of our normal deaths are just accidents, like hunting "accidents." You know, two buddies fight over a woman, they go hunting, one comes back—that sort of accident. There are the other kind, as well—real accidents, like with cars, a little too much drinking, high speeds, soft shoulders, tough trees. Some involve moose or deer. Others involve snowmobiles, boats and trees, though not usually in that order. Some, too many actually, are drug related overdoses. And others involve dementia, people wandering off and getting lost in the woods. Most we later discover suffered heart attacks and/or died from hypothermia. It gets cold in Maine. But we in Maine are working hard to develop our own niche specialty when it comes to the crime of murder and I'm speaking of domestic violence.

Domestic violence is the fastest growing category of crime in Maine. Speaking sarcastically, I believe this is because so many Maine husbands have failed to domesticate their partners and the upstarts are getting out of control. But seriously, this is a real trouble point in our society today. Married couples are actually killing one another. You'd think the men would suffer the worst; I mean the women are always toting those long knives around the kitchens, not to mention what they've been trained to do with a spatula or a whisk on the Food Network. But no, it's the men who usually do the killing.

Take heed of the warning signs, female-type Mainers. If you're a woman or a female type, and you and your man have just gotten into a big fight, be on the alert. If it's not deer season and he's sitting there muttering under his breath at the supper table, wearing an orange cap and a blazer and cleaning his thirty-ought-six, looking at you and drooling over a beer, I'd recommend you think twice about going to the Walmart for some cupcake papers, if you know what I mean. If you don't, I mean go get some cupcake papers now, woman! I mean they have Walmarts in Arkansas, right? Git to one, fast!

Drugs have become a scourge upon our society today. They run the gamut from tasty cough drops, to addictive codeine, from "over the counter" to Oxycontin, from medication for the piles to piles of medicating pot, from antihistamines to amphetamines, from an inhaler to heroin and from Crest to crack. It's all out there for the asking. Maine may be way out on a limb as far as states go, but there's nothing you can get at the trunk of the tree that you can't get at the tip of the twig either. Portland is known for its drug dealers working the coast, moving stash into Boston, New York, and beyond. Pot is grown everywhere, even alongside the interstate. We even have a yearly "Hemp Festival" in the town of Starks, for crying out loud. The DEA can't keep up with the level of trafficking going on. They're putting too many miles on their trucks hauling weed to be burned, much less dispersing the crowds that gather down wind. Washington County is swamped with Oxycontin users, as if nothing but cancer strength painkillers can relieve the agony of living in the middle of nowhere and picking blueberries for a living. What a crock! Where there's satellite TV there is no excuse for being bored, I say, shopping channels or not. Didn't you just read about TV in the prisons? Actually you didn't; it's in the next paragraph, so don't answer that question, just keep it in mind. As for dealing with drugs, I don't know what the answer is. The bottom line is that until people decide to "get a life," there is always going to be a problem with drugs; it's just that simple and just that complex.

I am so tired of hearing people complaining about prisoners getting to watch color cable TV to pass the time. Would they rather the inmates lifted weights only so that when someone takes an opposing view on current events they can tear off their limbs and beat them senseless, or would you rather have them able to discuss the pros and "cons" (sorry) of the subject intelligently? Not that they'd necessarily get that from TV alone, but you get the idea.

I don't think it's a bad thing to encourage interests other than how their cellmate might look in garters and a bustier. By the way, I don't think they have TV clickers in prison so they have to get up off their beds to change the channel, which in and of itself is good exercise given they have over a hundred channels to choose from. If you really want to punish someone, give him only the Home Shopping Network, the Weather Channel or Lifetime to choose from. Like he could place an order within the next fifteen minutes to double the knife selection and add the cleaver and paring knife at no extra cost, pay only for extra shipping and handling. As if he cares if it's raining in Spokane when he hasn't seen real sunlight in two years, or he wants to see "My Father, Axe-Murdering Rapist"; been there, done that. Want to drive him really nuts? Throw in the pay-per-view previews as well, the ones he can't get! Talk about your basic cruel and unusual punishment. I say let them have all the TV they want. It sucks to be locked away and they're not hurting you, so just shut up and get over it. And by the way, the world's in color now.

Speaking of killing time, and just plain killing, Maine does not have a death penalty. The reason for this is that the last person executed for murder was killed by accident. I don't mean that he slipped on his way to the gallows, or that when the hood was taken off, the executed man turned out to be Larry, the janitor who just happened to be mucking out the wrong cell at the wrong time, or that while the guards were playing musical chairs on the drop panel one of them inadvertently leaned up against the lever and whispered a half-hearted, "Oops." No, nothing like that. It's just that after the condemned man was killed, they found out he didn't do the deed! Imagine that! A prisoner who claimed he was innocent and really was! Who'd have guessed that would actually happen in real life?

Anyways, nowadays, when you're especially naughty, you are sentenced to life without parole in Maine. I think the state found it a little difficult to undo a wrong when that wrong took an innocent man's life. It's hard to call a "do over," when it comes to death—unless you're Dr. Frankenstein. There's a certain air of finality to the act of execution (excepting the aforementioned good doctor and certain religious affiliations). Anyway, I am proud of Maine for having taken this stance and even though I don't plan on killing anyone anymore, I think it's the right way to go. I cast my vote for life.

Speaking of which, again, Maine is also one of only two states that allows its prisoners to vote. I think that is mighty decent of the state and downright commendable. The voting booths are right in the prison and participation is encouraged, although I understand that absentee voting is not. But, really, why should a felon escape the same frustration and guilt that we outside those mighty prison walls suffer the day after election? Just because they made a big mistake in life, should that excuse inmates from having a hand in committing another mistake to office like the rest of us good citizens do? We need all the help we can get screwing things up politically and I thank them one and all for their assistance.

That's it. That's all I have to say about crime in Maine. I hope I didn't break any laws with what I've said, but if I did, I was only trying to do what's right, like exiting from the outside lane of those damn rotaries for God's sake! I don't care what the law says—call me a scofflaw and scum if you will, but I'm not exiting from the inside lane and if I do, it was only an accident, like the one I was trying to avoid. Sheesh!

Moose Crossings

There are approximately 20,000 moose either living in or visiting Maine at any one given time. By personal count there are approximately 100,000 moose crossing signs in Maine. It's impossible to have people respect crossing signs, crossing lights, and painted crossing lanes in our towns and cities, so why do college-educated conservationists expect our poorly educated moose population to cross our highways at moose crossing signs? It's ridiculous, if you ask me. All those signs do is frustrate tourists to no end. Now, that's not necessarily a bad thing, mind you, and I'm kind of in favor of that part of it, but if you're out and about trying to locate a moose to show a friend from away, it's just not right.

I've put a lot of thought into this and here's my solution. It would be a lot less costly in the long run, a lot less frustrating in the short run, and if you were just out for a jog and wanting to see the sights and a moose, a lot more satisfying, if our conservationist did this: hunt down the moose and put two sets of yellow blinking lights on them, one on each side. We could put a red light on the hindquarters (and a green to the fore if we wanted to get fancy), but I think that's just a tad lacking in good taste don't you? Anyways, we'd no longer need all of those phony moose crossing signs littering our highways any longer and from a mountaintop, every night would be the fourth of July, in a sense. Besides, in terms of safety, you couldn't get much safer than a lighted-up moose roaming the roads unless you put music to them as well.

But what with today's music, which is a generous euphemism for "rap," there's just no way I'd ever stand for walking down a dirt road on a quiet summer's eve and being greeted by a blinking moose, his lights hanging down below his ass, just strutting and jiving to a heavy bass "boom whappa boom, whappa boom, whappa boom, boom, boom." Yo bro! I'd pop a cap in that damn bitch's ass in a heartbeat. My guess is that any moose thus decked out and equipped would be extinct within a month.

No, on second thought, it's best we best leave bad enough alone. Forget the whole idea of lights and what not. Leave things as they are and just be satisfied with frustrating tourists. If we're going to drive our moose to the point of extinction, let's do it the old fashioned way, the way our forefathers have been doing it for centuries: I say put the Buick to 'em one at a time.

Snowshoes

Snowshoes are a great part of Maine life and lore, as they are in all northern climes in this and other hemispheres. They were originally developed by the Native Americans countless centuries ago, or about February 16, 523 BC, to be exact. No doubt, a clever brave, experimenting out back in the family garage one day, stumbled across the novel concept of keeping on *top* of the snow while walking as opposed to being mired up to one's red neck *in* the white stuff. Given that long johns were hard to come by before 1492, and that leather pants tend to shrink when wet, this was generally conceded to be a good idea, as this keeping on *top* of the snow also kept you dry.

Now, it has been long rumored that the Eskimo have over a hundred words for snow, and none for convertible or, say, coupé. I don't know if this is true or not, and frankly, I don't really care. I do know that native Maine Indians had over sixteen words for snow, fifteen of which were of course nasty curse words that I won't repeat here. Apparently, Indians back then didn't like shoveling out for the mailman anymore than we do now. As we all know, the snow in Maine can get rather deep, especially during the winter months, and as shovels were yet to be invented, the Maine Indians had to find a way to get around while visiting relatives during the Christmas holidays. Tunneling was tried and was fun, but not practical when Grandma lived several miles away. So, with the help of our young brave, the natives honed in and focused their attention upon the concept of keeping themselves above the cold white powder they so fondly referred to as %^*%, or *&%$, or $*^*%, and so forth.

Once the idea was born, the practical experimentation began in earnest. At first, they tried lying flat on their stomachs. Using a kind of rudimentary swimming motion, they managed to flounder a few feet in their intended general direction. However, they soon discovered that swimming in snow was akin to swimming in water in that in no time at all, not only were they soaked through to the bone, but onlookers derided their efforts, often commenting on how stupid they looked as they flailed about on their frozen bellies. They soon abandoned this approach.

One day, a very thin brave and his quite pregnant wife, decided to go out for a walk. There was a hard, but thin crust on the snow and at first, all was well. However, in short order, they both fell through. The thin brave disappeared over his head and was never heard from again, but his rotund partner fell only to her bloated belly and was buoyed up by her girth. This discovery led to everyone trying to get pregnant, which in turn led to many other societal problems, some of which were soon considered worse than falling through the snow. The idea of simply getting fat was tried as well, with the end result being that everyone fell through the crust all that much sooner. There had to be another way.

In southern Maine, near the Kittery Trading Post, an Indian whose mother-in-law was from Mexico and was visiting for the holidays, had prepared a traditional feast of tortillas and lobster succotash in her honor. He had burned a few of the tortillas and, after trying to make them more edible by generously applying a layer of maple syrup, gave up and threw them out his lodge door where they landed on a nearby snow drift. A few minutes later, his cousin happened by carrying a fruitcake his grandmother had given him because she didn't like him. This cousin was nearsighted and managed to step on the frozen, yet very sticky flour pastries. Realizing he had stepped in something, and that stepping in something is rarely a good thing, he stomped about trying to kick them off only to quickly realize that he while he couldn't shake or dislodge them from his feet, he also wasn't falling into the deep drifts and floundering up to his waist anymore, either. He had, in fact, literally stumbled upon what was to become the very first snowshoe.

From frozen tortillas and maple syrup, the Indians made a few subtle adaptations and improvements, tweaking the process here and there until ultimately settling on steaming fresh cut boughs of ash wood, forming them into oval or tear dropped shapes, sewing them together with rawhide strips, and fashioning a binding which enabled them to fasten the snowshoes to their moccasins. The snowshoe, as we now know it, was born.

Once the Indians managed to stay on top of their environment, life became a whole lot easier for them. For one thing, there were far fewer words to be learned to describe snow. Aided with snowshoes, they could now hunt game, travel long distances quickly and put out campfires much more easily than in the past. They no longer had to put bright orange safety balls on their heads, like those they placed on their toboggans to help find them in parking lots. The tribes flourished and snowshoe manufacturing became a wigwam, if not a cottage, industry. They advertised their idea, built up a demand, cultivated a market, and turned a handsome profit selling snowshoes at the Trading Post. However, it wasn't until the early white settlers arrived that production was expanded and evolved into a genuine factory process.

With the advent of the industrial age, manufacturing procedures were fine-tuned once more to enable lowered costs and increased quality controls through the use of the production line method. The advent of the Iron Age slowed the advance of snowshoe use somewhat, however, as iron snowshoes tended to rust and their weight proved a hindrance to sales when, in the spring, the bodies of those who had plummeted out of sight beneath the snow emerged from below and were retrieved. Those were tough times, but with the advent of modern advances in lightweight alloys and plastics, snowshoes were brought back into the twentieth century.

Today, modern snowshoes afford us the advantages of modern science, combined with the unchanged, enduring and simple pleasures of the past.

Aluminum and titanium snowshoes, available with metal cleats for icy conditions, enable the user to explore his wintry environs without concern for daily maintenance and such seasonal chores as oiling, shellacking, or restringing of the footwear. Plastic is used evermore to produce a durable and yet inexpensive product. More traditional craftsmen continue to produce snowshoes in the time-honored manner of steamed ash and use rawhide lacing and bindings. Prices can range from the reasonable to the "Oh my God, you've got to be kidding me" range.

There are many shapes of snowshoes, each offering its advantages and drawbacks depending on what you want to use them for. Traditionally, there are three shapes: the beaver claw, which is wide in the middle and tapered at the end, the bear claw, which is oval shaped, and the Yukon, which is very long and oval. Length and width vary with the type of snow and type of terrain, whether or not they are to be worn in the tight confines of the woods or in traversing an open field, for example. Uses are also traditionally divided into three categories as well, including mountaineering and hiking, recreational and racing, or sport. Sizes of snowshoes depend upon the weight of the person and gear they need to suspend above the snow's surface and, again, the type of snow. As a general rule, the square inches of snowshoe surface area should roughly correspond to an individual's weight. Really hard, really compact snow is called ice and snowshoes with a steel blade, often called skates, work best on such a surface.

Regardless of what kind of shoe you buy, like anything else in life, snowshoes are not worth a plug nickel if you don't use them. The finest equipment is useless unless it is used. So get out there and trudge away to your heart's content. Hunt snowshoe hare and other game with a gun or a camera out in the wilderness, or just explore the nearby woods of your neighborhood. Get out and learn about the world you live in, get a little exercise, and learn a little about yourself as well. Set out for a weeklong winter camping experience, or enter the snowshoe races in Lewiston, Rumford, Biddeford, Orland, and Ellsworth, among many others. Whatever you do, just do it. And remember to thank the Native American Indians whose perseverance and know-how allow you to enjoy winter's snowy bounty, not to mention needing only one word to describe the white stuff, and not sixteen.

Toboggans

Toboggans are familiar to almost everyone around the world with the possible exception of a few isolated Turkish Cypriots with a peculiar zeal for smoked owl jerky. Few realize, however, that they are yet another creation by the same folks who brought you the snowshoe, war bonnets and high stakes bingo, and yet, it's true.

The toboggan was a ubiquitous feature of the early aboriginal landscape in North America. (And my wife said I'd never use the word ubiquitous in this book. Shows you what she knows.) The toboggan was essentially the 4x4 pickup truck of the American Indian and everybody who was anybody had one, if not two, in their garage out back of the lodge. Of course, the toboggan not being a true truck, Native Americans were not required to buy license plates for them and thus we have no way of knowing the exact year or epoch when they were first conceived and manufactured. (Incidentally, the remains of an early toboggan factory were discovered on the outskirts of Detroit in 1914. We know this was an early factory because all the toboggans were black.) As for the exact date of the toboggan's conception, we could hazard a guess but that would just be whistling in the wind, and besides, I have no clue as to what that saying means. And what do people have against whistling, anyhow? Russians say it's bad luck to whistle indoors, we say it's useless to whistle in the wind, whistling hasn't been included in a major hit song since Bing Crosby whistled in "White Christmas," and whistling in the dark will get you nowhere but lost. What's a whistler to do these days? Hum? Use a Kazoo?

Anyhoo, it is clear from simply looking at the toboggan that it was, without a shadow of a doubt, an extension of the general concept of the ski, or the snowshoe, but certainly not both. Either way, the utilitarian nature of the toboggan made it an essential tool in the nomadic way of life enjoyed by the first inhabitants of our land. Without the toboggan, Indians would not have been able to get away on long holiday weekends, and roam, explore and hunt their continent's hinterlands during the long, cold winter months. Not only that, but the sight of toboggans careening out of control down a steep, rocky slope, haphazardly jettisoning screaming papooses lashed to their parents' backs on a sunny winter's afternoon, would have been replaced by hordes of cherubic, happy-faced children lying quietly on their backs, staring mindlessly at the heavens while endlessly making snow angels to pass the time. Just imagine the implications of this. Snow angels instead of the establishment of the proud, spirited warrior culture of which we are so enamored? I think not.

Getting back to the toboggan itself, it was constructed from the local, natural materials available to the local, natural aboriginal inhabitants of your basically local North American locale. Most were made from wood, but some early models were no doubt constructed from stone. Stone toboggans had the advantage of being extremely durable and long lasting, but their weight discouraged widespread popularity primarily due to the fact that they could not be moved. Most stone 'boggans ended up being used as planters or incorporated in foundation walls.

The earliest toboggans were, of course, created entirely by hand. Initially, they were no doubt carved out of entire tree trunks. However, the effort entailed in having to first fell a giant pine or spruce, well over a hundred feet tall with nothing more than a stone lashed to a stick and then whittling it down to the familiar toboggan shape with a fire hardened elk clavicle, was only the first hint of problems yet to come. The real trouble arose when the rugged brave tried to pull a loaded 100-foot-long toboggan without getting a hernia or, worse yet, rupturing a disc. It just wasn't practical.

Of course, if you lived near a lake as many Native Americans did, you could simply use the toboggan as a very serviceable sidewalk leading to the shore. If you lived really near the lake, your toboggan became a pier leading from your wigwam doorstep beyond the shore and on to your favorite fishing hole. No need for a birch bark canoe and paddle with that set up. Still, any sidewalk needs to be shoveled in the winter, so the idea was soon conceived to whittle down the size to say a more practical six-foot long toboggan that could be easily swept clean. The new size was great, but the effort and waste involved in taking a hundred-foot tree and paring it down to one six-foot toboggan proved slightly impractical (although the tinder generated and used for fire starting was greatly appreciated by mother).

Through time and experience, there emerged new construction techniques including the use of small strips of wood instead of entire trees. Steaming ash wood strips and bending them to achieve the traditional curved front part of the sled was an essential skill that any self-respecting toboggan maker learned to master. Joining the strips together created the necessary width for the toboggan. Individual strips could be used as skis if, say, you bought a cheap Japanese knock-off toboggan and it fell apart in the hinterlands leaving you stranded. Two toboggans strapped to the moccasins on your feet could be used in a pinch as snowshoes. Going downhill on snowshoes made in this fashion was not recommended as they are quite cumbersome, although it should be noted that the land speed record at that time was established in this very manner. Using three or more toboggans as snowshoes never panned out for obvious reasons.

To look closely at a toboggan is to begin to understand and fully appreciate the essential beauty and genius of its lines, and the simple functionality of its design. To begin with, the toboggan is flat. This is good. Having a large hump in the middle would render sitting or carrying items on the toboggan that much more difficult. Secondly, the toboggan has a rope on the front end (that's the end with the curvy part). The rope is used for pulling the sporting model toboggan back up the hill for another death-defying run, or the work edition toboggan to the store for essential larder.

Placement of the rope may appear random at first, but believe me, it's not. You can demonstrate this by means of a little experiment. First, affix the rope lengthwise from end to end. Now load the toboggan with, say, a cord or two of seasoned firewood. Next, try and drag that load of firewood back to your house. See what I mean? Keep trying and you'll soon discover why the wisdom of the rope-up-front concept prevailed. Besides, it's just plain stupid doing it the other way.

Having the curvy part up front is a good idea as well, as it both affords the rider a modicum of protection for his knees while fending off outcrops of rock, and offers a convenient means of holding on for one's life as well. The curvy part also tends to push the snow under the sled, though I think that was secondary to the knee rest/protection thing and just a fortuitous, though essential, happenstance.

In conclusion, we can say with a fair amount of uncertainty, that any toboggan must adhere to certain design basics including having a definite front and a definite back, and a definite top and a definite bottom. If you don't believe me, just try sliding down a hill ass-end forward, with the toboggan upside down. It's not going to happen. I know because I wasted several days trying unsuccessfully myself before a certain someone stopped laughing and pointed out that the whole shebang rides a hell of a lot better the other way round. Take my word for it: there's only one good way to ride a toboggan. You can ride the other way, but not for very long or for very far or unless your hill is very steep as in, say, a cliff, and very high one at that. Even then, the ride, exciting as that may be, won't last for long. Nor will the rider, for that matter.

If you want to enjoy a traditional wooden toboggan, you can't find a better place than Maine to do it. There's plenty of snow and plenty of open fields and hills. You will probably find it advantageous to make yourself a pathway to follow, a kind of chute if you will. By the way, that idea of steering a toboggan by twisting the curvy part, that's mostly a work of fiction. You might as well be whistling in the wind. Thinking of a toboggan as being steerable only makes you foolhardy; trying to stay on the damn thing longer than you should. My advice? Jump off the freakin' projectile before you hit that tree and save your body a trip to the hospital if you're lucky, and the morgue if you're not.

To my way of thinking, the ideal way to enjoy the toboggan is to have a nice icy chute already built and waiting for you when you arrive at the hill. Do you think that sounds too good to be true? Think again; it's not. The good folks in Camden-Rockport have a toboggan slide ready and waiting just for you and anyone else crazy enough to try it out. In fact, they hold the U.S. National Toboggan Championship there on Ragged Mountain each and every year. Teams from Maine and all over the world (really just Maine) come to pit their skills against one another and have a good time.

What's the key to a really fast toboggan rider? Basically it's the same key ingredient that determines why a big, fat, heavy rock falls faster than a small, paper-thin, light one; it all comes down to mass, baby, mass. All things being equal, the more equal your mass, the faster your mass, minus the "m," will go. So take my advice: find a big, honkin' friend (or your wife, for that matter), put down your Pepsi and go "slip slidin' away," as Paul Simon once sang. Who knows? You may end up a world champion, or just happy you're still alive. Either way, it's good, clean fun. And if you don't feel up to the stresses of the competition, you can experience the fun of a run for its own sake—that, and a small nominal fee. Either way, get out there and enjoy.

And remember, there really is a front and a back, and a top and a bottom to a toboggan. Once you understand those basics, the rest is as easy as falling off a cliff, but that's another story for another day—one that I don't recommend.

Snowmobiles

Snowmobiling is a centuries-old pastime in Maine, or it *would* have been had the Native Americans not been so fascinated with their feathered hats and war bonnets and instead concentrated on inventing the modern gasoline engine. Then again, they would have had to also discover petroleum reserves; perfect drilling and oil refining procedures; mining, smelting and casting techniques for metals and plastics; and so on and so forth. Actually, come to think of it, there's little wonder snowmobiles and ancient Indian culture are not usually mentioned in the same sentence. Still, if Indians had the opportunity to use snowmobiles, I bet they would have been quite popular with the tomahawk crowd to say the least. They sure would have made running around and around wagon trains in deep snow a hell of a lot less tiring, allowing them to put more energy into some really good whooping and slinging of arrows.

Anyway, snowmobiling is a fairly recent, but firmly established, pastime in Maine. The idea of snowmobiles is a simple one. Put a motor on a toboggan or sled, and off you go; no more just sitting there in the woods or in a field, in the cold, on that sled of yours, waiting for a hill to somehow just happen along. In fact, with a snowmobile, you no longer even need a hill. That motor sputtering beside you there is like a portable hill in and of itself. Fastened to your toboggan and chugging away, everywhere you turn is like having a little bit of downhill slope right there in front of you. With one of these babies, your life is always a downhill run. All in all, it was and is a pretty neat idea.

Now, snow machines were first invented around the turn of the century, the nineteenth to the twentieth, that is. Gasoline and engines were just coming into their own, and, as with anything else, once someone had a motor, they hooked it up with whatever passed their way or fancy. The 1900s saw automobiles, airplanes, motorbikes and motorcycles, motorboats, and who knows, maybe even a motorpogostick or motorpiano. I don't know for sure, but anything's possible and you can't prove otherwise—so there. The point is, it didn't take long for someone to realize that rather than trying to avoid the snows of winter when traveling, you could actually use them to help get you around. Again, the "over the snow" rather than "through or under the snow" concept rushed to the fore and took the coveted blue ribbon in the local "most obvious concept" contest.

The first actual use of the word snowmobile was apparently used when a Ford Model T was matched with tracks and skis:

"What in blazes do you call that cussed contraption Josiah?"
"I calls it a winter-use, snow trackin', ski-fronted, any-color-as-long-as-it's-

black, Model T auto-snowmobile, Lester."

"My hearing's off, Josiah. You say it's called a snowmobile?"

"Yes, that's it, Lester. A snowmobile. It's a snowmobile."

It didn't take much longer for the logging industry, as well as woodsmen and farmers, to realize this snowmobile machine could make their lives a whole lot easier, not to mention more fun. Not only that, there was the added benefit that it would make neighbors and friends drool with envy and it was cool to watch the drool freeze on their chins when it was really cold out. Everyone needs a chuckle now and again and the snowmobile brought that and a smile to everyone's face.

Anyway, it was industry that pushed the innovations associated with modern snowmobiles onward until, by the early 1950s, the idea of recreational snowmobiling began to take hold. With the advent of the Polaris Company in Minnesota, and the manufacture of what we would now consider a traditional sled or snow machine, the age of snowmobiling literally took off throughout the Great White North.

In Maine, as most places, it didn't take a genius to figure out that winter was the best time for snowmobiling. That's a good thing, because geniuses can be hard to come by here in Maine in winter. Of course, Chester Greenwood as a young boy invented earmuffs in Farmington, Maine, but that's another story. Still, like Chester, geniuses tend to be on the smart side. They tend to be wealthy and often head for Florida in December, January, February, and March. Fortunately, there remained then and is still today, a good supply of non-geniuses on hand and they proved more than up to the task at hand.

After many experiments over many seasons by many of those non-genius types, it was determined that the chances were far better for there being snow on the ground during the winter than in, say, in mid-summer. This had long been suspected but was not finally a proven fact until evidence-based practice came to be accepted in the mid '50s or thereabouts. It was also discovered that with winter layoffs in construction, extended school vacations, the many holidays and all, people had time on their hands during the winter season. And finally, with cabin fever affecting everyone, and all those kids home with the flu and sniffles, it was a good idea to get Dad out of the house before he killed someone or even everyone with that new shotgun he'd bought Mother to give him for Christmas.

Today, snowmobiling is multimillion dollar if not billion-dollar industry. Part of the reason for there being so much money involved with sledding is that the damn machines cost so much. I went online and happened upon a manufacturer's site. I won't say what manufacturer's site it was, but it rhymes with "bombard dee eh!" as in Canada-speak. I clicked on the first snowmobile I saw and brought up a price of $10,900! OUCH! Sorry, I was pulling the cat off the keyboard and he clawed me. Anyway, I went back to the computer screen. I added on a few upgrades and found I was now talking real money, something along the lines of $12,900. OUCH! *That* was the price, not the cat.

As I wasn't really intending to buy a snowmobile anyway and was just pretending, I went further and accessorized myself as well. You've got to look as snappy as your sled, you know, or what's the point? I bought a leather jacket ($500), pants ($400), boots ($180), and gloves ($90). I saw a spiffy helmet and bought that too ($480). My sled needed a cover ($240) and a windshield and skid plates that added roughly another $200. I totaled up the lot: $14,990! That didn't hurt as much as I thought it would. Pretending has its advantages. Then I added the tax! OUCH! Tax always hurts even if it's a pretend tax. Somehow, though, once I started clicking here and there, I warmed up to the challenge. Although I said I was warming up, just as though I were actually out sledding, I suspect I became increasingly numb as well and as time passed, the numbers didn't scare me any longer, except for the tax of course. I was warming, and numbing, and overall, really getting comfortable, too comfortable for my own good as it turned out.

I was actually beginning to think that this was fun and I wanted to share my excitement. I mean, no one wants to go snowmobiling alone, do they? No, they don't. What's the fun of showing off a shiny, new expensive sled and your duds to match, if there's no one there to show them off to? I mean, I have a family and we need to spend some quality time together. So, what the hell? I threw in a few more sleds for the kids and another just in case a friend stopped by. I also threw in a 4x4 Dodge Ram 350 Quad Cab. They start at over $40,000, but I wanted a Cummins diesel, too. How much for that little add on? Oh, I don't know, because the site wouldn't tell. I guess they feared I'd run and hide in my closet 'til spring. But they needn't have feared, I was immune to fear. No price was too high for my family and me when our pleasure was at stake. I'm an American, dammit, and I wanted the best or at least a reasonable facsimile, and so I continued to click away.

Having sleds and a truck, I'd also need a nifty enclosed trailer to haul my machines to the snow without actually getting them covered with snow, wherever that might be. I found a nice one for another five grand, but by then who was counting? Well, I was and I was just about set to total everything up. I checked out my list to make certain I hadn't missed anything of necessity.

Here's what one non-genius type in Maine, in winter, discovered. To get started enjoying the simpler things in life, like the great outdoors on a snowmobile with family and/or friends, I learned that by picking up four good sleds and gear, a trailer and 4x4 pickup truck, some clothes and other base necessities, my bill came to a grand total of somewhere in the vicinity of a mere $105,000, ballpark figure, give or take a few thousand, plus the unknown cost of the additional Cummins diesel. It could have been worse; I didn't opt for the cup holders, stereo, CD player, radio headset connections, and name brand socks and undergarments associated with and bearing the brand name of the sleds. What can I say? I guess I'm just cheap. I don't know what the DVD players, Ram-charged clothing, and other paraphernalia associated with the truck would have cost, either. I didn't really want to know and I didn't really care. As they say, if you have to ask how much it costs, you can't afford to buy it, and that's just not the American way, now is it?

So, filled with the frenzy of the hunt, I moved in for the kill. Like an idiot, an American idiot, I pulled out my credit card and in no time bought it all! OUCH! That hurt. And no, it wasn't the cat or the tax. That hurtin' was my wife clawing at me. "Stop it!" I cried. "We need this stuff. It's not for me, it's for you, you and the kids. Don't you care about your family? Don't you want them to have fun?" I guess she did, because she soon stopped her clawing, started to shake, then to whimper apologetically, and finally collapsed, curled up on the floor in a fetal position, which of course I took as an all approving yes! Let the good times begin.

Once all the goodies arrived, and we were all set with the sleds and our gear, we picked a date and a few short weeks later set off on our way to enjoy a wonderful weekend of bonding in the wilds of Maine. We headed north because when it comes to snow, north is a relatively safe bet, especially if you take that bet all the way to the North Pole. You could go to the South Pole, I suppose, but frankly that entails slightly more "dry sleddin'" than we were up for, at least on our first outing. There we were, bearing north on I-95—just me, the kids, the approving wife, and forty thousand other idiots with the same lame idea of heading out to the woods for some peace, some quiet, and some "solitudinal" communing with nature.

It was winter of course, and with our good fortune, we were headed out in a blinding snowstorm. This was good considering it had been raining for the past few weeks. It was January, and there were only so many weeks of good sledding left. To be honest, though, like it or not, we couldn't afford not to head out, what with all I'd invested, rain, blizzard or no blizzard.

The speed limit on I-95 was down to thirty miles an hour and there were whiteouts everywhere; you just couldn't see them because of all the driving, windblown snow obscuring them. Luckily, we were following the flashing blue lights of a Maine State Trooper accompanying an ambulance as it hauled another load of fellow outdoorsmen to the hospital or morgue or whatever. "It could be worse," I said, trying to cheer up the family, trying to get some color back into their white knuckles that were embedded in the new Ram's leather seats and dash. "It could be worse," I repeated. Suddenly the snow stopped for an instant and we saw what was ahead of us: a tow truck towing the police car while ahead of it, another tow truck towing the ambulance to the hospital or morgue or whatever. "See?" I said. "What did I tell you? It just got worse." Thankfully the whiteouts returned and we pressed on. Me onto I-95, them onto and into the leather.

The children were now complaining that they wanted to go back home. They had already seen the new DVDs I'd bought and wasn't there something to else to do and when were we going to get there anyway? My thoughts drifted to that guy with the cabin fever and the shotgun, regretting one necessity I'd neglected to buy. Then suddenly I was pulled back to reality as my wife told me to wipe that foolish grin off my face while she wiped the drool off my chin. She said I looked like Jack Nicholson in *The Shining* and I was freaking her out too. I took a glance in the rear view. She was right. I was freaking myself out.

Eventually, and I mean eventually as in "this is taking way too long," the kids' sobbing subsided to an occasional whimper here and there that actually perked me up as my eyes were drifting aimlessly, lost in the fading headlight beams, constantly trying to focus on the oncoming snowflakes that only served to draw them back to the Ram on the hood and out once again into space. Out and back, out and back; it all began to look like a *Star Wars* movie, with our Dodge rocketing along in hyperspace drive. Out to infinity and back to the Ram, out to infinity and back to the Ram, to the Ram, the Ram ... who in hell turned the Ram around so it was facing me?

How many times had I warned them? But no, they wouldn't listen, would they? They'd gone too far now, gone over to the dark side. I cursed them under my breath as I tried to figure out which one of them, and it had to be one of them, had done the dirty deed. I cast a quick glance around the cabin. They all had their beady little eyes closed, but they were all smiling. They knew. They knew I knew. I began to drool again as my thoughts returned to the good old days of cabin fever and sweet revenge when suddenly we were there; we'd arrived. There was our local snowmobile club, there at last. Five long, hair-raising, knuckle-digging, eye-closing, whining miles and we'd finally made it. I reached out and with a gleam in my eyes shook her.

"Wendy, we're home!" OUCH!

"I told you to drop that freaking weird look didn't I?" she snapped as she whomped me a good one upside the head, actually knocking that foolish grin off my face and onto the floor.

I looked on the floor and then in the mirror. "And I thought that was only a saying."

"What?"

"Nothing, dear. I said we're here. Wake up the kids, will you?"

The four-wheel drive had been worth every last penny we'd spent. The trailer had performed admirably; everything was dry, neat and above all, dry. I pulled up to a snow crunching halt only to be greeted by the moans and groans of the little evil ones as they awoke and realized where they were. They were not home.

"It's too cold out." "I'm missing my cartoons." "Wipe that drool off your face." But I didn't care what they said. I was beyond caring. This was the twenty-first century. Two could play with the dark side. I may not have had a shotgun at my disposal. I may not even have had cabin fever for that matter. It didn't matter. I had something better. I had a hundred thousand dollars and more of sweet, sweet revenge just waiting at my beck and call. I'd spent a small fortune for this moment and by God I was going to enjoy every second of it. I turned around slowly, relishing the pained expressions that stared back at me and I whispered ever so quietly, "Get out of my truck." There was a whimper, a moan, and a whine all of which warmed me to the core. I smiled. "Shut up and get out ... NOW!" I was not about to let some kids stand between me and my family.

Outside the snow had almost stopped falling. I looked around and there was a dozen or more of my friends and neighbors mulling about. I shouted out a few hearty hellos and they returned the courtesy in kind. I was in my element as I unlocked the trailer doors and began to unload the cargo, neat and dry. I was actually feeling proud, quite proud.

There we were, the four of us. The snow machines stood silently at the ready. "Gentlemen," I began slowly. "Gentlemen and gentle lady," I added with a bitter wink and that freaky grin. "START YOUR ENGINES ... NOW!"

Of course from that moment on out, things turned south, so to speak, taking a decided turn for the worse at every turn we made. Not every machine purrs, you know. Some, even new ones, tend more towards a smoking, choking sputtering resonance. I had to adjust a choke here, a throttle there and that infamous little "doo-hickey" the dealer told me about. Luckily some other club members were more familiar with my new machines than I was, and after exchanging some bitter glances with my family, and a few embarrassed "thank you very muches" with fellow club members, we were ready to head out into the white, into our adventure, into the land of dreams.

I looked back over my shoulder and signaled everyone to follow me as I grabbed onto the throttle and "throttled" her up. Just then, my sled, out of sheer coincidence I'm sure, rocketed across the trail, over a small stream and burrowed itself head first into a snow bank. Luckily for me, I'd fallen off the sled, startled by the first sounds of my twin V turbocharged engine's revving. Meanwhile, the machine quickly chugged and sputtered to a muffled stop and mercifully stalled out.

I stood up, more than a little shaken, while no one else stirred. I motioned the others to give me a hand as I trudged over to that smoking snow cave, that hole in the snow that hid my sled. I reached in and felt about. It was in there all right. Slowly I began to work it free. The clever little license plate I'd affixed to the back, the one that said "How am I driving? Call 1-800- LIKE I CARE," wasn't quite so hilarious as it had been when I'd bought it. I glanced back at my family standing there like little Darth Vaders one and all. I knew they were laughing at me the way their heads were bobbing up and down. Why did I opt for those tinted face shields? I couldn't see their grinning little smirks, but the fact that the shields were all fogged up and their shoulders and bodies continued bouncing up and down with their bobble heads was proof enough.

I thought to myself at that moment that it may be old fashioned, but the shotgun thing, that had a lot going for it after all and if I had to do it all over again ... Well, let's just say it was a good thing I was having so much fun with my family as we communed with nature or it could have turned nasty.

I managed, with not an insignificant amount of help, to free the sled and, in time, we all learned how to ride our snowmobiles like pros. My little Vaders aged, matured, and morphed into Storm Troopers and ultimately became the Jedi pals I'd always wanted. My wife didn't turn into Princess Leia, but hey, there are worse things than sleeping with a Wookie; at least we were warm. We traveled the ITS or International Trail System, its full length and breadth. We ventured hundreds if not thousands of miles, saw the backs of countless other sleds, breathed in their spewing, gray fumes as we sucked on the marrow of the pristine wilderness that is Maine, stayed at many a shabby, overpriced motel, ran out of gas more than once, broke down all too often and occasionally froze to death. Well, at least it felt like death or what I'd assume to be a reasonable facsimile of death. We certainly experienced despair, if not actual death, but all in all, what great times we had! What quality times they were! And when it was all over and the kids had grown, the best day of all came (as it does to all machine owners): the day we finally sold those damn contraptions, pickup, trailer and all—the whole "kit 'n kaboodle."

Now, my Sundays are warm and cozy like they used to be before we spent quality time with the kids in one of many traditional Maine ways. I have my mini-theater, my 42" plasma, my micro brews, my easy chair, and my Princess Leia back beside me. I can kick up my warm feet and turn on the sports channels and watch from the comfort of my home as those crazy snowmobile riding bastards spit out a flare of ice and snow, traveling over a hundred miles an hour as they challenge one another and the elements.

As for me, I can doze off, dreaming of my life and how it's turned out for the better. I never did buy that shotgun, by the way. I never really needed it. Quality time? Now this is what I call quality time. This is truly Miller time. It doesn't get any better than this. All I ever needed, all I ever really wanted, was to try; to try and prove a point. And having tried and succeeded, I can now say honestly that I've "been there, done that." My life is good again and I know it. I can smile now—a real smile, not that hideous grin.

"Wendy, now that I'm really home at last, would you get me another cold one? And make it a IPA, would yah? I'm a little warm and it's gonna be a three-beer night."

P.S. What you've just read is not totally true. I sort of made some of it up. I'm not really a snowmobile boy. But I have wondered what the fascination is with snowmobiling. I don't get it, but maybe that's just me. You see, I'm not good with engines and I don't like to tinker. When someone tells me they like to tinker on their sled, a voice in my head screams out loud and clear, "This snow machine sucks a frozen one." In fact, in my book, and this is it, to tinker in general is bad. I don't want to tinker. I want to say "I bought the Toyota of snow machines and I have never, not once, tinkered with it." That's what I want: a dream machine, not a nightmare that never ends. That would be my dream, if I ever had a dream about snow machines and so far, knock on wood, I haven't.

Like I hinted at, motors and I don't mix. I have enough trouble with my car or my lawn tractor. I don't need the headaches of needing to own something I don't need. I've thought this out over a lifetime and motors and I have come to an "arrangement," if you will. I feed them gas and they run. That's it. That's our "arrangement." If they don't live up to our little bargain, I kill them, plain and simple. "Don't want to start, you bastard? Fine with me. Say hello to Mr. Sledgehammer." Let's just say that's my idea of tinkering.

Now, a machine in summer is one thing. If it won't start, I may get a little worked up, may take out my frustration a little with the sledgehammer routine, may work up a sweat, but no big whoop; there's more than one cold one waiting in the fridge. I'll get over it. But what would I have to look forward to with a snow machine that won't start?

Not much! First of all it's winter, freakin' winter! Hello! It's cold outside, and guess what? Outside is where I would be because that's where the snow is. I'd be cold and my damn machine would be cold too. It'd just be sitting there. It wouldn't make a sound and that's a sound I've grown to hate. I wouldn't be happy, to say the least. I wouldn't have my trusty sledgehammer with me; that's in the cellar. I don't pack a traveling sledgehammer as a matter of course. I should, but I don't. And besides, the damn machine would be so expensive, I couldn't really bring myself to destroy it. I'd be trapped, cornered by my own wants. As for the beer, well, there would be no beer outside, thank God. I'd be cold enough as it was and I would never want to sink that low, so low that I wouldn't want a cold beer to cry over. I have my standards.

I knew it would come to that when I first thought of snowmobiling. I just knew something was up as in "wrong" when I actually did check out web sites for the snow machine dealers and found all sorts of accessories for "your snowmobiling pleasure." There was a message there, hidden somewhere in the one hundred piece Emergency Kit, complete with three days supply of nutrition bars and flares. There was a hint, a hint of things to come in the "snow claw," a clever little device that you can use as a shovel, and which can double as a splint! A real splint! That was not good. Then were the first aid kits, the sub-zero survival blankets and the folding shovels. I literally could have spent a fortune had I wanted to. Fortunately I didn't. I would have opted for the folding sledgehammer, but they wisely didn't choose to offer one. You see, I'm not good at reading between the lines. I don't take hints well. Why would I have bought any of this safety stuff? I wouldn't need any of it. Was snowmobiling somehow unsafe? Beats me.

One piece of safety gear did catch my interest though: snowshoes. I like snowshoes. I'll stick to the snowshoes, thank you very much. If they break, and they have, I have only a short crawl and cry back to the house and I'm fine once again, once my tears melt. You see, I know me. I understand me.

What I don't understand about snowmobiles is why anyone in their right mind would like them. I know people do because I see them everywhere. I've even talked to them. They tell me they like to get out in the fresh air on the weekends. But they're out there on a smoking, sputtering lawn-mower-powered toboggan, for crying out loud. They say they like to see the countryside, but unless they're paying attention, all they're going to see is the ass-end of the sled in front of them—that or a tree trunk. I know this because part of getting out and enjoying the quiet and solitude of the wilderness seems to be the prerequisite agreement that you're going to do this on a hissing, whining, growling menace of a machine with fifty or sixty of your good buddies in tow. And for the life of me, traveling like that, how are you going to see nature up close and personal unless you've just run it over and it's lying cold and dead at your mukluk-encased feet? Hey, I'm half deaf and I can hear snowmobiles coming from a mile away, and I don't have deer ears. Nature? Wildlife? I don't think so. I just don't get it and I never will.

Another thing I don't get is why Harley Davidson has let snowmobiling pass them by. I mean roaring, smoking behemoths of pure, unadulterated, primal power is right up their alley isn't it? Why aren't there Harley Hogs rooting up the woods? Why are there no "Hell's Snow Angels?" I close my eyes and I see a huge, black machine, emitting low, earth-shuddering growls as a black, leather-jacketed Hun, his beard encrusted in ice and snow like some pagan-worshiping Viking or Nordic god, revs his trail rocket to life. I see a Nazi helmet sitting on his head, with a spike coming out of the top and bolts off the sides. I see a pair of four-foot-long handle bars jutting up into the blue sky above, and a chopper front with a small ski sitting out ten feet ahead of this hulking, throbbing mass of steel and plastic. I see a black jumpsuit of leather, covered with stitched-on tattoos. I see a "biler" (pronounced "beeler") chick holding on tight for her life, anxious to feel the wind whistling through or around her tooth. And I see a thunderstorm of snow and ice erupt in lightening flashes, as, with a roar, the front of the Harley lifts skyward and forty some such "bilers" all do the same and roar off into the hinterlands searching for adventure and no good. I see all this, and wonder why not?

Then I drop to my shaking knees and thank my lucky stars it's not so. Why is it not so? Who knows? It's enough that it isn't. I don't know why it isn't, and I don't really care. I'm just thankful that it isn't. Aren't you?

Hockey

I love hockey. I really do. And I'm not just saying that because I'm writing a book and need to fill up some space on these pages. That's what the pictures (if there were any) and this sentence are for. I say I like hockey because I think it's the greatest game ever ... on ice. Okay, admittedly there's not a whole lot of competition what with curling and, well, curling. But even if there were another sport on ice, something say like basketball and NASCAR combined with some random gun play and perhaps cheerleaders with some really short skirts, I think I'd still like hockey better, except for maybe the cheerleaders. I may be lying, but I'm not sure about what.

You see, I played hockey as a young knave. Why did I use the word knave and not child? Because I got to use this sentence to explain why and that helps once again with the page-filling thing. Pretty clever, eh? Anyway, as I was saying, I played hockey as a child and though I was never great at it, in my opinion, I was pretty damn good just the same. Don't believe me? Well, just ask me.

There wasn't a lot of competition when I was a kid. Hockey was a miniscule niche sport back then, not the major niche sport it is today. When I was a kid there were only six teams in the National Hockey League and I could spell every one of them except maybe the "*Montrael Kanadiens*." My favorite team was the New York Rangers, but like I said, I was young and didn't know any better. They had guys like Jean, Jacque, Bob, the "Gumper" and "Injun Jim" Nielson. They were great just like me and just like me, they never won a damn thing, meaning they never won the "cup"—Lord Stanley's Cup. It didn't matter though, because the team I secretly loved was the *Montrael Kanadiens* and they won everything, meaning the "cup," the Stanley Cup. That was a long time ago and I've since grown up. My favorite team is now another team. It's one I can spell; the *Bostun Briuns*.

What's so great about hockey, you ask? I'll tell you. For one thing, there aren't that many other people who like it. That makes those of us who do enjoy it feel special and we like that. Besides, if you like hockey and you actually know something about the sport, well that makes you special too, because most people don't know much about anything, much less much about hockey. All they know is that hockey's played on ice, and you can't follow the puck on TV. In the wide and wonderful world of knowledge, generally speaking, that's not much to know. Those of us who know hockey, on the other hand, know all of that and more, much more. That's what makes us share a special bond and appreciate one another. We may root for different teams, but we're all fans and members of the same club, the hockey club. Actually, it's not a club, it's called a stick. The point is we don't have a secret club or a handshake. It's nothing like that.

Still, we know one another when we see one another, even if we don't know one another. How do we know? Well, if we use certain words or names like the "biscuit," "Moose" or "Bobby," the "Pocket Rocket," "dasher," "Gordie," "the box," "the Chief," or "the Gumper," we know by the look in someone's eyes just who's in the club and who's not. Take it from me; it feels good to be in the club.

Like I said, hockey is a great sport. It's the national pastime of Canada; that, making maple syrup, and saying "eh." It's also not too surprising. When you have ice underfoot ten months of the year, you have an incentive to make good use of it and Canadians do just that. If you go to Canada, and you should, you'll discover that there's a rink in every town. In fact I believe that's how the nation was built, one rink at a time. The government sent out expeditionary parties to build rinks at strategic points and the settlers simply gravitated to them. Regardless of how things came to be, that's the way it is.

What's the impact of this on Canadian society? Well, it's huge. On Sunday mornings people are in one of two places: either in church asking forgiveness for the fine Saturday night they'd enjoyed, or at the rink. They are in the pews or in the bleachers, hunkered down over a Bible or a hot, steaming cup of Timmy Horton's best. There are peewee leagues and hockey moms everywhere. And get this: the moms don't sit in their vans, listening to books on tape, waiting for the games to be over like soccer moms in the States do. No sir. Hockey moms help tape up their kids' sticks and their kids, pick up their teeth to be re-implanted (Thank God for free dental care!) and root for the home team. That's Canada and as even you "know nothings" know, Maine is way too close to Canada for some of that enthusiasm not to have rubbed off on us. It did and the proof is everywhere. Timmy Horton's coffee is the best!

Maine is currently going gangbusters for hockey. Leagues are popping everywhere you look, provided you look primarily around hockey rinks. And why is hockey growing so fast? Because it's a sport that anyone can play as long as you know how to skate, have two legs, two skates, a uniform, a rink, two teams (one for and one against), a stick, a helmet, some shin guards, a cup (recommended for girls too, by the way, or so I'm told), and a puck or two. That's it, so there's no excuse for anyone not to be out there on the ice.

We lacked for more than a few of those things when I was a knave, but we still played hockey just the same. For one thing, we had decent ice only two months of the year, not ten. Of course, being hockey fanatics, we still managed to play hockey year-round most of the time. At school, during recess, we used a piece of wood for a puck (we made these during shop class, while the teacher was looking for someone's finger), our feet for sticks, and literally kicked the hell out of it and each other until the bell rang or Little League Baseball began in the late spring, early summer. If you were the goalie, like me, you went back to history class with blood staining your torn pant leg, dripping down your shins and making for a squishy walk up the stairs.

We later played with sticks and pucks in our basements, on the linoleum floors. I made my goalie equipment out of a catcher's mask, some foam padding off the couch, a first baseman's glove and anything else I could scrounge up. The part about being able to skate isn't all that important either, because if you can't skate, you can be the goalie. Trust me on this one; I know what I'm talking about.

Once you're ready to roll, just go for it. The rules are easy to learn and in fact, you don't even have to learn them; that's what the ref is there for. Basically it's really quite simple. There are three lines, two blue and one red one in the center of the rink. There are six players for each team—three on offense, two on defense, and the goalie. The puck can't be passed over two lines and you can't go beyond the other team's blue line and into their zone until the puck goes in first. That's pretty much it. Oh, and if the puck goes the length of the ice, that's called icing the puck. That's pretty neat, what with the name thing, "icing," eh? The "eh" thing is cool too. There are a bunch of other rules, but to simplify matters, just remember this: anything goes in hockey unless the ref catches you doing it. If that happens, just punch the other guy until he hits you back and then you both go off the ice with a minor two-minute penalty for roughing.

Penalties are served in a glassed-in penalty box. It's like a time out for little kids. You have to sit for two minutes or whatever, but you can yell and holler and pound on the glass at the other guy sitting next to you in his box all you want. You can call him things like a "hoser" or maybe call "Gumby" on account of most hockey players have fewer teeth than their hat sizes. When the penalty is over, you throw one more punch at each other, whether you want to or not, when you both come out onto the ice and then head to your respective benches where everyone pats you on the back and says, "Way to go, hoser." "Hoser" is both an insult and a compliment. Kind of like a Canadian "aloha." It's good and bad, just depending on who says it to who.

Oh yeah, there is also the part about putting the puck in the other team's net, but that's for the fans' entertainment, not the players'. Hockey players keep score in their heads and they must like ties 'cause they're always talking about "evening up the score with Gumby, that hoser over there, eh."

In the good old days before helmets, you could tell who was scoring the most by the blood on the ice. It was akin to a gladiator battle back then, but on ice, not sand, and with Canadians in the stands, not Romans. Blood congeals quickly once it hits the ice so you had to clean it up and they would, and still do, scrape it up with a shovel and toss it. After the fight, the refs toss the players too; fighting's a ten-minute major.

Occasionally in a fight, someone's helmet is knocked off and he gets a bloody nose, but not all that often. I think there was actually less fighting in the old days, because without helmets you could really get hurt. With all the padding the players have today and the face shields, they take just a small risk fighting and so there tend to be more fights. I don't think it's good for hockey and slows down the game. On the other hand, not everyone has played hockey, but everyone's been in a fight so the fans can relate and they love it. There's still one rule to remember when fighting and that is this: the whole point in fighting is to pull the other player's jersey over his head, exposing his suspenders to the crowd and ultimately humiliating him. If you do that and bash him in the head until he slumps to the ice in shame, you'll win the fans' hearts and the fight every time. It's that simple.

Maine doesn't have a really long history of hockey, but it's a rich one. In the old days, Maine was a poor state. It still is, technically speaking, but poor today and poor yesterday are fortunately not the same thing. Thirty years ago there weren't very many rinks for hockey to be played on. There was pond hockey, but that involved a lot of work, what with the shoveling and all. Crashing the snow bank was a far cry from crashing the boards and if there was no snow, you got your exercise chasing the puck a half mile down the ice after a shot went wide of the net. As a "hoser" you either learned to shoot well and put the puck on net, or you learned to skate well. It was your choice.

The first really big move in hockey in Maine was at the wealthy, more elite schools of Colby, Bates, and Bowdoin. They had the "out-of-state" money to have the less common, more elite sports offered on campus. Towns like Lewiston and Biddeford sported clubs here and there filled with the sons of French Canadian mill workers, but overall, there was not a lot of interest (although Lewiston had a professional team for a time, the Nordiques). I believe it was when Portland got their first American Hockey League team, the Mariners, that the sport began to really take off.

Maine hockey at Orono became the focal point in the north central portion of the state. The Black Bears went on to have great success nationally with Shawn Walsh as coach and players such as Paul Kariya, Scott Pellerin and goalies like Garth Snow making it big in the pros and the National Hockey League. Back in Portland, the Mariners gave way to the Pirates and changed affiliations with their parent NHL clubs now and again as the beat went on.

Over the years, the hockey following grew steadily with new rinks being constructed and with powerhouse high school teams established in Lewiston, Yarmouth, Waterville, and elsewhere. Today there are exactly so many teams in the state, if not more.

My interest in hockey waned for a long time, until after moving to Maine in 1978, I began to follow the Mariners. In time, my wife and I began to discover the lower regions of Québec, especially Sherbrooke. We headed north to watch affordable hockey as played by the Québec Major Junior Hockey League and the Sherbrooke Castors, or "Beavers," translated to English. When we learned of the Castors being sold and moved, I was not pleased. Soon word came that they were heading from Maine, to Lewiston. I checked out the team on the Internet and put in my suggestion for the Name-the-Team Contest: the "Maineiacs."

I wanted the name to reflect the entire state and not just one city. I wanted all Mainers to take pride in this fast-paced product from the north. And I wanted the name to reflect our passion for not only hockey, but for our state as well. I was shocked when I was called and told the team had selected Maineiacs for their name. I now know the name is not unique, and that I didn't originate it. But back then I didn't know of the Maineiacs air refueling squadron in Bangor. I only knew that I was happy and proud of the name and the team. I was especially proud when a few short years later the Maineiacs won the President's Cup, emblematic of QMJHL champions!

So, that's my claim to fame, my one and only claim. I've had my fifteen minutes of notoriety and I must say, I enjoyed it. I have a stairway at home leading to our second-floor bedrooms that I love and my wife despises. It's my "Hall of Hockey." It's full of pucks and sticks that I've screwed to the walls. It has posters and jerseys of the Maineiacs, the Black Bears, the Bruins and the Canadians jersey I wore as a kid. There's a plaque saying I named the Maineiac team, too, and an autograph from Ray Bourque from the night of the first game. There are also pins from all of the QMJHL teams stuck into a map of Maine, Québec and the Maritimes that was painted on the wall by my daughter, Jenny. There are mementos of the Castors and the Black Bears too. But most of all, there are my memories of the countless hours I spent, listening to games on the radio, watching on Saturday nights and playing on ponds, cellar floors and parking lots.

I love hockey. I really do. And I don't mind taking up space to tell you.

P.S. On a sad, personal note, the Maineiacs have disbanded and no longer exist. My infamous "Hall 'O Hockey", once a living museum, is now a dusty archive that needs vacuuming. The Québec Major Junior Hockey League has lost its sole American franchise and with it has broken one more arrow in my quiver of pointed logic for Maine being a part of Canada.

The idea of saying "She looks like a million bucks" is to imply that she is priceless, which is to say she is very costly, which is, in fact, counter-intuitive. Whatever. The "Million Dollar Bridge" in Portland cost a hell of a lot more than a million bucks, so why not say so? Why not brag it up and simply call it "The hell of a lot more than a million dollar, Million Dollar Bridge?"

Curling

Curling is a wonderful pastime, a pastime whose time one might have thought had inconspicuously and mercifully passed. But fortunately, such is not the case. Curling exists and while it may not exude a rosy pink blush of health, it is not exactly on the gray brink of death either. And for the life of me, I don't know why. Really, what can one say about curling that is, well, good? If you look at it from a distance, a real long distance, curling looks a lot like shuffleboard, without the "shuffler" or whatever that stick thing is called that pushes the "shuffle" or whatever that plastic disc thing is called. Remember, I said to look from a real good distance? I said that because up close and personal, curling is not shuffleboard at all. Curling is something else altogether.

Let's examine the sport, and I use the word "sport" loosely, to say the least. I say sport, but I think in all fairness, curling should be called a game. I think of a sport as something you actually could train for if you wanted to, not that I ever would. I'm thinking of running, aerobics, weightlifting, and calisthenics. That kind of training. When I think of curling (and God help me here), there's not one thing I can think of that would make anyone a better curler: nothing, nothing other than just curling. It would be like training for the sport of gin rummy. Go ahead. Try to train. You just can't do it.

First of all, curling is played out on a sheet of ice. Do you know of a less resistant surface for a game to be played on? I don't. I don't think there is one unless you can freeze Teflon. Secondly, there is a heavy granite weight. I'll give you that, but here's the catch; you don't lift the bloody thing at all! You just kind of push it, or shuffle it along on the ice and after a few moments, you simply and slowly let go. That's it. You don't throw it hard. Hard is counterproductive in curling. You don't chase it, even. You have someone else do that for you. You don't even stand and watch as it fades away; you kneel, apparently to conserve your energy for the next stone you "throw." And while you kneel, you yell at that someone else, at your teammate, telling them what to do. Could you possibly participate in any other sport and exert less of an effort?

And those others you tell what to do while you're "resting," do you think they chase the stone down the ice as it ever so slowly "hurtles" towards the awaiting circles that you are aiming for? NO! Of course not. This is curling. They're standing halfway there, waiting for the stone to come to them! And what's more, they have brooms to lean on while they're waiting. Now I'll grant you that sometimes they have to get out of the way of the stone, and sometimes they feverishly sweep the ice ahead of the stone, but that's it. Besides, if they were really the industrious types, they could have swept the ice anytime, while they were waiting. God knows they have enough time while you, the finely trained athlete that you are, kneel and point and work out your strategies. They shouldn't have to wait until the last second when the stone is, as I've said, hurtling in their direction at a slow walk. If they have to sweep hard, well, it's their fault for waiting so long in the first place if you ask me.

Well, that's it for curling, except for when the stone eventually arrives near the circles on the ice, then some things sometimes happen. Like sometimes the stone hits another stone and knocks it out of the circles and then again, sometimes it doesn't. There's a lot of whooping it up on the sidelines during a tournament, but other than that, no one works up much of a sweat except for the fans rooting from above the ice, who are sucking down Molsons like there's no tomorrow.

When I consider everything I've learned about curling, I've got to admit I like it. It's my kind of sport. I mean, I feel like I've been training for it all my life, and who knows, maybe I have. I will tell you this. I was in Canada where I often go and believe me, Canada is one hotbed of curling fanaticism if there ever was such a thing. I turned on the TV to kill some time and there it was, "Curling Night in Canada." I laughed and laughed. I couldn't believe what I was watching. This was a nationwide TV broadcast, mind you. This was ridiculous. I laughed and I watched, and I watched and I chuckled and I watched and I watched. Then I left to get something to drink; I think it was a Labatts. I opened the beer and then I sat down and watched some more. Somewhere over the next few beers I even stopped smiling. The beer was good. And do you know what? The curling was even better! I've got to admit it: I like curling, I really do. It's a neat sport and I don't use the word "sport" loosely. It's neat and it's unique. I dare you to actually sit down, with a cold beer of course, and watch an entire match and not get caught up in the "action." It's addictive and the curling is habit-forming as well. I watched, I'm addicted and I think you will be too. I know I'm not alone, because since I've written this chapter there have been two Olympics and guess what? Curling has turned out to be one of the top attractions at the games, and one of the most watched on TV. People just love curling.

If you want to see curling first hand in Maine, you may not know this, but you *can*, you lucky dogs you! Just go online and check out the Belfast Curling Club. It's situated right off Route 3, just outside of town. They are up and running and they are some kind of busy. Oh and by the way, tell them I sent you and watch the expressions on their faces when you do. They won't have a clue.

Sopstix

I have a close friend—well, not really *that* close a friend, but a good friend. I know her, and I work with her. Well, I don't exactly work with her, but I work somewhat near her. She's in the same building. She's a friend and I invited her for Thanksgiving dinner, but she refused, so I guess she's not really that good of a friend when you think of it. All right then, she's not really a friend at all, but she doesn't exactly hate me either. I've seen her and I could pick her out of a line up if the lighting were really good. Okay? Are you satisfied? I have no friends, all right? You've made your point. You don't have to rub it in.

Anyway, she says that the Japanese like to think of themselves as a superior culture, superior not just to ours, but to everyone's. I'll admit they have mastered the manufacturing and selling of small cars for just as much, if not more, than our large Detroit cars, so I'm willing to give them that. That's a pretty neat trick, but there's more to culture than just cars. If that were the case, Americans would have the biggest if not the greatest culture in the world, wouldn't they?

When you think of culture you think of language, arts, the theater, food and more. But for me, it comes down to the basics, the little things and that's where if you ask my opinion, the Japanese come up short. I ask you this: What superior culture doesn't have a fork? The Japanese don't have forks. They eat with sticks—little, pointy (but not too pointy) sticks.

The girl I don't know says they don't have forks, but they have a "kind of spoon." Fine, I said, they have a "kind of spoon," but can they eat soup with this "kind of spoon"? And can you have a "kind of spoon," but not a real spoon and still call yourself a superior culture? I don't think so.

She said they really don't use the spoons for soup, that they prefer to slurp their soup, that it's customary to slurp, that it's a sort of compliment.

Fine, I said, but as far as I'm concerned, they are soup-slurping savages. I'm not impressed. You call that culture? I don't.

She said they use the chopsticks to pick out the solids in the soup, then pick up the bowl and slurp the remaining liquid or broth.

I thought, and I didn't think hard mind you, for two seconds or less and came up with this idea: Why not use chopsticks that are also hollow, like straws? You can pick out the solids in the soups with the chopsticks using them in the traditional manner and then, when there's nothing left but the liquid soup, suck it up. No putting down chopsticks, picking up "kind of spoons" or bowls, and no slurping: simple, neat and functional. If you like the soup, just say so. How many thousands of years of superior "culture" did it take these people to *not* come up with this idea when an idiot, such as yours truly, thought of it? Cultured? Maybe. Superior? I don't thinks so. And then there's that whole

Godzilla thing, but let's not go there.

P.S. Some people might think this racist, but I don't. I don't believe in races. I believe that all humans are just that: humans, with the possible exception of certain of my ancestors who were found clinging to the family tree in a prehensile sort of way. But that's my problem and I'm dealing with it. Our problem is much larger and it's this: Why are there no ugly Chinese people? I was driving in my car the other day and the thought hit me. I know there are ugly white people; hell, I'm one of them. There are ugly blacks, ugly Hispanics, even ugly Swedes, if the truth be told. So why can't I ever remember having seen any ugly Chinese people? I mean I saw a Chinese beauty contest on TV with twenty-five contestants. When it was all over, they had ten tied for second and fifteen tied for first! That's just not right. We had a beauty contest in our town here in Maine and the winner came in third. Trust me. That was the right call. But, I don't get it and it's not racist. I just don't get it and I thought I'd mention it while I had the chance.

Almost Electricity

People say to me, "It must be nice to live way out in the country in Maine," and to be honest, it is. In fact, it's down right wonderful. Why? Well, there's a different answer for every person who lives out here "in the country." For me, the answer is simple: I don't have any close neighbors. Don't get me wrong, I like my neighbors and even though I really don't care, for the sake of being civil, I'll go so far as to say I hope they like me too. We just don't associate a whole heck of a lot and frankly I think we all benefit from that lack of contact. Knowing me as I do, I *know* they do. When our paths do cross, it's because it's either a necessity or mere serendipitous happen chance: there's a reason, or it's a natural and spontaneous occurrence, as in "I didn't see you coming and it couldn't be avoided."

You see, when you live apart, you have to go out of your way to interact, and that's a good thing. People who live too close to one another are always interacting, like it or not, intentional or not. They can't avoid one another and that's not a good thing. Having a reasonable degree of separation makes for better, if not good, neighbors. The farther the separation, I believe the better the neighbor. The point is, I get along very well with people I don't associate with or even know exist. Eskimos, for instance, fall into this category. I don't know any. I have nothing bad to say about them. As far as I'm concerned, Eskimos make great neighbors.

As I said, here in the country we don't tend to arrange our meetings; they tend to just happen. In the country this is not as bad a thing as it is in the city, because being farther apart, we don't run into one another very often at all. We're never at a loss for words because there's always something to say, if only something such as, "So, you don't look good, but I see you're still alive aren't ya?" If our paths cross we just rack it up as an unavoidable accident, like hitting a deer at night. I tried to buy insurance for just such accidents (that's running into people, not deer), but I learned they don't sell any such thing. Anyone who has run into me would tell you; they should consider it.

Here in the country, we don't visit one another just to socialize and shoot the shit (I always duck where I hear that phrase. I always have. I firmly believe it's why I'm living today.) We meet because we have a reason to meet. It's real, not faked or fawned. I like that and we like that. We meet because there's a need, a definite purpose to our meeting. Either that or it's an accident as I said before. Truth be told, mostly we just keep to ourselves.

We like our privacy, that's why we live where we do, here in Maine. By the way, for clarification sake, by "we", I mean me. We, meaning me, didn't move out to the "boonies" to find friends and share tea with the neighbors. In fact, the opposite was more the case by far. To us, and by "us" I mean me, neighbors are like relatives. It's nice to see them come bringing us, meaning me, gifts on Christmas, for example (actually that's a lie, I don't like receiving gifts at Christmas or anytime), but it's nicer still to see them, meaning them, go, leaving their gifts behind with me, meaning me. It makes you, meaning me, appreciate the distance between us, meaning us and them, and reminds me of you and the reason I, meaning me, came to the "pucker brush" in the first place, which was to avoid you, meaning you, as in them. You see, there are just too many of us— you, we, me, they, them and I—to be tolerated and that's why I want to live alone with the rest of us, out here in the country: to get away from us all.

I'm sure my neighbors feel the same as I do, if not more, given who's likely to be heading down the road in their immediate direction.

Now, a man's home is his castle, upon that we can all agree. Me, I like my castles tall, thick, with impenetrable ramparts surrounded by a moat and drawbridge filled with knights, knaves, and maidens in distress, not to mention an alligator or poisonous serpents. That's my idea of one big, honkin' home. Too bad we all can't have castles. I know I'd like to own one and I'd like to have serfs too, now that I think of it. I think having serfs would be fun, but unfortunately for me, and fortunately for the serfs, I suppose, that's just not practical in today's world. Society and the "liberal progressive types" always have a way of ruining things with their so-called "human rights agendas." So, instead of thick walls of stone and enslaved minions, I have to settle for mere distance and my wife. It's not fair.

I think I deserve at least one serf, muck- and shmuck-raking humanists or not. I don't think that's too much to ask, but, no, apparently society can't abide, can't sleep well at night, should God find it in his heart to grant my one little request. I'm sorry that it's come to this, that we've come to this sorry state of affairs. I'm sorry there's no tolerance for differing views nowadays. I wish I got to make the rules once in a while. Life would be a whole lot more fun, at least for me. And be honest, wouldn't you like to own a serf or two yourself? There's a lot you can do with a serf, you know. We'll have to talk when it's safe.

Getting back to neighbors, just how much distance between homes is necessary to encourage a healthy state of interactions? Well, I have a little test that I've evolved over the course of my life that works quite well for me, much to my wife's chagrin. Try not to think of me as being crude, though I suppose that would be only natural if you're the civilized type, and remember, though we may wear really neat hats for certain events, we are all animals under our fur or skins.

My rule is this: I don't want to live any place I can't go outside and take a leak without having to a take a peek to make sure no one's sneaking a peek back. Take a leak, no peek and no need to sneak. That's it, that's my rule and my test for living the correct distance from the next residence. If I want to step outside my back door and unzip my pants, I don't want to have to concern myself with what the neighbors might think or say. I'm not interested in having that discussion. I don't appreciate the laughter. I just want to relieve myself and take a leisurely look at the stars while doing so. That's it. It grounds me and makes me feel free and complete, at one with the world. If the best things in life are free, you can't get much freer than lifting your thoughts up to the heavenly hosts while you're peeing down on dear old mother Earth. If that's a crime, then I'm a criminal. It's not a crime is it? I hope it's not a crime. And what's with cats not paying attention to what you're doing? It's their own damn fault if they get it on the head stupid, curious, always rubbing up against you, creatures that they are. And if you, my dear neighbor, want to live so close to me that you can observe and be offended by my actions, well don't take this the wrong way, but to hell with you Mr. Way Too Nosy For His Own Good Goody Two Shoes You. Just look the other direction or move farther away, will you please! And no, I'm not going to look out for your stupid cat. Now get out of here, Boots, before I step on you or worse!

Suffice it to say, I have good neighbors where I live and we all get along just fine. I have my distance and my privacy. My nearest and, well, *only* neighbor whose house I can actually see, lives a quarter mile up the road and we're separated by a stream and some woods. True, the stream isn't wide and deep and the woods aren't thick and dark, but they do the trick. Besides, the neighbors live in New Jersey and only visit a few times each year. Now that's my idea of a good neighbor.

I remember when we first moved here over thirty years ago, how whenever a vehicle approached, the whole family would all run to the window to see what was happening. Who was it? Would they stop? Would they pass by? Did they want our bottles again? Would they dim their lights, cut the engine and slip silently into the driveway, only to emerge and slit all our throats in the middle of the night? How exciting is that! Or worse yet, were they Jehovah's Witnesses and would they leave *Watch Tower* magazines and slip away in the darkness before we could tell them to go to hell and never return?

Those were the good old days, what with all the excitement and anticipation of not knowing what might happen from one moment to the next. It was like hearing reindeer hooves on the roof when you're eight! Everyone was so pumped. Looking back, I suppose that when you only get two channels on TV, and one of those is public broadcasting and you can't see any of Big Bird's four heads clearly, our reactions were to be expected: expected and pathetic. Still, when you're sensually deprived, you find your entertainment where you can and we were nothing if not entertained.

But times have changed and so have I. You would think that after thirty years of living as I do, out here in the pucker brush, on a dead end dirt road and all, I would get lonely and welcome guests to my home just to break the monotony of my existence, but you would be wrong. Such is not the case. In fact, if anything, I've gotten more reclusive over the years. Even now, when I hear the sound of an approaching car or truck, my blood pressure rises and I become anxious. But, being older, I've mellowed and I'm wiser in my ways. I don't over react anymore as I once did. I don't explode in a "hissy fit." My Paxil is working just fine, thank you. My Molson is working too, even three! I am at peace relatively speaking. I just sit and wait in anticipation and acceptance of what will be. Then, as the muffled engine sputters and fades up the road and the lights dim from view, I calmly release a long sigh of relief and the twitching pressure on the trigger of my .308 Enfield, the one with the telescopic sight, eases. There will be no crimson flash of light tonight. No sharp, cracking snap of thunder piercing the night air. There will be no *Watch Tower* to start my next fire with. Life is good.

Like I said, I like where I live and I've mellowed with the years.

Understand this, however, and don't be so quick to judge me: I am not an anti-social type of person. Okay, I'll amend that statement to this extent: I *am* an anti-social type person, but I have good reason to be so. I have satellite TV now. I have hundreds of channels at my disposal instead of just two, and some of them aren't even those damn useless home shopping channels or religious programming they make me pay for even though I refuse to watch them. I have a life to live now, people, so please, don't interrupt me while I'm hard at work living it. Simply let me live it in peace, will you? Surely, that's not too much to ask.

And what a life it is! There must be at least one Seinfeld episode I haven't seen fifteen times, and I'm willing to continue watching reruns night after night until I find it or die trying. And if I don't find it, I'm good with that too, except the dying thing, I just threw that in for effect. In fact, I'm good with all of what I do. Just let me do it, alone. I have George, Jerry, Kramer, and Elaine. They're wittier, more clever, and funnier than anyone I know in my "real" life, including me. I like that and I like them. I am not lonely. Do not try to help relieve me of the drudgery of my solitude. I don't want to be rescued from the "opium of the masses." Okay, that refers to religion, but TV is my religion and I'm addicted.

And no, I don't need any help watching my TV, thank you very much. I am fully capable of sitting glassy-eyed in a stupor staring at a flickering screen in a darkened tomb of a room alone with my beer. I don't want to have to put on my pants just because someone's coming over to "visit" me. I don't like having to get all dressed up for "occasions." I don't like being "visited." Do it to somebody else. I don't want to have to be polite and presentable. That's asking too much. That takes too much effort. I want to fart when I want to fart, pick my nose when I want to pick my nose, and fall asleep when I fall asleep. To me, that's what owning a castle is all about. To me, this is a good life, or at least a good enough life for me. I'm not complaining. It may not be good enough to suit you and it may not be pretty, but it's who I am and I like it just the way it is. Now be a good neighbor; go away and never come back. I'll consider sending flowers to your spouse when you die.

Fine, be that way. You don't take advice well, and I see you're still here, so I'll try some more to explain to you why I have come to live in Maine. Early on in life I learned a most difficult lesson and that was this: I just didn't fit in being where I was and who I was. Now, a person doesn't come by such knowledge easily. It's a painful process, this self-discovery and realization thing. You feel lost and alone at first, but you soon find that "fitting in" makes you feel even more lost and more alone. You find yourself grinding against everyone's expectations of what you should be and the friction burns deep to your soul and fires up your insights. You learn, as your true nature is revealed to you, that it is your job to figure out how to recognize your personality for what it is and to make it work for you. You can't go back to what you're not and you've not yet established whom and what you are to be. You're in limbo my friend. It's a painful contradiction of self-exploration and until you simply accept it and then do something about it, you are stuck in unending misery.

In my case, I tried to fit in, tried to enjoy doing, being and thinking like everyone else, but I quickly found that for me there was simply no pleasure in it and in fact, there was a considerable amount of pain to be endured. I learned that when I wasn't being true to myself, I didn't like me very much and I suffered. I began to shun myself. I wouldn't talk to myself for days on end, the hypocrite. I deserved it too. This life simply wasn't working. I decided I would have to like myself, even if no one else did, and that made me feel better straight away. Once I accepted who I was, my life was a whole lot easier to live and I was a whole lot easier to live with, not that I was living with anybody. She had wisely divorced me years ago.

I found that I didn't care for things, for possessions, and I never really have. I don't care about shiny and new, and I don't care about valuable. Something is only valuable if it means something to me. That thinking freed me of being jealous of what others had and what I didn't have. I didn't have to satisfy anyone else, only me, and I'm easy, especially when it comes to being easy on me. I appreciated that and I began to get along with myself much better.

I learned also that I didn't and don't care much for money either. Sure, I have worked my entire life, literally, from the very day I turned sixteen and was able to get a job, but I never did it for the money alone. I got paid, don't get me wrong, but that was an added benefit. I worked for two reasons: to do the best I could for my own self respect, and because I had to live up to being the man my father had been—to earn *his* respect.

My father and I never seemed to agree on much although I respected him immensely. Looking back, I think he and I were very much the same kind of person in principle. We just didn't share the same principles. We seemed to clash constantly. His values were sacrosanct to him and mine to me. He was his own person and I was learning to be who I was. We were the same in the nature of who we were, but so very different in what we were.

One thing my dad and I did agree on was that there is no value in spending money for its own sake. He was cheap and so am I. It was from him that I learned that I could be just as happy as the next guy, and do it for a whole lot less too. I simply adjusted my tastes and discovered it's true—everything is relative. Thank you, Mr. Einstein. I learned to live within my means and have always lived comfortably no matter what those means were, no matter what I had or didn't have. I have what is to me a lot of money now, but I still cut coupons and always will. I like to play the game.

My dad was special. He would ask me how many clicks there were in a ballpoint pen while I anxiously punched the button in and out. He thought I was wearing it out and wasting it. I thought he was a nut back then for saying that and I still do. It wasn't his fault that he grew up during the Depression, I suppose. Ballpoint pens were an "invention" to him. "Waste not, want not" was the message he had learned. What did I know? Ballpoint pens were there when I came into this world and I for all I knew, if I'd ever bothered to even think of it, they had always been there. It's just the way generations' perspectives differ and no one generation's right and the other wrong, although you have to admit, my father was wrong. As for me, I still can't get over how something so large and heavy as a jet airliner can fly. I am still amazed to this day and my kids think I'm nuts. Go figure.

Anyway, my dad instilled in me a cheapness for which I am forever in his debt. My wife and kids, on the other hand, no doubt hold it against him to this very day. My dad also built his own house, so what choice did I have, but to do the same? Why did I do it? Because my dad did it, and because I wanted to prove to myself and anyone else who was listening (though no one was, or is) that anyone could build and own his or her own home. You didn't have to be rich either. You also didn't have to be particularly talented. (I'm living proof of that.) You just had to set your sights low and go for it. If you failed, you succeeded and if you succeeded, you surpassed all expectations. You just had to want it and be willing to follow your dream. It was an adventure and a risk and, thankfully, because my father lived it before me, I got to live and share the dream too.

And no, I wasn't lucky. Luck had nothing to do with it. It was work, hard work all the way. I dreamed it, I worked it, and I earned it. I am lucky to have had the opportunity to earn my dream, and for that I thank myself and a few select others, but mostly, I thank myself, and my dad.

I've walked most all of the Appalachian Trail too and it was much the same journey. People told me I was lucky then, too, but there was no luck involved. I walked it. It's pretty simple. You know—right foot, left foot, get back up, that kind of thing. You just do it. There is no luck. I don't believe in luck, except for bad luck and I've had my share of that too. But I must say, I've always had good luck come out of bad. I've worked hard at making my good luck. So again, I thank myself and my dad once more.

And if you think I'm selfish for saying that, you just don't understand luck and life at all. Maybe you haven't lived a dream and accomplished something from your heart, with your hands, something you weren't sure you could do. So, once again, my poor, deprived friend, if you tell me I'm lucky, you just don't get it and I respectfully say to you with all sense of sincerity, just go to hell my friend, go to hell and close the door behind you, it's hot enough in here as it is.

My dream was to live my life, not to buy a life. I never wanted to be any-thing because I already thought I was something. I just didn't know what, a thought I share with others who know me. I still don't who or what I am. I never wanted to retire because I saw that as giving up, akin to moving to Florida. To me, life is a struggle and man's dignity is derived from that struggle. That's it. It may not be a happy philosophy but it's mine and I share it with one hundred and sixty million Russians. We can't all be wrong, no matter what McCarthy said. I have scars all over my body, carpal tunnel in one hand, a crooked, "fro-zen" finger on the other, and a bad back and bum leg, but I have my dignity and sense of self worth, delusional though it may be. And when I get old, if I am "lucky" enough to live that long, I will have a cane too. I'll have a nice, hard, hand-carved cane—one I carved myself. Pass my way and you'll find yourself poked in the ass by a gnarly old codger with a surprisingly self-satisfied look on his face. That would be me and oh, how I am looking forward to the day.

Like I said, I didn't want to buy a life, but live it. If others wanted to be rich and elitist, I wanted to be, shall we say, less rich and more common. Being less rich, I had to find a place where a little money went a lot farther. And I was fortunate enough to find just such a place. I found a place where people lived life, and didn't play at it. I found a place where it was harder to live, but it was real living. I found a place where one's entertainment came from life itself, and you didn't have to buy it, not all of the time. I found a place where you cut your wood, split your wood, and stacked your wood or you froze your ass off. I found a place where your pleasure came from a job well done, from next year's cordwood sitting in a neatly stacked pile. I found a place that measured you against yourself and no one else. It was simple, it was good, and it meant something to me. I found Maine, and in finding it, I found my soul was warmed by who she is and who she demanded I become.

That inner warmth is like the warmth you get heating with wood. Maine is special. Wood heat is special. It means something more to those of us who burn it. If you flip on a switch for your heat, you can't help but take it for granted. Sure you're warm, but you don't appreciate it because you weren't cold to begin with, were you? You don't enjoy the heat because you have no perspective to judge it by. You only know that if the thermostat is raised a few degrees, you're going to pay more. What a shame. You've missed out on so much. A simple pleasure lost is a lessening of your life. We need to live.

When we wake in the winter, our house is often 40! That's a tad on the nippy side, even for us. But under the covers upstairs, we sleep like the dreams we dream and are toasty warm. Still, on the AM side, once out of bed, we're freezing! We, and by we I mean most times my wife but occasionally me, have to build a fire. Most days I have to head off to work early and my wife remains to perform the chore. On weekends, I gather the kindling and split the sticks of firewood. I crumple the newspaper just so. I take care to build and create, layering the kindling and placing the sticks. When I'm done, I strike a match and put it to the paper bed, watching in amazement and satisfaction, as the tiny flame spreads, and takes off on a life of its own.

I watch as the smoke and the flames rise and swirl. In short order, the dog and the cats have gathered beside me in front of the stove as it begins to crackle and hiss, slowly emitting a warmth like an exhaled breathe, a warmth you can actually feel penetrating into your skin. The fire gains strength and I move closer. I'm hotter now, too hot: now too close. I move back and away. The contrasting coolness refreshes me. My senses rebound and drink in the heat, luxuriating in the differing temperatures I experience as I move about, adjusting my position for comfort. I sip my coffee slowly and exhale through my nose, savoring the nutty flavors, extracting all the sensory pleasures I can. The coffee warms me in a different way as I sit nearer the fire once more, warming myself both inside and out. I enjoy this. I love this. My soul is better for this. This means something to me.

The growing sense of warmth is wonderful and I feel heartened knowing that the animals are enjoying that warmth as much, if not more than I. This matters; something so small as this fire matters in such a big way. In a cold, dark world, this fire, this day, this here and now matters. My life is grounded once again. My perspectives are re-calibrated, adjusted and corrected. I know what's important again. I know what's real. I am alive and the coffee and the fire are good. No, they are great. I'm warm now and the coffee has circulated. I head outside to take a much-needed leak. What, you don't like that? You're offended? Well then, look the other way. I told you I didn't like company didn't I? I told you why I came to Maine. Did you think I was kidding? I wasn't. This is why I came. This is what I live for. Now, for the last time, get the hell out of here, Boots!

I came to this land a complete fool, armed only with the dream of building a future for my family. I didn't want to change the world for everyone else; I just wanted to change my world, for me. Some might think that a selfish goal. Some might think that. I don't care. It's worked for me. I live with me, not you. You will have to please yourself. Don't expect me to please you. I'm too old and tired for that now. That work is your own. My advice is get to it before it's too late.

I built my house with my own hands. It's not a great house by any means. It's not built of the finest materials and certainly was not constructed by the finest of craftsmen. But you know what? I did mention that I built it myself, didn't I? It's mine and I did it. It wasn't always fun. In fact, it was seldom fun. It was a challenge. It may not mean anything to you, and it shouldn't, but to me it means more than I can ever say. I did it. It feels good to know that. It feels good every day. I lived my dream and I'm the better for it. And, oh yes, my house is not finished and neither am I, but I think you suspected as much.

I started this piece expecting to write about living life in the country. I ended up writing about what I've learned about living life in general. I started out expecting to talk to you about electricity and ended up expounding on a life. What can I say? You never know where you're going to end up, do you?

As you live out your days, your life changes and changes you, but accepting that, that's the secret to enjoying it, isn't it? If we knew where it would all end, then we wouldn't be truly living it. We'd just be going through the motions and passing the time. If we live our life correctly, in my opinion, we'll never know, but we'll always be open to the moment. It's there, it's hidden in there, in the unknown opportunity of the moment, that life which is truly lived.

In the end, it's the journey, not the arriving that matters in this world. Life is not something that can ever be achieved. There's nowhere to get to, no medal to be pinned to your chest for a job well done, where you can sit back in satisfaction and rest on your laurels forever. It's only through the daily grind that, if we're lucky, we eventually discover that our final destination was trudging beside us along that our final destination was along the way all the time.

So finally, if you think you've arrived, get over it big boy; you're either delusional or dead. Take a moment to kick back, reflect, and enjoy what you've accomplished—then find something else to do. Get moving again. Life is movement, it's not just standing around. This isn't curling, you know. When we've stopped moving for the last time, we're dead. That's when you've finally arrived at your ultimate destination and guess what? It's too late to enjoy it. You're dead. On the other hand, you're dead, so there really isn't any time to regret what you didn't do, either, is there? I guess not.

Just pretend you didn't read what I wrote. And if you haven't already, forget what was said. And if perchance you can't do either, well, you won't be any worse off in the end, will you? No, I suspect not. But as for me, I feel better, not for having succeeded in reaching you, but for having tried and made the effort.

Dogs, Sleds, and Sled Dogs

Dog sledding in Maine is becoming a popular pastime. It's a fun way for dogs to get out and socialize with one another aside from tearing into the neighborhood garbage cans with their buddies or getting it on with Fifi, the local miniature French poodle/whore dog who summers down by the lake with the "snoots" from away.

The idea of having a dog pull you around the countryside is a good one in my estimation. Whoever came up with the idea of chaining man's best friends together in front of a sled and yelling "mush" instead of "here boy, come on boy, come here, come, I mean it, I'm not kidding, come on, get over here, get over here now, I swear to God you're going to wish you'd come when I catch you, here's a 'treaty treat,' be a good dog, if you don't come here, now, you're really gonna get it, I mean it, here boy, come"—that man is a genius. I also like the idea of having your means of transportation also serve the function of keeping you warm in an emergency. It's like leaving your engine running in the car, only it's "green," and it's environmentally friendly. I like the idea of the dogs warming up my sleeping bag at night. A "three dog night" is fine with me especially when the alternative is freezing by your lonesome out in the middle of nowhere. In that case, "one *is* the loneliest number," if you know what I mean. If you don't know what I'm talking about you're probably not a "boomer" or a fan of classic rock, don't own a dog and if you do, haven't taken it camping with you on a really cold night. Poor you.

I have always thought that if I were to believe in reincarnation, which I don't, I would want to return to this world as a dog. I like dogs and I think I'd make a good one. I like to be loved, and I like to eat and sleep. I would especially like being loved simply because I was a dog and liked to eat and sleep. I like to do those things now, but I don't get credit, much less loved for my indulgences. I also like to ride in cars and I like to feel the wind my face, which is why I ride a motorcycle. Being able to lick your eyebrows among other things is pretty cool too. I like the idea of there being "dog days" not to mention the idea that "every dog has his day." There's a lot to like when it comes to being man's best friend.

But, unfortunately I'm not a dog. I have a dog, Diesel; he's my best friend, and I work for him. His idea of lying around all day long and waiting to be fed and petted is fine for him, but what do I get out of it? Whoever said "It's a dog's life" got that right. For those of us who own them, however, it's anything but for us since we have to "work like dogs" to support our canine buddies in the style to which they've become accustomed. As far as I can tell, my life has "gone to the dogs."

So you see, I like the idea of dogs pulling sleds. It's a payback kind of thing with me. You know, sort "life's a bitch and then you die." That didn't come out right, did it? Anyway, you get my point, which is that it's about time our dogs did something to make us feel good, isn't it? Don't get me wrong, I like making our "muttly" happy; it makes me happy too. But if doing good to feel good is the point of owning a dog, I can feel a whole lot better with a whole lot less effort just by buying myself a six pack of Shipyard's best. Good boy, me (pat on the head), here's a treat for you (sound of a bottle opening). By the way, are dogs really smiling or is that just some genetic trait they've cunningly evolved? They look like they appreciate everything we do for them, don't they? I suspect it's the latter, the genetic thing, but I still fall for it every time, don't you? I think we like being appreciated and since our wives don't tend to sit at our feet, tongues hanging out, drooling, just waiting for us to pay them a tiny bit of attention, our dogs will have to do.

Anyway, in Maine, the sight of dogs pulling sleds through the snow is becoming ever more common. There's an entire circuit of regularly scheduled dog sled races now, not just in Maine, but covering the entire North East coast and on into Canada. Families load up Spot, Rover, Blackie, Rex, and yes, even Fifi, into their little kennel shacks stacked precariously on the back of a pick up, throw on some teetering bales of hay for bedding, strap down the sleds on top of it all, and head on out to the races looking like "Sooners" setting out for the start of another land grab. Yee haw!

We usually travel up to Rangeley to watch the races there every February. They're part of what is called the "Snowdeo" celebration. For those of you who don't know, a "snowdeo" is just like a rodeo only there are no horses or cowboys and everything else is basically different too. There aren't any horses, but there are dogs, and if you like dogs, you're going to love dog sled racing. It just couldn't be any other way, could it? And if you like to gamble and drop a dime on the races, well you're out of luck. You'd better stick with the horses. They're your best bet.

As for the races themselves, I like the starts best. There's no trumpet blowing like at the Kentucky Derby or the Preakness, but there is a lot of barking and milling about. I like milling about. I'm good at milling. When you're milling about correctly, no one bothers you. They know you're milling (they're probably milling too), and they let you mill without disturbing your milling, which is how milling is best done. It's during the milling about before the start of the race that you get to appreciate the true ambiance of the spectacle. That's when you get to see everyone and everything at their pristine and primal best. The snow is mostly all clean, fresh and white lying thick upon the pine boughs bordering the trails and surrounding the starting gate. There are food vendors and souvenir tents too and the smells are inviting. By the way, only accept red, blue and purple snow cones. Definitely do not pay for a yellow snow cone: just a word of advice from one of the not-so-wise.

I like to mill at the starts, cup of coffee in hand. There's excitement and anticipation in the air as the racers are wearing their numbered bibs, waiting to be called to the line. You just know when someone's wearing a numbered bib that this is all official and sanctioned and not just some group of "hosers" running their dogs for the fun of it, though it *is* fun. The dogs look sharp, fresh and clean, straining at their harnesses. By the way, the plural word is harnesses, not "harni." I looked it up to be authentic, too. As for the dogs, they're happy, ready to please their masters, and raring to go. Their masters, meanwhile, are checking and tightening the straps one last time, adjusting the gang lines here and there, and securing the little booties the dogs wear to protect their feet when the snow conditions require it. How can you not like dog booties? They're like little moccasins for mutts. If I were a sled dog, I wouldn't run without booties and I'd want my name made out of tiny, colored beads to be sewn on the sides. I'd demand it or I'd bite you. It's as close a dog is ever going to get to lacing up a pair of Nikes. One thing I wouldn't do is wear a handkerchief tied loosely around my neck, though. That's just gay, not that there's anything wrong with that. It's just not for me. I'd leave that to Fifi and her pampered crowd.

Once all is set and ready to go, the teams are called to the starting gate. There is no set number of dogs for a sled team. It varies by the class you're running in. Some sleds have a dozen, others only a few. There are limits and classes like any other sport. There are sprint races, long distance endurance contests, and there are stage races. Everyone's heard of the Iditarod race in Alaska. That's the oldest and greatest of the stage races. Well, there's no such famous race here in Maine that I know of. But don't despair; there are plenty of other races and your chances of enjoying the experience of dog sledding here in Maine are likely a whole lot better than the odds of your being in Nome, in thirty below temperatures on a given day in the middle of winter. Few people are that unlucky. The thing is, you can experience the joys of dog sledding right here in Maine and as an added benefit, you won't have to pay the Rosetta Stone folks a small fortune to learn how to speak fluent Alaskan.

Just another word of advice: take your pictures at the start of the race. That's when the dogs and the drivers are looking their best. You'll have a slew of teams and dogs to choose from so don't worry if you miss one; another will soon come along. That's when you get to snap shots of those beautifully groomed Malamutes and Siberian Huskies in their full, thick and lustrous coats we've all come to expect at the start of sled races. But in my experience, those are not the dogs you're likely to see at the finish. The dogs you see finishing first are likely as not going to be a pack of thinner, wiry types, bred for running, not for looks. They may not be the stereotypical team you've been led by Disney to believe in, the ones that always win the grand prize, but they're just as beautiful all the same. You just have to love dogs and, like I said, I do.

If you catch the bug and want to experience a sled ride for yourselves, there are an ever-growing number of opportunities for you around the state. Check them out on the Internet; you'll find them there. You'll also find that, more likely than not, you'll have the dogs you've always pictured in your mind running in front of you. Cuba Gooding, Jr. won't be there, however. This is Maine.

It's not a racial thing. It's just the way it is. But celebrity musher or not, it's a beautiful sight to see and experience and remember, your view is much better than the average dog's view. As they say, it's only the lead dog that gets to appreciate the changing scenery; for all the rest, the view never changes and yes, that tends to stink.

You might also want to try a new sport that's quickly catching on called "skijoring." Skijoring is when you harness a single dog to yourself while you're also strapped to a pair of skis. It sounds like fun. It sounds like payback, "mano y mano," for that particular dog of yours who never comes when you call. If he's going to run away from you anyway, you might as well put his instincts to good use and harness the rebel in him, so to speak. It sounds like fun, though I must admit, I've never tried it. Still, if you don't have the room, the time, the money or the inclination to house, feed, and care for a dozen or so of man's best friends, and few people with an actual life do, this might just be your thing. Check it out.

In conclusion, I would have to say that if I were going to be reincarnated as a dog, I think I'd prefer this old-in-the-tooth canine to come back to Maine more than anywhere else. In Maine we treat our dogs like they deserve to be treated, like the best friends they are. We own dogs because we love dogs and like to see them happy and enjoying their lives. It's that simple. We have the open space, and we certainly have more than enough trees, don't we? Yes, we do. We have plenty of trees, and as you know, many trees make for happy dogs and we like our dogs happy. Like I said, what makes our dogs happy makes us happy and really, for a dog lover, isn't that what it's all about?

We also have a few rules or standards regarding our dogs. Maine is not like down south where a dog is often treated like a tool used to perform some chore or task such as hunting coons under a full moon, or keeping the neighbors' kids from swiping parts from the junk cars out back. When you use a tool, like say pliers, do you really care if they're happy pliers? I know I don't. Here in Maine, we like our dogs to be happy and friendly and our tools to be functional, well oiled and from Sears. Aside from our children, and well to be honest, maybe even more so than some of our children (yes I'm referring to you), our dogs are our most cherished family members. They wag their tails and they love us. They don't change on us, become teenagers, shun us, mooch money from us, borrow the car keys and keep us up half the night worrying about them or what they're up to. Dogs are nice to us. They appreciate us. And did I mention, my dear children, now that you've grown up and no longer fear Santa's good and bad list—we neuter our dogs. We do that. We sleep better that way. We don't have to worry about puppies and disgusting behaviors. I just thought I'd mention it, seeing how the weekend is almost upon us.

Our dogs here in Maine tend to live in the house with us. If they don't have their own monogrammed beds from L.L.Bean, they sleep on our beds, not in a small pack under the front porch like down south. They lie on our couches (living room couches, not porch couches) and watch our TVs. We know how many of them we own. They have collars, dog tags, regular vet visits and we call them by individual names, instead of "you mangy mutt." They eat in our kitchens and often eat the same food we eat, just a few days later. And they pee in the backyard just like, well, like some people I've heard tell of. They are one of the family and all things considered, one of the better ones. Oh sure, they'll still sniff a stranger's crotch, but so didn't uncle ... but let's not go there. No need to bring that up is there? No. That's all said and done and besides, he won't be getting out for a long time.

As I said, we like our dogs here in Maine, but we like them to be real dogs. Being a miniature this or that just doesn't cut it here, at least not with the people I know. We like our dogs to sit and still be in the picture if you know what I mean. We don't like cat-sized creatures that somehow manage to bark. It's not fair to do that to a dog. In my eyes, a dog has to have some modicum of self-respect, or it's just simply not a dog. If you're six inches high, I'm sorry, but you are not a dog. If you're six inches tall, or better said, six inches short, you need to go live in New York City or Boston with Aunt Gertrude. She'll knit you a nice sweater so you won't get chilly when she takes you out for your constitutional. You need to be somewhere where someone follows behind you and scoops up your "deposits" and yet doesn't feel like a freak. And by the way, how do you people do that? Yuck! You need to be somewhere, but you do not need to be here in Maine. So, no offense, but please, go away will you?

We like real dogs like Siberian Huskies, Black Labs, Chocolate Labs and Golden Labs, Golden Retrievers, and Irish Setters. We like Pointers, Blue Tick Hounds, and Newfies—hell, some of us, but thankfully not many, even like Beagles. Down south they tend not to have distinct breeds. They tend to have one breed: mutts. They like mutts, cheap mutts, cheap, replaceable mutts. And they like their mutts to be lean, mean, and nasty-tempered hunting machines. Toss them some red meat, be it coon or cat (cats are red meat, right?) or kids, they don't care none, just so long as they can "rip 'm up," know what I mean?

In Maine, we like our dogs to bark, not yip. A yip, even a yap, may be fine for some, but it is not a bark and it is not acceptable here. Here, a good healthy bark is what we're after. We want our dogs to let us know when someone's coming up the road, but we don't want to have to worry that if that someone stops and gets out of their vehicle, old rover is gonna "rip 'm up." We like big dogs here, fierce-looking dogs, but friendly dogs. We like to say, "He's just a big baby. He won't hurt you, will you, Thor?" We don't like to hear "You'd best not step out of that vehicle mister unless you've always had a hankerin' to walk on knotty pine legs. Lester there, he don't cotton to, don't take too kindly to, strangers. Does you, Lester, you mangy mutt you?"

As I said, I live in Maine. I love Maine. And in Maine, we love our dogs, don't we Diesel? Yes we do, you good boy you. Now get back under the covers, I'm freezing. When is your mother going to get up and make that fire?

Electricity, Not Almost, But Really

This is the chapter I really meant to write on electricity, but somehow got side-tracked. That won't happen again, I promise. Not unless the electricity goes off and I'm left in the dark. Then all bets are off. It's stormin' outside right now, a real wintry nor'easter, so I'm not really sure how this is going to turn out, but let's have a go at it, shall we?

Maine has electricity, lots of it, and since I'm a Mainer, I have it too. It's not my birthright, of course, since I wasn't born here, but I have the same right to it that a native Mainer has, just as long as I pay my light bill. My daughter was born here and she says she doesn't have to pay for her electricity, but I know my daughter—I don't trust her and I think she's just lying to get back at me for something I must have done to her when she was little. At least I hope so. Anyway, I can't imagine my life without electricity. I can't think of it. I won't!

Descartes was a philosopher and once said, "I think, therefore I am." Well, I have electricity, so I don't have to think. Somebody else did that for me. As for me, I can just sit in the dark, so to speak, flip a switch and voila! There I am. My philosophy is, "I flip on a switch, therefore I think I have electricity." Eat your heart out, Descartes. You didn't have it. You didn't even think of it. And besides, you are not a Mainer like me. You are French, or at least were. And you didn't have electricity, so in my humble opinion, you didn't really live at all. Think on that.

You thought that if you think then therefore that proves that you are, that you exist. Well, that's real clever, that is. A rock doesn't think, but I think it still exists. You can disagree with me if you want to, but if we were arguing about it, and you kept it up and I had smashed you in the head with a big honking stone on Bastille Day to prove my point, well, dollars to donuts that head of yours would have been headed for some significant hurtin'. Think on that, Mr. "I'm oh so much smarter than you are," Descartes. So much for a life's work in philosophy. Outsmarted by a stupid stone. I'm no genius, but if I saw a rock approaching my noggin, come to think of it or not, I'd duck.

As for me, I like my philosophy better than Descartes'. Why, you ask? For two reasons: first of all I think his philosophy was just plain stupid and sec-ondly, because with my philosophy I get to have electricity, that's why. There is only one slight caveat or qualifier when speaking of my philosophy and enjoy-ing electricity in Maine, or at least where I live in Maine. We have it, most of the time, but not all of the time.

My daughter insists that the reason I lose power is because I'm not a real, full-fledged, dyed-in-the-woolens Mainer and since I wasn't born here, I guess technically she's right and I never will be. Rats! Still (I hope she's yanking my chain and I really did do something to her as a child), my philosophy works pretty well most of the time and that's good enough for me. No philosophy is perfect, I always say. Just ask Descartes once the swelling goes down.

Anyway, when I first moved to Maine, we didn't have electricity and I didn't have a philosophy. I built my house without any power or doctrine to guide me. All I had was dumb, brute strength, or, in other words, I relied on my own attributes and power. My neighbor Merle had power and he would let me load my lumber on his truck and haul it up to his house where I could unload it, measure it and cut it to length with a skill saw. Then I loaded the cut lumber back onto the truck, and hauled it back down to my home site where I unloaded it and nailed it all in place. This worked well provided I had made the correct cuts and didn't have to reload, haul, cut, re-reload, re-unload, and nail. It was quite a process and served to build character, or a character, as well as what passes for a house. It also made me despise CMP.

Back then, Central Maine Power (CMP) produced and operated all the power and power lines in Central and Western Maine where I live. They insisted that I build my house before they would hook me up to and with any power. I guess they wanted to make sure I was really going to stay. They didn't want to run the risk of planting five or six poles and running power lines and a transformer to another person "from away," not with all the "tree hugging nuts" running around with their ill-conceived dreams of living off the land in the wilds of Maine. They were—let's be kind—prudent. Prudent bastards.

Now, I like the "wilds of Maine" as much as the next guy, but I also like to be able to enjoy those wilds after four in the afternoon in mid-December when it begins to get real cold and real dark outside. I am no Euell Gibbons type, living on and eating off the land. I like my luxuries and yes, I count electricity foremost among them. I am a child of the fifties, and therefore joined at the hip to television. I was raised on TV. I am a product of TV and if there is one thing I have learned about TV, it is this: TV works best when combined with electricity. To me, no electricity means no TV. No TV means I don't exist. I don't want to not exist. It's not healthy to not exist. Ask Descartes. He's not around. Ask him how he feels, lumpy noggin and all. I want to exist. I want my TV. And so, I also want my electricity. It's as simple as that.

Once the house was built and I wasn't desperately in need of its power, CMP was so kind as to hook us up. Once we had power in the house, I was in heaven, although I'm still sure I'm going to hell for what I said about CMP despite the fact that I'm not religious. For a non-believer like me, heaven is a maybe, but hell is a given. Here in "maybe" heaven, I was able to wire the house myself. Back then, the state of Maine thought that if you were actually stupid enough to run the risk of electrocuting yourself by wiring your own home just to save a buck, then by all means go right ahead and remove yourself from the gene pool. I was that stupid and that cheap. Fortunately, and through no fault of my own, I somehow survived the experience. I didn't do a good job of wiring, but then again the house didn't immediately burn down, so I had no complaints. That is excepting for the TV reception (or lack thereof).

You see, we live in a secluded valley and could get only two and sometimes three stations with the antenna that was strapped somewhat securely to the chimney protruding through our roof. The rabbit ear contraptions you could buy back then worked as well as if we had used real rabbit ears. As luck would have it, they didn't work much at all either. I guess we should have tried a rabbit's foot and not the ears for better luck, but that doesn't really work as advertised—just ask the rabbit.

With no other choice, we, meaning I, had to go up on the roof and rotate the antenna to get different channels, ones that you could actually see and tell apart from one another. Those were the good old days that older people like me like to reminisce about, but would just as soon forget, but can't. Dementia is something I look forward to in some respects. But as for now, I can recall clambering up on the icy roof in good weather and bad (somehow, at least as I remember it, there was always ice up there), trying my best not to fall off, loosening screws and bolts with frozen tools, turning and twisting the antenna shaft to the left and then back to the right, hollering down to my wife who was running between the living room and the front door, screaming back at me, keeping me updated as to whether the reception was better or not although I couldn't hear her because the wind was howling and all the while I was choking on acrid plumes of smoke pouring out the flue. Oh yes, those were the good old days. It was at moments like that, teetering on my perch, in the icy cold, angry and frustrated, that I thought back to the stories my parents had told me about their good old days. Of course, they weren't so lucky as to have TV, but they had their stories. I thought then, and I do now, that everyone's good old days stories have one thing in common: they really sucked. Suffice it to say, I didn't enjoy my good old days at times, but hey, they were all we had back then, so we made do. Now, looking back at those times from the comfort and perspective of another century, I can honestly say, they really did suck.

Today we have satellite TV and I am just soooooo spoiled rotten. I love it. I have all the TV I could ever want. I even have "sound around," as I call it. You may call it surround sound, but I don't. I have hot water and a shower too. I have a refrigerator and a coffee maker. I have fluorescent bulbs, tungsten bulbs, low-voltage lights, CFLs and powerful, juice-guzzling floodlights. I have a computer and a microwave. I have everything at my fingertips, at the flip of a switch: that is, when there's power.

There are however those times when the power goes off. I don't like those times nearly as well as when we have power. I don't take to not having power very well. I tend to sulk when there's no power. I tend to sit quietly in the dark, sipping my warm beer, sobbing softly. And it is quiet, deathly quiet, at least when I'm not cursing at CMP and the other "powers that be," raging at the top of my lungs. You see, I am not what is referred to as a "happy camper" without power.

It's the same with water. I have been without water in my life, and I don't like that either. Being without water made a big impression on me. Today, I don't even like being someplace where I can't see water, or hear water running, or at least dripping. My wife is not happy with my phobia because, for instance, I won't repair the leaking kitchen faucet. I like water. I must have water.

Like water, I have lived without power and I didn't like it. I must have power. I don't like being someplace where there isn't a refrigerator humming or a commercial blaring on TV. TV is my friend. TV is a good friend. TV is my best friend, my wife and dog aside. I don't like not having my best friend with me. I like my TV.

In 1999, I was working at home on my computer. It had been misting out and we had been warned about possible power outages due to the weight of the gradually collecting ice that coated the wires and trees everywhere. Just as it had been predicted, light rain fell and an icy shroud soon engulfed the little corner of the world that we like to call "the entire freakin' Northeast."

Now, I like natural disasters as much as anyone, and probably much more than most. There's a part of my personality, a significant part (if not the largest), that revels in the misery of others. It makes me feel fortunate and believe me, I like to feel fortunate. Feeling fortunate is a good feeling. No matter how bad things are, at least I can say that I've got it better than that sorry so-and-so I'm watching suffer on TV. Well, there I was, that day in the winter of '99, in a pretty good mood for me, all things considered. Actually, I was quite happy, if not downright giddy. I was working on the computer, running downstairs from time to time, turning on the TV, checking in on the disaster that was going on in other people's lives all around me. Those poor souls were losing power everywhere. Lines were down everywhere. Everywhere it was a disaster, an unprecedented disaster, but not at my house. At my house everything was hunky dory. Now that was my kind of disaster. One I can watch on TV. It was cool. Like I said, I was happy, that is until ... until the very moment ... the power went ... off.

The house went silent. My heart stopped. Then the house and my heart fluttered and sputtered back into life for a brief moment. My emotions flared and then suddenly were extinguished when everything went dead once more. Someone, the big guy, had FLIPPED THE SWITCH!

We were out of power. I hate those words. We were out of power and would remain so for the next seven long, dark days. Our lives became one of campers and I was not a happy camper. My wife was not a happy "camptress." Our once happy home was no more. This wasn't cool. This was a freakin' disaster!

Now at first, once the initial shock of not having electricity wore off, I must admit, it was sort of not all that bad, if not actually somehow fun. You know, like when you break your foot and get to use crutches for the first time. Or when you snap a bone in your wrist and have everyone sign the cast. It was that kind of almost fun. But that kind of almost fun doesn't last long. Soon your armpits ache from the crutches and your arm itches under the cast and what's that smell? Is that what gangrene smells like?

We got out the candles and the lanterns and lit them even though it wasn't dark out yet. And why not? We were ready. We were ready to be without power for an hour, maybe even several hours. We were prepared, but not prepared for a week without power. No one prepares for that, not even an Eagle Scout is that prepared. It was bad, and yet, as bad as it was, we had it much better than most. We heat with wood, so that was not a problem. We would be warm. We cook with gas, so that was not a problem. We would have hot food. What we didn't have was water: no working pump equals no water. That was bad. What was worse was this: no TV. For me, this was a devastating double whammy. No TV. It couldn't have been any worse. I can't live like this, like some kind of Neanderthal in a warm, snug cave eating hot wooly mammoth potpies. This is too primitive. I don't like to play board games. I don't like to participate. I always lose. I don't like to do my entertainment. I like my entertainment to do it for me. I like radios and noise. I like lights. I like TV. If I have to think, I therefore am not, am not who I am. Damn you, Descartes! You just may have been on to something.

After a few hours we thought the power would come back rather quickly; maybe we'd be out a day at the most. We wouldn't like it, but we could handle a day. That was not to be. My neighbors and I checked the road and the wires. There were no trees snapped. No limbs were bent under the weight of their icy shroud. Nothing was touching the lines. Our best guess was that the breaker on the transformer at the end of the road had somehow tripped. That was all. It was a simple matter of resetting a breaker. Hell, I do that all the time in the cellar, on the panel. CMP would just have to flip the switch, or so we thought.

As it happened, we thought wrong. You see CMP has this plan that if power goes off in a widespread manner such as it did in '99, they restore that power according to a list of priorities. Hospitals, nursing homes, police and fire departments, and major business centers come first. Once these necessities are up and running, the centers of population are next restored to power. Then the trucks and work crews fan out and bring back those lines with the most people, and so on and so forth. This is the only fair way of proceeding and I would usually go along with that, but not when it comes to electricity. Fair is just not good enough a reason for me to be without power. Fair doesn't cut it if, like us, you live on a dead end dirt road, just you and four other houses . At times like this, I don't give a hang about what's fair or not; I just want my power back. We can discuss fair over a hot cup of freshly brewed coffee, after I have my power, but not before. As far as I was concerned, it's my opinion that (and when I don't have power I don't want to hear any other opinion) CMP had their wires crossed. Their thinking was short-circuited. According to their way of thinking, I was a "non-priority." It's not that I'm insulted being referred to as a "non-priority," not at all. I've been called worse. It's just that being a "non-priority" insinuates that I don't have power, and insinuations of that nature irk me to no end. We all know that a tragedy is something bad that happens to us, and a comedy is something bad that happens to the other guy. Being a "non-priority" is not funny, it's a tragedy, and don't laugh.

So, here we were living in the midst of the greatest natural disaster to ever befall the region, and I couldn't even sit back and enjoy watching it on TV. How cruel is that? I couldn't see the videos of the tumbling towers of high power transmission lines. Now that was funny. I couldn't see the maps outlining the blackened areas of New England. Now that's comedy. I couldn't see the twisted metal pylons stretching their twisted arms towards Montreal or the ice enshrouded TV towers and bridges. How can you not laugh at all that? Let me tell, it's easy when you don't have any power, that's how. I thought at the time that this was never going to be one of those "back in the good old days" tales I was going to tell my grandchildren. I was wrong again. This really, really sucked.

To make matters worse, I began to realize as the days wore on just how stupid I really was. I mean how many times do you have to flip on a light switch before you realize that it's not going to turn on? If you're me, the answer is apparently a whole lot more times than you would think for a college-educated, quasi- (almost a semi-) grown-up adult. As it was, I couldn't enter a room without flipping the switch. I just couldn't do it. I'd try to use the TV remote because it ran on batteries. Is that dumb or what? It's dumb. I thought if I used a little thing, a small radio perhaps, that would work as if a little electricity could be pulled from no electricity. What I really grew to hate was going into the bathroom and instinctively shutting the door and hitting the light switch. Sitting on the toilet in the dark is pitiful. Trying to clean yourself when you can't tell, aside from smell and feel, if you've done the deed or not, is disturbing in and of itself not to mention unhygienic as well. If you're wondering, it's not '99 any more and I'm still traumatized. I haven't gotten over this, people. I still have to look, just to be sure and just because I can; I don't like doing it any more than you like reading about it, but I can't help myself. I did learn one thing, though. I learned that I would much rather be deaf than blind. That and that it's the simple things in life, like not having to smell your fingers in the dark, that make life worth living.

After a few days, when the trees stopped snapping and the limbs stopped falling, the weather began to let up a bit. We could get out and actually go places, places where there was power, to town and all, but that wasn't really fun knowing that we would soon be heading back home to darkness and another night of going to bed at six o'clock. What else was there to do? Talk to each other? You've got to be kidding.

"So, how do like sitting here in the dark without power, dear?"
"Shut up or I'll kill you, honey!"
"You can't see me. You don't even know where I am."
"I can hear you. I can hone in on you. So just keep it up the chit chat (click) and this gun may 'accidentally' go off a few times in your direction."

This was cabin fever, concentrated cabin fever; you didn't mix it with water, you took it full strength, all of it at once, and it got old fast—real fast.

In a few days' time, we gradually got used to the fact that we were not likely to see the light of night for some time. We gave up hope and accepted our plight, which, surprisingly, made life easier. We ceased to struggle and fret. I guess it's the same thing that enables strict Catholic couples to look happy after thirty years of marriage. Our thoughts turned to making the best of what was clearly not a good situation.

I cut a hole in our nearby stream and hauled water for the toilet and drinking. It wasn't easy, but it worked. Besides, what else did we have to do? We actually began to feel pretty proud of ourselves. We were like pioneers. I took an old, discarded fifty-gallon metal drum and buried it in the snow, covering it with ice and snow. We put all our frozen foods in there and we didn't lose a thing to spoilage. I liked that. We were making ends meet here. We were learning how to adapt. You couldn't call it fun, but it wasn't half bad either. We found that we could do this, and do it rather well. And we even began to talk in the dark. Or at least I did, once I managed to hide the shotgun shells.

By the seventh day, we were on cruise control. We knew we could last this out, however long it might take. It didn't really bother us anymore. We had survived. We were surviving. We were actually doing rather well. And then it happened.

I think we sensed something was different before we actually realized what was going on. We heard the first whir of the fans on the fridge, and the humming of the appliances coming back to life. It all sounded so foreign, so unnatural at first. It was as if a living creature had suddenly been awakened from a long hibernation and was shaking off the cobwebs. Lights came on randomly having been left on or off. Who could tell in the dark? It was amazing. We were stunned. We hadn't expected this. We all just sat there looking dumbfounded at one another. True, that in itself wasn't all that unusual, but this was different. After a moment of stunned silence, I ran to turn on the TV and see if it were really true, that the power had been returned. Sure enough, they said so on the news. Power was being restored here and there and we just happened to be lucky enough to live here and not there. The picture was the best it had ever been. The colors were vibrant and alive. The sound was exquisite. I stared in disbelief. Life was fun again. This disaster was happening to someone else once more. Life was good and I found myself enjoying the news just like in the old days, just as though we had never lost power at all. But we knew that wasn't the case. We knew we would never take our power for granted ever again, and though over a decade has passed, we haven't.

Now when the power goes off, and it does quite often here in the foothills, I don't miss a beat. I don't think back to that winter's day in '99. My reaction is quicker than that, faster than thought. I have PTSD now. I have Power's Terminated, Someone's Demented. I turn instantly into a frothy, angry, nasty, self-centered baboon, ranting and raving at the powers and lack thereof that be, twitching uncontrollably all the while. It's like flipping on a switch, the way it turns me off, the way I carry on.

Summing things up, let me say this: I hate life without electricity. I don't want to live it anymore if that's the way it's going to be. I hate it. I'm serious about this. I wouldn't wish power outages on anyone, ever again. Maybe not even on New Hampshire, but I'll have to think some more on that before I commit myself.

I suppose I would feel the same about earthquakes, hurricanes, floods, and other such events if they happened to me as well. I sure hope they never do, because I still really enjoy watching them on TV. What a wonderful world we live in. There's always some kind of natural disaster devastating someone someplace else and it's only the flick of a switch away. I feel so fortunate.

I like my life again. I am a happy camper and all the world's my campground. I am a good person once more and nothing will never, ever change that ... until the power goes off, and then you'd just better watch out, keep your mouth shut, and keep your distance. That, my friend, is not a pretty picture. That, my friend, is best left for the dark.

Portland, or Why I Just Don't Understand Antiques

Portland is Maine's largest city, both in terms of the number of its inhabitants and population. It is a popular place and therefore is populated by a large population of people which explains its being Maine's largest city. I thought you would have already guessed that, but then again, I don't know you very well, and well, maybe there are gaps in your education. If you already knew this, don't bother reading the last line. If you didn't know this, well, you do now so don't bother rereading the line before the last line. Let it suffice to say that to us Mainers, Portland is a really, really big city.

In fact, and fiction for that matter, it's our only big city. It is so big that it has more than one Kentucky Fried Chicken/Taco Bell. That's how big it is! And that's just another reason why it is so popular with us Mainers. It's also popular with those "from away," but for a slightly different reason. They seem to like Portland because it's so quaint and "small," and it's not cluttered with all those Kentucky Fried Chicken/Taco Bells like back home. Go figure.

Now, the name "Portland" is comprised of just two syllables (like M-Maine if you stutter): "port" and "land," not "portl" and "and," or "po" and "rtland." It's "port" and "land." To be sure, "port" and "land" is a good combination to have if you want to be popular, especially with sailing merchantmen looking for a place to dock their ships, unload their cargoes and make a buck or two. If you just have a port, that is to say you just have a lot of water, with no place to land your vessel, you basically have what is called an ocean and there's a surplus of that, as we all know. If you have only land stretching as far as the eye can see, land bordered by more land, brushing up against still more land, surrounded by land piled on land, boring land, hot, dusty, dirty land, land, land, land—well, then you have what sailors call a real problem when it comes to sailing, or Kansas, for short.

Portland is fortunate in that it has both an ocean to float a ship on and land on which to dock it when the need arises. It's got it all. Portland is a great city and like any great city, there's a surplus of things to see and do there. If you're hungry and sick, Portland has Kentucky Fried Chicken and Maine's largest and best hospitals, for instance. You could go there, order some extra crispy and have your kidney removed, like I did. But let's say you're not at death's door, you have some money jingling in your pockets, and you want to have some fun. Well, there's always the Old Port.

The Old Port was really just the "port" part of Portland, but then it got old. Since we now have modern fire departments and there is no way to simply burn the "old places" to the ground and start over again like in the "old days," the city fathers simply threw their arms into the air and gave up. "It ain't going away no time soon," they decided, "so what the hell, let's say we just embrace the problem and call it a success?" Thus was born the Old Port.

So now here you are at the Old Port, money in hand, looking for something to do. Not a problem. That's what Old Ports and other attractions are made for: separating tourists from their money. And the Old Port is good at this, catering to all sorts of needs. The Old Port features everything from the lowlife to the high life, from life in the gutter to life at the top, from the way life should be, to the way life really is and all of that which lies in between. You can buy plastic lobsters and real lobsters, junk food and fine food, fine art and crap—and by that I mean those velvet paintings. You know what I'm talking about. Something like that but with a Maine touch, like a sequined Elvis peering out of a lighthouse with his eyes shining like beams of light that seem to follow you around the trailer. You know, something like that. Or worse.

But most of all, there's antiques and antique shops.

Now, I just don't understand antiques. Antiques are old things. I'm getting to be an antique. But I'm not valuable. And I'm certainly not becoming more valuable simply because I'm getting older. If that were the case, I would have sold my grandmother years ago and been living on easy street instead of writing this stuff. No, when it comes to antiques, I just don't get it.

Just take a look at today's society. Those of us who are married and have kids have families. We love our families. But as we age, we just don't like, much less love, to live with them or even near them for that matter. In point of fact, for most of us, if we didn't have major holidays we'd never see our families at all. As semi-adults, we moved away to get away. It's that simple. Oh, it may have taken moving away a couple or three times, but eventually we did it and here we are, happy and alone, or at least until the most recently troubled one of our dear children moves back in. But for now, life is good.

And then one day the getting old thing starts to happen. Earth, moon, revolving, solar system, comets and stars, revolutions, seasons, years, time ... you know the story: getting old, it happens. Not to us, mind you—we're too young for that—but to our parents. They get old and before you know it, you're making so many trips to their house to do what they can no longer do, that, well, it just makes sense to have them come and live with you, what with the price of gas and all, right? Whatever were you thinking? *Were* you thinking? Are you crazy? Have you lost your mind? Have you gone senile? Have you forgotten what it was like, you living with your family? What didn't you learn the last time before you moved out for the last time? Can't remember? Not to worry. You're about to learn it all again, and this time in spades.

Now don't get me wrong; I like old people, but with two slight qualifiers: they have to be old people I don't know and old people I don't live with. Those are the only old people I like and that's a good thing because most old people meet those criteria. I like to listen to old folk talk about their lives, their adventures and their families. It's interesting. What I don't like is listening to my parent's talk about their lives, their adventures and their families. That's boring.

It's not only boring, but I've heard it all a million times before and I have to be honest with you: I don't remember it having happened like that. I mean I never acted that way, or said those things. In fact, just about the opposite is true as I recall it. But do you think I can get them to admit to that after all these years? You just try setting the record straight with the old people you live with. You can't do it. And why can't you? Because they remember too damn much, that's why. They'll swear to you that they can't remember if they turned off the TV set they're actually watching, but they can remember all the details from July 17, 1962. They can recall it like it was yesterday. Well, not yesterday, because that memory is gone forever, but you know what I mean.

They've got rusted old minds that won't let anything new in, and won't let anything old out. They are what they are and it's not pretty and it's not fair. You want to argue the past? Good luck! They know all the facts and you only have inklings of what it felt like to you at the time. You were just a kid with feelings. You may have a college degree, be fully-grown and a pillar of the community and they may be seventy, wearing diapers and out of their gourds, but they're still right and deep down you both know it.

It's only a matter of time before you're in your room listening to "oldies" on the radio while those stupid really old people are sitting in what was your living room watching Jeopardy. There they are, talking to the TV at the same time, oblivious to one another, and gloating, saying things like "I'll take 'My Son's Childhood' for a thousand, Art!" It's Alex, you idiots, Alex! It may have been Art twenty-five years ago, but it's Alex now and even Alex is getting old! He's got white hair for God's sake, so get with it before he's dead too. And I don't care if you do have $58,000 and you're wagering it all on "Rude Things Our Unappreciative Offspring Have Said to Us," you're still wrong and I hate you and I'm never coming out of my room or talking to you again! So there! So. So there! So there you are, a grown child pouting in your bedroom in your parents' new home (what used to be your home). Does the price of gas seem so high now? I don't think so. And what's with that smell? But, hey, at least you have the solace of knowing you did what was right by the folks who brought you into this world. Now if it comes to the point that you have to kill your parents to preserve your sanity, of course that will take the shine off the good karma you've accrued, but hey, a child's got to do what a child's got to do. Besides, you're still just a kid in their eyes, a juvenile. You can't be held responsible can you? You could always plead temporary insanity. You'll be getting off easy if that's all you have and not the full blown kind of permanent insanity they seem to have.

And that is why we move our old people, our families and loved ones, out of our living rooms and into their nursing homes. There they can die in peace and contentment at Sunny View, away from their children, their constant sobbing and random threats of violence.

Which brings us back to antiques and why I just don't get it. Now, everyone says that the most valuable things in our lives are our immediate family, our parents, but when they get old and time gets short and is ever more precious, we spend a fortune to have them sent away. Well, I'm simply confused. I'm at a loss. It makes no sense. It's crazy. Which as I've just explained is why we're driven to do it in the first place. But, here's what really drives me nuts. Because they are now old we have sent our parents away, but because the things they lived with and grew old with are now old also, we treasure these things even more because they're more valuable and they "remind us of them." When it comes to understanding antiques, I'm from away. Go figure.

Which brings us back to antiques once more. I picture America as a city, a city existing over time. It's grown and developed, changed and transformed with the centuries. As a country, the South and Southwest are its booming suburbs and strip malls. The Midwest and Central areas are its industrial belt and mature neighborhoods. The West Coast and Florida are its eccentric, artsy retirement centers. And the East Coast, and more specifically New England, is its Old Port that never burned down. Maine is the largest antique shop in the nation's Old Port.

So why do antiques trouble me so? Here's why. How can a nation that is ever growing ("burgeoning," if you will believe whomever currently resides in the White House), how can a nation like that continue to produce antiques from way back when? There can only be so many old things, and I mean really old things, right? So where does this endless stream of antiquity derive? Where do they keep coming from, these antiques, and what makes them so valuable in the first place?

Wouldn't you think that by now all the antique shops would have sold all the antiques? I mean, ask any of them and they'll tell you business is good if not great. Old things are flying out of the shops like this afternoon's special edition newspaper hot off the press. Will we ever run out? Aren't antiques a finite resource, like, say, oil? Shouldn't there be warnings about buying antiques, something like if we don't conserve our old things and stop selling them, pretty soon we'll all have to muddle through life with the latest and the greatest whatever it is to hit the market? Someone has got to put a stop to these antique-guzzling new colonial-style home developments, for instance. Interior decorators and Country Living magazine must be put to the stake and torched before the last hand pump, pewter dish, shaker table and Victorian armoire is gone forever.

Now I know that most of Maine, and a few unexplored regions of northern Vermont and New Hampshire are still being thought of as our nation's antique reserves, but they can't be tapped forever. We must preserve our antique wilderness. Traveling Maine's back country roads, you may still run into a yard sale offering up a classic, but I'm telling you, the mines are playing out and playing out fast. You may find a nugget here and there, but the mother lode of history will soon be just that: history. The attics and barns, these mines of Maine, are dwindling to a precious few. We may soon find ourselves a nation of now, of no heritage, of Walmart and IKEA. Is there nothing that can be done? Well, I have a few suggestions.

I will suggest a remedy by way of rumor. In Maine, I have heard that duck decoys are a hot selling antique item. In fact, this phenomenon is not relegated to Maine alone, but is spreading like warm margarine across the hot bread basket of America, dripping sweet rewards onto the laps of decoy merchants and auctioneers near and far. The demand for collectible decoys is on the rise. Unlike our genius forefathers who in their foresight apparently fore-produced enough spinning wheels to fore-power the universe forever (and which, by the way, if they were placed end to end would form a line), duck decoy carvers were not so keen on anticipating the future needs of our society. Apparently, the shortsighted fools, sitting and whittling on their front porches, only produced enough decoys as could be sold and used in their time. Economically speaking, they supplied for the current demand. They didn't plan for the future and that is where they fell shy of the genius of, say, an Edison or a Ford, and that is why we suffer today from a shortage of antique duck decoys.

Now, what makes a good antique duck decoy or at least one that is collectible and sought after? There are three basic and fundamental criteria. First of all, a decoy can't be in great shape, all shiny and freshly painted, or no one will believe it's like really old. Secondly, it can't be manufactured to perfection, or no one will believe that it was hand crafted on a front porch and unique. And thirdly, it has to kind of resemble a duck or at least a bird of some kind. It needs a beak or bill and maybe a feather and wing or two, but not three. That's it. Not too difficult, not too demanding. So what's the solution to our dilemma?

Well, I have heard through the grapevine over a can of Old Milwaukee Light, that Mainers are stepping up to meet the challenges of this economic conundrum. Rumor has it that before the last of the many local wood turning mills were put out of business by poor, hapless, ignorant, ill-clothed and ill-fed, modern, international, Chinese, industrial entrepreneurs, they produced a windfall of poorly made wooden duck decoys. These decoys were secreted away in the dark of night and have since, like a fine vintage wine in an oaken barrel, been aging, or shall we say "antiquing," in the back yards of some of Maine's most industrious citizens. Soon, these superb examples of early American craftsmanship and ingenuity will flow into, if not flood, the antique auction houses of our waiting hinterlands and buoy our economy once more.

Maine is on the move and is becoming a leader in a new industry, namely the manufacture of new antiques. I may be wrong, but all that junk we see aging and weathering in the back yards of Maine's backwoods may not be what it at first appears to be. In fact, it just may be the wave of the future that will feed the flow of the antiquing juggernaut of our times.

So, we may have figured out where antiques of the future will come from, but what of antiques of the past, the old kind? Where do they come from and what exactly constitutes an antique?

The gist of what I gather from my Webster's is this: an antique is simply something produced some time ago that somehow remains with us today in somewhat limited numbers, that is in some kind of fairly fine and original condition, and is somewhat in demand of some sort and therefore is something of some value to someone, somewhere. Think about that, but not too hard. An antique is not something for the most part that was really popular and commonly used or it would have been worn out and replaced and it wouldn't be around today. Maybe, just maybe, the reason antiques are still with us is because they weren't very good, very useful, very practical, in demand, or all of the above. If they were a good idea, well crafted and put to use, they would have been used to death, worn out, repaired, or simply replaced with another of the same. So by way of such reasoning, it was the odd, the not-well-thought-out, the useless, the unused, and the discarded remnants and rejects of society that survived to become our valuable antiques of today. That is, unless in 1792 someone threw plastic over all their furniture and wouldn't let anyone actually sit on it or bring food into the living room to watch TV, but that can't be true because my grandmother wasn't even born back then. Nope, it has to be because the stuff was just no good junk and therefore not valuable, or at least valuable in a pre-antique sense.

In summary, I have reviewed my thoughts on antiques and I still just don't get it. They still make no sense to me. I've thought and thought, for instance, on antique Victorian parlor chairs. Why are they seemingly so valuable and so in demand? Everybody has one, but why don't they have two? Why don't they have a house full of Victorian chairs and couches? All I can come up with is this: that Victorian chairs—straight and upright, backs at 90 degree angles to their seats, inflexible, padded with lumps of small animal bodies, wooden arms, claw feet, rusted metal roller balls and all—are a true torture device if ever I've encountered one and they only exist to this day because no one in their right mind actually wants one to sit in one which is why they last forever and therefore why everyone simply must have one.

You may say my thinking is a little twisted and off-base. I don't care what you think. I think I'm right, and I think you're wrong, and I think I can prove my point with one simple statement that is indisputable and true and that is this: you will never, never ever, find an unused, in original condition, unstained and pristine, antique Lazy Boy recliner anywhere in the world. Ever! Point proven. I win!

Maine to Florida, Pine Trees to Palms: A Rite of Passage

If you know anything at all about cartography, or map making, you know that whatever format you choose to use, there will always be some distortion to the land masses and waters depicted. You can't get around it; it's just the way reality transfers to paper. It's why this book sucks. It's not me and my lack of writing skills—it's reality. It just doesn't translate well to paper.

Keeping this in mind, if you look at a map of the eastern United States, you will see that Maine and Florida are represented as being on opposite ends of the North/South axis with some other meaningless distances, states, districts and commonwealths scattered between for filler. I say that with all due respect to these entities, excepting, of course, New Hampshire. From north to south they are the aforementioned and totally disrespected New Hampshire, Massachusetts, Connecticut, New York, New Jersey, Delaware, (perhaps Pennsylvania,) Maryland, Washington D.C., Virginia, North Carolina, South Carolina, and Georgia. I'm sure they are all fine in their own way, except New Hampshire, of course, but Mainers just don't care. It's nothing personal, again excepting New Hampshire, but we just don't care. To a true Mainer, these thirteen colored areas on the map may as well be a barren desert wasteland, devoid of all meaningful life. They are nothing but distance, space and time. To us they represent fifteen hundred miles, thirteen states, districts and commonwealths and twenty-five or six hours to be tolerated and endured at best. To put it bluntly, to a Mainer, they are nothing but "in the way." In medical terminology, Maine and Florida are joined at the hip and separated by one big, festering, hunk of "stuff" that a whole lot of people call home. That's nice and we hope you're happy, but we just don't care.

As we all know, Maine has but three seasons, not one of which happens to be spring. We have a short fall, followed by a long winter (okay, a *very* long winter) and then it's too warm to snow. The snows melt suddenly with the rain, our rivers swell, our cellars flood, flowers and trees bloom, black flies bite, and suddenly it's summer. That's it. We really don't have even a vague concept of what spring is or should be. We don't understand it and don't want to. It's just not a part of our reality. What we really want is just a longer summer, not something that hints of summer, but summer itself, and to get that in March, April and even May, we head for Florida.

Now, as I said earlier, maps are can be deceiving. To a Mainer in March, the eastern seaboard consists of Maine and winter, some stuff in between, then Florida and summer. There is nothing else. A Mainer's map would have Maine and Florida abutting with a thin line separating them and reading "1550 miles, 13 states, districts and commonwealths, one pain in the ass, and 25 or 26 hours of time." But it really doesn't matter because we just don't care. We have but one goal and that's Florida.

Ask a Mainer how far it is to Florida and they'll say twenty-five or six hours unless you have an accident and/or get killed in New Jersey. To us, if you're going to spend any time in New Jersey under sixty-five miles per hour, you'll wish you were dead anyway. There are only five reasons to even slow down in New Jersey: 1) you're out of gas and always wanted to see someone in a turban who talks like Apu on the Simpsons fill your tank for you, 2) your wife needs to use the rest room, 3) you're paying another damn toll, 4) traffic has ground to a stop, and 5) you're dead. I've tried the first four and have seriously thought about the fifth on more than one occasion. None of the options are pretty, but I digress from my true purpose here, which is to take you on a mythical journey to Florida and back, experiencing things as a typical Mainer might. To save time, which is what this trip is all about, we'll just take the trip back.

Our vacation is over now. We've had our sun and fun. We have sobered up. We're essentially broke and living off credit cards. We have to get back to work in a day or two if we still have a job. We're all packed and anxiously waiting for the alarm clock to ring, so watch out.

It's dark outside as we open the door to the parking lot. It's always dark at 4:00 A.M., I don't care where you are. That's when we like to leave for home. It's the best time to set off because for one thing, the women in our lives are still essentially asleep and easily managed in their semi-conscious state. They may grumble and take a swipe at you, but their co-ordination is off this early in the morning so the danger of being hurt to the point of requiring medical attention is significantly reduced.

We've loaded the car the night before so there's nothing to do but head out the door. I don't know about you, but I like the morning and I like to sing to the melody of the old Rawhide TV show. "Get 'em up, get 'em out, get 'em in, get a goin', Roadside! Yeah!" Crack that whip! Move 'em on out! I like to sing, and I like that it drives my wife crazy. She hates my singing because she can't sing, and she hates the morning because, well, because it comes so early in the day. If morning came around evening, she might like it, but it doesn't and it doesn't get much better than this if you're me.

We settle in and I adjust my seat just so. I turn the key and the engine purrs to life, raring to go, just like me. We're on our way home now and we "don't need no stinkin' map or God forbid, GPS" because there's only one direction to go and that's north on I-95. It's a real man's dream come true. No directions to follow at all, no chance of getting lost, just "follow the yellow brick road" home. I click the heels of my sandals together silently, close my eyes, and whisper to myself, "I wish I was in Maine, I wish I was in Maine." I open my eyes and the "Wicked Witch of the West" is staring at me. I guess we're not in Kansas any more, eh Toto? I switch on the headlights, momentarily blinded as they pierce the warm darkness surrounding us like a coal miner's lamp. We are miners in a way, I think to myself, miners in a dark shaft called I-95, digging and clawing our way to the golden light at the end of the tunnel: Maine, Auntie Em, and home. I glance to my right. Flying monkey! My simian canary isn't looking so well. I roll down my window a smidgen and give her some air spiced with the sweet scent of hibiscus.

I release the parking brake. It's a habit from back home. There's no way to roll in Florida, nothing to roll down. I ease her into gear and we're off, off to a fantastic start of a fantastic journey. We're going to break all our old records. We're going to average seventy-five miles per hour and thirty-five miles per gallon this trip. We're going to make it home in twenty-five or -six hours tops. We're going to, we're going to, we're going to run out of gas! _X%#@#_!

All right, take it easy. Somehow I overlooked that one. I'll just pull into the nearest station here and—"What the hell is this?" Their gas is two cents higher than the one we just passed a block back. I'm not paying that price what with all the cheap gas around here, and I'm not heading back either. I'm on a mission. There's got to be a cheaper station just down the road. There isn't, of course, and I end up paying considerably more at the next gas station, but what the heck, that's just a minor setback in the overall scheme of things. Besides, we were running on fumes so I really had no choice did I? I tell myself that it wasn't my fault, that somehow the canary did it, that there was nothing I could have done. Anyway, the tank's filled, the windshield's clean, and the oil is fine. Now just to dip inside for a quick, steaming "cup o' Joe," and we'll be on our way. Life is good. It's still early, it's a new day, the coffee's hot, and this time, this time we're really good to go. Or so I foolishly think.

Leaving the store I see some motion up ahead near the car. Someone, a shadow of a figure, shuffles out into the darkness and I hear a door slam shut. It's my wife. "I've got to use the ladies room," she mumbles as she wobbles past. I begin to say something about wanting to get back on the road and why couldn't she have gone to the bathroom while I was filling the tank and why didn't she go before we left the motel and suddenly the wobbling stops and she turns. It suddenly hits me. I've seen that look before. I know where this is headed. Thirty years and I still haven't learned when not to open my big mouth. That's one big, nasty-looking beak on that canary. I sputter something like, "I'll be waiting in the car, dear," and scurry off into the darkness and safety of my late model, four-door cave. "That was close. She's waking up, coming back to life. I've got to be more careful from here on out," I remind myself.

Ten minutes later, ten precious minutes later, the shadow eventually shuffles over towards the car and asks me for some money. I give her my wallet without comment. I'm getting wise in my old age. She flits off again towards the gleaming glass doors. I want to say something witty like, "Go into the light, go into the light," but don't. What's the use? She's waking up, but her sense of humor won't show itself until sometime after noon, so why chance the pain? Besides, we've already lost our jump on the day. It didn't last long, but the dream is over. The coffee is having its effect. I'm waking to my reality. We haven't even hit I-95 yet and I've already given up any hope of breaking records. This trip isn't going to be any different than the rest. What was I thinking? She shuffles back, this time with a cup of tea in her hands, opens the door, drops my wallet in my lap, and settles down onto her perch.

"Can we go now?" I ask half sarcastically.

"Don't push your luck," she replies coldly.

"I guess I'd better not sing the Rawhide song then?"

"That would be a wise choice," she responds. We head off into the darkness in complete silence, but in my little head, I'm singing out loud "Get 'em up, get 'em out..."

I-95 is the great funnel of a tunnel that connects Maine and Florida at the hip. President Eisenhower is the culprit who was responsible for its creation along with the rest of the interstate system. It was originally intended as a military highway system to protect us against an invading enemy, say Canada or Mexico, I suppose. No one thought that life's a two-way street, did they? Still, Eisenhower was a smart man. The Canadians couldn't have gotten far because their money isn't accepted at the little wire buckets at the tolls where you have to toss it in. Trying to pass a "loonie" by a collector would have set off all kinds of alarms. As for the Mexicans, they don't use the roads anyway. They hike the desert, swim the Rio Grande, or whatever. Now that they're here, the roads allow us to ship them back as fast as they come. I guess it was a good idea. What was I thinking? I was thinking that what the interstate system really did was open up the country to tourism for Americans, and Mainers, quick as we are, soon picked up on the fact that Florida was now a viable alternative to shivering in the dark. The Rite of Passage began in earnest.

In the old days, Mainers didn't go away on vacation to Florida, unless they were really, really rich. In those times you either were working and had money, but no time, or were laid off, out of work, and had all the time in the world, but no money. That's all changed now and Maine has become a little wealthier and a little more like the rest of the country. Of course, I am speaking in general terms and in particular referring to myself, and my own circumstances. I've gotten to that stage in life where I have both the time and the money to join in the fun. I have noted, though, that the more time I have on my hands, the less money those hands have in their grasp and the more of it that falls through my fingers, which brings us back to our journey north.

The first thing you see, other than the red taillights of the cars in front of you—the taillights of the many cars in front of you, the many cars of the others who just like you got up early to beat the traffic and get a jump on the day—is a sign offering a rest stop. I'd hoped to sneak by at least the first one, but no, the wife's able to somehow see through her closed eyelids and asks me (tells me actually) to pull over; she's got a need to partake of the facilities. It's the damn tea, but it's not just the tea. There's something more going on here. It's that general rule of thumb that while traveling with a woman, if there's a restroom, there's gonna be a stop made. Accept it and get over it, men. We have to relieve ourselves when we have to relieve ourselves, while they, on the other hand, can go whenever there's an opportunity to go. It's part of our "on demand" society, I think. It's like walking a dog, only a male dog, that can't pass any tree, bush or post without marking it. Women somehow have the remarkable ability to generate water on demand, and the equally remarkable inability to hold it in. It's going to be a long day anyway, and unless you want to make the time and the miles feel even longer yet, I suggest you accept your reality, and pull over whenever and wherever the opportunity presents itself. Besides, extending this courtesy will make you look like a caring individual in their eyes and that can carry benefits well into the night, if you know what I mean. Having control of the TV clicker is no small matter in my book.

Now that we're on the road, you will notice that you and all those other tail-lights are heading north at a considerably quicker pace than we in Maine usually tend to travel. The speed limit in Maine is set at sixty-five mph, and strictly enforced if you go above a hundred or so. That's fast, but there's just not a lot of traffic, just you and the state trooper. Down here on I-95, the limit is seventy, which means, by law, everyone is obliged to be doing a minimum of eighty and above and that includes semi's hauling trailers, pickups towing campers, vans towing boats, Buicks with little, old, blue-haired ladies towing U-Hauls full of whining cats, and even convertible car loads of vacationing nuns with both hands on their heads, trying to keep the wings on their hats from pulling their heads off and that includes the driver. It's a madhouse and it literally scares the crap out of me. Thankfully, and I don't know if I've mentioned this before, but my wife likes to occasionally stop at rest stops, as in every one that comes by, so I have the opportunity to clean up and re-gather my composure.

Everyone it seems is on a mission, just like me. I don't feel unique and special anymore, but more a part of a herd, a migrating wildebeest or a Johnny Reb soldier in Lee's Army of Northern Virginia, marching in formation as we swarm north towards the hated Yankee heartland. But I have something Johnny Reb, or even a wildebeest for that matter, never had. I have a little cruise control button on my steering wheel. You just slap her down at the speed everyone else is going and you're all set and good to go. Now I'm free to stomp my feet to the Acadian rhythms throbbing on my CD, much to my wife's obvious disgust. Nothing can stop me now, nothing, and yet, there's always something, something to bring the melody to a screeching halt.

Suddenly, without any warning or reason, this flowing artery of life suffers a major coronary thrombosis and the heartbeat of traffic shudders to a pitifully, erratic, occasional pulse. For several minutes we're actually, clinically dead. I'm waiting for someone to collect my retinas and kidney. Then, again without warning or reason, we come to life and surge forward for a few hundred yards when suddenly little clots of vehicles begin to form, collude, and once more the ebbing flow is stemmed.

Stalled and bored, I wave to the other cars from Maine and they wave back.

We have a fraternity here that others don't seem to share and I savor it. We pass things back and forth between our vehicles, like key chains from Kennebunk, and insults about southerners and their so-called hospitality. We chat about back home and how this would never happen back there. And then suddenly, just as it had begun, the traffic jam dissolves into open space and it's everyone for themselves as the speeding cars and trucks pass out of view. Why did we stop? Who knows? We pass a nun's hat. Who cares? Stuff just happens, like lint or that fodder stuff that collects between your little toes.

When the sun rises, for us at least, it rises on Jacksonville. Jacksonville is where the Patriots won the third of their Super Bowls, so I'm looking everywhere to see the stadium, everywhere but where I'm heading, and so I never saw the highway split until it was too late and I looked up and realized I was on Route 10 heading west. That's how we got to see a lot more of Jacksonville than your typical Mainer heading for home might have. Ten minutes and a lot of curse words later, we're back on I-95, streaking towards Georgia. Jacksonville was okay, but I don't think we'll stop and visit the the next time.

There's just one more hurdle before the border, but I fail to clear it and fall flat on my face, gazing at a billboard sign proclaiming a thirteen-foot long alligator and free samples of fruit. I'm up for anything that's free, we needed to buy some oranges for everyone back home anyway, and besides, my wife thinks they must have a rest room out back as well.

These tourist traps are really good down here on I-95. You can't miss them because unlike in Maine where they've been banned, there are billboards everywhere you look proclaiming the glory of everything under the sun, from fireworks and fruit to firewater and fine velvet artwork. You can't avoid the signs and in time, you find yourself enjoying them as much as a form of entertainment as for their information. Not everyone has a DVD player in his or her vehicle, you know, and besides, unlike reading every billboard that passes by, watching a movie while driving can sometimes prove dangerous and even worse, boring. I'm thinking Nicholas Cage here. It doesn't matter what movie does it? If he's in it, I'm looking for a rest room.

Having been lured into one of these traps, you find yourself staring at all sorts of junk you never knew existed much less thought you'd ever need. To me they're like a super supermarket of what the British call tat and we call crap, and I love them. Don't get me wrong; I like to think I'm sophisticated, but honestly, who can resist a shake up snow scene with palm trees, bathing beauties, and manatee? Or is that a manatee? I remember seeing something like that on the beach at Cocoa, but it was wearing a pink bikini.

Speaking of which, thank God for my wife. She has better sense than I do or I'd be showing off rolls of generic, discount toilet paper proclaiming in black and white that it's "for cheap a-holes" to everyone who visits our home. "Now that's funny, I don't care who you are," as Larry the cable guy might say. I did manage to sneak by her a couple of post cards of the "fat ladies on the beach" series, though. I mean good taste can take you only so far in life. Know what I mean?

Heading out of Florida, we run smack into the Peach State, Georgia. If there's one thing I learned from this trip, it's that Georgia has the finest rest stops I have ever seen. They are a sight worth visiting unto themselves and I would recommend them to anyone traveling with or without a wife. They have azaleas in bloom along with countless daffodils and other flowers and are manicured just as if foreigners were living there. If we had these in Maine, they'd probably charge admission to get in and I'll tell you something, cheap as I am, I'd pay it. Georgia, like Florida and every southern state, also sells fireworks and each and every store is advertised as the largest and the cheapest one you'll find, so you can't go wrong. They also seem to specialize in all-you-can-eat, topless diners and pornography stores. I suggested that these might also have restrooms, but that didn't pass muster with the old lady. Somehow she managed to hold it that time. I would recommend you consider a visit only if you're traveling without your wife or prefer to drive in silence for a thousand or so miles and then never hear the end of it once you're home.

Speaking of scenery, South Carolina has an ambiance all its own. It's called South of the Border. There are fifty-five billboards advertising Pedro and his village; I know, I counted them all and I don't think I missed any. You can't help it. You find yourself waiting anxiously for each and every somewhat cleverly worded ten by twenty foot sign until like every other idiot who has ever made the run, you find yourself pulling off just before the North Carolina border, approaching the giant sombrero lookout tower just to see what the hell it's all about. The hell of it is this: South of the Border is the ultimate tourist trap carried out to the nth degree. I learned that every bad idea for a souvenir gimmick has a home here in a bin and I bought most of them, or at least tried to. I also learned that while South of the Border may have fourteen individual stores, it seems that they all sell the same tat. Luckily for me we were on a mission or I'd still be there shaking my head, trying to explain just what it was I was thinking when I bought this or that piece of plastic crap. On the positive side, they do have a very nice collection of plastic, no doubt handmade, clawed, back scratchers that work quite well thank you very much.

North Carolina is just like South Carolina, only different. It also has the nicest rest areas I have ever seen. The palm trees have gone now, replaced with miles of pines, but the azaleas continue to flourish. If Florida is orange and the land of theme parks, North Carolina's theme is the military and its color is camouflage. There's a fort or base, or so it seems, at every exit and every base has its own museum dedicated to the "fighting" number this or the "fighting" number that. Stop at a rest area, and if you're paying any attention at all, and you will, you will discover every other person there is wearing a hat with the name of some army unit or ship on it, which brings us to the battleships and aircraft carriers that have been strategically placed along the coast to further entice the traveler off the beaten path.

This seems to be another of I-95's influences upon our culture. Every state with a river emptying into the ocean has an old battleship and/or aircraft carrier, with a few destroyers and submarines thrown in for good measure, anchored to its muddy shoreline. They're all big, all gray, and all guaranteed to inspire awe. Be sure and stop and visit each and every one; that way you'll make up for me and the other Mainers taking a pass on the opportunity. Maine has somehow managed to avoid the "old gray lady" syndrome, except for our U.S. Senators.

Speaking of old, gray ladies, North Carolina also has cheap cigarettes. I don't smoke, so I'm not interested, but judging by the number of billboards, a whole lot of other people are. And like South of the Border, North Carolina has its own billboard overkill in J&R's store, offering discount everything from tobacco and cigars to sheets and towels. I didn't count the number of signs for J&R's on this trip, but I will on the next trip to be sure and if this book is ever revised, God forbid, I'll fill you in on exactly how many there are. As for now, there are way too many for my taste.

Virginia is just like North Carolina, only different as well. It has the nicest rest areas I have ever seen. Traveling through the Commonwealth, you begin to get the feeling that you're somehow leaving the South, though the constant signs for the Confederate museums and Civil War battlefields remind you that you have a ways to go yet beffore you reach the land of the hated "blue bellies." On the plus side of the ledger, there are now things to see along the roadway other than billboards and trees—things like actual cities you actually pass through and can actually see rather than only signs that warn you about their existence. I was beginning to think southern cities were like Maine moose. You see warning signs everywhere, but never the real thing. Virginia, on the other hand, has the real thing. No, not moose, but it does have cities and these cities have buildings, and sports venues, and shopping centers, and homes. It almost feels like a real place, just somehow not quite.

Now as you head north out of Virginia, you merge into even greater traffic than before, and even though it's going slower, there are more cars so it feels just as dangerous and out of control. We're approaching our nation's capital, Washington D.C. I found myself cursing the many expensive SUV's with tinted glass surrounding me, guzzling gas and blocking my view ahead. Four-wheel drive behemoths in a land where, if it snows, they proclaim a holiday. Go figure. I'm still "down south" in my mind, so I call them all "sumna bitches" as I holler out my window for them to get out of the way so I can see the Washington Monument and the Capitol dome as I cruise by, swept along by the flow of vehicles surrounding me. They can't hear me. All their windows are rolled up tight and besides, they have tinted glass, so even the deaf ones won't be able to read my lips.

They say Washington is a dangerous city to live in, with many homicides. If I had to live there, there couldn't be enough homicides to suit my taste. With my luck, I'd never be car-jacked, robbed and murdered. I'd have to commit suicide. The only way I could live in Washington would be to kill myself and get planted near Arlington. I never served, so near Arlington will have to serve me if I'm ever to live and die for my country in D.C. Enough said.

Maryland is a whole lot nicer than Washington because I can see more from the highway. Baltimore is close by, in full view, and with the Raven's stadium and the Orioles Park at Camden Yards, it provided a much needed pick-me-up. There's also the tunnel for entertainment, not to mention the impossible quest of trying to find Fort McHenry in the harbor. Still, all too soon for me, Baltimore is in my rear view mirror and I can only recall the many interesting sights I didn't have the time to see. Quote the raven, nevermore.

Up until now, the southern part of I-95 has one thing that the rest of the highway can only dream of, and that is this: can you say no tollbooths? If you didn't have to get gas, eat, use the restrooms or buy the necessary crap offered along the way, you'd never know you were in the South, and you'd never hear that familiar southern twang. You'd be isolated from the inhabitants just as though you were on a raft, floating at sea on four rubber tires. That is, if you never turned on the radio and listened to the non-stop preaching that goes on day and night, well, pretty much non-stop. But, there's a price to pay for progress and here we are approaching Delaware. I'm warning you now, pull out your map and take a look. Delaware is shaped a lot like New Hampshire, if you know what I mean. It's like a mirror image if you will. Looks can be deceiving of course, but not here.

"Welcome to Delaware," the sign reads, "home of tax-free shopping." That sounds all too familiar to me as I feel the road etchings thumping against my tires and see the tollbooths looming ahead in the distance. This is getting eerie. They want my money, and the state motto is "Liberty and Independence." It's not live free or die, but it's close, too close. They want me to donate to their tax-free society. Their nickname is the Diamond State. Diamond? Granite? Both are hard rocks. They want me to stop and shop. Unlike New Hampshire, Delaware is the second smallest state, and there are no mountains, but maybe there is a "man of the mud flats" lingering somewhere about. I begin to muse. They want me to buy things, but what is this? These are real things, not fireworks, smokes, liquor, and pornography. Whoa! It's not as bad as I had feared. I'm not in New Hampshire after all. This is not her identical evil twin. At least not exactly. There are differences. Still, I'd better get out of here as fast as I can. Fortunately, Delaware is smaller than Maine's evil stepsister and we soon pass on into Pennsylvania, but not without another toll. They're small. They have another nickname too, the "Small Wonder." They're small, but they're good, real good. It's not New Hampshire South, but just the same, I wouldn't trust Delaware if I were you. That's just me. You make your own choices. You take your own chances.

Pennsylvania is altogether different from anything else we've seen so far. Even though we're in the Commonwealth for but a short time, it's easy to see that this is actually a pretty cool state, what with Philadelphia and all. The city is to me akin to a Baltimore North and I enjoy passing by the sports stadiums, ballparks, the mandatory battleship, and vistas of the bridges and towering skyscrapers. I'm feeling like I'm "up North" for the first time since we began this trip. It feels good. I'm getting comfortable again. I should have known the warning signs, the comfortable feeling, but I've been away for a week. I let my senses down. They've atrophied. I was dreaming, in La La Land but this shook me out of it and fast. Something was about to go bad, to go "south" up north if you will, and did it ever: The sign read "Welcome to New Jersey."

I wasn't ready for this. I never am. Before I moved to Maine from New York, New Jersey was my own personal semi-equivalent of New Hampshire. I relished despising the state and honed my viscous diatribes on its pathetic, bland, cream-colored "Garden State" license plates. I knew it as only as something scummy, smeared with oil refineries, factories, small houses packed tightly together, and roadways peppered with tollbooths every couple of miles. I hate tollbooths and if Delaware was good at them, New Jersey is even better. The Garden State Parkway invented stop and go traffic. Stop and pay a toll. Go and pay a toll. You even have to pay a toll to simply get off it, get off it anywhere. Every exit has its own toll. The memories come flooding back. I can't avoid them. I give up the fight. This is too much for me. I become paranoid. If traffic even begins to slow down, I reach into my wallet, pull out a dollar, roll down my window and just throw it out. I'll give the money to anybody, to nobody. I just don't care anymore. Just take my money and let me go, I'm begging you. I feel like I've been captured by Somali pirates sailing in little concrete block boats. But before I can pay them all off or escape, there's the restroom scene to be experienced yet again.

"You've got to be kidding." There was no response. No verbal response. The look said it all.

"Fine," I said, "but I bet they have coin-operated toilets." Again, no verbal response, just the outstretched hand.

When will I ever learn to keep my big mouth shut?

New Jersey has the worst restrooms I have ever seen. They are worth avoiding at all costs, even worth running the risk of having your wife glare at you for a hundred miles with a full, occasionally leaking, bladder. By this point in the trip, though, I don't care. I don't care at all. I should never have pulled over. There are people everywhere, milling about, horns are honking, diesel and gas fumes fill the air, and strange accents and dialects slosh against my eardrums. These must be the Somalis themselves. There are gas lines at the pumps like back in the seventies; I begin to experience flashbacks to Vietnam and I didn't even serve. I can't buy anything to eat because the lines are too long and the people remind me of Napoleon's army returning from Moscow: dreary, expressionless, wet, and covered with melting snow. And besides, the prices are too high. I'm not going to pay that much for something I don't want in the first place. The place is a dump, but everyone is rich. I'm baffled and confused. I'm beginning to have a panic attack, an anxiety attack. This, this place, this represents all I have come to despise in life. This, this mob scene surrounding me, this is why I moved north. This is what I fled thirty years ago. I've got to get out of here, now. And I do. Just barely escaping with what's left of my sanity. Ha!

Ha! Just try and catch me, New Jersey! Ha! Ha! Just try!

Then suddenly it's over. I'm in New York. I feel relieved. I don't even hate the Yankees and George Steinbrenner for a moment, but that mental lapse quickly passes and I regain my senses. A weight's been lifted off my shoulders, a hunch off the back of this Quasi Motor Man. I'm ringing the bells in the tower of my cathedral of joy, ringing them for all I'm worth. I'm free! Free at last. Free at last. Thank you, you the guy who built this car. I'm free at last! And I'm in New York. Can you believe it? I'm in New York and I'm rejoicing. That, my friend, is how badly I despise New Jersey. And as if all you've read wasn't enough, did I mention my wife was born there? Well, she was. Someday New Jersey, someday.

We've only three hundred and eighty miles to go, "only" almost four hundred miles left. That's how warped my perspective has become. We've driven eleven hundred miles and what was once a dreaded trek for the holidays has now become a mere afternoon's joy ride. This is a piece of cake. I know these roads like the back of my hand even though I thought I'd washed the memories away. I checked my hands. Where did that liver spot come from, and did I miss my turn? This is no joy ride. New York and then Connecticut only seem better when compared to New Jersey and those memories are setting as fast as the sun in the western sky. The traffic is relentless. It's night, a Sunday night, and there's more traffic than on New Year's Eve on Cumberland Avenue in Portland. It just goes on and on like in the South, only slower. Up north the speech is quick, it's the traffic that has the slow drawl, y'all. The traffic picks up speed then slows. It stops and it starts. Again, there's no rhyme or reason. I hate this place.

I think back to Washington and my thoughts of suicide. We're getting close to home, but I don't know if I can hold out much longer. I begin to stare at the bridge abutments, as we slowly pass by, not fast enough, not yet, but soon. My wife is staring. I wipe the smile from my face.

"You want me to drive?" she asks. She's knows, she's on to me. It's that damn "Wendy, I'm home look." "There's a rest area ahead. Pull over, I need to use the ladies room."

She's right. We're getting close. I can taste it. I pull over and hand her the keys. "I'm feeling relieved already," she says. I nod my head. I am too.

The rest of the trip is pretty much uneventful. I can't see anything, which is not a bad thing because my eyes are closed and I'm trying to catch forty winks. There's not much to see anyway, but red taillights running off into the distance. I know what a sockeye salmon must feel like as it heads up stream to spawn, or a sled dog on a team with hemorrhoids, just one red butt behind the next.

We leave Connecticut at Sturbridge and I pick up a much-needed coffee. I'm recovering now. I take the wheel again. The Mass Pike takes but a moment. I-93 peels off most of the traffic surrounding us as it heads towards Boston and its environs. New Hampshire lies just ahead as the hairs on the back of my neck rise instinctively. We approach the tollbooths. I don't want to give away my money anymore. I'm getting well again. I read the sign that says "No Stopping

Except in Emergencies" (paying tolls is an emergency in New Hampshire's eyes) and I think to myself, "Yeah, right! As if I'd stop in New Hampshire for anything less!" As we approach the bridge over the Piscataqua River, I wonder why New Hampshire hasn't placed a last tollbooth on its bank. Could they actually be doing something nice? I shudder and shake off the insanity. It's an oversight on their part. One they surely will correct in time.

"Pull over," I say to myself as we land on Maine's fertile soil once more. "Pull over and let me take a deep breath."

It's good to be home again: only two and a half more hours to go. I step on the gas, close my eyes, and the rest, as they say, is history.

Yes, it was quite the journey, quite the Rite of Passage. I've done it once and will never, not now, not ever, not never, do it again. I've traveled to Florida now by bus and by plane, by thumb and by train, but this was the worst of all, by car. I've learned my lesson, and learned it well. Don't nobody have to hit me over the head with no tire iron twice. I'm all through with driving to the sun and fun.

Still, it only took us twenty-seven hours or so, and we did get thirty-five miles to the gallon. And did you see what the airfare is lately? Never say never, I always say. Who knows what next year will bring? I kind of liked those rest areas down south, and maybe, just maybe I'll pick up some real cheap fireworks for the Fourth of July. Why, I might even forget about New Jersey by next year. Nah! There's no medication or therapy that will ever cure me of that.

What I really think we'll do next time, is take our sweet time. We'll take our sweet time and take a big, wide curve around New Jersey. That would do it. We'll take a week. Maybe make the trip itself the vacation. Who am I kidding? I'd have to be retired to do that. Or fired! Nah, my wife's not ready for that, not yet. Still I'd love to see the look on her face when I can say, "Wendy, I'm home. For good!"

Evolution: Myth or Fiction?

Maine is no different than any other state when it comes to the ever recent controversy regarding whether mankind evolved through evolution or was created by divine intervention and planning: we don't know the answer either. But that has never stopped anyone from Down East or anywhere else from believing what they will and asserting that everyone else is wrong. Now, I firmly support everyone's right to their own beliefs (excepting of course my uncle who wanted us all to believe he slept with squirrels. That was just wrong. The mere thought of it has adversely affected me down through the years, but that's another story altogether). The point is, I have a hard time believing in evolution. I know that this sounds ludicrous to many, but here's why I feel as I do. You see, I don't sleep well, never have, and probably never will. I wake up at odd times from rather bizarre dreams that often involve midgets, various sauces, and linen. I don't know what it means and I don't care to know. I just want it go away. That's why I was so surprised to wake up one night thinking about squirrels: surprised and happy, but at the same time perplexed. It was this vision about squirrels that got me convinced me that evolution is not for real.

You see, squirrels have existed for countless millions of years. That's a fact unless of course you choose not to believe it. Still, it's a fact and you're wrong. Maybe it's a factoid, I'm not sure, but I am sure that squirrels have been around forever or at least a pretty long time, and you're still wrong. Now pull out your calculator and begin to do the simple math with me. Take those countless millions of years and add them all up. That's a pretty large number isn't it? Of course it is. Now, take that number and multiply it by the number of squirrels that have ever lived. That's probably an even bigger number if I remember my geometry correctly and I don't. Take that number and multiply again by the number of oak trees that have existed during the same time as those squirrels and, I think I'm on pretty solid ground here, add the even larger number of acorns that have fallen from those trees. Finished? Okay, so we're talking a whole lot of zeros and to the power of this or that, and such and so. Big time numbers—certainly enough numbers to hazard an educated guess about something. I mean, if elections are predicted by a couple hundred phone calls to within an accuracy of plus or minus three percentage points, then I guess the number we just came up with will yield a degree of accuracy slightly more than akin to shall we say certainty? I think we can reliably do that.

So here's my point. A bazillion, billion, million, quintillion give or take a couple of years, squirrels, and nuts and today, what have we got to show for all these ingredients of our potential evolutionary soup? NOT ONE NUT-THROWING SQUIRREL! THAT'S WHAT! Tell me that makes any sense at all. You can't. Think of it. It doesn't seem possible, but have you ever seen a squirrel throw a nut? No, you haven't and neither have I. I've seen a lot of squirrels and a lot of nuts, but never have I seen a squirrel even attempt to throw one of them. Me, I've thrown nuts, even thrown them at squirrels, so it's not like they haven't been shown, haven't seen it done. I've even managed to hit a few, so it's not like they don't know it hurts. It's not like they haven't witnessed a demonstration of the potential here. And yet, for all of that, not one squirrel has attempted to drop, much less throw a nut towards me. It makes no sense at all.

Ponder this if you will. Leave a click-top ballpoint pen in the woods so a red squirrel can reach it and I guarantee you within five minutes he'll be up that tree, sitting on a branch, just clicking away endlessly. That's how smart and damn annoying red squirrels are. But what else could a squirrel do with a pen, you ask? And that's just my point. What the hell can they do with a nut? Pick it up, put it down, eat it, hide it (this is usually from themselves, which is why they hide so many. It's like squirrels are born with Alzheimer's), and, oh right, there's one more thing they could do with it—they could THROW THE DAMN THING! But they don't and it drives me crazy, so crazy I can't help but bring it to the attention of anyone I run into.

For instance, I mentioned all of this to a receptionist the other day. She wasn't at all impressed when I asked her to consider the advantage of being a nut-throwing squirrel. So, I asked her this; "If you had ten nuts and I had just one and I wound up and bopped you off the head with it, what then?" She thought for moment and said she'd have eleven nuts. Well, I don't think so. I think what she'd have when she woke up was a knot on her fuzzy gray scalp the size of an acorn and a vague recollection of ten other acorns and that's all, that's what I think. And they wonder why they're receptionists.

Darwin pointed out that various sub species of finches on the Galapagos Islands have evolved various types of beaks over the eons, each suited to eating just a particular type of seed or fruit. These variations enabled a particular finch to become more adapted to its particular environment and thus more successful than the other finches in accessing a particular food. This in turn led to more finches of this kind living and breeding and there you have it: evolution. But squirrels? No such luck. I don't get it.

Going back those millions or billions of years, to the age of the dinosaurs, I'm sure there existed a reptilian equivalent of today's fuzzy little nut eater. This creature no doubt was a fearsome, especially fearsome if you happened to be a nut. I imagine it with a crested, leathery head sloping to hardened stegosaurus-like plates on its back, leading to a spiked, club-like tail. Its hind legs were no doubt roughly similar to the legs on a vicious T-Rex. Its mouth likely sported saber toothed tiger-like fangs. Now that was a squirrel to end all squirrels. That was a squirrel to be reckoned with and of course if you looked like that, you didn't need to throw nuts to have your way with the world around you, so those little T-Rex arms may have made sense at the time. But today, with our modern, furry, cute little rascals roaming the woodlands, a strong right arm makes all the sense in the world, and yet, where is it?

Not only should there have evolved a strong right arm, but what with all the time squirrels have had to develop, it's a wonder they can't throw spitters, knuckle balls, cut fastballs, and wicked ass curves as well. That's ridiculous, you say? Why is that, I ask? Baseball has only been around for a hundred and fifty years or so and we've got all that and designated hitters too!

Okay, you say, even if they had evolved a throwing arm, a squirrel lacks an opposable thumb to grasp a nut for a two seam slider. Big deal. No thumb. That explains why they aren't successful as hitchhikers, not as nut throwers. Anyway, why would you want to ride in a car if you're so small you can't see out the window once you're strapped in? I don't blame squirrels for not accepting rides. I do blame them for not throwing nuts.

Okay, but they can't get a good grip on a nut without a thumb, you say. Hogwash. They've still got two hands and have you ever even seen them grab a nut with both arms and raise it over their heads in a threatening fashion like a medieval knight defending a castle rampart with a large rock? Maybe that's because their arms are so short that if they attempted the stunt they'd only succeed in rapping themselves in the throat. Evolution would work against any squirrels trying to do that, so maybe those two-handed, over-the-head nut-raisers were eliminated. I'll give you that one.

Still, I can't get past why they don't throw a nut? Their little arms are just too short, you say? Well, they could have evolved longer arms, couldn't they? Isn't that what evolution is all about? And even if that couldn't have happened, haven't you ever seen girl's fast pitch softball game? Those honeys can wind up and windmill a mighty fast, high and tight one with the best of them. But there's no Eddie Fanner out there with a gray head and a bushy tail is there? No, there isn't and that's my point.

So that's it. That's why I can't believe in evolution. So many squirrels, so many nuts, so much time and not one nut thrower to show for it. I'm sorry Darwin, but I just can't buy your theory. As for divine planning, who in their right mind would create a world without a nut-throwing squirrel? I know I wouldn't, but I could be wrong. After all, I never believed my uncle slept with squirrels until I saw it with my own eyes. Who'd a thunk it?

Elixir, The Beer of Life

I have two beers each night when I come home. I like my beer. Sometimes I come home two, three, maybe even four times a night. Whatever it takes, I say, whatever it takes.

I like to drink beer and I like to talk about drinking beer and that is why I have included a chapter on beer in this book. If you have a problem with that, you teetotaling, non-alcoholic miscreant you, just move on to the next chapter and don't judge those of us who may imbibe on occasion, any occasion. But before you act too hastily, consider that Maine was once the leader of the temperance movement—well, before prohibition became the national disaster that it was. The point is, we wised up, and you can too.

Now, I have been waiting with baited breath to write this chapter for some time now and I have baited that breath with the finest of Maine's quality malted brews. As a welcome result, I have passed many an evening in a satisfying stupor reminiscing about something I couldn't recall then, and can't recall now. My research has been thorough, dedicated, and unrelenting. I have pursued my thirst for knowledge with unswerving dedication. I have done my duty nightly and over a period of years without regard for my own personal safety. (Will the need for personal insight never cease? I sincerely hope not.) The wisdom I've garnered has been laid out for you on the following pages and I pass it on, filtered and refined by the kidney of my mind for your reading pleasure. (I regret that I have but one kidney to give for my book, having donated one to cancer early on in life. I have no other regrets, however, as my one remaining kidney is a very contented kidney and I intend to keep it in its slightly pickled state for the foreseeable future.)

I like my beer as much as the next guy, provided the next guy really, really, really likes his beer. If he doesn't, "Move aside my good man and let a real human being 'sidle up to the bar.'" I've always wanted to use that phrase, "sidle up to the bar" and now that I've done it, I must admit it feels as good as I had hoped it would. In fact, I think it feels better than I thought it would. I think I'll use the phrase again.

Personally, I don't "sidle up to the bar" (ah!), there being a number of legitimate reasons. First of all, my sidling skills have never been of the highest quality, though not for a lack of trying. I've attempted to practice and improve, but as you are likely well aware, there are damn few things one can sidle up to, especially for a sidling novice like myself. For instance, if you sit on a park bench and try to sidle up to a complete stranger you're likely to get knocked upside the head with a quick left hook. It hurts. I know.

If you try to sidle up to a close friend, on the other hand, without first explaining what you're attempting and why, you will likely encounter a confused look, followed by some raised eyebrows, a rapid shuffling motion, some quick sliding to the side requiring additional, mostly ineffectual sidling efforts on your part, all of which leads in time to the end of the bench and ultimately, that sideswiping left hook once again. It hurts. I know.

If you take the precaution to forewarn your friend that you intend to sidle up to them, you may avoid the left hook, but your sidling will likely not take place either. In this case you've saved your friendship, for the moment, but are still burdened with inferior and inadequate sidling skills. This is my sad plight. I'm stuck with poor sidling skills. I guess I will have to simply accept the fact that I'm just no good when it comes to sidling and never will be. It's painful to have to accept one's being a second-rate sidler, but not nearly as painful as that damned left hook. It hurts. Believe me, I know.

The second reason I don't sidle up to a bar (and it still feels good to say it, by the way) is that I am cheap, really cheap. Though I love my beer, I have my own personal standards to live down to, and being cheap is prominent among them. I must be true to my ideals if I am to look myself in the eye with even a modicum of self-respect. I need my self-respect. It's what keeps me going, but if I can buy it for less, I like it all the more. Unfortunately, I have discovered that being cheap is not only a part of who I am; it is perhaps the largest part of who I am. In fact, I've discovered I can afford to live with a little less self-respect if the price is right. I mean after all, self-respect only goes so far when you're broke.

Being cheap, I know the current price of beer at the store and I've heard of the current price of beer at a bar. They are not the same price. I fully understand that there are reasons for this price differential and I respect them, but I literally don't buy into it any of it. I realized early on in life, having been to college and taken Economics 101, that sadly, bars are in business to make money, not to give me beer. I accept the concept, if not the reality. I also understand that making money is not a crime, though financing a condo at the 'Loaf by selling beer at inflated prices is a criminal act in my mind. I don't like feeling victimized even if the atmosphere is "très chic." The only "atmosphere" I'm interested in is reached by drinking a brew that contains approximately 5% alcohol by volume and should not be consumed while operating farm equipment, while pregnant with a defective birth defect or child, or something or other, blah, blah, blah. Like I care to hear that kind of depressing blather when I'm drinking. Hey, I'm trying to tie one on, and have a good time, not get a medical education so spare me the lecture.

Besides, enjoying beer, but not being any good at sidling as I've already explained, I know there is just no way I'm going to get my money's worth heading out for a night at the bar. I'm only going to get what I pay for, and being cheap, that's never been enough for me and never will be. Some may say that you can't put a price on sidling. Still, I swear that if you could, whatever that price might be, it's more than likely too high for poor dregs like me. Let me demonstrate what for me would be a typical night out on the town and why I don't go.

First of all, I'll begin by saying that I know I'm not cut out for the bar scene. Experience has taught me that I'm just not comfortable sitting at a bar, or anywhere for that matter, conversing with others, and trying to have a "good time." I would like to think that I could enjoy myself like everyone else, but I can't. Meeting strangers and carrying on an intelligent conversation while drinking and trying to sidle is quite simply too much for me to handle. Hell, I'm not good at either when I'm sober, much less sitting drunk at a bar.

You see, it should come as no surprise to anyone who knows me that I'm not an accomplished "mingler," I feel too awkward and self-conscious to mingle. Mingling only leads to awkwardness, which leads to my drinking more to compensate, which leads to my spending more money, which leads to my losing my tenuous grip on that modicum of self-respecting cheapness I cling to, which leads ultimately to guilt, and I hate guilt because guilt makes me feel guilty and I don't like that feeling. Besides, try to do all those things while carrying on a witty conversation about the meaning of Leonard Cohen's lyrics with an attractive wench and see where that lands you. I can tell you from experience, if you really want to know. It lands you flat on your keister on the floor, that's where it lands you and I don't like conversations where I'm being talked down to.

But it's not that I don't enjoy the actual drinking of the beer; I do. Or at least I try to. It's just that, being cheap, the good taste of a brew is soon diminished exponentially by the price differential between the wholesale and the retail exchange rates that my brain keeps tabulating and washing down my throat. Expensive taste is hard to swallow if you're a curmudgeon like me, and with each sip the experience becomes ever more bitter and less satisfying. "You could have saved two bucks, that's two beers, if you were back home," my conscience chastises through the smoky din surrounding me. "Four dollars. American money. What would your father say?"

I soon find that what began as a simple attempt to quench my thirst, to enjoy a cold one, and meet someone new, has transformed into an increasingly frantic attempt to drown my self-contempt in the foaming swill before me. I soon order another, masochist that I am, and drift ever downward. It's no good. I'm no good, no good at all. "Sorry, Dad." I down another. Then another. I raise my head off the bar and look around. Whoever it was I was talking to is no longer there. The wench has moved aside, silently sidled away. She's good. She's also gone and I'm going fast. I've lost her and if I don't act fast, I'll lose what little chance I ever had of finding "Miss Right."

I have also lost my mind. Feeling a combination of my wild oats, the brew's barley, yeast, spring water, and damn little else, I have obviously lost what little semblance of a grip on reality I ever had. Buoyed by a false bravado, semiconscious, I try to rise above myself. I attempt the unattainable, try to make up for lost time, and become someone I'm not, never was and never will be. I try to be like everyone else. I fake it, or at least I try to fake faking it. It's not much, but it's the best I can do. I throw caution to the wind and make my move.

I sidle up as best I know how. I sidle up and pause. I wait. I'm not swiped upside the head. Interesting. Bolstered by my success, I sidle again. I wait and again, I feel no pain. Looking back, I should have looked to the side as any accomplished sidler would have done. But an accomplished sidler I'm not. I sidle once more, and pause: again, nothing. I'm on a roll. I sidle a final time, and feel the presence of another next to me. I've found her. Things are going well. Now to toss in a bit of mingling and some witty jargon perhaps. I think of something to say, an opening line, but I realize, there's no time for such nice-ties. It's too late in the evening for such niceties. I cut to the chase and with-out thinking, obviously without thinking, I begin to swoon in as masculine, testosterone-soaked and sexy a voice as I can muster. "You know babe, I got a hankerin' for some pankerin'. What do you say? Your place or yours?" That didn't come out right, but what the hell, it was worth a shot and I took it.

Almost immediately (as in no pause, no wait), I experience something vaguely familiar. Something I take to be a quick left hook, to be exact. I note almost simultaneously both an increasing sense of pain upside my head, and a distinct loss of satisfaction with my present lifestyle. My companion, whom I had assumed was the rather cute and demure young lass with the nice set of gams I had been chatting with, has somehow transformed into a rather surly figure of an apparently happily married logger or lobster man who was clearly not in the mood for some "pankerin'."

I don't remember which he was, but I distinctly recall staring at a pair of rubber boots as they danced merrily upon my skull for, oh, ten minutes or so. I remember thinking that this guy, whatever his profession, was obviously, aero-bically speaking, in great shape and I wanted to compliment him on this and his dancing, but it's hard to speak with a size 13 steel-toed whatever in your mouth, so I let it pass. In hindsight, it's probably just as well as he didn't appear interested in receiving another compliment from me just at that moment.

As I lay shuddering in a pile of sawdust and in what would have been real pain (had I been in a condition where I could feel real pain), I surprisingly found myself tapping my toe in time to the beat of the man's boot stomping my head while a song of unrequited love filtered somewhere from above. I was reminded once again that the price of sidling, not to mention mingling, what-ever it may be, is high, decidedly too high for my tastes and my abilities. I am cheap and I am getting older. I simply can't afford to attempt to sidle or mingle any longer. It was there and then, on the floor of that bar, that I decided I either had to give up drinking or sidling and mingling. For health reasons, I gave up the sidling and mingling. That's it. I know my limits. No more goddamned sidling or mingling for me—not now, not ever, not never!

So, now do you understand why I do my research at home in the safety of my trusted recliner? Given that I'm on my back, with two comfy armrests securely encompassing my body, I am prevented from even the remotest chance of a haphazard attempt at sidling in any direction at all. Besides, I have taken the proper precautions. First of all, I tricked someone into marrying me so I wouldn't have to sidle to begin with. I also decided to avoid polygamy so I wouldn't have to mingle either. And secondly, I swallowed a big dose of reality and self-reflection. I met the enemy and looked me square in the eye. I understand my thinking processes or lack thereof. I know my vulnerabilities and have taken all necessary and appropriate measures to ensure my future success. I am after all, no fool. I don't sidle, and have no need to mingle, ever, not even at home, and especially not while I'm drinking. And did I mention that drinking at home is cheaper? It is. It's also far safer too. I like that.

Getting back to beer and Maine, I can say without hesitation, that the status of beer in Maine is good, very good and getting better all the time. Maine beer is damn good beer. It's as simple as that. I checked out the Internet to determine just how many establishments there were in our fair state producing beer and I was pleasantly surprised to learn that we have a slew of them to be exact (a "slew" being a precise scientific and mathematical term that equates to a number that is both greater than one, and yet slightly less than infinity, leaving unending room for improvement). We have what I like to refer to as "sleweries of breweries," and they process some of the finest "brewskis" this or any other country has to offer. But before we go much further, we need to define exactly what it is we're talking about when we discuss our vaunted elixir of choice.

When talking beer, we must establish certain ground rules and the following are mine. There are two certain and undeniably vital components to any real beer and they are these: alcohol and flavor. All beer must contain alcohol, at least by my definition. This is my book, you bought it, and with that, you bought into my definitions as well. I have your money and therefore I'm persuaded you're persuaded and in agreement with me. If you're not, I don't care. As I said, I have your money. I'll get over the rest. For our purposes, however, we agree that beer must contain alcohol.

Now, the exact percentage of alcohol you can adjust to suit your own taste, but the bottom line is that alcohol must be present. Part of the experience of beer drinking, and no small part I might add if it's to be done right, is to experience the buzz of the brew. Without the buzz, it's not beer. It's just beer-flavored water. Flavored water is fine and while it may have fizz, it's not beer. Technically speaking, its scientific name is Kool-Aid and it's meant for kids and mass suicides only. It's certainly not for me.

The second ingredient of real beer is flavor and it is essential to a beer's true enjoyment. When I was young and dumb, I used to think that all beer was good beer by definition, but that was only until I tasted really good beer. By really good beer I mean beer that tastes really good. Well, that's goes without saying, you may think. You may think that, but you'd be wrong. For a beer to taste really good, it must have flavor. Not all beer has flavor. If you don't believe me just drink any mass-produced American beer and certainly any, and I mean <u>any</u>, light beer. (All mass-produced American beer is light beer by definition, according to my definition of beer, kapish? Case in point: Coors Light is an oxymoron and/or redundant. It's also not beer in my book and this is my book.)

American mass-produced beer is manufactured to exacting standards of excellence that for some reason include the guaranteed elimination of any real beer flavor. I don't know why this is so, but take my word for it, it just is. Most Americans don't realize this because they only drink the same brand of beer at a time, be it Miller, Bud, Coors, or whatever. As the alcohol effect kicks in, to wit, "the buzz," the drinker's ability to discriminate and discern true flavor lessens resulting in a falsified, or "faux" sense of satisfaction. Don't be fooled. Alcohol affects thinking. You only think you're satisfied with the taste. You're not satisfied. You're buzzed. There is a difference.

America's entire mass-produced beer-making industry is based upon getting consumers to literally buy into this false satisfaction by choosing one beer over all others. Once you've fallen for the advertising and have a preference, you'll never know the difference. You'll be satisfied with the buzz alone, but you'll be missing out on the other half of the equation, namely the flavor. And here is the truly sad part of our tale: you will never know what you've been missing until, when, and if, you drink a real beer: that is a Maine made micro brew.

Remember, life is made up of ying and yang, not just ying. Drink just one "yingy" beer after another "yingy" beer you "yingers" you and you will never know what you are missing, namely the yang. Now, drink a "yingy" beer and then a "yangy" beer and whoa! What was that difference? That, my friend, was flavor. So, I say, wise up America. Put down your so-called traditional, mass-produced American beers. They're not worth crying into. That only dilutes an already weak and relatively flavorless beverage. Step up and try some real beer, some truly unique beer. And there is no better place to do this than Maine, because—trust me on this one—Maine has a host of really good beers to choose from. That's an amazing fact, truly amazing given our "hooch" history.

The fact that Maine has become a hot bed of brewing is both remarkable and ironic once you realize that Maine was once one of, if not the most, vigilant of the Temperance States. Perhaps it's exactly because we lost the ability to legally manufacture and imbibe our favorite brews for so long, that we now value and cherish them so much today. As Joanie Mitchell sang, "Don't it always seem to go? You don't know what you've got 'til it's gone." Well, they "banned paradise" from sometime in 1851 until July 1, 1933. That, my friend, is one long, dry stretch of Maine history and I for one am damn glad they parked it.

In point of fact, the stretch was long, for sure, but it wasn't all that dry. Mainers, bless their souls, are not only idealists by nature but they are pragmatists as well. We tend to be tolerant even of the most intolerant that there are. If there were those among us who wanted to attempt the "noble experiment" of banning the manufacture and sale of alcoholic beverages, intolerant as they were, tolerant Mainers were willing to let them have their way. If, on the other hand, there were those among us who wanted to have a drink now and again, well, Mainers, tolerant as we are, were more than willing to look the other way at that as well. In Maine it was possible to have your cake and eat it too. In other words, you could ban your beer and drink yourselves into next Tuesday if you wanted! Life the way it should be and life the way it really was: philosophy in action. What a state!

Today, of course, there is no thought given to banning breweries. The industry flourishes from one end of the state to the other. There are breweries and brewpubs literally everywhere. Each one produces truly unique and flavorful beers and ales of all kinds. I can't begin to list the many varieties of brews from which to choose, but I will mention that you must try some Wild Blueberry Wheat ale. To the best of my knowledge, you can't get it anywhere else.

Yes, as far as I'm concerned, the status of beer in Maine is wonderful and then some. It's like I died and went to Québec, only better. I don't have to go to Mass with a hangover on Sunday morning and miss my son's hockey practice, and I can also somewhat understand the language.

Here's a partial listing of the major breweries here in Maine: Geary's, Kennebunkport, Casco Bay, Allagash, Kennebec, Freeport, Rocky Bay, Sheepscot, Gritty McDuff's, Atlantic, Sea Dog, Shipyard (can you say "Pumpkinhead"?), Belfast, Sebago, Acadia, Sunday River, Sugarloaf, Bar Harbor, Maine Coast, Oak Pond, Sparhawk, Stone Coast, The Granary, Great Falls, and more. You get the picture. It's a big picture. There are a slew of them, as I said before, and catch the buzz; they are all great. If they're not exactly what you like, so what? Try another, or another. Like I said, there's a slew of them and you're bound to find your calling.

So get off your Duff (sorry Homer, but it's a mass-produced American beer) and get out and do your own exploring of the available elixirs out there. Be an adventurer, a Lewis and Clark in search of the next great, unknown beer or ale that awaits you just beyond that yonder towering pub. Go out, find your own Sacagawea and make merry. It's okay. It's legal. Prohibition is dead. Let's all drink a cold one to that. And for God's sake, whatever you do, take my advice and don't attempt to sidle up to anyone or anything. And don't mingle unless you're damn sure you can pull that off too. Trust me on this one. It's the truth and if the truth hurts, don't go there. I know what I'm talking about.

Do vampires bother you? They bother me too, but probably not in the same way. You see my problem with them is this: they're too damn neat. Have you ever noticed how nattily they dress to the nines and how just damn perfect they look all the time? How do they do that? I mean how is it that they are perfectly coiffed, not a hair out of place, not one nose hair protruding, not one whisker not shaved, no ear hair, no lint on their collars, no nothing wrong or out of place at all, ever? How do they manage all that and yet, they can't see their own reflection in a mirror? How do they do it? It's just not possible is it? I don't think it is, and that's what bothers me about vampires. That and they suck

Parking Brakes

Just a thought, but couldn't Floridians save some jingle on their vehicles if they could purchase them without an emergency brake? I don't know a single Floridian who uses their emergency brake anyway, and why should they? It's not like their vehicles are in danger of rolling anywhere. I mean the highest point near my sister's home is a speed bump at the local Publix for God's sake.

Now in Maine, we always use the emergency brake (if it works) no matter where we park because, just like not using the brake, using it is a habit and one not easily broken. For example, when we visit my sister's and her family who live in Cocoa, we borrow one of their vehicles because, well, they're there and I'm cheap. Besides, we're not going anywhere anyway, but we still need a vehicle to get there and renting one involves the exchange of money, signing your name, etc., etc. In short, it's an unnecessary hassle, so we borrow. It's free for me, which makes me happy, and I like to think it makes my sister feel better about herself, as well, you know, being generous and all.

So when we're done "not going anywhere," like to the beach, we head home, park our car behind the one they use, and out of habit, I pull on the emergency brake and we go inside to tell them how much fun we had while they were out working all day. So far so good, but not so good for so long, because eventually night gives way to morning and a new day begins. Inevitably someone, usually two cranky people who have a life and somewhere to go, like to work, disturb my richly deserved vacation sleep and ask me to "fix" the car blocking their exit because for some unknown reason they've started it up, put it in gear and stomped on the gas, but it still won't move, and they suspect I may have had something to do with it.

Now, my sister's been to college and my brother-in-law works at Cape Canaveral on the Space Shuttle program. They live in Florida, but still, even with that, I've never thought of them as idiots. Ed's a computer engineer, a rocket scientist, and you'd think releasing an emergency brake on a car would qualify as well, "not rocket science." But you'd be wrong my friend. It seems they can't release the emergency brake because they don't know what it is, why it is, or where it is. So, I'm lying there, sweating although they have the air conditioning on, and thinking to myself, "Just guessing here people, but I don't think there's an emergency brake on the Space Shuttle. If there were, we'd all have known about it by now."

"Three, two, one and we have ignition and launch of the Space Shuttle Whatever!" Silence.
"Three, two, one ... one ... one." More silence.

"Something's wrong! Something is terribly wrong." The Shuttle is just standing there amid the rocket's intimidating roar, standing there, buried in a swirling cauldron of steam and vapor, vibrating, straining and yet somehow unable to move!

"What is happening? And what the hell is that God awful smell?"

The Canaveral mission launch commander's voice crackles across the continent: "Houston, we have a problem ... again."

"This is Houston," comes the frantic reply, "we copy you. We're working on it as we speak, Frank. We think we've narrowed it down to ... what is that? You're kidding me. Oh, my God no! Someone left the emergency brake on! How could that have happened? This is NASA, for Christ's sake! This is Florida. Why would anyone... Somebody grab a manual and figure out how to release that damn thing before all hell breaks loose. Oh, my God!"

Then, from the Shuttle itself, comes a calming voice of reassurance amid the ever-mounting crescendo of overwhelming chaos. The first ever astronaut from Maine speaks: "Sorry 'bout that fellas, just a little habit of mine don't ya know. I'll just give a flip to this heah toggle and pull this levah some, and theyah!" (The Shuttle, free of its restraints, bursts upward in all its majesty, arcing heavenward.) "We're on our way, ayuh. Now, that weren't so bahd, were it?"

No, I don't think there's an emergency brake on the Shuttle or we'd have known by now.

But getting back to my story, I'm now being rudely awakened from a much-needed beer-enhanced sleep. It's been twelve hours, so I've sobered up some, I mean woken up enough to catch the gist of the problem, and answer sleepily, "Sorry 'bout that fella, just a little habit of mine, don't ya know."

I tell them the emergency brake is on and explain in detail just what to do, but that does no good. They just stand there, slack-jawed, their eyebrows furrowed, and with a dumbfounded look on their faces say in unison, "Huh? What's an emergency brake?"

"It's that levah you engage when you pahk so your cah won't roll away, you idiots," I snap back, clearly annoyed. Their dumbfounded look becomes even more pronounced, even more dumbfoundeder. "Huh? What's 'roll away'?"

So you see, Floridians could save a bundle and stop annoying me if they'd just remove the parking brakes on their vehicles. But what about when Floridians travel out of state, like to New England? "What then?" you ask? Well, it doesn't matter, people. Or should I say I don't care? Using or not using the parking brake is just a matter of habit. They're from Florida; need I say more?

Imagine: A small family shivers on a hot July afternoon in the White Mountains. They're wearing "hoodies" that say "Go Gators" and gloves.

"What are all those people gawking at over there?" the father says to his wife. "Here we are on top of Mt. Washington and they're all looking down instead of out at the beautiful view all around us. What a bunch of morons!" He walks over towards the ruminating throng and speaks out to an old timer who's standing off to the side and slowly shaking his head in obvious disdain. "Hey there, what's all the commotion about?"

The man looks up, puts his hand to his whiskered chin and shakes his head again, this time with a slight grin creasing his face. "Well sah," he begins in his measured pace. "It's the damndest thing, but seems some 'idjit' didn't engage the emergency brake on his vehicle, his cah. Imagine, no emergency brake up heah on the highest mountain in all of New Hampshah, New England fah that mattah. No sah! Must be a 'flatlander,' no doubt 'bout it. Where do folk like that come from, I wondah?"

The father drops his head to avoid eye contact and mutters something under his breath. "Whad'jah say?" the old timer prods. "My hearin' ain't what it used tah be sonny."

The man stops and turns, still avoiding the native's eyes. "I said, 'They're probably from Florida.'"

"Good one!" The old-timer drops his hands to his knees as he bends over, bursting out with a good belly laugh. "That'd fit the bill, some 'idjit' from Florida. I like that. Seems 'bout right don't it?" He raises his voice towards the receding, slumping figure slowly moving away.

"Say, you're a pretty smaht fella you ah. Where ah you from?"

Sports in Maine

Maine is a state that loves its sports, but it's not crazy about sports like, say, Texas for instance, is crazy about football. That may not be the best example for me to use, come to think of it; Texas is just plain crazy, George Bush aside. But I don't want to belittle Texas. I have nothing against Texas, George Bush aside, so I'll leave demeaning Texas to the Oklahomans, or maybe the Louisianans, or the New Mexicans, or the Mexicans for that matter. I want to concentrate on Maine and Maine alone.

I think there are many reasons for Mainers not being insanely fanatical about any one particular sport like football and the reason for this is that Mainers just have too many damn choices when it comes to sports and sporting activities. Why is that? I like to think it's because we are not limited in our thinking. We are also not limited to events that can take place only on flat, relatively dry playing surfaces such as baseball fields, football fields, basketball courts, tennis courts, and bowling alleys. I think that pretty much covers Texas sports. Oh no, I forgot car racing and yeah, shooting things dead. Oh no, I'm bashing Texas again. Oh no, I'm beginning to enjoy it. Oh no, it's too late. I forgot fishing on flat reservoirs and hitting golf balls on flat fairways. There, that's everything you can do regarding sports in Texas. Did I neglect billiards, ping-pong, and darts? Whatever was I thinking? Throwing darts at a picture of George Bush is a popular pastime anywhere. And it's not easy. Just try to get something to stick in his thick skull, even if it *is* only a picture. I don't think you can do it. I think you'd need a "nucular"-tipped dart for that. Sorry George, just kidding. NOT!

Back in Maine we have what are referred to by geographers as "not-flat places." These "not-flat places" enable us to do many things, like go up and down as well as back and forth. This may not seem overly important at first, but it makes downhill skiing, for instance, a whole lot easier what with the hill and all, not to mention the snow. Try skiing on your so-called flat, dry "ranch," Georgie boy. And here's another thought for you to try, just a thought. When you're in Texas and limited to going forward and backward and left to right, but you choose to only go backwards and to the right, you're kind of limiting your options. You might want to consider that the rest of the country moves and thinks in a broader sense with more options. Hell, even NASCAR goes forward and to the left. It's just a thought you might want to consider. I don't want to keep you up at night. It's just a thought. Sleep on it.

In Maine, we also have what we call "different times of the year," or seasons. You may have heard of them. True, we may not have as many of these times as some other states who have say four, but we have more than others like Florida, which has but one, plus that "unusual cold snap" that seems to coincide with every vacation I take there.

Now if you do the mathematics, and I prefer you do it rather than me, you soon begin to understand why Maine's sporting options are so varied. We have three point something seasons, multiplied by the concepts of back and forth, up and down, left and right, over and under, wet and not wet (some call it dry), frozen and thawed, hard and soft, in and out, windy and still, with leaves and without, green and not green (gray and white are other options), with ocean and without, white water and blue (no brown, sorry Texas, you can claim that one), rock, dirt and sand, etc., etc. The end result is that rounding off to the nearest number, as with "brewskis," what we have is a "slew" of ever increasing combinations and choices when it comes to sports and activities.

An exact figure is difficult to ascertain, but I like to go with 3,458 choices depending on which way, and if, the wind is blowing, and if it is, factoring in exactly how hard. If there's a gale flag up, kiting, boating and just plain holding on to your hat are three options that come to mind and the later comes literally off the top of my head. That's a lot of sports and activities to select from, you've got to admit. So, if you come to Maine and can't find something to do, you'd be best advised to have written a living will because I can see someone, an heir perhaps, pulling your plug sometime in the very near future. Know what I mean?

In Maine we have two categories of sports, organized and unorganized. If you've ever witnessed "youngstahs" playing soccer, you'll understand what constitutes an unorganized sport. Kids under ten playing soccer; uniforms, refs, and whistles aside, is unorganized sport. Don't believe me? Just try to coach it.

As for organized sports, and by that I mean ones with clear, precise rules that are enforced by knowledgeable officials and played by honest, ethical and noble participants, well, we don't have them any more than does anyone else. What we do have here in Maine is this: everything else.

We have baseball with the Sea Dogs at Hadlock Field in Portland. Sure they're only double A ball, but they're the mini-Sox, and the field's a mini-Fenway. That's pretty cool in and of itself. Besides, at least you can afford to see them and you don't have to battle traffic for three and a half hours just to sit behind some green support column while you drink an overpriced Samuel Adams beer at the real Fenway. Still, we love the Red Sox and they are our adopted major league team. Do you hear that Steinbrenner? Oh, you can't because you're dead? So sorry about that. Mainers love the Sox. And if there is any curse left in baseball, it's you, dead or not, you and your damn Steinbrenner kids!

We also have, or had (I'm not sure) the Bangor Lumberjacks of Class A ball, not to mention our own Black Bears from UMO. These are the big three, except of course for the Lumberjacks, but I'm feeling generous tonight so what the hell, these are the big three. There's also a myriad of other college (USM has enjoyed great success) and high school teams as well as summer leagues and more, but they're too numerous to mention. True, we sometimes have to shovel snow off our diamonds on occasion, and the ground doesn't really dry up until June, but with the snow and the mud, you don't get any of those cheap Baltimore chops passing for hits. This is baseball the way it was meant to be played, up close and personal, just like Maine.

Now, pay attention, Texas: we also have football, as in the Patriots, three-time Super Bowl Champions. We also have the Black Bears and all you have are the Cowboys, the Texans, the Longhorns, the Aggies, Rice, Baylor, UTEP ... Okay, you win this one. But your water's brown, and who was the last to win a Super Bowl? You or us? I'll you a hint. It wasn't you.

As for basketball, we have that too, what with the Celtics. Ever hear of them? The Celtics? Ever hear of sixteen, count 'em, *sixteen* world championships? You say Boston isn't spelled M-A-I-N-E? You've got education; I'm impressed. Okay, you win this one too, but who was the last to win the NBA Championship, you or us? Okay, let's forget that one and move on.

We move on to the greatest sport of all, hockey. We have it and it's good hockey at that. We have the Maine Black Bears from UMO, Orono and the Alfond Arena, sometime-champions of Hockey East and perennially ranked nationally year after wonderful year. Go Bears! We also have the Portland Pirates, affiliated with the Buffalo Sabres of late and the Phoenix Coyotes of not so late. They play in Portland at the Cumberland County Civic Center. I know that seems obvious, but there are people from Texas trying to read this, so bear with me. No Child Left Behind? Yeah right!

And speaking of hockey, we have my favorites, the Lewiston Maineiacs, of, yes, you guessed it, Lewiston, Maine. They are the only American team in the Quebec Major Junior Hockey League and my own personal pride and joy. I suggested the name, great wit that I am, and received the official honor of having named the team. I know I didn't come up with the name of Maineiacs—I stole it if you must know—but I stole it first, so there.

Anyway, we have the Maineiacs, not just Lewiston, but all of us. And by the way, Maineiacs management, a lot of people think that I won season tickets for life, not just one year. I hate to have to keep telling them they're wrong, hint, hint. You might want to consider a lifetime, two-seat pass for say, any available seat? You don't sell out very often you know. It's just a thought, but you're getting a lot of free advertising here and I would have asked the editor, if I had one, to put the Maineiacs' logo on the cover of the book in anticipation of your making the right choice. I thank you, I truly do. I'll keep bringing the kids too.

As for other sports, but not of a professional or major league stature, Maine abounds with options. We have some of the finest natural brook trout fishing you can find anywhere in the world, as long as you don't look in northern Quebec. We also have landlocked salmon found nowhere else, or at least I'm pretty sure they're found nowhere else, and certainly not in Texas. And unlike fishing in all too many places (can you say Texas?) you can actually see your trophy fish before you pull it out of the water! There's trout, bass (large and small mouth), togue (lake trout for those of you from "away"), perch, pike, pickerel, and so much more. Then there's the Gulf of Maine and the Atlantic Ocean and all they offer the avid angler. Yes, when it comes to fishing, Maine has it all, except for marlin. Marlin and sailfish. Marlin, sailfish, and tarpon. Marlin, sailfish, tarpon, and bonefish. I'm gonna stop now, since I'm getting depressed, but when it comes to fishing, Maine has it all.

Speaking of hunting, we have some of the best, and most of it's legal. In Maine you can hunt for white-tailed deer, antelope, musk ox, caribou, cheetahs and leopards, although you'll likely only see white tailed deer. Still, if you're stupid enough, you can hunt for the others and elephant, as well—you're just not going to bag any. We also have moose. Got any moose, Texas? I don't think so and "Moose" Johnson doesn't count. We have black bear too. Then there are wild turkeys, partridge (read "grouse") pheasants, and starlings. We don't actually have a season on starlings, but it's all right by me if you want to hunt them, them and the elusive red squirrel. They're not necessarily legal game but they're fair game if you know what I mean.

We also have golf here in Maine and yes, you can play with a white ball for more than just the month of July without fear of losing it in the snow. We have caddies you know, and Maine Guides if you've got a real bad slice. We have some really great courses such as Sugarloaf, Sunday River, Penobscot, Falmouth and Samoset to mention a few, and whole bunch of good ones as well. Not only that, they're accessible and most all are open to the public and me too. They're not crowded, either, which is another way of saying we'll happily take your money and actually say thank you for the privilege.

I'm glad someone mentioned water, because we have a whole lot of it here in Maine. Canoeing, kayaking, sailing and motor boating are all real big once the ice melts and, yes, it does eventually melt. We also have fast flowing rivers such as the Penobscot, the South Branch of the Dead River and the Kennebec where you can experience the thrill of white water, white-knuckle and purple-lipped rafting. Yes, the ice eventually melts into water, but it's still not exactly what you might call warm. On the coast, sailing, surfing, sea kayaking, and yachting (provided you can afford a yacht) are all always in vogue. If you can't afford to own a yacht, there's folk who'll rent you one, or take you out on their schooners for day trips. We also have ferries and group fishing boats for those who like to experience the water in, shall we say, a less personal manner. Be forewarned, however, that unless you have your sea legs, take the precaution of ingesting a few seasickness pills before you head out. They might just be your best investment for that trip out on the Gulf of Maine. I know. I didn't take them and I spent four luxurious hours lying on my back, dreaming of the plains states, yes even Texas, and clicking my heels together repeating over and over again, "I wish I were in Kansas, I wish I were in Kansas, I wish." You get the picture, and no, that's not chum the captain spread on the water, that's my breakfast. I don't remember eating that, and my apologies mom. You were right. I guess I really don't chew my food enough.

Maine has so many other activities that I'm just going to gloss over them quickly. We have all the major winter sports such as skiing (both downhill and cross-country), snowboarding, snowshoeing, ice-skating, ice fishing, not to mention snowmobiling and polar bear clubbing. I'm speaking of taking a dip, not slaughtering cute little animal babies, and besides, they're seals, not polar bears. Hit the wrong one with a club and you'll find out what the difference is. We also have tobogganing and even curling if you're so inclined.

There are opportunities for four-wheeling, great backcountry roads for biking and motorcycling, and trails for hiking including the rugged terminus of the famous Appalachian Trail high on Katahdin's crest. We have stock car racing for those of you visitors with a drawl and a twang. We have resorts with pools and hot tubs galore, tennis and yes, even shuffleboard for the over, over whatever, I guess pretty much over-*life* crowd if you come right down to it. We have croquet aficionados too, or at least I recall reading about one once up Bar Harbor way.

Well, that's about all that comes to this limited brain of mine for the time being. I know there is more out there to do and if you can think of it, you can find the opportunity to do it here in Maine. Not only that, but no matter how far-fetched your particular pastime might be, there is likely some nut who lives here who shares the same passion and who'll even be willing to do it with you provided you bring the beer. God knows we have a lot of those and working at Walmart can't be all they do in life.

As for yours truly, I like to think of myself as a competitive drinker of sorts. Stop by and we'll pop open a couple of brews and watch the sun set. Now that's my idea of a sporting activity. Whoa boy, is it ever getting dark out here and it's only three in the afternoon and July. Pass me another one, I'm feeling up for it. I've been training for this all winter long. Pass me another one ... talk about cold, talk about dark.

On a sad note, the Maineiacs have recently disbanded and disappeared from the hockey scene. I miss them now that the weather is turning cold again. I missed them when it was hot too. They're gone and I'm sad. Go Bruins! Stanley Cup Champs for 2010!

If an amnesiac has a second attack of amnesia and then regains his original memories, does he know who he was before he forgot? Or better put, does anyone know if he knows that he didn't know he knew? Don't ask me. I don't know. In fact, just forget I even brought it up.

Marceller Butlah Says Auguster

When it comes to basic Maine-speak, there are a few simple rules to keep in mind. In Maine, words that end in the letter "R" are pronounced as though they ended in "ah," thus "lobster" becomes "lobstah," and "letter" becomes "lettah." On the othah hand, words that end in "A" are pronounced as though they end in "er," thus "idea" becomes "ideer" and "Augusta" becomes "Auguster." Only in Maine and only to a true Mainah, such as my cubby mate Marcella, would the simple sentence "Marcella Butler has an idea for Augusta" be considered a tongue twister, or should I say "twistah"? Now, you try to say the same sentence as she would naturally say it: "Marceller Butlah has an ideer fah Auguster," and that sentence instantly becomes a tongue twistah, at least for the rest of the world. Go figyah.

Now, I have a theory on why true, old time, Down East speaking Mainahs speak the way they do. You know the style of speech we're talking about, the somewhat slow, halting manner sprinkled with pronounced pauses which are often thought by the listener to be used for emphasis or effect. Sorry, not the case. An example would be "That lobstah feller theyah. (Pause.) He's a keepah. (Pause.) Ayuh!" Sounds quaint, doesn't it? Quaint, yes, but if we look closely we see that it is also necessary if you're going to use Maine-speak. Why? Because if you have to constantly change the endings of words, you need some pauses here and there to get it right. Don't believe me? Well just go back to that "Marcella Butler has an idea for Augusta," sentence and try to say it your way and the Mainah's way. Seriously, try it out loud (pause, not for effect, but to give you time to actually say it). All right what did you discover? Two will get you five you discovered your way was not a problem, but Marceller's way was. To say "Marceller Butlah has an ideer fah Auguster," in a rhythmic and timely manner, takes effort. But I think you can do it and here's how, and it's simple. If you slow down and make the attempt like a Mainah would say it, it becomes doable. Now try this: "Marceller Butlah (pause now, just for effect of course) has an ideer, (interject the old standby, and draw it out to a semi-pause), ayuh, (now convert the remaining two words in your mind and finish her off) fah Auguster." There, you did it. Not near as difficult, is it, and you were actually beginning to sound like a Mainah.

The key to the whole process is the use of judicial pausing and the throwing in of the "ayuh" word to buy you time while you convert the rest of the sentence to Maine-speak. As you get better, you'll learn to use other "effect" words and phrases such as "wicked good," or "jissiky." Practice makes perfect, so get to it, keep up the good work and soon you too may be sounding just like a true Mai-nah, ayuh! Now that's wicked good Maine-speak fah an outah-statah, ayuh, wicked good it 'tis!

The Portland harbor area contains an actual working dairy. It is comprised of a few real live fisherman, DeMillo's Floating Restaurant, several other restaurants that would sink if you pushed then into the harbor, and roughly ten thousand small eclectic shops owned by "farmers" dedicated to the milking of the prover-bial tourist from "away."**

Weather or Not

Maine is very much like most of the other states in that we, too, have weather, just usually a little colder than what you may have. And while Maine is unique in general, it is not especially unique in terms of its weather, just a little different. It's those differences that keep life here between New England and the Maritimes interesting and life here in Maine is nothing if it's not interesting.

Now, weather is not something you can avoid unless you live in San Diego, which claims to have the best weather in the whole of the U.S. of A. That may sound like heaven to you, but it would be hell for someone like me. I don't know about you "perfect weather" people, but if there are sunny skies and mild temperatures for most every day of every year, well that's a surefire recipe for driving someone like me to contemplate suicide. The same weather day after day, over and over again? I don't think so. I don't care if it's perfect; it's also perfectly boring. If I wanted to live like that, I'll just stay inside with the thermostat set on 72 and the lights set on a timer: perfect temperature, perfect lighting ... perfectly horrible.

Excuse me, but I'm a human being—sort of. I have emotions that I need to express and I find a palate for that expression painted in the changing weather. To my way of thinking, if warm and sunny is all you want, just take your Valium every morning like One-A-Day vitamins and call it a life. Phone it in for that matter. As for me, no thank you. This may sound crazy, but as my mother once said about Florida, there is such a thing as being "too perfect." I understand now what she meant, though at the time I just racked it up to her becoming a crazy, senile, old coot like I hope to be someday. To put this in a positive way, she was trying to say in her negative way, that to live is to change and vice versa. If everything's always perfect it's not alive: it's plastic. We may like to think that we'd enjoy having perfect weather, but if you have perfection all the time, I'm sorry "it's too perfect," and that as we know from my mom, is not nearly perfect at all. It's not even satisfactory. In fact, for me it's intolerable. Call me a crazy, senile, old coot, but I'd rather be real, perfectly insane and perfectly alive, imperfect though that may be.

Now, weather, in and of itself, is not a good thing or a bad thing, it just is. That is unless it's always perfect and that of course is a bad thing, as I've already pointed out. But, no matter what the weather may be, there's going to be someone who doesn't like it. That's life and that, my friend, you can take to the bank (only you can't put it in the vault and you'll accrue very little, if any, interest). That someone who doesn't like the weather, that someone who is always complaining, the person who doesn't like what normal people like, that person is yours truly: me. Or as the French say, "Heem over zere in zee funny hat drooling."

Don't get me wrong, it's not that I don't like weather, I do. In fact, just the opposite is true. I love weather. I just don't like the same weather or the same weather everyone else tends to like. You know, your typical weather. I like more extreme, more atypical weather. I like the really black storm clouds, or the pure white puffy clouds, or gray, overcast, gloomy clouds you can't see because it's so cloudy, so foggy. I'm fussy. You see, I like to delude myself. I like to think of myself as a complex individual and as such, I have a lot of different moods to fit my different personalities. I've counted over a dozen of me so far. My favorite me is one I like to call "Mr. Contrary." It's an easy mood for me to be in as it comes rather naturally. Ask anyone who knows me and they'll tell you straight up "Yup, he's Mr. Contrary." With me, if you like it, I don't. If you're happy, I'm not. And I'm not alone in this. There are a lot of people just like me. It's just that they won't admit that they're contrary because, well, they're contrary.

Contrary people aside, most normal folk tend to like pleasant weather. You know the kind I'm speaking of, relatively warm and sunny summer days, with an occasional cloud scattered about here and there for that dramatic and inspiring 3-D effect that was so appealing to classical painters and animated movie people. Normal people prefer this kind of weather, but they don't dislike other kinds of weather. They understand that we need rain, they just prefer it not rain everyday. Normal people like to watch the snowfall in winter too, just let's not have too much of it fall at any one time, say like two feet in two minutes. That's not healthy. Normal people like to feel the wind blow in springtime—it "keeps the bugs down"—just let's not have a hurricane while we're at it, or a tornado that can turn that bug into a bullet and pierce your thick skull. And normal people like the cool, crisp nights of fall counterpoised with the sudden warmth of the ever-shortening days, just no killing frosts or ice ages lasting tens of thousands of years—not yet.

You're probably saying to yourselves, "Yeah, yeah, I know all this. Tell me about Maine." Fine, I will, but first I want to say this. I want to make a comment on the weather. I want to comment on the one comment that permeates all comments made by just about everyone commenting on their particular weather just about anywhere. I don't like that comment. That comment irritates me to no end, like my rambling on is probably irritating you. That comment is this, "If you don't like the weather, just wait a minute." That's it, that's the comment and I'm irritated just having written it.

No matter where you go in this country or any other country to that matter, you keep hearing that same saying being said over and over again. It's just spoken with a different accent, or in different language. I've heard it here in Maine, and I've heard it said in Florida. I've heard it in Montana and I've heard it in Arizona. I can't say that I've heard it said in San Diego, but I've never been to San Diego. I've never wanted to go there. I hear it's boring there. Nonetheless, perfect weather or not, I'm sure someone has said it there too, by someone who's contrary, no doubt. I just wish everyone would shut up and stop saying it. Stop saying the saying. I'm just sayin'. I mean it's weather, people, what did you expect? It changes. I get it. We all get it. One minute it's this and the next minute it's that. It's time, it's physics, and it just plain has to be that way. It's the way it is. It's the way things are. That's why we have weathermen or women, or weather people, or whatever. Things start and things stop, it's not all that special. Let's do us all a favor and everyone, please just stop with saying the saying already. All right? Enough said.

Having said that, having said "enough said," Maine weather *can* change really fast, sometimes in a matter of minutes. I've seen it happen. It doesn't usually work that way, but occasionally it does. It's just not worth commenting on. Like the other day, I didn't like the bright sunshine we were having a week ago and being "Mr. Contrary" I made the mistake of commenting and complained to my wife about it. She told me if I didn't like the weather, to just wait a minute, which really ticked me off because I hate it when people say that, especially people who say it just to tick me off like she does. Unlike the weather you see, I'm predictable and my wife knows it. I said, "Fine, I'll wait a minute just to make you happy." And I did. I waited a whole lot of minutes, but guess what, the weather didn't change. It was a nice day and it stayed nice. I tolerated it. I went inside and got myself a beer and the paper and went back out on the deck. I sat it out. It's not like I'm going to kill myself over a sunny day. I knew in a day, or a couple of days, things would change and I'd be happy again. That's it. That's what our weather here in Maine is like. And unless you live in San Diego, I suspect it's not all that different where you live, either.

In general, though, Maine is apt to have rather unique, extreme, complex and varied weather and weather forecasts for the state as a whole, especially when compared to the rest of New England and the nation for that matter, and there are good reasons for that. For one thing, Maine is further north and east than the rest of the other New England states, so for starters, it tends to be colder and, well, more easterly. Keep in mind that being colder is the more significant of the two. We are colder and we are a (relatively speaking) much larger state as compared with any other in the region. When it comes to weather, size matters. If it's raining one place in Rhode Island, for example, it's a good bet you're getting wet if you're outside somewhere else in Rhode Island. Not so in Maine. Since Maine is relatively pretty big, the weather is more likely going to be different in, say, York than in Fort Kent or Calais.

Maine's different in other ways besides size. With a long coastline and a large, deep interior, right there you're going to have two different sets of general weather patterns. The coastal areas tend to have a more temperate climate due to the moderating influence of the waters off in the Gulf of Maine. The interior of Maine, removed from the shore by what we call "distance," has greater temperature extremes, higher highs and lower lows, over the day, and over the course of the seasons as well. The interior climate is also influenced by the elevation of its foothills and mountains, especially in the western region. Most of the coast tends to be at ocean level, especially the beaches. It's just the way it works.

What's so special about Maine is that with the cold and the proximity of the Gulf of Maine, we are far more likely to experience the infamous "nah'eastahs" you've all heard so much about. Nor'easters can herald extreme weather conditions. I like northeasters. That's what they are too, "northeasters." Some weather person came up with the "accentuated" classic Maine "nah'eastahs" and it stuck, but it's not authentic. It's not authentic, but what it is, is a big bad boy of a nasty storm that hangs on and on.

Simply explained, storms tend to move across the country from west to east, as the prevailing winds generally dictate. The winds of a storm turn counterclockwise. When a storm crosses Maine, it heads for the Gulf where it meets up with a storm's best food to snack on –warmer and wetter air—which it not only snacks on, it positively gorges itself on. It reinvigorates itself, turns up the power and like any self-respecting soul who's stuffed to the gills, it tends to burp and belch more than usual. When that belch occurs and the colder air on the land meets up with the warmer, wetter belching air being blown in from the Gulf, carried on the strong winds that blow in from the northeast, you have yourself the ingredients for one big dump of a snow storm if it's winter. You have yourself the makings of a classic "northeaster."

Well, that's it for weather in Maine. It's different than weather in other places, certainly different than, say, Miami Beach, but it's still pretty much the same too. It gets cold, but it gets colder other places. It gets hot, but not that hot. It gets snowy, but other places get more snow. It rains. I guess it's just the combination of what it gets, and the complexity of how it gets it, that makes Maine's weather so special. I like it. You'd like it too. And if you don't, well, just wait a minute. Gotcha!

Fifty State Impressions

1. Maine—"The way life should be."
2. New Hampshire—"The way life shouldn't be."
3. Vermont—Benjamin N. Gerald for President. Think about it. "Love those Teddy bears."
4. Rhode Island—"The 'Why bother?' state"
5. Massachusetts—"Taxachusetts," "Tax-is," "Massholes," etc.
6. Connecticut—"Desperately Seeking an Identity"
7. New York—Should be two states: New York City and the rest of it. Both would prefer it that way.
8. Pennsylvania—"Coal, Corn, Chocolate and Quakers"
9. Indiana—"Answer to the question, 'How far is it from Ohio to Illinois?'"
10. Ohio—"I get it. I know what a Buckeye is; ask me another."
11. New Jersey—"I have never heard anyone say with a straight face, 'I'm hoping to move to New Jersey someday.'"
12. Virginia—"Rebel suburb of Washington, D.C. where they fought the Civil War, y'all"
13. Maryland—"Yankee above 'burb of Washington, D.C."
14. W. Virginia—"Where you're related to all your neighbors 'ceptin' them slickers from town."
15. Delaware—"See Rhode Island, south."
16. North Carolina—"Pine trees, army camps, and cheap cigarettes"
17. South Carolina—"Pine trees, palms, 'South of the Border,' and cheap cigarettes."
18. Georgia—"Squeal like a pig, cause 'crackers' is for real." (P.S. Idea for a really bad t-shirt to be sold in Atlanta: "I'm with Sherman, which way to the sea?")
19. Florida—A nice warm place to die.
20. Alabama—"They're still fighting the Civil War there, and they're still losing."
21. Mississippi—"That's a lot of dogs to fit under one porch, mister; how much for the lot?"
22. Louisiana—"One of kind beats everything else. Katrina was a bitch."
23. Tennessee—"Bourbon, blue grass, Bobby Joe, Billy Joe, Robbie Joe, Willy Joe, Jo Joe"
24. Kentucky—"Where they love fast race horses and slow cousins"
25. Illinois—Lincoln had to be born somewhere.
26. Iowa—Answer to the question, 'What is the one state you've never planned to see?'"

27. Michigan—"Upper & lower, white & black, city & farm, Chevy & Ford"
28. Minnesota—"Did you really count all those lakes? Are there really ten thousand?"
29. Nebraska– "Corn, huskers, Corn Huskers Lotion, and Corn Huskers"
30. North Dakota—"Used only in the question, 'What's the capital of North Dakota?'"
31. South Dakota—Montana is big. Texas is bigger. Why not just Dakota?
32. Missouri—Your arch should span something; that's what arches are for.
33. Kansas—"World's largest producer of 'flat'"
34. Oklahoma—"Is it really so hard to spell that you need a song to help you?"
35. Texas—After George W., I'm wishing Santa Ana had won.
36. Arkansas—"Not quite the sum of all around it, and a little less to boot"
37. Colorado—"South Park and the Broncos; not too shabby, except for the Broncos"
38. Wyoming—Casper should be a ghost town.
39. Montana—"Do you really think your sky is bigger than mine? Really?"
40. Idaho—"I like my potatoes brown and my football fields green, thank you very much."
41. Utah—"Mormons, mountains, more Mormons and Moab"
42. New Mexico—"I'll take Charley Weaver in the lower right corner to win, Peter."
43. Arizona—"Florida without Mickey or a coastline"
44. California—"There's just too many pretty people, in them thar hills."
45. Oregon—"What you thought California was actually like"
46. Washington—"Rain, rain go away."
47. Nevada—"Las Vegas: Disneyland on Viagra"
48. Alaska—"Really big, really cold, really cool"
49. Hawaii—Aloha means "hello" *and* "goodbye." You need some more words in your language.
50. The missing state. Can you guess which one it is? If you can't, I guess we don't need it after all.

Ice Fishing

All you need for ice fishing is ice, some fish, a hole in that ice, some fish for the fish, and a completely different attitude than the one I have. I don't like ice fishing. I'd love to like ice fishing, but I don't. Ice fishing is an affliction to which you are born, not bred. To my way of thinking, ice fishing is a lot like freezing, only with beer. Having heard that, you know I must have some serious issues with ice fishing if I don't like it and there's beer involved. Let me explain.

Maine is a great state in which to ice fish. I mean, we have all the ingredients: the ice, the fish, and good beer. What more could you ask for? I don't know, maybe warmer weather for a start? I know that would wreak havoc with the ice, but hey, there's still the beer, right? And if you brought along some bait fish that were big enough to say eat, well then, it appears to me that you've just completed a successful day of ice fishing and it's time to pack up the traps and head home for another cold one.

But seriously, ice fishing is just lacking, in my humble opinion. I know it's a good excuse to get out and enjoy the weather, but it's winter in Maine, folks, and while I like the winter season as a whole, the daily weather generally sucks. Or more precisely, on an open lake, without cover, it just blows, as in the blowing wind sucks. And where there's wind in winter, there's that damned wind chill factor to be considered. "Wind chill: you've heard of it, now experience it for yourself." Not the best slogan for a hobby that I've ever run across, I must say.

No, standing stiff on a frozen body of water (and I remind you that as humans we are 95 percent water) with your back to a forty mile-per-hour gale, with snow whipping about your frigid face, down your neck, up your back, and you waiting patiently for a flag to jump ... well, no thank you. That's not my cup of iced tea. I don't want to be out on the ice. Isn't this exactly where the Eskimos send their elderly when it's time to ring the doorbell to St. Peter's gate? That is not my idea of a good day's fishing. It's more like thermostatically challenged masochism with a demented twist of frozen lemon. You know the old saying, the one on all the hats and ceramic wall plaques: "A bad day fishing is better than a good day at work." Well, as far as I'm concerned, "a good day ice fishing is worse than a bad day at work," and there are times I don't like my job all that much either. What I do like is having ten bendable fingers and a nose that doesn't resemble Michael Jackson's; mostly white, half missing, and clearly headed for dead.

Then there's the matter of equipment. People say that ice fishing is an inexpensive hobby that the entire family can enjoy. Hogwash! Believe me, there's money involved here, my friend, real money if you do it right and I can tell just by looking at you that you're a first rate kind of guy who does everything right. You have class, standards you live by. You bought this book didn't you? Well, didn't you? No? If you didn't, I take it all back. You suck, but don't take it personally, that's just my opinion and what do I know? I'll tell you what I know. I know you and your ilk by just looking at you and take it from me, you suck.

But getting back to ice fishing and first class fishermen unlike yourself: as with any hobby, you need special equipment. I didn't know this at first and being a fly fisherman (flies emerge when it's warm, like me), I spent many an hour trying to cast a sinking nymph into a ten-inch pool of rapidly freezing water. Needless to say, I didn't catch any fish, but my casting accuracy improved immensely. Eventually I wised up and employed the use of a flag. It made for a much better target, but still I caught no fish. Being no fool, I soon (and by "soon" I mean within a matter of but a few short weeks) picked up on the difference between fly and ice fishing and changed my methods.

First off, I found that it pays to put down the fly rod and buy some ice fishing traps—good ones, not like the ones I bought from the discount dollar store. The ones I purchased were made in Guatemala, not exactly a hot spot famed for its ice fishing. For one thing, the flags were white, which is not a real good strike indicator against a backdrop of ice, snow, and angry, prowling polar bears. Of course, if you're surrounded by a nasty crowd of angry, prowling Guatemalan ice trap builders whose sales have fallen flat and who want to take out their frustration on the nearest gringo (meaning you), that white flag might just be what you need. But save yourself the time and trouble; cough up the few extra pesos and steer for the traps with the red flags, the cheap red plastic flags.

How many traps will you need? Well, when it comes to ice fishing, the more the merrier, I always say. That's the theory behind buckshot, isn't it, and that works just fine for red squirrels and unsuitable suitors. When shooting red squirrels or ice fishing, chancing overkill is not a bad way to go. So, you'll purchase a smattering of traps, but since you're an adult and you're honest (I may be assuming a lot, but what the hell, this isn't golf and there's no money involved), you're only allowed five traps per person according to your fishing license and last time I looked, you're just one person so you're limited to five, count 'em, *five* traps. Not fair I grant you, but not to worry; no problem either. This is where the concept of wholesome family fun comes into play.

With kids around, lucky you, you now are entitled to five more tip-ups for each child on the ice. Sure, you may have to plan ahead some for your winter safari, and this can take years of hard work, but with perseverance and fortitude, not to mention those long, cold winter nights under the covers with the missus, in no time at all you'll have three or more little cherubs to drag out onto the ice with you. With an additional three sports in tow, you've now got a fighting chance to catch a real Maine trophy fish. Three kids! Oh, and a wife. Did I mention you'll probably have to get married, too? You know your mother has expectations, not to mention your wife's father, and besides, you only get married once. Did I say once? Yeah, right! Did I say inexpensive hobby? Yeah, right! But hey, suck it up. Catching a woman and having kids was why you dodged the buckshot in the first place, wasn't it? Yeah right!

There might be some other paraphernalia you may want to have as well, things like an easy means of making a hole in the ice, your dog and dog food, bait fish and a bait bucket, good beer and lots of it, an ice strainer to keep your holes clear, lip balm, snowshoes, a jigging pole and lures to occupy your time while waiting for another beer, extra hooks, tackle and line, a cook stove, a cooler full of food to be cooked, more good beer and lots of it, your wife to do the cooking, plates, cups, utensils and napkins (remember your wife? She's neat) a radio, extra clothing, (Did I mention beer?), hats, gloves, boot warmers, sunglasses, a snow shovel to reach the ice to make the holes, matches, and I don't know, maybe some more beer just in case the fish aren't biting. I know there's more, but that's all I can think of at the moment.

Okay, you've got your family and you've got your traps, your associated paraphernalia, and you're all set to go. What more could you possibly need? Well, for starters, you need to somehow get all that stuff out to the lake and then out there onto the ice where you can make use of it, you idiot. And, as your dear wife reminded you the last time you attempted to literally drag her and the family out for a fun day of quality bonding, you can't expect the kids to actually walk out onto the lake and back again. After all, they look like three Charlie Browns, unable to bend at the waist, bundled up as they are in the finest L.L.Bean winter fare Leon and his clan has to offer.

And you thought you'd pull them out on a toboggan! That's right: "pull" as in "drag." Ha! You'd best think again, Mr. Admiral Perry. How many trips would it take with you hitched up like an ox to that toboggan to drag out the kids, the paraphernalia and the food, not to mention the beer? Too many, that's how many. Yes, you'd best think again, and think hard.

Luckily, you're a good thinker and you planned ahead. No, you didn't want to, but you were going to have to buy yourself a snowmobile sooner or later anyhow so it might as well be now. You're gonna need one since there are five of you and the dog. Did I mention the dog? I think I did, but if I forgot, I apologize. There is always a dog here in Maine. And come to think of it, you'll need two snowmobiles. They're not that long. Of course then there's the snowmobile trailer, the toboggans to load and tow, the 4x4 vehicle, etc. You get the picture and the picture is a group photo of smiling ex-presidents if you know what I mean and I think you do. (Reacquaint yourself with the chapter on snowmobiles if you don't.) You haven't hit the ice yet, but you've certainly got yourself a good head start on a nice, adult, toy collection you can be proud of.

So there you are, finally, out on the ice, just you and every other well-intentioned fool and their reluctant families, all out to have themselves a memorable, wholesome day of good, clean, healthy winter fun. Well, good luck!

Did you remember to bring the ice auger? Yes, that's the sound, that chainsaw-like sound, you've been hearing off in the distance. No? You thought you'd save a few bucks on the power auger and go with a V8 or a Hemi instead of the standard six. Good choice for a truck, but you're on the ice now, on the ice with nothing but a freakin' metal chisel and a hammer. Nice try. Good thinking. First of all, time-wise, it takes exactly, well not *exactly*, but damn near "forever" to chisel a hole through the ice, any ice, by hand. In fact, my first experience with ice fishing was limited to just this, chiseling out one measly hole. It's amazing how much you can learn from one little hole, but if you're stupid enough in the first place and smart enough in the end, you can learn a lot.

But let's say you're tougher than I was and you actually stick it out and chip a hole all the way to liquid water. Then what? Well then you can scoop out the floating ice chips with your strainer and take a peek down your little porthole to heaven. What do you see? Togue? Salmon? Brookies? Not likely. What you're likely to see is a lake bed littered with chisels that somehow slipped through their frustrated owners' frozen hands, or were slyly and simply dropped through the ice where they are now lying, rusting. If you learned anything and are smart in the end, you'll add one more to the collection. And by the way, you didn't really pay attention to the fact that ice water lurks below the ice, did you? Well, it does, and it's cold, damn cold. It's a fact that won't be lost on you either, as your gloves quickly begin to solidify around your quickly numbing fingers. Having fun yet? No? You soon will. Trust me, you haven't even started to have fun.

So, smart man that you are, you've lost your chisel and have but one hole to set all your many traps in? Not to worry, ice-fishermen are a friendly breed. They'll soon notice your plight and come over to stare and laugh at you with their buddies over a cold beer. Did I say laugh at you? I mean *with* you. Sure I do. Anyhoo, once they've stopped politely chortling and pick themselves up off the ice, someone will soon offer to drill you a few holes. Not the twenty you had in mind when you set out, but a few, just enough to get you started. Let's say five if you're lucky, but hey, you've had nothing but good luck so far, so why should it change now? Good thing you brought along the kids and the wife, isn't it?

As for the holes, you won't have to pay the others for drilling them for you. They're happy to do it. It gives them something to do. You see, ice fishermen are a friendly breed for a reason and that reason is this: once you've managed to set your traps, there's nothing, and I mean absolutely nothing, to do. You just stand there, open a beer, drink and wait, and open, drink and wait and sip and wait, and wait.

Here's where the family enters the picture again. You've got kids. And since you didn't get to set their traps, they are useless to you—useless and worse. We all know how much children like to do nothing than stand, stand and wait, wait and watch you drink, and wait. If any kid has ever told you they like to stand and wait, there's medication and a truly gifted therapist involved. To a kid, ice fishing is like one long, cold, miserable time out: standing and waiting, waiting and standing, waiting, waiting. They're too young to drink, remember. For them, the only noticeable difference between being punished and going ice fishing is that with ice fishing, there's no corner to stand in, just the cold, the blowing wind, and the waiting. If there were a corner, they'd all gladly huddle in it to get out of the wind, but there isn't. What were you thinking? You're cold now too, but were you that numb before you actually went out on the ice? Did you actually think kids would like this sort of thing, would take to this kind of "fun"?

Well, surprise, Einstein; they don't like it, they don't take to it, and they are not afraid to let you know, either. What are you going to do? Punish them? How? Make them stand in time out? Nice try. You couldn't even swat them on the bottom to get their attention if you wanted to. With ten layers of fleece enveloping them amid the roaring gale you'd have to write them a note to let them know what you're trying to do.

You look at your brood, standing there, waiting, shaking, and yes, now they're crying, their tears freezing halfway down their reddened, wind burned cheeks. You try to apply that lip balm you brought along, apply it to their entire exposed faces, but just like their faces, it's frozen solid too. Your wife makes you check them for frostbite. Nothing, thank God. No frostbite; they're just frozen. They're fine, they're good to go, and I do mean go. The thought of their leaving has crossed your mind more than once because the kids have been shouting their intentions since you began to drag them out, and I'm talking out of bed, not onto the ice. The chanting only got louder with time, but now it's strangely silent and you notice the only sound is that of the wind. An icy chill passes up and down your spine. You feel it stab through your down coat and layers of clothing. Your wife!

You turn around and the icy glare stops you cold. And then there's your wife looking at you. She's done trying to light the damn, paltry gas stove that the howling wind keeps blowing out. She's muttering something about the next time she and the kids will be going ice fishing, muttering something about the end of the world and hell freezing over. You're running up another bill, my friend, adding to the tab that's going to come due for the rest of your life.

You try to avert your eyes. Glancing downward, they fall upon your faithful dog. You notice he's glaring at you too, staring with a strange glint in his eyes, a glint you've never seen before. You wonder why you never noticed just how long his white, canine fangs were until now. You wonder what he's thinking. You hope it isn't something like he could be lying in the sun on the porch, or in front of the wood stove, if only you weren't so hell bent on playing Nanook of the North. You hope that, but you know better.

And suddenly in the midst of all this joy, it comes to you. Maybe now would be a good time to suggest to the wife and kids that you call it a day, gather up your traps and paraphernalia and maybe think about heading back home. You start to gather some stuff to get the ball rolling and turn to tell them your thoughts, expecting to see some sign of appreciation on their faces, but when you pivot around and up, all you see of your family is their snowmobile slowly, silently receding into the distant white distance.

There you are, alone on the ice, just you and the silence of nature at rest, hibernating. It's just you, nature, and that odd, strange growling sound that seems to be getting louder and louder. What is it that? What can it be?

"Whoa boy! Good doggie. Good boy."

So there you have it. That's Ice Fishing 101. Sound like fun? Well, if it does, try a dose of Prozac. Prozac, "it's good for what ails ya" and if that sounds like fun to you, trust me, *something* "ails ya." Come to think of it, there must be a whole lot of people on Prozac in Maine and especially in the winter, because there are a whole lot of fishermen out on the ice come Sunday afternoons in February. There must be something that lures them onto the frozen lakes and ponds that you've missed. There must be something that keeps them contented and satisfied and coming back for more. And I think I know what the secret is: it's the ice shacks.

Now, I know what ice shacks are for and why there are so many of them. At times there are veritable villages of ice shacks on some, if not most, of our lakes. They are often laid out in grids with actual streets and parking lots. There are vehicles in these towns as well. Snowmobiles are there for sure, but there are also cars and trucks. Some loonies have actually tried to bring wood skidders onto the ice, and got an excellent view of rusting ice chisels for their efforts. But aside from the occasional large hole, mostly there are ice shacks out on the ice.

These ice shacks run the gamut from rustic, makeshift huts to, well, what would pass for a fine, stout home in some sections of Florida. The worst look like temporary outhouses but without the scent and atmosphere. The best may have wood siding and be cedar shingled, but most are likely covered with foam insulation, silver foil and Tyvek house wrap. Most all have a wood or gas stove and a stovepipe exiting the roof unless the inhabitants are into smoking their catch. There's likely as not to be a generator purring away just outside the front, and, for that matter, only door. The generator is there to power the TV. The shack also has a window, usually a very small window, for occasional glances out to check the traps for flying flags, not to mention a table for playing poker and cutting sausage and brats. There's obviously no need for a refrigerator what with the ice and snow. And did I mention, there is usually beer, cold beer. By the way, do you know why ice fishermen put their beer in a cooler? Here's a hint: it's not to keep it cool. It's just the opposite, actually: to keep it from freezing. That's what the cooler's for. So, what exactly is an ice shack for? Well, the short answer is that it's for men; single men, men who wish they were single, and maybe a good buddy or two, as in a good drinking buddy.

As I understand this, an ice shack is just another way of saying clubhouse. It's a refuge for grown-up boys where they know they are safe, hidden in plain sight from the rest of the prying world, meaning their wives. It's a place where they can go to get away from the daily grind—the daily grind and their three yapping kids. It's like Las Vegas on ice; what goes on in there, stays in there. There is no way on God's sweet, frozen earth that any wife and any kids are ever going to venture out on the ice again; not now, not ever, not never. Not after what you and every other fine figure of a father has put them through.

Everyone thought you were crazy when you said you wanted to take your brood out ice fishing lo those many years ago! Wholesome family fun my sweet @#$! But now? Perhaps that's the whole point! Crazy? Crazy like a fox! "Pull that trap," you say to your other single male friends, each with no family in sight. "Think we've caught another? By God, you were right. Yes sir! This one's a sixteen-ouncer! Let me get my measuring mug. Yup, she's a 'keepa!' And is she ever cold! Pass the Cheetos and turn up the sound, ole buddy. I can't hear the game. Brady did what? No way! Go Pats Go."

You, know, I'm beginning to think I may have been wrong about this ice fishing thing. I may have judged it unfairly, been a little too hasty in my thinking. I might just be able to acquire an affection for this sport after all. And who knows? Maybe, just maybe I'll learn to love it. After all, any sport that involves beer is a sport I'm willing to try, and try, and try.

How to Dress Like a Mainer

Here's the thing of it. If you consciously try to make the effort to dress like a real, true-to-life Mainer, you've already failed. You can't think and dress yourself at the same time and be a true blue Mainer. That takes too much effort and we Mainers don't have either the time or inclination for that. What we do have is the inability to care and that makes all the difference. We don't care and within that secret, you will discover the key to dressing like us. Ask a Mainer how to dress like one and they can't tell you. They're not trying to be coy or tight with their words like some "Bert and I" character. They truly don't know because they don't care and they don't think about it, ever. Try to look like a Mainer and, well, you just can't get there from here. It just won't happen. What will happen is that you will begin to resemble the preppie types that frequent stylish magazines and pass themselves off as real Mainers. Them you can look like if you try. Go 'head, by all means.

To dress like these mostly mythical people you have to have class and style. Few Mainers I know, myself included, have that kind of class, or any kind of class for that matter, and we all lack style, any style. Style doesn't travel well from the big cities. Those that want to think they have both, live in a narrow belt just to the north, west and down east of Portland and its immediate environs. I think that about covers it; anything else is on water, be it fresh or salt. This is where the "summer folk"—the preppies and the small number of actual Mainers who actually do dress like faux rustic models—this is where they live. There are a few notable exceptions to the general rule, but none of any note. Have you seen the way some of our elected reps dress? Do you see what I mean? Some of us try, but let's face it: we can't cut it.

Let's try an experiment starting from the ground up and dress like a Mainer, mythical style, and compare that to what real Maine people wear. Keep in mind, Maine and money are not synonymous and that fact plays a role of great importance in how we dress.

We'll begin where the rubber meets the road: footwear. If you were to believe those fashion mags, all Mainers wear either L.L.Bean hunting boots or dock shoes and they wear them all the time. It just ain't so, people. It's not that we don't like L.L.Bean hunting boots and dock shoes, we love them. But what we tend to wear when we wear those particular shoes, are spin-offs, knock-offs or just plain offs from China. In fact, by and large, if the truth be known (and that's what we're here for, the truth, isn't it?), most Mainers wear sneakers and they wear them year round. And our favorite brand of sneaker happens to be the one that's on sale on the day we stumble across it. Except for the kids, and that goes without saying, it's price that determines what a Mainer wears more than style or what's in fashion. We don't mind being in fashion, mind you. We're not against it, but that's secondary to say the least. If you keep price first in your mind when you shop, you will begin to understand how we Mainers really dress and why so little we wear seems planned and coordinated much less in style or fashionable.

It should be noted that during the month of summer, some Mainers will be seen wearing sandals. We prefer the simple foam rubber, one or two-dollar kind that come in all colors as long as they're hideous. If we do wear a more expensive variety of sandal, likely as not, we wear them with socks. It's the class thing, or lack thereof, again rearing its ugly head.

Let's move on to socks. Wannabe's take note: socks and underwear are in the same category and, basically, we don't care about socks. I myself wear gray athletic socks all the time. Everything goes with gray and if it doesn't, so what? They're socks. You can't see my socks and if you're noticing or trying to notice them, you've got a problem and need professional help.

Underwear is in the same category as socks. It doesn't really matter unless if you're over, say, fifteen and/or not married. If you're under fifteen and married, well, that's another subject altogether and likely involves a probation officer and community service if you're lucky. As a kid, who cares about underwear? In fact, as a kid we'd all wear the same pair of underwear everyday if we could get away with it, but we can't and that's why we own at least two pair of underwear if not more.

As a married person, again, we don't care. It's not like we're out to impress anyone. Hello, we're already married. If we even begin to pay attention to our underwear then our spouses become immediately suspicious of us and that's just not worth the hassle. Once they're married, women move on to losing the thongs and "skimpies" that ride uncomfortably up their butts, and move on to those tent-like things that you once saw billowing in the breeze on the clotheslines in the neighborhood and that you thought as a kid only your grandmother or Mrs. Mullins wore. You, my friend, were oh so wrong. When you look out on the clothesline now and are greeted by what look like multi-colored tents flapping like some kind of Central Park artwork what's-his-name concocted, you, my man, are being subtly reminded that you are oh so married. Never forget, lest the reminder becomes not so subtle, as in upside the head.

As for married men, we have a choice to make: briefs or boxers, boxers or briefs. Price is not what we choose by, because as men, we really don't shop for underwear or much else. Our wives do this for us, as in "I got you some underwear. You needed them and they were on sale at Reny's." Like I knew either of those things. As a result, I myself wear some of both. I guess my wife thinks I might like to mix things up and be spontaneous, but there's more and you may not want to know this. I've discovered that briefs need to be changed on a daily basis or at least in some kind of a reasonable time frame. Briefs are prone to skid marks and as such, tend to be more, how shall we say this, odor-challenged than boxers. Boxers can also be so challenged but being 1) roomier and airier, and

2) colored with a print, they can easily double the brief's shorter staying power and can last up to three days with a little care and preventive maintenance. It may be more than you want to know, but I thought you should know it.

Time to cover up and pull on a pair of pants. Khakis, corduroys and even the infamous gabardine are all fashionable, permanent creases or not. If you're a state worker like me, or another "professional," then you're kind of restricted to wearing the above, but only during the workweek. We wear them, but we don't buy where the "fashionistas" shop because they cost too much. If they are from some famous store, they were either a gift from someone who lives "away" and bought them from a catalog, or my wife picked them up at an outlet store in Freeport or Kittery. Outlet stores, it's where Mainers tend to do their brand name shopping. In fact, I'm on a first name basis at most seconds shops.

On weekends and/or vacations, most Mainers all dress the same and yes, you guessed it, we all wear blue jeans. They're acceptable, they're functional, and they're always on sale somewhere. Blue jeans can be worn washed or not, with holes or without. We don't care. It should be noted that blue jeans are mandatory if one is attempting to imitate the "crack" effect so well known throughout the rest of the nation. The effect is attained through use of the basic blue jean, carpenter variety preferred, coupled with the extended belly/no ass body type so prevalent here in the far northeast. Squatting is recommended for full effect coupled with an occasional bounce on the heels.

By the way, old time Mainers occasionally still wear those woolen green or red-checked pants, but count yourself lucky if you come across an actual walking pair. And for Pete's sake, don't ask the wearer if the pants itch. It's a stupid question and a moot point. There's usually woolen underwear beneath them. Just let him climb into his Buick or rusty pickup and leave him be. Besides, he probably didn't hear you anyway and beware the cane; it's as much a weapon as a tool. And if he's wielding the gold capped Boston Post Cane, please, don't make any loud noises or sudden moves or you may be trying to rinse the taste of Fixodent out of your mouth following a bout of CPR. Consider yourself warned.

The only potential rival to the above mentioned pant types are worn by the totally fashion-oblivious Mainers who stick to their tried and true sweatpants regimen. In the sweatpants category I, of course, include the ubiquitous stretch pants as well. Husbands and wives often share in the wearing of these fashion non-statements and interchange their favorites as "one size fits all," whether it does or not, thus doubling their wardrobe while halving their costs. Sweatpants can be worn to all social functions except weddings, but look best on those cruising the aisles in handicapped motorized chairs available at selected large chain stores. As with boxers, the proportion of sweatpants in your drawers decreases proportionally the projected use of your washing machine. Thus sweatpants save you money all around. Wardrobes that are sweatpants-heavy can be coordinated with designer sweatshirts including but not limited to those touting Elvis, NASCAR, your favorite beer or rock band, last year's festival somewhere, the Dallas Cowboys, and "I'm with Stupid." I don't believe L.L.Bean carries a line of "sweatwear." I don't think that's the market share they want to cater to. It may not be top of the line-ish, but it sure as hell is Maine-ish.

Short pants are another fashion item that actually don't translate well here in Maine. Here, shorts are primarily "cut-offs." We have no need for formal, khaki, trendsetting and sophisticated Bermuda's except along the coast, and take note, those folks will be wearing the dock shoes as well. Warning: do not under any circumstances approach anyone wearing Bermuda khakis revealing bony knees, tall black, elastic socks, L.L.Bean hunting boots, a Hawaiian shirt, and a hounds tooth hat. These people are best left alone. There is nothing you can do for them. It is too late.

Getting back to shorts, as Mainers, we have no need for machine-made shorts because as every Mainer knows, that's what old blue jeans are for. Our drawers are full of potential shorts. When your wife won't let you wear your jeans any longer, out come the scissors and voila! We wear cut-offs as shorts and we wear them as bathing suits, both men and women. You must wear underwear with cut offs while swimming to get the authentic "falling out the bottom, hanging over the top," effect that only soggy underwear affords.

Shorts in Maine are also not just for summer. Pass any bus stop in mid winter and you'll understand my point. Someone, usually a chunky someone, will be wearing those baggy, mid-calf half pants and a t-shirt. That's all. Snow can be falling and the temperature in the single numbers. It makes no difference. Don't think about it. Chances are whoever's dressed this way didn't either. It's just Maine; accept it.

Belts in Maine are optional, given the numbers of sweatpants that typically come complete with either elastic waistband or drawstring. Professional dress, such as khakis, are worn with narrow, quality belts, the kind you may find in L.L.Bean. White belts are restricted to foreigners, Pat Boone wannabe's or those who are "from away," only. You must prove you are a member of AARP to purchase such an accoutrement. Having spotted a white belt, take the time to look around and you will usually spot a large tour bus somewhere nearby as well with a bus driver standing to side having a smoke. Blue jeans may be worn either without a belt for the famous Maine "crack" effect, or with a wide belt and a huge belt buckle denoting you as some kind of aficionado of something or other. The larger your buckle, the more likely some kind of trailer is attached to your vehicle. Rope belts are "verboten" although I must admit out of necessity on more than one occasion I've headed down Little Abner's road towards the "holler."

Maine shirts are puzzling to me. There are just too many options to categorize. L.L.Bean has made inroads here but so has everyone else. As Mainers, we are not at all distinctive regarding our outerwear shirts. We wear whatever we like to wear, but keep in mind, we like what's on sale so you may see just about anything that can be stitched together, and I mean anything.

One thing we do the same, is that we all tend to wear undershirts, but not the muscle kind. Muscle shirts are restricted to those below the Mason Dixon line, or below an IQ of 63, or more than likely both in my humble opinion. In my experience, the two usually coincide quite nicely. We in Maine prefer the pocket shirt for some reason and I think that reason is that pocket shirts can be worn in many social settings. Pocket shirts are like the salt of fashion; they are that basic to our lifestyle. They're great for work, either on the farm, in the woods or at a construction site. They're great around the house for informal lounging. They make fine summer sleepwear. They're ideal for wearing under a more formal shirt as at the office or at church precluding the necessity of changing into another shirt when you get home and strip. They can be worn as a golf shirt provided you don't belong to a club. And last but not least in Maine, with a pocket shirt, you have the option of carrying your smokes in the pocket, or if you're really cool, rolled up in the sleeve. Try that, Mr. Muscle shirt. Oh right, no need; you chew.

Other Maine shirts are the printed logo t-shirts that are universally worn everywhere on Earth and will likely be found on aliens and wherever life exists in the universe and beyond. These shirts are by law sold as three for ten dollars or four dollars apiece at gift shops everywhere. They carry the same logos as sweatshirts and then some. They are often stained, warped or otherwise unsuitable for daylight except around the house or on vacation. And best of all, they make great gifts for friends and relatives "from away."

Where Mainers truly express themselves is in their outerwear, as in coats and jackets. Here L.L.Bean has tapped into reality somewhat. A lot of us ski, so we wear those jackets made of non-tearing fibers with tall collars, lots of pockets, a removable liner and Velcro sleeve cuffs. We also put a ski tag from Sugarloaf, Saddleback, or Sunday River on the zipper pull just for the effect. That way you others will know we're for real and not faking it even if we've only been to Sugarloaf once, just to get the tag, and we usually ski closer to home (like Titcomb in Farmington in my case).

We don't, however, tend to wear windbreakers. I think that's because windbreakers are for spring and we don't have spring here in Maine. What we like is fleece. Fleece is great. I think it's made from the wool of mountain "sheece," but I'm not sure. Whatever it's made of, fleece can be made into anything and anything that's made of fleece we will buy. We have fleece gloves, hats, neck-ups, vests, jackets, and coats. I don't know if anyone's made fleece underwear, but I'd buy it if they did. I'd estimate its staying power in the two-day range, somewhere between briefs and boxers. Its comfort rating, however, would carry it into a range bordering on the obscene. Oh yeah, I'd buy a pair or two of fleece underwear and oh yeah, I'd be smiling.

On our heads, Mainers are again a varied lot. Very few of us wear yellow rain hats like lobstermen supposedly wear, so get that picture out of your head right now. If we're bald, we tend to wear a hat regardless of our profession. If we're bald and a professional we try to wear a distinctive hat such as a houndstooth that lends a certain amount of panache to bolster our aura. If we're bald and regular Mainers, or just regular Mainers, we wear baseball hats. We don't wear baseball hats that say anything about Maine on them. You don't do that if you live here. Our hats have a red B on them. That's it. And unless you're young, and by the way, you young people, you're wrong, we wear them the way God intended, brim to the front, squared up and rolled to perfection. If you think you're cool, go ahead and just move to New York and get it over with. You'll be back and your cap will be on the way it should be. As for the rest of us, if we're older, we also wear those hats with the name of our ship on the front, provided we were in the Navy of course. They're okay too. They're even more than okay. Of course there are some nuts among us, those who wear huge Russian fur hats while snow blowing the driveway or skiing, but hey, let's not talk about me.

To sum up our dress, we Mainers don't, as a rule, wear raincoats (true down east slickers aside), we do wear ski jackets with identifying slope tags, we wear baseball hats, we don't wear a lot of leather (motorcyclists being the exception, and they're mostly Hogs), we do wear a lot, and I mean a lot, of fleece, and we layer, we do wear blue jeans, we don't wear much madras (me being the exception, the cheapness factor is unavoidable), we do wear pocket shirts, we have mixed feelings about bathing suits, we do wear sweaters and turtlenecks, we do wear underwear (maybe for too long, but we wear it), we don't wear as much flannel as we used to (see fleece), we wear pastels and faded clothes (but we didn't buy them as pastels and faded clothes, to us, faded is earned, not bought), and above all else, we like to buy what is on sale, but not necessarily what is cheap. It just has to be a bargain.

To that end, we like to shop at outlets and "seconds" shops. The first choice of many Maine shoppers is to shop "seconds." "Seconds" are "seconds" because of a small flaw in the manufacturing, such as they're missing a sleeve, the number of buttons and buttonholes when divided into one another results in a fraction, or they spelled "Maine" with two "N"s. Please note: there are two things you must do if buy a "second." First, you must tell everyone you have purchased a "second." You can't try to pass it off as something expensive and good. Second, you must point out what the flaw is that made your item a "second." And second, you must by law tell everyone both how much you paid for your "second" and how much you saved by buying it. That's one first and two seconds, but I don't care. You must do both of these things—all three of them, in fact. It's the law. It maybe an unwritten law, but it is still the law and while you can't be arrested, well, word gets around. It's a small world up here. And please, no, none of this is offensive to anyone here. This is Maine. It's expected of you.

So there you have it: a quick guide to dressing like a Mainer. Still confused? Still not sure what to wear? Just bought a lot of great stuff, quality and bargains all, but nothing matches? Why I think you're beginning to get it. Now just totally give up trying and begin not to care at all and you'll almost be there. When you don't notice what you're wearing anymore, when you just put on what you've got because it's yours and it's there, when you don't think at all while you're getting dressed, then, then you will be dressing like a Mainer. Dressing like a Mainer requires a kind of Alzheimer's gift of fashion sense. You're getting close when your wife says, "You're not going out like that, are you?" Yes, you're getting close. But the magic comes when you get there. When you *both* get there. And when you get there, it won't matter because when you get there, you won't know it. Then again, once you're there, you won't care, either.

I want to here and now apologize for any untoward remarks that may have been taken in context or even the wrong way. I intend no insult to any company, its minions or its products and none should be assumed. In fact, I wish I owned more of them myself; the products, not the minions, that is. My point is that while Maine is catching up to the rest of the country in terms of wealth, for the most part, we're still not there yet. I'm sure in time we will all be able to dress in the tastefully, well tailored and rustically casual mode that the rest of the country thinks we wander about in, but for many of us, that time has not yet arrived. Still, if the truth be known, as regards L.L.Bean, I really like them and as a Mainer, I'm proud of what they represent; the very best Maine has to offer: quality and integrity. Besides, if you buy the right stuff and it breaks or wears out or you just don't like it, you can usually bring it back and get another. Try that with your in-laws and you know who. See where that gets you. I know where it got me and trust me, I'm not going there again.

Cold, Maine Cold

"Cold" is a relative term, which is to say that it's a distant cousin to the term "hot." They're not exactly blood relatives, but they're in the same relative family. They get together infrequently in early summer or early fall for a rare, comfortable reunion that is known in Maine as, "Who'd a thunk it'd be this nice a day?" When you talk about Maine, in most folk's minds you're talking about cold and, for comparison sake with most other states, that is a fairly accurate assessment of our climate. Maine is cold, or at least colder than most other places in the good ole U.S. of A. It's not Alaskan cold, Montanan cold, or even Minnesotan cold, mind you, but it is cold nonetheless. It is cold in general and at times can be very cold in particular. Exactly *how* cold, you ask? Well, the coldest temperature ever recorded in Maine was a negative something on the Fahrenheit scale. Negative something is a rather vague term so I'll narrow it down to what it actually was, a positively big negative number: a negative 48. That's a negative 44.4 on the Celsius scale for those of you who are interested. You hosiers know who you are, eh?

As you can see, it's not exactly balmy when the Fahrenheit and Celsius scales approach one another at around negative 40 and achieve "Celsienheit." I'm not sure what happens when they meet at "Celsienheit," but whatever it is, I'm sure it's not good. I'm also fairly certain you'll want to have pulled on an extra pair or two of long johns that morning as well. By the way, that low negative temperature was recorded in Van Buren, Maine. Van Buren is tiny town of several hundred frostbitten souls, tucked away up in the northeast corner of Aroostook County, hard by the Canadian border. God bless whoever went out to check the thermometer that morning because there's just something wrong with that boy. I'll bet the significance of the moment wasn't lost on whoever it was, though. I'll bet an icy chill of awe ran up and down their spine when they saw just how frigid cold can be. I also suspect there was an outhouse involved because unless there was a really pressing need such as nature calling, no one in their right mind goes out at negative 48.

Now, when I think of real cold, I think of real quiet. Quiet is what comes to mind when I've been out and about in really cold temperatures. The reason for this is that my wife is not stupid enough to venture out with me when it's really cold, so I'm always alone. The coldest I've personally experienced was a minus thirty. I can't tell you much about what that was like, but I can tell you this about that: negative thirty is pretty damn cold. I can't imagine that another eighteen degrees less could possibly feel any more cold. Now, you go from 90 to 72 and you can appreciate the difference between feeling uncomfortably hot, and comfortably comfortable. You go from a negative 30 to a negative 48, and there's not all that much difference between freezing your ass off and well, freezing your ass off a tad bit quicker. Point is, your ass is frozen either way. Those kinds of differences simply aren't worth noting. It's like the difference between steel and hardened steel. You hit me in the head with a piece of steel and all I can tell you is it hurts. I can't tell you whether it's hardened steel I've been hit with or not. You hit me hard enough, and I don't think it matters what kind of steel it was. That's the kind of cold we're talking about here: steel cold, the kind of cold that hurts.

Imagine coming home to your house on a chilly evening, taking off your coat and settling down in your comfy chair only to realize after a few short minutes that you're not so comfy after all. You check out the thermostat and the temperature reads about sixty. That's not family reunion temperature, is it? You turn up the thermostat to 72, curse the sheiks and/or oil barons that be, and presto! You hear the clank and rattle of oncoming heat. In no time at all, you're basking in warm comfort, smiling and shaking hands with friends and family as opposed to just shaking. Now, imagine ninety-degree weather. That's hot. One hundred degrees is pretty much unbearable to us Mainers, so we won't go there. Anyway, just think of this: you'd have to go almost one hundred and ten degrees due north on the rungs of your trusty mercury ladder from that bitter cold morning in Van Buren just to get to the chilly and uncomfortable temperature of sixty. That's what's called mighty cold, folks.

As I said, when I think of cold, I think of quiet. When it's a negative twenty plus something, from my experience, it's usually quiet and especially calm outside. Thankfully, there's seldom any wind blowing at those times. I think Mother Nature knows when to take pity on her earthly dependents. The heavens are usually crystal clear and the skies are bright with stars such as you've seldom if ever seen. For some reason I always recall a full or nearly full moon at those times as well. The snow is pure and bright white and haunting shadows run dark and deep. It's a surreal experience, like an old Fritz Lange movie come to life. And it's quiet, dead quiet. That is until you take the time to listen more closely and begin to hear the snap and crackle of the trees as they freeze ever more solid than solid and the moisture from deeper within them transforms into ice, expanding like the gases in a diver's blood expands when one suffers the "bends." What you're hearing is the surrounding woods and waters suffering the "bends" of another sort, but the "bends" nonetheless. That cracking and snapping becomes ever more pronounced the longer you're out in the cold, so take care for safety's sake to be sure to make certain the clacking you hear is not your teeth rattling about in your head as that can sometimes be the case on a really cold night.

I suspect that at first your senses are simply overwhelmed by the shock of entering this inhospitable and alien realm, but as you become more accustomed to your surroundings, they slowly recover. The snap, crackle, and pop of crispy trees is mixed with a deeper whooping sound that emerges from the streams and the frozen beaver bogs as the ice that encases them freezes ever colder, ever deeper and expands and splits like a giant lobster shell being shed to make room for what lies beneath its hardened mantel. Those are my memories and impressions of a really cold, still, and deceptively quiet night at thirty below zero. Those and how good it felt to get back inside where I practically sat on the wood stove, thawing out that frozen butt we discussed earlier.

Getting back to my first impressions, I still think cold and quiet are joined at the hip don't you? You don't? Well consider this. Do you notice your refrigerator when it's running or not running? No? Well then, you have a fine, working appliance my friend and you should be proud. On the other hand, if you have a "Kelvinator" or the like that is making a whole lot of sounds like chirping, whistling, clanging and crunching, chances are that baby isn't long for this world and neither are the perishables you have stored inside. If your fridge is making noise, it's probably not making much cold. It's that simple and that's my point. Cold is quiet and in my mind, they're joined at the hip.

Quiet is also the sound your car makes at thirty below if you haven't charged and maintained your battery and sometimes even if you have. That's a "not going to work today" kind of sound. Those are the true sounds of silence. That's a "hello darkness my old friend, I've come to talk to you again," early morning, Simon and Garfunkel "Sounds of Silence." That's a "you're not going anywhere but back to bed" sound of silence, my friend.

And why not go back to bed? At thirty below, your vehicle is in a deep slumber so why not you? At thirty below, vehicles hibernate like big, burly bears up on the mountainside. They are in a state of suspended animation and as Newton said, an object at rest wants to stay at rest. You wouldn't poke a sleeping grizzly with an "agitating stick," would you? Hell no, that would just agitate him. So why disturb your vehicle on such a day? Now I don't think Newton ever experienced thirty below zero, so his car probably turned over quite easily most mornings, but at those temperatures, most vehicles are downright grumpy if you try to wake them. But then again, you have to try. After all, we're talking cars, not real, live grumpy bears.

Now, compare notes with me and see if your experience with cold is anything like mine was on a recent, frigid, early January morning. I'd slowly, ever so slowly, awakened to the sounds of a really cold house. Those are those "sounds of silence" things again. My body was toasty warm under the multiple layers of flannel sheets, woolen blankets and my fat down comforter. My shoulder was icy cold though, and my head and nose were feeling a bit frosty, so I pulled the covers over my aging noggin and tucked it underneath to enjoy the warmth. These in-between times are a favorite of mine. I'm in a nether land between asleep and awake, between hot and cold, between up and about and down and under. I've got that Ying and Yang thing going big time and I'm working the differences for all they're worth, just relishing the moment. But then, sadly, it's just that, a moment and I know I have to get up sooner or later, so reluctantly I throw off the covers and jumped out of bed. Ouch!

This next is probably more than you might want to know, but I don't care.

I don't wear pajamas. Now don't get panicky, I'm not stark barenaked for God's sake. I have some couth—not much, but some. You see, I sleep in my shorts and a t-shirt no matter what the weather, so when I jump out of bed in the cold of morning, I've learned to keep jumping just to keep warm. I always suspected that those Indian braves jumping around in the early misty mornings and chanting "Ay, yi, yi, yi! Ay, yi, yi, yi!" weren't doing some mystical, sacred dance. Not at that hour. They were just trying to keep warm and saying the Indian equivalent of "Oh great father, it's freakin' cold! Oh my God, my ass is cold!" And that's pretty much exactly what I yell out on a really cold morning myself, much to my wife's dismay. I suppose I should show some consideration for her after thirty years of marriage and try not to disturb her rest, but hell, she's warm in bed and I'm the one who's up and freezing my "tuckus" off. I'm cold and I don't care who knows it. I also know that she will smile, chuckle to herself and fall back to sleep directly. God, I hate her on mornings like this, on mornings when I have to go to work.

So you see, I couldn't care less when I tromp noisily downstairs where (if this is possible) it's even colder yet, because as we all know, heat rises even if it's a cold sort of heat. That's why our bedroom wasn't frigid and coated in frost. That's why it was just unbearable outside of the bed covers. That cold sort of heat is a good thing if that's all you've got going for you. Of course that's all we've got going for us, because I don't keep a fire burning the whole night through. I don't keep a fire going because I'm cheap with my wood and I say that's why they invented blankets. Besides, by morning, unless I've been up all night stoking the fire, it's still going to be cold in the house anyways and I'm just going to be out that much more wood, not to mention feeling really tired and cranky from lack of sleep and did I mention, cold? So, I say, what's the point?

Actually, I told a half lie. We used to burn only wood, but now we are civilized and have a kerosene, direct vent heater, so all I have to do is go to the trouble of pushing a small button to get the heat generating. That heater has been a godsend, although it came from the friendly folks at Monitor and God had nothing to do with it. In the bad old, good old days of a few years back, I'd have had to head down another flight of stairs to the cellar to get the heat moving. Here's another odd thing about living in a cold climate, the cellar is about as cold as the upstairs is warm, being acclimatized by the surrounding earth it's been dug into.

Anyways, once in the cellar I would have split some wood, gathered some paper, chopped up some kindling, and so forth, and worked up the beginnings of a fire. That's all there is to it, that and wait patiently for nearly an hour or more before any meaningful (by which I mean detectable) heat could be discerned escaping from the floor registers. That being done, once the fire was roaring in grand style, my wife, hearing the clanking of the duct work as it expanded with the warmth, would quietly venture downstairs where she would then deposit herself directly over a waiting register. There in her inflated, hot air bathrobe, she'd sit balloon-like, hogging all the heat and wallowing in its warmth. She'd look exactly like one of those fairies in Sleeping Beauty with their billowing skirts, only she wasn't wielding a magic wand in her hand, just a steaming cup of tea.

Getting back to the Monitor heater, I don't have to build fires nowadays; I just have to exert the effort required to push the little red button and when I do this, the temperature gauge lights up and digitally informs me that our home is now a toasty—get ready for this—thirty-nine degrees! Shocked? Me too. I expected worse. "Not too shabby," I think to myself. "That insulation really did the trick." You see, I thought it was going to be really cold. As the heater ignites and clinks and clatters to life, I turn my attention to elsewhere and wonder what the temperature is outside. I'm a weather junkie after all, and I like to know just how bad things are. It's what keeps me going. The worse things are, the happier I am. That's the way it is with us weather junky types. If we're happy, you probably don't want to be living next to us.

I open the front door onto the pitch-black sun porch, struggle to free the now-frozen slider, eventually win that fight, and dash out onto the deck to check out the thermometer reading. These are the times I live for, I'm sorry to say. For me, this is my Christmas morning and I'm about to open that one present I've been waiting for all my life. I stare at the thin red ribbon on a stick: twenty-six below. Damn it! I tear at the wrapper and toss it aside. Tube socks again! I knew it wasn't that cold. I was hoping for a record cold and all I got was a tube sock cold. I never get what I want for Christmas. Why, Santa, why?

Where I live in Maine, twenty-six below zero cold is just an annoying cold. You freeze your butt off, of course, but you can't hang your hat on it, and you certainly can't brag to your sister in Florida about it. If you lived back in Connecticut, this would be one of those all-time bragging to the grand kids kind of cold; but up here in Maine, it's only some kind of pretty cool cold.

I'm disheartened, but my disappointment soon fades as I realize that I'm standing in my underwear at 5:45 in the morning, in early January, at twenty-six below zero on a dead end road in New Vineyard, Maine. Something stirs me. I see my reflection in the frosty window. I begin to light up inside. I think I might have set a new record for stupidity. The thought of being able to brag about something, even if it's just stupidity, warms me up some, but then I quickly realize it's not near enough and I flee back inside for some real heat.

Ah, inside; now that feels good. What feels so good, you might ask? Well, for starters, thirty-nine degrees and rising, that's what. Thirty-nine degrees and rising is downright toasty when it's a full sixty-five degrees warmer than where you've just been standing, standing in your cotton boxers, t-shirt and bare feet. And no, I don't wear socks to bed. That would be stupid, and well, I'm not that kind of everyday stupid. So, there I am, standing in my living room, basking in the differential warmth for, I don't know, maybe ten seconds or so, until I realize, "Hell, it may be sixty-five degrees warmer in here than out on the deck, but it's still only thirty-nine degrees in here!" Like I said, I'm not *that* stupid so I point my clanking knees towards the bathroom and head for a warm shower.

Before I get there, though, I stop and turn about. I have to put on my coffee. I run back out into the kitchen and flip on the light switch. The switch plate is covered with frost; cool! The fluorescent lights blink, and blink some more. They can't believe I'm waking them up on such a cold morning. They shudder, they flash and finally, they give it up, throw back their covers and relinquish a grudging, subdued glow: not quite on and not quite off, kind of like me before my coffee. Either way, there's enough light now so that I can make my way around and quickly get a pot of java brewing before I run back to the bathroom, my body covered now with goose bumps running along my arms like the Andes down the spine of Chile. Get it? Chilly? Now I can take that shower, "gracias por favor."

Once in the bathroom, I turn on the fan and listen to its growl. That's not an "I'm happy to be a fan" sound. I'm not surprised. Nothing makes really happy sounds when it's this cold. I pull back the stiff shower curtain and turn on the water, wait a couple of seconds and flip on the shower control. It's hot! There's hot water and it's really hot, not just differentially hot. This is great. I throw caution to the wind and jump in. Immediately I'm scalded to a rosy pinkness, but I don't care, I can't feel anything anyway as I stand in the steaming El Niño-like cauldron of swirling steam that envelopes me. This is heaven, I think, or at least as close as I'm ever going to get. Isn't it funny that heaven is something that's hot and burning, just like hell? Whatever; this is some kind of "muy bueno" good. If this is hell, well, so be it. Move over Donald Trump and make room for Daddy. This is that kind of good.

Then suddenly and without any warning, my senses recover, the Ying is gone and the Yang takes over. I realize this is not heaven at all, this *is* hell: this is some kind of "Diablo" hot; this is some kind of bad, "muy" bad. I screech in pain and frantically adjust the temperature knobs like someone, maybe Homer Simpson himself, at a nuclear power plant trying to avoid a meltdown. Somehow, unlike Homer, I manage to rise to the occasion. There will be no Three Mile Island this morning, not today, not in New Vineyard, not on my watch.

The moderated heat of the water now slowly begins to penetrate my flesh. I'm only cooking slowly now, not burning. I could live like this, encased for the day in a permanent, steaming hot shower. I stand there, leaning against the shower wall, luxuriating and just taking it all in. This is just great and believe it or not, it only gets better. Now I get to play with the soap and the liquid soap and that silly, "poofie, scrunchy, thingie thing."

I don't know about you, but I like to use different combinations of soaps. I'm a little different myself, so I'm in my element here. I like to imagine myself a kind of bathroom chef on the cooking channel, roasting my body, and doling out my spices and herbs as I slowly simmer away. I'm the Emeril Lagasse of the shower set. Let's see, I'll use a pinch of Dial first, BAM, with maybe a swipe of mango Zest, BAM, before reaching for the scrunchy thing and the citrus Soft Soap, BAM, BAM. Now I squeeze on some manly scents, some Gillette products, to balance the fruity sensations that pampered my feminine side. BAM,

BAM, and what the hell? BAM! I begin to scrub away.

Tell me if I am crazy, but do you ever think about this? I'm right-handed and it strikes me as odd that I always scrub my left forearm first, hardest and most when I'm taking a shower. My left forearm is never dirty to begin with, forearms seldom are and hey, it's my left forearm, but that's where I start to scrub, nonetheless. I don't think I sweat particularly much on my left forearm either, but still, that's where I begin to clean myself. I pay a lot of attention to my left forearm when I wash. In fact, my left forearm is by far and away the cleanest part of my entire body. The least clean has to be the center of my back. That area gets the least effective cleaning. I can't reach there. No one but a contortionist can reach there. Besides, there's all that hair to deal with, too. Well, that's life. What are you going to do? But my left forearm? I'd match that baby up with the most sterile operating room in the state on any given day of the week. That baby's clean.

The liquid soap is fun, but it doesn't last for long, so I grab a bar of soap, a different spice formula, and set to work on my left forearm again. I rinse and as I do, something catches my eye. It's Zest, some new, liquid soap Zest. I don't remember buying it, but I must have. I have coupons so I buy every kind of soap and liquid soap I can. I squeeze some out and again set to work, on my left arm of course. I rinse again. I'm just about done. I reach for another bar of soap, a small, sharp bar. That's my shampoo soap. I lather up my head, and rinse off for the last time. Then I take the full bar of soap and lather up my neck to shave with. I'm done. I turn off the water, open the curtain, reach for a towel and begin to briskly dry myself off.

I don't know why, but I always begin toweling with my left forearm, too. I swear, it's the most pampered, stuck up, and self centered part of my body and I'm helpless to do anything about it. Go figure.

The entire shower that I've just described has taken me, I'd say, about three and a half minutes, maybe four tops. I'm not one to linger. I tend to slowly luxuriate at a fairly rapid pace. But don't get me wrong; I get a lot of pleasure out of those three and a half minutes. It's not much in terms of time, but it's enough for me. I'm one of those "swish, swam, thank you ma'am" kind of guys. That was great. Maybe I'll call you and we can do it again next week.

The exhaust fan stopped complaining and did its job well. Or maybe it just stopped. I can't tell because I can't see across the six feet that separates me from the other side of the bathroom. I'm living in a steam room now. Lucky me. One of the benefits of living in Maine is that when it's thirty-nine in your house, you can have a bona fide steam room experience for the price of a shower. You can't do that at seventy degrees!

I wipe off the mirror and there, peering back at me, is some fat, old, gray haired guy, standing where I should be. He looks like a nice enough guy, so I say, "What the hell, I'll give him a shave." He has a beard so a shave only takes about 27 seconds, more or less. He looks good. He's smiling. He seems happy and that makes me happy. I smile too. I've done someone a good turn. Then the mirror disappears again as the fog bank rolls back in and my friend fades. It's funny, but metaphors are everywhere. People come, people go. Life goes on.

I dry my hair and run my wife's brush through it. I'm in my fifties and I have hair. Some of them I later discover are six inches long and blonde, but hey, they're hair and I'm happy. I slap on some deodorant. I have several different kinds. I choose the sport scent. They have coupons for deodorant, too, you know. Then I pull on my clothes and I'm good to go, but first I have to smear my face with aftershave. I choose Old Leather. I know that none of these fragrances match or compliment one another in the least, but I'm good with that. I may smell like I was standing next to a suicide bomber in a Walgreen's personal hygiene section, but I don't care. I like the way, or should I say "ways," I smell. It is, shall we say, unique and odd: just like me.

I emerge from my alternating morning ritual a new man. The temperature in the house is now a toasty fifty-four as the heater is working its butt off. My coffee has brewed and is waiting. I pour it into my special Official Maine Black Bears insulated travel cup that my daughter Jessie brought me from college, and doctor my Maxwell House just as I like it: a teaspoon of Hannaford store-brand cream substitute and a smidgen of sugar. I take a sip. It's good. It tastes like hot. I shake a few plastic pill containers, swill back my psycho pills, the ones that in my mind at least make me semi-normal, and head into the living room.

The cats have encircled the heater. The dog is a heat magnet in the center of the circle of the cats. The fish stare at me. They need feeding. I ignore the cats and they ignore me. I hate the cats. I think they hate me, or at least I hope so. I trip over the dog and feed the fish. I fall into the sofa, turn on the TV and settle in. This is my time and, next to not getting up, my favorite time. I relax in the growing warmth, stretch my legs out on the coffee table and sip at my coffee as I watch the "I-Man," Don Imus. This is my time and I milk it for all it's worth, which is about ten minutes and then it's my time to go.

I reach for my jacket, the fleece one, and then reconsider. No, it's too cold for that. I put it back on its hook and grab my ski parka. I also grab my Russian hat, the furry rabbit one that I picked up on the streets of St. Petersburg, outside the Hermitage. I haggled the price down to where I wasn't actually robbed blind, just ripped off. It's a hat that looks silly to everyone but me, but as with most things in my life, I don't care.

As you may have guessed, I've been to Russia and I know what's warm and what isn't. And speaking of hats, I've learned that there are two kinds of hats for the cold. There are Russian fur hats, which keep you warm, and there is everything else, which doesn't. If you've ever been to Russia, you know that the Russian cold is a real cold kind of cold and only a fur hat will keep you warm. I tug down the earflaps of my hat, pour myself another cup of coffee into my insulated mug, grab hold of my lunch bucket, and head out the door.

It's strangely quiet outside, dead silent as a matter of fact. It must have gotten colder. I feel insulated from the world around me and everything is somehow muffled. And then I remember: oh yeah, the hat. I lift an earflap and I hear some snapping and whooping, but still it's pretty quiet for the most part and I cover my ear once more. It's still pitch-black out and the air is hard and biting. It stabs at my throat and pokes with sharp, icicle knives. You don't breathe deeply in cold like this; if you try, you quickly learn you can't. You have to ease the air into your lungs slowly, letting it roll on your tongue like a fine wine, warm and mellow with age, savoring it in your mouth and nose before it melts and sweetly slips down your throat. Breathing in really cold weather isn't crude work; it's an art form. So if you want to be an artist and have much of a career, you had better learn the trade quickly. Personally, my breathing is a work in progress, it's serviceable but you won't see it framed on a museum wall anytime soon. Still, I am breathing and that's always a good sign. I head for the car.

The snow makes that crunching sound, like walking over frozen popcorn, as it breaks beneath my felt-lined Sorels. I know the sound well and I like it. It's a familiar sound that reminds me of where I live and brings back boyhood memories from last year and the year before and the year before that and so on back into time, to when I really was a boy. It's a dry, compacted, grating sound with slight, squeaking undertones. It's a sound you only hear on cold days like this. It's a special sound and I like it a lot.

Once at the car, I reach out for the door handle but I can't open it. I'm wearing my mittens, my L.L.Bean, Gortex mittens, and they're too big to grab at the handle. Like hats, there are two kinds of hand coverings for those really cold days like today: mittens like the ones I'm wearing, which keep your hands warm, and fingered gloves, which look good, but don't "do jack." Fingered gloves only serve to help you keep track of your fingers after they've become frostbitten, blackened and brittle, after they've fallen off your hands like dried, dead, crackling leaves. I like my fingers and I don't like doing math, so I wear mittens.

If there is one problem with mittens, though, it's that they tend toward the awkward and clumsy. As I said, I wear mittens because gloves with fingers are less than useless in real cold; in fact, they're down right dangerous. With finger gloves, real cold forces you to retract your fingers and clench them in a ball to conserve heat, like a nest of wintering rattlesnakes in a cave. This defeats the purpose of having finger gloves in the first place, so, you may just as well dispense with the now hollow, flopping about empty fingers, but admittedly good-looking, glove altogether and opt for a pair of mittens like me. Besides, I have gloves in the car for when the heater warms it up—if it ever warms it up, that is.

Standing outside the car, I pull off a mitten with my teeth and tug at the door handle. Finally, it gives way and, with a sharp cracking sound, loosens. In the past I have actually broken off a handle, but this time I'm lucky and the door slowly opens with a prolonged groan, just like you might hear in a haunted house movie. Pulling my mitten back on, also with my teeth, I slip into my seat. I'm glad I have cloth seats. I like cloth seats. I especially like cloth seats at twenty-six below zero. Vinyl seats at these temperatures are like thin, sculpted ice creations. You slide on them and being thin, they crack like the ice they've become. Thin ice is never good ice and an icy, hardened steel, spring suppository is not a welcome treat first thing on a cold January morning. Trust me on that one. Don't ask any questions. Just trust me. I like my cloth seats just fine, thank you, and I'll take my suppositories the way I prefer them, if I can say that, in capsule form not shaped like some primitive, corkscrew, Spanish Inquisition torture device.

Now that I'm finally in the car, I realize I have to take off my mittens once again to reach into my pocket and pull out my keys. If you don't have to take off your mittens to retrieve your keys, you're some kind of special person with large, funny-looking clown pockets and I tip my furry Russian hat to you. If you can pull car keys out of your pants pocket while wearing mittens at nearly thirty below zero, all I can say is that there's a nightclub in Fairbanks just waiting to headline you and your act. I can't do it.

Latching onto my keys, I quickly put them between my teeth, slip on my mitten once more and then mouth-feed the keys between my mitten thumb and the rest of the mitten. The keys are now securely in my grasp. At least I think they are. Or at least they look like they are in the waning moonlight. I can't feel them, of course. I can't feel much of anything. I puff myself up inside my parka, like a chickadee, grab the parka by the neck and pull it out and blow down the opening just to see if I can sense the warmth of my breath against to my skin. I feel something, so I guess I'm okay. I poke around the keyhole opening with the key, the one I can't feel through my mittens, the one I have to watch to make sure it's still there and pointed in the right direction, right side, tooth side, up. Finally it disappears. I dropped it. I fumbled around amid the noise of me cursing, and go through the procedure again. Again the key disappears. It's in there all right. It's in and we are ready to rumble!

This is the moment of truth. This is what the whole dang morning has been leading up to. This is it! Come on baby! I turn the key and sense a sound. It's not a natural sound but a mechanical, steel-on-steel sound. The bear is disturbed, but he's not awake. He's just disturbed. I've poked him with my battery powered, electric agitating stick and he senses it; he just doesn't want to acknowledge it. He releases a short, "leave me alone" grunt and slumps back into slumber. I give him another twist of the key, jabbing again, agitating the slumbering giant. This time he grunts haphazardly a couple of times and then, as before, nods back off to sleep. He hopes I'll go away, but I won't. I can't. I have no choice. I have to get to work.

I also have to be careful and monitor my strength. If I poke him too many times, too fast, I'll weaken and he'll win. He knows this. I'll have to space my prodding just so. I'll have to time my prods, put them to a rhythm and build up a momentum. We both know the dance. I begin and the bruin grudgingly responds. Again I poke, and again he answers. We do-si-do. We tango. But my warmth, what little I brought with me from the house, is fading fast and with it, my patience. I prod. I stop. My warmth is gone now, replaced by cold, not bitter cold, but cold. This is it. With my patience ebbing away, I stab one last time and manage to almost count to ten. I don't care if you are a big, old, bad boy bear; we are about to have at it. This may be my last chance and we both know it. I poke and twist and go for it. I hold the key firmly and hang on for dear life. There's no turning back, not now. One of us will win. One of us will lose.

The bear can't ignore me any longer. He rumbles and sputters, he jerks and shakes as he moans and groans, spitting out his anger. The sounds, notes separate and alone at first, slowly begin yield to my rhythm, to meld together forming from a jingle, a tune, and soon, maybe even a melody. With a final transformation, the bear rises from his slumber and stands tall. He roars a loud, steady roar as the car shudders and explodes into a symphony of orchestrated life. This is sweet music to my ears indeed and if I weren't wearing my furry Russian hat, I could probably hear it, too!

The bear and I sit there in the darkness shuddering and shaking in unison. The fan belt is squealing in a high pitched, piercing agony that will only abide when friction softens its frozen spinal cord and numbs its stinging pain. I fumble for the headlights and switch them on. The beams appear to actually take several seconds to penetrate the cold, black nothingness in front of them. They extend their range foot by foot as they slowly feel their way into the darkness. One hundred eighty-six thousand miles per second, my ass. I don't think so. Not on this morning. I nudge on the fan and am greeted by a sound that can only mean one thing: "now, now." I switch on the radio and lift an earflap. I swear that the sounds feel stiff, slow, and frozen. The voices seem to drawl and I expect a good ole boy's, "Y'all can't always get what you want" to emanate from Mick Jagger's cockney lungs, but of course it doesn't come. And there I sit, in the center of this cacophony of sounds and wait. I have to wait. I have no choice. This is Maine in early January.

I can't believe it, but the engine is actually running, the patient is alive, but though the operation was a success, he still can't move his legs. The gearshift is locked in place. I push at it slowly, rocking it back and forth in an effort to loosen it up. It grudgingly obliges me, or at least in a fashion. After a few minutes I can actually manage to put the car into reverse. I depress the accelerator, ease out the clutch and hope for the best. Like a Coast Guard icebreaker on the Kennebec edging towards Bath, the vehicle shudders, creaks and then methodically begins to break free of the icy hold that grips it tight. I hear that same, dry snowy crunch beneath my tires as we begin to grind towards the road. Once there, we pause, catch our breath, stop, and rest.

We're good to go. I push against the gear shifter, feeling its resistance weakening as I force my iron will upon its steely core. It's finally there, I have it: first gear, I think. I release the clutch and depress the gas pedal. The car doesn't move, it only groans in mocking disgust. I thought wrong. Sorry. I try again, pumping the clutch this time, and willing the gears into lock synch place. I give it the gas and the car grudgingly responds obediently, despite its better judgment. Slowly we begin to work our way down the dark dirt and snow-covered road towards the highway leading to town. The car bumps and thumps along on oval, nylon tires. They won't become round again until I'm miles down the black top, well on my way to work. But I'm not concerned with the tires. I'm reaching for my ice scraper. My windshield has fogged up on the inside and it's frozen, opaque, encased in a frosty shroud. I scrape it clear for the moment, the snowy flakes falling onto my lap where they sit laughing in little groups. They are not about to melt; they know it and so do I.

We creep along, scraping, hitting the washer fluid that freezes instantly and streaks, driving with one hand on the wheel, one on my privates, blowing into my mittens, cursing, all the ten miles to town. I look at the time and temperature clock: minus nineteen. Sometimes even I wish I lived where it's warm like that. Eventually the car is finally able to move without making so much noise that I can actually hear the radio. I turn on MPBN as I always do on my way to work. I have to know what's going on. I need to know. I'm a news junkie too. It's who I am. I am "Mr. Up to Date on Everything Man." I know it all and I need to know more so I listen, but what was that? What did I hear? What did he say? No, that can't be. That is something I don't need to know, not now. "Mr. Up to Date on Everything Man" does not need to know that it's going to be clear today, that the wind is going to pick up from the north and briskly gust at thirty miles per hour, that the temperature is going to peak at almost zero, to almost warmth, if you can call it that, and that all of this is going to make for a beautiful, gorgeous weekend, beginning today, a SATURDAY, in January.

Ten minutes pass. My tears have frozen to my cheeks. I look in the mirror and see a porcelain reflection staring back at me. I'd like to literally crack a smile, but I wouldn't risk it, even if I could. Ten more minutes pass. A door cracks opens and then icily closes. There follows a slow crunching of snow and another door cracks open momentarily, than snaps shut with a thud. The stairs creak beneath measured steps. The bedroom door eases open as a shadow sheepishly approaches.

"Hey, wake up."

"Stop that, your fingers are cold."

"Of course they're cold. Not everyone gets to sleep in like you, you know."

"So, where did you go?"

"Never mind, I just went. Now blow on my fingers will ya?"

"But why did you go out on a Satur ..."

"I said never mind and stop talking. I need you to blow harder and don't stop."

"Okay, but you didn't try to look cool in those stupid gloves you bought, did you? I warned you about them. I told you ..."

"Stop already with the gloves. Just blow while I count my fingers ... five, five and a half, six and a half ..."

Hot, Maine Hot

Maine can get hot, very hot. Maybe not Arizona Sonora Desert Hot, but pretty hot nonetheless. At least at times it feels very hot to me, for Maine that is. And to be honest, the longer I live in Maine, the hotter it seems to get. I think the reason for that is that as we get older, and by we, I mean me of course, the more we tend to find our own individual comfort zones, our personal niches if you will, and huddle within them. By settling out, I'm not just speaking of our succumbing to gravitational forces exacting their inexorable toll upon our paltry human frames (to wit: some of us get fatter and grow a well-earned beer belly). I am speaking of that, but not just that. I'm referring to our climatic preferences as well.

In terms of temperatures, as we age, we tend to gravitate to a nice middle ground of about 72 degrees Fahrenheit. Anything above or below that number becomes an increasingly intolerable extreme for us to endure as we move up in years. If you doubt my argument, I offer up this conversation I recently had with my wife as proof positive:

"I'm dying of the heat in here," I said moaning and tugging at my sweater neck. "I'm tanning, for crying out loud. It's December, the full moon's out, and I'm getting a freakin' tan. It's like a sauna in here. This isn't natural, I tell you. It's 74 degrees in Maine in winter and it's just not normal. Are you trying to kill me or something?"

"Yeah, I'm trying to kill you," snapped back my dearly beloved of many, way too many years. "It was 70 in here all day long and I was freezing to death so I turned on the heater without written permission from your highness, King of the Hottentots. Is that a crime? You want me to die of hypothermia? Is that what you want you old cheapskate you? You want me to die?"

"I should be so lucky."

"You should be so lucky? I should be so lucky as to not have to put up with you!"

"You want to know why I'm so hot? It's because I'm always hot under the collar, which, by the way, is a self-defense mechanism I've had to resort to counteracting the cold shoulder you're always showing me. If you'd lose the cold shoulder and warm up to me you may find yourself quite comfortable."

Well, you get the picture. We have our preferences and these likes and dislikes get stronger and increasingly flavor our personalities with age, just like a fine Tennessee whiskey. Speaking of which, I need a drink just thinking about talking to my wife. My point is this: If I've convinced you of my proposition regarding temperatures and physiques, forget about it, you're all wrong. What really happens is that as we get older, whatever extremes we experienced at a younger age, become ever more extreme in direct proportion to how far removed we now are from them. It's this exponentially charged "factum extendum" that dictates that snowfalls of one foot as a child were twice as deep as one-foot snowfalls nowadays. Of course we were half as tall as we are now. Forget that one-foot snowfalls were about a third or more of your total height as a child and are now about a sixth of your height. Forget about that reasonable way of thinking. I'm talking about emotional memories here, the real thing and not some factual reality. Walking uphill to school and uphill back home again. Walking uphill in both directions? Not rational? No, but it's possible if you don't think about it and just feel it, experience it. As a kid, your brain simply doesn't function correctly anyway. Rational people don't explode into tears followed by hour-long fits of rage just because Scooby Doo was pre-empted by a news bulletin. Scooby will be back tomorrow. As an adult, knowing that is bad enough, but you don't see me crying, do you? Of course you can't, and like you care anyway. Scooby will be back, sure, but it won't be the same show, will it? Who the hell knows that? Let's just assume the worst and no, it won't and you don't care! I hate you and I never want to talk to you again. EVER!

Now, I researched the highest temperature ever recorded in Maine and discovered much to my surprise that it was 105 degrees and occurred on July 10, 1911 in North Bridgton, Maine. I wasn't surprised that it happened in North Bridgton. I've never been there and aside from it being able to claim the hottest temperature ever recorded in Maine, I've nothing against the place. I also don't mind that it happened in 1911, although that's not entirely true and I do mind that a bit. What really peeves me is this: I remember visiting Maine in the 1970s before moving here for good. That's "for good" both literally and figuratively, although in the early years it was mostly figuratively.

Be that as it may, it was mid-August and my family and I experienced what I clearly recall as 107-degree temperatures although I will admit that I was somewhat delirious at the time. I want to tell you, that was some kind of hot. I remember that as a fact. I don't care that apparently it didn't really ever happen. That doesn't make my memory, my emotional memory wrong. That only makes me mad and hot under the collar, but not as hot as I was in that 107-degree heat. That was hot. I don't remember 105 degrees in North Bridgton in 1911 because I wasn't even born yet. My father wasn't even born for that matter and if he were alive today he'd tell you he doesn't remember it either, even though he lived in New York and wasn't born until 1918.

The fact is, I was trying really hard not to exaggerate anything in writing this book and I was willing to tone down the facts and report a temperature of 106-degrees during my visit. Now I find out that's too much as well. It seems an honest liar just can't win anymore. So, here's what I'm going to do. I know it was 107 degrees, in the shade. My factual memory was not wrong. I also know that the record is officially 105 degrees in North Bridgton, no mention of shade or no shade. Being a reasonable man, I'm willing to compromise just to prove I'm not pig-headed and from here on out, I'm going to recall a 106-degree record temperature sometime in the '70s, somewhere in Maine. If you don't want to believe me, that's too bad for you. I don't care. Those are the facts and I just report them. What you believe is up to you.

So, here we were in Maine on August 4, 1974, vacationing, and I'm proud to say that we were here for the 106-degree Fahrenheit temperature recorded as the hottest day ever during a Maine summer. I suppose I didn't have to say it was summer. If it had been 106 degrees in winter, that would have made headlines all the way to Boston. But it was summer, so you probably don't know about it. We were at Acadia the day it got that hot. It wasn't that hot at Acadia, but it was somewhere inland of the shore. We were at the shore, and whatever the temperature was, it was hot, maybe not 106 degrees hot, but hot. Being hot, and being at the shore, we headed straight to Sand Beach. That is, our family and about two million other pathetic optimists of a similar mind. I think we were at Sand Beach, but I can't swear to it as there were so many people there it would have been better if it were called People Beach. Anyway, we were there.

Now, when you're at the beach and it's hot, you go swimming, don't you? Yes, you do, but not at Sand Beach when it's 106 degrees somewhere inland in Maine. It's not that we didn't go in the water; we did or at least tried to. It's that Maine water on the coast is meant for looking at, not really swimming in.

You'd think that with temperatures at 106 degrees somewhere inland in Maine, the water on the coast would be warm, or at least tolerable. You'd be wrong again. I've been in the water on the coast in summer in Maine and it never felt like this water did on that day. It's not that it felt cold, though it was. It was that it just hurt. Usually we wade about in the shallows, waiting for our legs to go numb. Then, as our legs pass beyond our consciousness, we venture in deeper until we are either refreshed, or rescued by a lifeguard. This day, we never got to numb. We couldn't get past pain. I think it was the contrast between hot and cold that did it. We were getting sunburned from our heads to the water line on our bodies. From there, we were turning bluish purple down to our feet. The splash of the surf on our baking bodies was like acid thrown on limestone. Our chiseled bodies smoked and burned and the pain was excruciating. It can best be likened to a full-body ice cream headache. It was as though Ying and Yang were out of control. It was like sweet and sour sauce: the sweet being pure sugar and the sour, the bitter taste of almonds (as in arsenic).

By the way, I get Ying and Yang; they were the original Siamese twins. What I don't get is the word "Yo Yo." I know what it is, like anybody. What I don't know is what a "yo" is. There's string—that I know. And there's this other thing which I assume is the yo. That's it. There isn't anything else.

Moxie

Moxie is a soft drink—not a popular soft drink, but a soft drink nonetheless—that was originated and is still "manufactured" in Maine. It is also now the official soft drink of the state of Maine. I can only believe that it became the official soft drink of Maine for two simple reasons: 1) it was a particularly slow, hot day in Augusta and some aged legislator decided we needed yet another official something or other and that something might as well be a soft drink, and 2) there was no other soft drink in the legislator's hand or choice in the soft drink category except Moxie.

Moxie was introduced prior to the turn of the century, the twentieth century that is, just before science became associated with the term scientific. The inventor (it tastes like it came directly from a chemistry set and should be packaged in a test tube) surely was simply out to make a buck in the old, time-favored American way of the age: by way of duping unsuspecting citizens out of their hard-earned money. Sensing something might be amiss, he must have offered it to former and future former friends.

"What do you think? Tastes somewhat different doesn't it? Something akin to a rusticated Coke but without the mitigating factor of cocaine to ease the pain. Packs a right hard kick, don't you agree? Refreshing and yet it has that bite, don't it?"

To which his friend no doubt answered, "It tastes like medicine."

To which our quick-witted "concoctor" must have replied, "And that's just what it is, my friend: medicine in the form of a soft drink. Good for what ails you. Good for the rheumatoid and the digestion, the dyspepsia and the con-stipation, not to mention the vapors. Did I mention the vapors? Rub it on the skin and it wards off mosquitoes and black flies too. Helps with flat feet and restores hair to the knuckles while preventing cavities and halitosis as well."

Moxie was born of, or should I say "hatched from," natural ingredients, but is so unnatural. Of course, over time, science became evermore scientific, and laws were enacted to prevent such hoaxes from being perpetrated on an unsuspecting public; thus, before you could say, "Excuse me Aunt Ethel, I just 'vapored' despite the Moxie I took," you couldn't market a cure-all simply based upon the placebo effect no matter how "mediciny" the elixir tasted. As a result, Moxie was transformed into a soft drink that may not be good for you, but it didn't really taste good either. Moxie moved on over from the pharmacy counter to the soda counter. Actually, over the years, Moxie has evolved into more of test of fortitude than a refreshing beverage. It's now considered a test of man-hood here in Maine. You can't own a gun unless you can down a can of Moxie without wincing. It's also considered an "acquired taste," which means I assume that, wisely, the body's defense mechanisms initially reject any introduction of Moxie into its system. Over time, with persistence and determination, and in the past when other choices were few and far between, the taste buds become numbed and deadened and voila! There you are. You have arrived as a bona fide Mainer. You think you begin to actually like the stuff. You mistake tolerance for preference. In my mind, it's as if someone decided that Kaopectate would make a great new flavored drink and suddenly you found gray packages of Kao Kool-Aid on the supermarket shelves. You know someone would buy it just because it's there and it has a reputation. I know I'd buy it. And suddenly you've got a new beverage cult on your hands. It's as if NyQuil were to be manufactured without the alcohol and offered as a liqueur for the under aged. That kind of thing. Suddenly there's a festival, a state proclamation and it's the official new drink of somewhere. Well, that somewhere happens to be Maine—Lisbon Falls, Maine in particular—and the festival is held every summer. See you there, if you're man enough!

How to Eat a Lobster

So, you've decided to come to Maine and eat lobster like a true Mainer. The only problem is, you don't know how and you don't want to embarrass yourself in front of friends, family and other diners at a restaurant. Well, my friend, I've found that ignorance is as good a place as any to begin an education. Open your texts to where you are now and we'll begin. Class is now in session. I will be your instructor, and as a perceptive educator, the fact that you're reading this book to learn how to eat lobster tells me several things about you as a student, such as: you are truly a desperate individual, you don't have a clue, and you are easily intimidated. No matter, you've come to the right place, you stupid, pathetic wimp you. Shut up, sit down, take that gum out of your mouth, and pay attention. You just might learn something, but then again, if you've gotten this far in life as you are, what are the chances of that, eh?

Nonetheless, to begin with, a lobster is an animal, and we are humans, though animals too. Lobsters are crustaceans, meaning they have a crust of 'acean' or something very close to it. They are hard. They are also bottom feeders. If you're reading this book to learn how to eat one, you and the lobster have at least that in common. If you also have claws, a shell and a segmented tail you have way too much in common with lobsters and need to consult a specialist. I'd suggest one living far inland just to be on the safe side. If that's not possible, don't bother to make any appointments after lunch. If you fit the above description and are married, you and your spouse both scare me and I just don't know what to say except go back where you came from. That would be somewhere near "the depths" and never return again.

The lobster is unique. There is nothing like it except another lobster. In fact, excepting for size, it's impossible to tell one healthy lobster from another because they don't wear hats, have no hair to fashion, don't speak with an accent, don't wear glasses, are not particularly fashion-conscious. What they are, and this is the important part, is good to eat. They are tasty little buggers.

Native Americans picked up on this and consumed lobster like we eat chicken. Unlike chicken, however, southern fried lobster never caught on, but like chicken, lobsters could be had at most any market for a fairly reasonable amount of wampum. In fact, large piles of lobster shells, plastic sporks, and discarded handy wipes discovered along the coast of Maine have identified long abandoned MBL (Maine Boiled Lobster) fast food franchises that were once quite popular with visiting tribes during the summer tourist season.

In short order, lobster became such a staple of the local native diet that it was literally known as the original "chicken of the sea." How can a tuna be called the chicken of the sea? It makes no sense at all. It's obvious that the lobster is the

231

true chicken of the sea. Witness the fact that a lobster is exactly like a chicken in all respects save it lives in the ocean under saltwater, doesn't have feathers, and doesn't cock-a-doodle-doo while sitting on a fence in the wee morning hours. Other than that and the hard shell and crushing claw thing they've got going, they are almost identical. They have drumstick-like appendages and tails and, just like a chicken, hardly ever fly. In fact, for some reason I've never understood, a lobster with only one claw is called a chicken lobster. Look, I'm not going to argue with you about this. If you want tuna, I suspect you're capable of opening a can, so go for it and call it what you will. As for lobster, you know nothing. That's why you're here. You've come to learn. So stop thinking, turn your little brain to "off," and let's learn already.

Here you are in Maine at last. You've journeyed hours, days, whatever, from some God forsaken place and are finally here in the land of the lobster and the pine tree. You are famished and ready eat. You don't feel up to a whole pine tree, but you're more than ready for your first lobster. Where do you begin? My suggestion (and it is a strongly held suggestion) that you, you wuss, should take as a command, is that you, as a beginner, and an easily intimidated beginner, should begin at home, alone. This will allow you to experiment without being self-conscious and will avoid having other innocent bystanders harmed in the process, either emotionally or physically, should they become curious and sneak a peek. Besides, if you want to eat like a Mainer, you will be eating on the cheap because, as every Mainer knows, "you can't eat ambiance." You can have two lobsters or more for the price of a fancy sit down restaurant with picnic table, checked plastic tablecloth and everything. You want ambiance? Turn on the radio and sit in front of an aquarium. I want lobster.

You're in the local supermarket in Anytown, Maine (or a reasonable facsimile) and are ready to begin your culinary experience. You are standing, awestruck or dumbstruck as the case may be, in front of large tank of water the bottom of which is crawling with lobsters. Cool! Selecting your lobster is the first step. As I said, except for size, and therefore price, lobster all look the same. Now, you can't judge a book by its cover, but you can and should, judge a lobster by its shell. Lobsters come in two varieties: soft shell and hard shell. Soft shell is cheaper, although I hear that hard-shelled lobsters are better eating. As far as I know, that is just hearsay, a rumor. I have no experience with hard shell lobsters, so, I'd suggest you select the soft shell. You are, after all, just a beginner, not a connoisseur of cretin.

You'll note that hard or soft, lobsters are green not red (the blue ones are really expensive and outside of an aquarium you're not going to see one). These green lobsters are what we Mainers call "alive." When speaking of lobsters, red is dead. Maine once had a dead lobster on its license plate. That was just wrong. It was like Connecticut putting a majestic, breaching, rare Right Whale on its plate with a harpoon stuck in its head and blood spewing red, staining the pure blue sea. But I digress.

Back to the tank. You're standing there excited. This is like a visit to the aquarium only better; in Maine, it's free. Free is good. You're catching on. You're also ready to choose your lobster. I recommend spending some time getting to know your lobsters rather than just selecting them willy-nilly by saying, "I'll take two, please" and leaving it up to Chance or Lester or who ever might be waiting on you. No, get to know your lobsters personally. Watch them closely as they lie there, barely moving. You'll soon begin to pick up on their vibes and get a sense of just who they are. Somehow, their personalities will emerge and you'll strike a rapport here and there. Some you'll like, and some you won't. Focus on the latter despite your instinctive attraction to the other. Identify the couple of lobsters that you somehow just don't like at all, the ones that rub you the wrong way, the ones you're really beginning to detest. Tell the clerk you want those two over there, those ugly SOB's, those right there in the corner. Yeah, that one, and the one next to him. If no one's in the market but you and Chance, you may even want to yell out something like, "I got your sorry asses now, you bastards. You're gonna get what's coming to you, but good!" Or maybe not. I'll explain why in a moment.

You've broken out the Visa card and now you're driving home with two live, green, ugly, and obnoxious creatures whom you detest lying next to you in a brown paper bag. Please, resist the urge to open the sack and have a look. Lobsters are slippery. They are not fast, but they can move or at least fall off a front seat if you're not careful. They fit neatly under a gas pedal too, if you must know. Trust me on this one, unless of course you enjoy swapping strange and funny accident stories with police officers while you're waiting for a tow truck.

Okay, you took my advice and made it safely home where you're in the kitchen and raring to go. Get yourself a large pot, one that's plenty big enough for your twin lobsters and fill it half-full of water. Add some salt. Add some more. Remember, the lobsters have lived their entire existence in saltwater and they will need the salt in the pot if they are going to be happy lobsters. Happy lobsters are sweet, tender lobsters. Now light the stove, turn up the gas, and begin to boil that water.

While you're waiting for the water to boil (and stop taking the top off the pot, you idiot, it's only going to take that much longer), turn your attention back to the lobsters. It's safe—well, sort of safe—to open the bag and take a look now. There they are: two green, hard, soft-shelled, lobsters. Pretty cool looking, aren't they? Now, picking them by their bony backs, place them on the floor and let them roam about. Look at them, green, hard, clickity-clackity lobsters. Wicked awesome. Don't worry, there's no need to put a bell on them; they won't go far. If you have pets, call them in. See how the cats like to play with the lobsters. No? They don't play? They hiss and swat? They run and hide? What could they possibly be afraid of?

You notice the steam rising from the flopping lid of the pot. The water's boiling and you're really getting hungry. What's next, you ask? Nothing, nothing at all, except killing your two innocent, trusting little buddies by plunging them both head first into a cauldron of boiling liquid death until the very essence of life itself vaporizes and is removed via a fan, forced outside without any due respect or ceremony for what once was a living, almost breathing creature, spewed into the ether of the great outdoors!

Oh no! What's that you say? You can't do it? Right, we're civilized and civilized people don't like to murder what they're about to eat. We like to think we're above all that. We like to think we wouldn't eat something if we had to kill it ourselves. So we hire killers to do the deed, tear off their skin, or hairy coat, and chop up the victim until it no longer resembles whatever cute little animal it was that we like to put barbecue sauce or whatever on, and then we stuff our fat faces for all we're worth. We like our meat ensconced in a plastic tray, with plastic wrap clinging to the "product." It's neat, it's safe and antiseptic, and best of all, it's guilt free. Well, get over it. You're in Maine now. And in Maine, we get hungry and we kill our food or at least our lobsters. You want to eat like a gastronome? Well, get ready to murder like Al Capone. But how? How can you do it, you ask?

Here's how my friend, here's how. Take a good look at those two culprits lying there on the floor. Remember what it was that turned you away from them back in the store. Remember that of all the lobsters in that tank, these two somehow revolted you, angered you and made your skin crawl with hate. Sure, you didn't hit a tree because of them, since you had this book to warn you, but still, those two bastards have it coming to them. Still not sold? See those little rubber bands on the cute lobster's hands? Take those off and shake hands with the adorable little creatures. Go ahead, it's all right, make friends with your little buddies. Stick out your finger, that's right and ... " Son of a bitch ... that hurts! You're going in the pot you little #@&%^&#@! Die you $^&%&$, die! There! Now for your co-conspirator! Guilty by association! In you go and good riddance you freakin' $%^&(&##!"

Congratulations, you've done it. You're a hunter/killer now! Well, at least, sort of. Take a moment to collect your thoughts and catch your breath. Feeling a little ashamed of yourself? Feeling a twinge of remorse? Then take a long look at that throbbing finger you offered those two in a spirit of true friendship. What did it get you? "I hope they suffered," you mumble under your breath. So much for civilization eh?

In the future, realize that you won't have this personal enmity with every lobster you'll eat, so you'll have to figure out a means of quickly dispatching them humanely and without any unnecessary vitriol. I use a hammer. I smash their heads before plunging them into the boiling water. Some folks shoot them. Really. They go to the trouble of having a mock trial, convict them because, hey, look at them, they're guilty as all get out. They tie them up against a small wooden post, put on a little blindfold and place a cigarette in their bony little mouths. I think that's going a bit far, but hey, that's just me. I use a hammer. By the way, hanging just doesn't work for a number of reasons.

How long do you cook a lobster? Good question. I suggest you keep them boiling at least until they stop moving around and cursing. Wait 'til they've stopped and then give it another minute. The last thing you want is a vengeful lobster on the prowl. Total time for most folks is about five or ten minutes. Remember, lobsters, like chicken, are conveniently born with built-in timers telling you when they're done. On chickens, these pop up out of the breast. With a lobster it's easier (unless you're color blind); they simply turn red. Remember, when it comes to lobsters, red is dead and dead is always good when you're planning on eating something, so let's eat. But first, remove the lobsters from the pot ... with tongs, you fool! Remember the boiling water? Now your hand's bright red. Put it under some cold running water, or better yet, cover it with butter. Come to think of it, don't; don't do that. That's what you're going to do with the lobster and seeing that you're now ravenous, you don't want to mistake your hand for a claw. There, now that you've removed your colleagues from the pot and placed them on your plate, you're ready to begin. Take a look about and make sure you're alone, then set to.

Eating lobster correctly is like eating chicken correctly: it's messy if you do it right. In my humble opinion, if you don't make a mess and don't get your fingers in there, ripping and tearing about, you're missing out on half the experience and depending on your personality, if you're like me, you're missing the better half. It's as though lobsters and drumsticks have been scientifically designed by Charles Darwin himself. They're meant to be picked up and handled, so grab on. Oh, but wait, we've forgotten the infamous lobster bib! You know the one, with the bright red lobster on a sheet of flimsy plastic that blows in the wind, sticking onto your face, making a fool of you in front of all your friends. You're indoors and alone, but right, let's forget the bib. We're Mainers now. You're wearing your lobster-eating T-shirt, the one with grease stains from last week when you changed your oil before you went to the store to pick up your meal. Besides, you're alone and who's going to see you? Better yet, you're beginning to think and act like a Mainer and you just don't care one way or the other. Resume handling the beast.

The first step is to gently rip off the largest of the claws. See all that boiling hot water surging out onto your lap? I bet you're some kind of glad you're alone now, free to scream in agony to your heart's content. Didn't think you could hit that high a note, did you? Well, don't worry; it only burns for about five minutes or so. Lobster's revenge? Maybe. I like to think not. I like to think it's just genetics. Now grab your pooling plate and drain it into the sink while you're up and you've pretty much stopped hopping about. Now you see why Mainers don't eat lobster on stupid, flimsy paper plates. You're learning. You're learning the hard way, my way. You're going to have a lot of common sense by the time this meal's over. You're gonna learn not to wear pants with cuffs, either.

So, you're back in your chair, your (let's be kind) upper leg is now the same color as the lobster's shell and your still-throbbing hand. You're feeling better again, and taking satisfaction once more in having plunged those criminal crustaceans head first into their boiling fate. Thus, you resume your meal. You've got the crusher claw in your hand. You know, the one you "shook" with earlier. So, crush that sucker with the hammer. I recommend you use a hammer. I use a hammer. Restaurants don't supply hammers so I suggest you bring your own; ball-peens perform best by the way. Restaurants, being sophisticated by nature, will supply you with a clever, specially designed, nutcracker-like device. If you're a true Mainer, true to form, you're likely to use a plain nutcracker, or what works even better, a set of Craftsman offset pliers. One way or another, once the shell has been shattered, you put down your weapon of choice and like a dentist surveying his shiny, sterilized tools, select the sharp, pointed meat extractor you bought at the expensive culinary shop in the mall in preparation for this adventure. How much did that cost? A nail works just as well. A sixteen-penny nail, preferably galvanized. And they're cheap. Rusty ones hold onto the meat better if you don't use the galvanized ones, so save them. But enough about the picks.

You probe about the corpse and finally, you see something pinkish, and soft: that must be the lobster meat! You pluck it out of its womb or is it tomb, and plop it into your mouth. Ahhhh! Haaaa! "My God, that's hot!" You spit it out in agony and rush to the sink for relief. Lobster's revenge? Maybe. I'm beginning to suspect in your case it's genetics too. But not to worry, the pain will subside and eventually pass. Once again you're back at it, consuming now in earnest. You've located the luscious morsel of succulence you had spit out and just by fate, it landed by the melted butter dish that you had forgotten to dip it into. By the way, unless it's ninety degrees out, melted butter does not stay melted. Lobster eventually cools as well. Do you get the picture? I use a liquid butter spray because I'm lazy, but be careful where you aim; you might overshoot your intended target and hit another diner in the face. Then again, there's whole lot of fun to be had in that endeavor, as well. It's your choice.

Finally you have what you came here for: warm lobster, dripping with melted butter. You slowly raise it to your lips. You savor its aroma like a fine wine as you allow it to breathe. You drop it into your mouth and experience its texture as heavenly, and succulent flavors dance upon your taste buds. Delicious! You slowly swallow, allowing the meat to gently slide downwards and back with the assistance of gravity alone, and you ease back satisfied, sinking into your chair. You exhale through your nose and enjoy another fleeting reminder of what you've swallowed. That was worth everything: the journey, the pain, the guilt, everything. You could eat fifty of these babies, fifty. Well, Bucky, your baby has only got two of these claws, and you just ate the larger of them. Welcome to the wonderful world of lobster. Tempting? Yes. Enticing? Yes. Alluring? Yes. Satisfying and filling? Well, I wouldn't go that far.

You attack the smaller claw. Chicken lobsters only have one, like I said, but they're cheaper so if you're like me, there is no smaller claw or larger claw. There's just a claw. I hear that lobsters with two claws are very tasty and somewhat more satisfying. But then, you're from "away." You've got the Spudders, rich boy. You're rolling in Spudders. Your lobster probably has two claws, too. So, you devour the other, but guess what? Yes, the flavor was there, that intoxicating flavor, but you haven't begun to dent your hunger. You're still famished. Where to now?

All that's left is a red, submarine shaped "shelly" kind of thing. Aha! "To the tail!" Grab it and break it off. Meat! Lobster meat! Now just start tearing off the exoskeleton working towards the very end of the tail itself. You did it! It wasn't even all that difficult, but then again, you were driven with lust, lust and hunger. There, lying before you is at least one quarter of one half of sixteen ounces of the finest seafood Maine has to offer. Unadulterated Maine lobster tail! Good thing you splurged on the big boys, isn't it? You tear into your prize, devour it, inhale it, and are left staring at what remains. Nothing but what looks like a grisly red car wreck.

You're wrong of course, but you're new at this and you move onto the next victim, repeating the process except for the boiling water in lap routine you now manage to avoid. Been there, done that. That's what common sense is all about. You're learning. In another five minutes it's over and you're all done. Of course you're still hungry, but you're all done, regardless. You sit there in silence.

"Is that it?" You think you must have missed something and you're right.

You've had two lobsters, but you're not satiated and you want more. You're not in a restaurant, and you're not heading back to the market, so what the hell? You're alone. Let's experiment with what's left. What's left, aside from the shattered remains of that red car, looks like a rudimentary tank from WWI: a tank with ten legs instead of tracks. Legs! Ten legs! There's meat in them thar legs! Pull, crack, pick, and now, yes, you've heard of this, suck! Meat! There wasn't much. Maybe it was just flavored water, but it seems there was something in there. Pull, crack, pick, and suck nine more times. Now what? That was tasty, but you're still hungry. Rip some more and dig deeper. You'll discover that there's more meat around the base of those little legs, pull, crack and pick some more. You're getting the hang of it. You shake out your pants cuffs. What's this? This whitish, fibrous material? You pop it in your mouth and chew. That tastes just like lobster-flavored insulation doesn't it? Why, those my friend, are the gills and by the way, if you acquire a taste for these little treasures and are at a neighborhood lobster chow down, you are not going hungry any time soon. Good luck with that.

Well, that's it. That's all there is, or was, in the thorax section, except for this little oddly colored bit of what looks like edible soft tissue. You have located the "tamale." Good for you. Some people consider the tamale a delicacy; personally, I don't. Some people put shotguns in their mouths. I haven't for years. You want my tamale? You can have it. I'll toast your courage with another round of Moxie.

Now, that's really it. You're done. Your exploratory surgery is over. If you want, you can crack open the head and take a gander, but you won't find anything. It's not like lobsters are scholars, you know. There's precious little there, just enough brain to make them curious enough to wander into a lobster trap and as far as I'm concerned, that's all the brain they need. They do have those stalk-like eyes you can play with, and of course the antennae that make you look really funny when you hold them on your eyebrows, but that's about it. You are truly done. Fin! (As in "the end" not as in pretty good.) You did it and besides yourself and that evil pair of keratin creations, no one was harmed during the reading of this food channel, culinary epic, with the exception of your finger, your hand, and hopefully your thigh.

You push away from the table and peruse the remains. Your plate looks like two Iraqi insurgent, suicidal, bomb-toting, soft-shelled, off-on-a-Jihad terrorists just saw an opportunity to greet seventy virgins coming their way and opened the gate leading to their own personal stairway to heaven. You yourself are covered with bits and pieces of their remains: shell, butter, and salty water. But what's this? What's that smell, that odor emanating from your water-shriveled fingers? That? Oh, that's lobster smell, the odor of satisfaction well earned. Your hands and you exude the aroma of cold, damp, dead lobster. And they are going to smell like cold, damp, dead lobster for the next two days so you'd better get used to it. Don't waste your sweet time trying to wash the odor off. It's not going anywhere. I don't care if you soak your mitts in kerosene for an hour and light them, the charred remains will still stink of lobster. So save your money—kerosene is expensive these days—and wait it out. In the meantime, I suggest you partake of Aqua Velva, copious amounts of Aqua Velva.

As for the rest of the meal, well, there's not much to it. You have some French fries, coleslaw, rolls, and some corn on the cob and that's about it. Don't, and I mean don't with a capital DON'T, don't use those stupid, plastic, yellow, half corn cob things with the two pins sticking out that you bought when you bought the meat picks. Just don't use them. They are stupid, stupid, stupid! They have no place at the table when you're eating lobster. I mean, really, you're a mess aren't you? You've done it right, and like a true Mainer, you don't care what you look like. So what now? You don't want to soil your dainty little digits by actually touching corn? Yeah, right! Save the cob handles for your guests. That way you can have a good laugh at them while serving up your own authentic Down East extravaganza and at the same time, subtly make note of just how sophisticated you truly are in the colloquial manners of coastal Maine eating.

One last point; if you're going to order a lobster roll at McDonald's, I ask why? Just tell me why? I don't get it. Lobster salad on a hot dog roll? "This is really good! Tastes just like seafood salad, what with the mayonnaise and the celery, onions and all the seasonings. Only difference is that it costs ten times more than what I could make at home. Hey, I think I'll get another one. These fries are great too. I only wish I had some corn on the cob so I could use these yellow, plastic cob-holders I bought at the outlet store in Kittery. There goes that damn bib, blowing up in my face again. Down boy, down! Yessir, I wish I had some corn on the cob. Then I'd be eating like a real, authentic Mainer. Ayuh!" At least now you know better.

Bean Hole Suppers

Maine has a great history of eating beans. I think we inherited the habit from our colonial connections with "Bean Town," and it continues to this day. We especially love our baked beans. We even have a great baked bean producer located in Portland along the harbor-side in B&M Baked Beans. B&M have been baking beans in the old-fashioned way—hand-stirred in brick ovens—since 1867. If the wind's blowing inland, and you haven't eaten for some time, and you like baked beans, and you were thinking of food anyway, you find yourself drooling as you drive by on 295; they're that good. And here's an interesting factoid: few people know what the B and the M on the label stands for and if you don't know yourself, you still won't know when you're finished reading this. I wouldn't tell you, even if I knew, which I do. Look it up. Hint: it's on the can."

Now, Bush's Baked Beans are really tasty, too, but they are not made in Maine, or hand-stirred by real Mainers. Real Mainers eat only B&M Baked Beans, unless Bush's Baked Beans are on sale when it's then permissible to buy the cheaper brand provided that later, all things being equal again, you only purchase the B&M brand. Other brands are right out. You can't eat them and pretend to like baked beans. If you're going to eat these others, you might as well buy the ones with the little hot dogs inside as well. They're not real hot dogs either, but what the heck, we've already determined you're no connoisseur of beans, so go for it, you loser you.

Having said that, baked beans are a staple of life here in Vacationland. Every family has someone who has their own special recipe for making baked beans. Even if we open a can of B&M, we often "doctor it up" with fresh onion, bacon bits, green peppers, and so on. Hey, we're home, not in the army fighting the Kaiser and eating K rations. We can do this and so we do.

There is one special recipe, however, that tops them all, bar none, and that's the revered "Bean Hole Baked Bean." What does this mean? Well, it's subtle for sure, but if you read between the lines you can figure it out. Bean hole baked beans are beans baked in a hole. Clever, eh? What's a hole, you might ask? Well, think back to your early childhood years. Have you ever walked through a field, looking up at the sky, gazing into the clouds only to trip and fall full-faced onto a cow patty? You haven't? Well, aren't you the lucky one! I have. If you had too, you might have muttered something like, "Son of a freaking $^%))%# hole!" That, my friend, is the kind of hole we're talking about: a hole in the ground.

Here in Maine, we like to keep things simple. You know, fire, water, a pot, beans and a hole. That kind of simple. We don't like complicated recipes that require exotic ingredients. We don't want to go hungry for lack of marjoram or toasted coconut flakes. We like to eat every day. We don't mind if what we consume is simple as long as it's "a lot." But, we don't want to spend "a lot" of money either. We want our "a lot" cheap, and want it good. And we want "a lot" of it. For most Mainers, that means baked beans.

Now, the idea of a Bean Hole Supper is two-fold. It's usually a means to get people together raise money for something special, like when someone is sick and needs help with their medical bills. We could ask for donations, but that's not our way. We don't beg. We have to have a product to sell, a cheap product that allows us to make a hefty profit, but a good product nonetheless. Beans fit the bill all around. In winter, we do the same thing with spaghetti dinners. Similar idea, different product. Mainers get to eat some good food, socialize, and contribute to a worthy cause all in one swift move. Personally, I'm an anti-social animal and would gladly pay big bucks to avoid a community event such as a Bean Hole Supper, but I'm originally "from away," so what do you expect?

Now Bean Hole Suppers are traditionally located along a lake or a pond. Every Maine town has one of these. I think town lines were set up to ensure this. We all seem to have a town beach and it is there that the bean hole is dug. There are several reasons for this. First of all, it's a convenient gathering point. Then there's the open space. We don't want to dig a hole, build a fire and poten-tially burn down the town by baking beans in the woods. If we did that, we'd have to have more and more bean hole suppers to meet the needs of the victims of those fires. You can follow the logic of this and come to the same conclusion I did; Maine would end up being a smoldering shell of a state. I think the idea would work in New Hampshire, though, and I'm going to suggest it become law there. Being a state of rugged individualists, they should have the right to burn the place down if that's what they or we want, and to tell the truth, I for one wouldn't shed a tear.

The second reason is that if we had the Bean Hole Supper in town, we'd have to have it on community property and the only community property available would be the concrete sidewalk. Have you ever tried to dig a bean hole, or any hole for that matter, in a sidewalk? It's not easy if you can do it at all, and you're more than likely to simply end up with a fire and beans strewn all about where people are trying to walk to church or to visit one another. It just don't work.

That's why we dig our holes in the beach. A beach is made of sand, and being sand, it's easy digging. By the way, don't dig the hole too near the water's edge, however, as it's rather difficult to keep a fire going in standing water unless you live in Cleveland, Ohio. Dig a dry hole.

Okay, you've got your hole, now you need to gather your basic ingredients, which include a reason to raise money, a shovel, a pot you don't mind burning and burying, a copious amount of beans, some mustard, an onion or two, a hefty chunk of salt pork, ketchup, some wood, matches, and a lot of time (say a day or so). You've dug the hole half again as big as your pot so that's all to the good. Now, build a fire in the hole. Build up a good base of coals, up to two-thirds of the hole. Bring some hot dogs and beer to while away the time and make use of the fire while you're waiting for the coals to accumulate. Parboil the beans until you can blow on them and their skin wrinkles and resembles your late grandmother. If you drink as frequently as my grandfather and brush your tooth as infrequently, find someone else to do the blowing. His breath could wrinkle metamorphic rock, not to mention what it did to grandma. Once the beans are ready, dump in all the ingredients and cover them, adding water. Don't cover the beans with the pot lid and then add the water as you're going to reek havoc with the fire. Add the water, and then cover the pot with the lid. I shouldn't have to explain this, you know. Now, dig out the coals until you have about three inches on the bottom. Put the pot in the hole and cover it all around with the remaining coals. Again, be sure that the lid is secured on the pot before you fill the hole as this has a direct effect on the taste and edibility of the final product. Cover the pot and the coals with dirt and/or sand, making sure that no steam is escaping. That's it. You're all done, except for disposing of the rest of the beer. No sense having to lug heavy beer cans back to the truck, is there? Once you're soused, all you have to do is wait.

I like to put the beans in the ground as the sun sets in the west and then go home to cook them, adding a few more beers to the mix. I've found I wait best in a slight stupor, overnight, with my eyes closed. The next morning you shake off the stress of cooking all night and head out to check up on your bounty.

That's all there is to it. You're ready to dish it out and dish it out you will as folks will come from all around to partake of the scrumptious victuals. You add some coleslaw, a few biscuits, and plenty of coffee and everyone ends up happy and content (provided you restocked the beer). You've made some money, had a few beers, met some nice folk, filled your belly, and have done someone in need a good turn to boot. Job well done.

If you haven't participated in a bean hole supper, do it. If there's a roast pig involved all the better. The price may be a tad more, but it's well worth the extra jingle. As for me, I'll mail you the money from my recliner. As I said, my genes don't work this way. I'll sit to home and down the B&Ms, no maple flavor thank you very much, just passing the time and passing ... Did I mention the end result of eating beans? I like to eat my beans alone, and if my wife has anything to say about it, and she does, sleeping off the after-effects alone as well. But that's another story.

"Ka-Ching-Grala"

It goes without saying, that every right-minded person who wants to reside in Maine has a dream vocation, and that is to retire and own a Bed and Breakfast. Notice that I didn't say own and run a B&B, just retire and own a B&B. Notice also that the word "retire" comes first. This is important, so pay attention. You must understand the rationale, if it can be called that, behind the B&B phenomenon if you are to avoid the almost certain disaster that awaits you should you attempt to go there. Fortunately, I have done the legwork for you, so I'll walk you through this fantasy while helping you avoid the pitfalls of reality. Trust me, you'll be a better person for it.

Bed and Breakfasts are the wave of the future. They're the moneymaking dream you have literally been sleeping on your whole life. You just haven't awakened and smelled the coffee—until now, that is. You're up and about, alert, and on to the hunt. Perhaps your nose is a-twitching at the scent of easy money. You're about to "release the hounds" of self-enterprise. But heed my words and beware; sweet dreams can quickly turn into nasty nightmares if you're not careful. So, watch your step, and follow me.

Before we can proceed to the how-to, the nitty-gritty of B&B's, we have to examine closely the premise that I've stated. To that end, let us review the first sentence of this chapter in detail and dissect its true meaning.

On the surface, it appears to make perfect sense. "It goes without saying, that every right-minded person who wants to reside in Maine, has a dream vocation: that is to retire and own a Bed and Breakfast." A fairly straightforward declarative sentence you say. Wrong! "What's wrong?" you ask. Just about everything, that's what's wrong, I say.

First of all, "It goes without saying." Why do people say that? It makes no sense at all. If it did, you wouldn't be reading this now, would you? No. Therefore, the sentence should begin, "It needs to be stated that." There, I'm feeling a little better already.

Moving on, what's with "every right-minded person"? What does that mean? I suppose if you read on to the "wanting to retire and own a B&B" part, you might say to yourself, "Yeah, I've thought of that." I can only assume that you therefore include yourself among the "right-minded." Makes sense doesn't it? No, it doesn't, and I'll tell you why. It's really this simple. I too have thought of retiring and owning a Bed and Breakfast. I know me pretty darn well, perhaps too well. After all, I've lived with me almost all of my life, and I can assure you I am not to be included among the "right-minded." In fact, the truth is quite the opposite. Therefore, this segment of the sentence must be revised and should read, "It needs to be stated that every somewhat askew person who wants to reside in Maine." See how that's better? Now we're starting to get somewhere. But wait, there's more.

I can live with "dream," as in fantasy, but "vocation and retire" is where I sense an irritating rub against the grain, if you will, a grating sound on the chalkboard of my reason. The raised hairs on the back of my neck tell me something's not kosher.

So, my suspicions aroused, I dusted off the old, red Webster and looked up "vocation." It reads as follows: "a strong calling to a religious life." No, that's not it. "A strong impulse, or inclination to follow a particular activity." We're getting a tad closer. Finally, there it is: "A particular occupation, business, or profession." That's it, I'd say. But just to be certain, I looked up "occupation," as well. The definition read as follows: "A person's usual or principal work or job." Spot on! "Work or job," it is.

Referring back to our opening sentence we read: "Blah, blah, blah, dream work or job is to retire and." There it is again, the sound, the hair; something is painfully amiss. Let's look up "retire." The definition of retire is "To give up or withdraw from an occupation." Whoa, that's it right there. That's the problem. We have the culprit cornered at last. It's clear why the sentence simply makes no sense at all. Let's put what we've learned together and you'll see my point.

Summing up all we now know, the sentence should now read as follows: "It needs to be stated that every slightly askew person who is crazy enough to want to retire to Maine has a dream: that is to work at not working, at a job they don't have, or want, and owning a Bed and Breakfast is the perfect way to do it." Does that make any sense at all? Can you honestly say that you understand what this sentence means? Or do you finally agree that it doesn't make sense and that it doesn't mean anything and that we need to start over from the beginning? Well, you're wrong on all counts.

Our beginning premise now makes all the sense in the world and it clearly explains why B&B's continuously fail to succeed. Fail to succeed? Let's try again. It makes all the sense in the world and it clearly explains why B&B's continuously fail.

Get it through your thick skulls, people: You can't retire to run a Bed and Breakfast. You have to work at it. Owning and operating a B&B is a job. It is work. You have to work, and you have to make money. If you don't work at it and if you lose money, you will soon find yourselves "unretired" and working for real—perhaps making beds at someone else's bed and breakfast!

The simple reason B&B's fail is that people don't think their ideas through. The reason their so-called "train" of thought regarding B&B's often leads to derailment is simple. Theirs is a one-track train of thought. Theirs is a one-thought express train to disaster. Theirs is an engine fueled by visions of easy money and nothing more. They're chugging along, high-balling it down the tracks, oblivious to the pitfalls that lie ahead, around the curve. There is no one at the throttle. There's no striped, capped head hanging over the side, lantern in hand, peering through the darkness, watching for the crossing lights to flash their warning. Instead, if anything, they're asleep at the wheel. And if by chance they are startled and look behind, they'd see that there's no train there at all; no boxcars of planning, no flatbeds of sum totals and bottom lines, nothing, not even a caboose to find refuge in. Nothing. Is it any wonder that, statistically speaking, B&B train wrecks cause more personal harm each year among the retired than yo-yo or shuffleboard accidents? Check it out on the World Wide Web. Everything else is there, why not that?

As I stated earlier, I too have thought of my dream vocation of retiring and owning a Bed and Breakfast. But unlike the rest of you slackers out there, I have put some serious thought to the matter. I have come up with a business plan that can't fail, not even if I really do open a B&B. It's fool proof.

Now, most people who open a B&B are nice people, very nice people. They open a B&B because they like people. They like to meet new people. They see themselves as mingling with their guests, sharing good times and small talk in the kitchen and before the fireplace. It makes them happy to simply think of others enjoying their home as they themselves do. What could be better than finding one's own enjoyment in making others happy? In fact, these people are so nice that they even feel awkward having to charge their guests money for their stay. After all, don't they get almost as much out of the experience at their guests? What's not to like? Well, chew on this bitter pill, Pilgrim. What you've just read is a surefire recipe for failure. Swallow hard and read on, you just might learn something.

To be sure, you knew this all B&B chatter sounded too good to be true, and it is. It's just not based in reality. To be a success, you have to not only charge your guests for their stay if you're going to be a viable business, you have to gouge them deep and enjoy doing it. "The more it costs, the better the experience," both theirs and mine. That's my motto. In fact, if you're really good at it, I believe you can revel in the gouging of the guest with a twinkle in your eye and actually have them thanking you for the privilege of being gouged so royally. "If it costs this much, it must really be good!" That's what I yearn to hear them say. That's what I live for.

Now I'll admit, I have what many will see as an unfair advantage over the usual B&B owner. I don't particularly like people and I don't care if they know it, just so long as I end up with their money when they leave. I like to keep things simple; it works for me. In my mind, I have opened up my home to these cretins, it's my castle not theirs, and believe-you-me, their intrusion upon my lifestyle is going to cost them, and cost them dearly. To this end, I have thought my business plan through. My plan is vague and clear, complex and simple, viscous and endearing, subtle, yet obvious. A nick and nickel here, a cut and a quarter there, a penny for your thoughts, two cents for mine, I tell you what I'm feeling for only a dime. It's my heaven. It's your hell. Welcome to my Bed and Breakfast. Welcome to "Ka-Ching-Grala."

Was it the large, ornate, hand-carved, hand-painted and embossed wooden sign with the gilded gold lettering that drew your attention to the oh-so-catchy name of my beloved B&B? I thought as much. Tourists are such suckers for gold foil lettering. Go to the expense of a neon light and they'll ignore you, but a plain wooden plaque? No way they can pass that by. "Budweiser Beer" on Main Street, USA, flashing on and off in high octane, garish red rays guaranteed to penetrate two and a half centimeters into pure chromium steel? Didn't catch _my_ eye. What about yours? But what's that over there, hidden in the shadowed nuances of the alleyway? Is that a hand carved, gold lettered sign above a plain, unpainted wooden door? Is it whispering something subtle about a pale wheat lager offered within? This we need to investigate further. Boring Bud is a buck a big bottle, but this brew is a niftier, four-fifty a snifter, and bitter to boot! Lucky thing we saw that sign! Lucky indeed. Lucky for someone.

So here you come, slowly working your late model luxury car up the non-descript dirt road, so as not to raise the dust, looking at the ... well, the trees. Cresting the hill, you ease your foot off the accelerator and pause, gazing at the ... well, the trees. Realizing what you are seeing, having seen enough of the trees already, you catch your breath, taking in the expansive view, across the valley, beyond the fields, towards more ... well, trees. You're descending now, in measured steps of roadway, peeling the veneer of distance from the fruit of your journey and suddenly you are there. This is it. This is "Ka-Ching-Grala." Let the death by a thousand cuts begin.

The key to my little scheme of a successful B&B lies in its basic format. As in restaurants, there are many of these upon which to base your enterprise, but for our purposes, we'll narrow down the choices to three: 1) one price for an all inclusive meal (appetizer, main course, dessert, beverage), 2) the buffet format, and 3) the à la carte format.

The one price inclusive is reserved primarily for the upscale dining experience where price is not a factor, the kind of a place where they accept American Express only and don't take coupons. You know the type I'm talking about, the ones where the waitress refills your water glass by tipping her pitcher on its side, fancy-like, and where someone is always asking if every bite of food you stuff in your pie hole meets with your satisfaction. I'll get my own water, thank you, and for love of God let me eat in peace. Just go away and die.

These establishments are too fancy for me. They usually require reservations, sometimes even a jacket and tie, and include an appetizer and wine list. Well, first of all, I don't like to plan ahead for anything, so I sure as hell am not going to call ahead for a table at five o'clock. If the place is that crowded, I'll go somewhere else. And, I'm a "drop in as you are" guy, a spur of the moment creature of impulse. I don't travel about with a suit jacket handy, and I won't wear a tie or jacket (I own only one of each) outside a courtroom, your honor. Also, I don't like wine, especially old expensive wine. I'm a beer guy. I want it cheap and I want it fresh. And I don't go to places whose names I can't pronounce or understand, so if your restaurant has a fancy name like the Chez or the Maison Grande, I'm not going in. And finally, when I'm done eating, I'll go up to the cash register and pay myself. I'm not going to trust some guy or girl who can't hold a regular job with my credit card, even if you hand me one of those little book-like things. And what's with that tip line on the check? I'll give you a tip if I want to give you a tip. I've got the coins in my pocket and I can figure out for myself what five percent of ten dollars is. And finally, I want a toothpick, not a fancy little foil-wrapped mint. God, I hate those places. To summarize, high-class restaurants are a neighborhood in which I don't live. Option number one is off my list.

Now, option number two, buffets, are another story altogether. All you can eat for one low price I understand. This is a neighborhood I like to frequent. I don't need a navigation system or a GPS device, I know my way around a buffet table. Yes, indeed I do. I know its intricacies, its ins and outs. I know the logic behind it. I've studied the format for some time now and I feel I am quite proficient in my exercising my culinary approach. I understand what the owners are trying to do here. I know the logic behind the sneeze shield, and I know how to abuse it, for I am a Taurus, a bull, and a glutton.

The interesting thing about a buffet set-up is that most of these places offer an upscale approach as well. You can order the inclusive meal if you want, but you might as well ask for a party hat and sign to hang around your neck as well—something proclaiming yourself to be an idiot. You can get the same stuff and more at the buffet table and for less! What were you thinking, Wall Street boy? Fiduciary expertise be damned. You are a fool, son.

Now I hit the buffet like a general plans the siege of a city. This is going to take some time and it's not going to be pretty. If I'm to win, I've got to be focused, rational, and disciplined in my attack. The enemy is two-fold: my waistline and the restaurateur. I've got my gluttony and inherent cheapness going for me. The restaurant has training, guile and the food. It's a battle of wit and will, but I will not be defeated.

I love to eat and I love to shop, so I know what I want and I know how much it costs. I'm headed for the food I can't normally afford or better phrased, won't pay for. I beeline for the salmon, the shrimp, and the crab legs. I fill my plate, avoiding the French fries, the rice, and the macaroni. I attack, and I attack, relentless, again and again, plate after plate; roast beef, frog legs, and stuffed mushrooms. I charge on, chicken fingers to the left of me, salad to the right. I ignore them all and persevere. No bread, no Jell-O, no pudding for me. I'm on a mission. If I fail, everything I stand for fails with me. I will not fail, and I don't. I pay my tab, pick my teeth, and waddle out to the car. I won, but I have suffered mightily for the victory. Like a boa after gorging on a suckling pig, I am spent. I won't eat again, at least not for a few hours.

No, my friends, I know the buffet racket all too well to employ it as my own business enterprise model. Sure, not everyone was born in May, but there are many others out there like myself. I just know I would cry if ever I had to watch one of my ilk defile my business plan as I would if given half a chance. No, option number two is not an option for my B&B. For me, there is only one choice, and I will select it from the menu, thank you kindly: à la carte.

Yes, à la carte is the way for me. It makes sense to the consumer. The word itself is derived from a foreign language spoken by foreigners in a foreign place. It translates in the literal to mean "from the cart." It refers to the selecting off the cart or haberdasher's conveyance, only those specific items in which you wish to indulge. It's the perfect ruse to use in a Bed and Breakfast. My thinking is thus. In Option One, you charge a very high price but include everything. Now, no one I know is that stupid, or rich, so that's right out. In Option Two, you offer everything at a low price. Now *I'm* not that stupid or rich, thus Option Two is also out. That leaves me with Option Three, à la carte. The consumer buys only what he wishes to buy after paying a basic, menial fee. The consumer is thinking, this is good, I won't pay for what I don't use, this is fair and this is good. He or she is thinking, "I can do this." Yet the consumer is wrong, oh so wrong. He's coming off the street, usually on impulse. I'm lying in wait, prepared. This is no contest. I like this. This is *not* fair, but this *is* good.

As the long black car pulls into my driveway, I am awakened by the raspy, excited, chortling of what I like to think of as my flock of imperial peacocks or Guinea hens, but is in actuality, the insane, incessant barking of my stupid fifteen-year-old mutt, Moochie. I yell at her to shut up, but she's deaf. I know she's deaf, but I yell anyway. What can I say?

"What the hell is it now," I whine. "Not some damn youth league out collecting my hard-earned bottle money again, I hope," I yell to my wife as I put down my beer. "And if it's those damned Jehovah's Witnesses again, tell them to put their magazine in with the rest of the trash and hit the bricks. Maybe they think Sunday is on Saturday, but I don't. This is Sunday. This is my day of rest. The Red Sox are batting, for crying out loud. Jean! Help me out here."

She replies, "It looks like it's someone interested in the B&B! They've even got luggage with them. Get up."

"But I don't want to. I'm retired."

"George, this was *your* idea, remember? Besides, we need the money. Try to be nice."

"Money," I drone through my drool in a voice closely resembling that of Homer Simpson. "Money."

"Why, hello there. You must be tired. Come right in and take a seat. May I offer you something to drink? It's mighty hot out there and you've probably had a long drive," I say, my strained smile reflecting the artificiality of my words. "Where are you from?" I ask as I turn my back, not waiting for a reply as I walk into the house, assuming they will follow. I could not be more disinterested in these people if I were related to them. "Somewhere, something, so many hours, whatever ... And how many nights will you be staying with us? You there from where you come, with the nice car and all."

Our conversation is brief but to the point as I lie and sincerely assure our guests that we are more than happy to have them share our home. I next explain our pricing system, Ka-Ching-Grala-à-la-carte: "That will be twenty dollars

American for the night at the base rate. That includes your room. We offer a sauna for your health, a spa for your regenerative pleasures, and a fireplace for your evening's relaxation, ready at your disposal, and each for but a small, nominal fee. Don't use them, don't pay for them. We also have ponds, both vegetable and flower gardens, and balconies outside your room and overlooking the gardens. There are also bridges crossing the gurgling brook leading to a short walking trail out just beyond the tri-posted flagpole where flutter the American, State of Maine and Canadian colors."

They are stunned by the reasonable cost for the room. They speak to one another quietly off to the side and return, approaching with a genuine smile. They like the à la carte system, they say, and suggest that they might take us up on the use of the spa later that evening. They sign up for two nights, in fact. I take their credit card and punch it through. While waiting on the machine, the gentleman comments upon my speech, noting that I don't have the traditional Maine accent he has always heard so much about and was expecting. I explain that I'm not a native "Maine-ah" but I can put it on for him if he'd like; however, it'll cost him a nickel a word for my efforts. He laughs. I let the nickel he already owes slide though he doesn't know it. He's new to this. Handing back the American Express Platinum Card, I thank them and tell them that they are all set to enjoy their stay. And I remind them, "From now on, it's pay as you use, that's the ruse. You have the room, the rest is extra, but reasonably priced so you won't get perplexed-ah." They look a tad puzzled. I laugh and nod my head, encouraging them to join in the mirth.

They begin to chuckle along with me, and turning as they pick up their bags to head for their room, the gentleman, a kindly looking man in his late sixties, dressed in a dapper fashion and obviously quite sophisticated and experienced in travel, asks matter-of-factly, "Might I trouble you for a brochure, please?"

"Certainly," I reply. "No trouble at all. That will be fifty cents. Should I put it on your tab or would you rather pay now?" I lift up my shirt revealing the freshly oiled, push levered, chrome plated, coin dispenser I have fastened to my belt. He appears taken aback, as if stunned for a moment, and mumbles something about how these things are usually free. I remind him that true, such is usually the case, but then the base rate is inflated to reflect such incidental costs and after all I remind him, he is paying à la carte. He smiles and hands me a dollar. My waistline piggy bank spits out two quarters in change and I hand him the brochure.

"It'll make a nice souvenir," I venture with a smile in return. He forces a stiff smile himself and stuffs the brochure into his blazer pocket.

"And now if you'll kindly show us to our rooms, sir?" he asks.

"Certainly," I reply cheerfully. "That will be fifty cents and would you like me to take your bags for you and the missus?"

"Fifty cents?" he replies instantly. "For what, might I ask?"

"Fifty cents to show you to your room. It's a dollar a bag for the luggage,"

I respond.

"Are you crazy?" he asked in astonishment. I tap my coin holder indicating a dime for the response. He stops. "You want me to pay you a dime just to answer my question?" he says in utter disbelief. I tap my waist a second time and our eyes lock.

"It's just a dime."

He dejectedly shrugs his shoulders and nods his head in submission, "All right."

I answer, "Yes, I do. Yes I am. And, please follow me. That's seventy cents, plus two dollars for the bags. I'll put it on your tab with your permission," I say as I pick up the suitcases and head upstairs.

"What in blazes is all this," I hear from behind me.

"It's the Hall of Hockey," I answer, not looking back. "It's very interesting and reasonably priced at two dollars."

"Two dollars?"

"Yes, only two dollars, but it's good for the day and you can spend as much time looking as you want. Quite a bargain, really, if you think of it."

"Two dollars each?"

"Yes. Plus ten cents for each of the two questions I just answered, but don't trouble yourself now, I'll make a mental note of it and put it on your tab. With your permission, of course." I hear something I can't quite make out. "I'll take that for a yes. Enjoy."

I open the door to the main bedroom. The walls are painted a pastel green, and are hand-decorated in the quintessential French Canadian manner. There are stained glass light fixtures, paintings by noted impressionists, and subtle, traditional paraphernalia thoughtfully placed throughout. Our alternative bedroom is characterized by a more rustic décor highlighted by knotty pine and earthy tones. However, as these are sophisticated folk, there was no question as to which room was appropriately theirs.

With a sunny view to front of the grassy meadow and another of the garden and stream to the side, our guests seem rather pleasantly surprised at the cultured yet folksy ambiance surrounding them. And then it suddenly hits them like a burning Sirocco wind. They try to catch their breath. The day has been unusually hot for a Maine summer, and the room temperature must register a sweltering 95 degrees at the least. "My God, man," our new boarder stammers. "It's positively stultifying in here. I'm literally roasting." I place the baggage at the foot of the bed and point to the wall. There, positioned in the wall, sits an air conditioner. "Thank God," he says wiping his brow as he approaches quickly in desperation. "How do I turn it on?" he pleads. I watch his face lose expression as his eyes fix upon the apparatus and the reality of the situation sinks into his mind and pocket at the very same instant. A connection has been made. "A coin-operated air conditioner. I don't believe I've ever seen one of these," he says dryly.

"I've got two," I intone equally dryly. "I found them on the Internet. They operate with quarters, American money only. I have a ready supply should you need them. Feel free to ask."

"Free?" he queries expecting the worst. He's catching on.

"Well, that may have been a poor choice of words on my part," I reply. "It's practically free, just a nickel."

"Helps keep the base price down," we recite in unison. I'm smiling, while he whimpers to himself, a pained look etched upon his melting face. He stares at me in awkward, ensuing silence. I break the tension by extracting a quarter from my waistline and offer it in a gesture of appeasement and good will. "On the house, just to get you going," I say, as I drop the coin in the slot and the machine begins to whir in compliance as it stirs to life.

From across the room, his wife speaks up, staring at a brown stain under the pillowcase. "I think it's chocolate, or was," she offers. I nod my head in agreement. "Rochefort."

"Is that included in the price of the room?" her husband asks sarcastically.

"It was, until you felt the urge to ask," I reply equally sarcastically. The veins on his neck are protruding clearly, visibly throbbing with each pulse of his heart. He glares at me. "You think you're pretty smart, don't you?" I didn't rise to the bait and instead peered out the window. "You think because your guests are polite that you're going to somehow profit off their civility and humanity, don't you?" His temper is rising, making the room only all the more uncomfortable. "Talk may be cheap sir, but you can't put a price on it; not a nickel, not a dime!" he continues, his voice rising along with his temper. I make no reply and think to myself, "He's really getting it now."

"What makes you think you're so special?" he finally spits out at me with a roar, spittle lacing his lips. "What makes you think you're so special? Answer me, dammit," he finally shouts out in frustration.

"That last question was rhetorical wasn't it?" I ask in barely a whisper. "YES," he screams. "YES, IT WAS RHETORICAL!"

"Well then, there's no charge for that, is there?" I answer in as charming a manner as I can muster.

"GET OUT!"

That's how the afternoon begins. It gets better as the day wears on, at least from my perspective. Our guests, now accustomed, or resigned (whatever word you'd like to use, you get the idea) to our little game, cease their petty protestations. Quietly, and without question I must add with regret, they play along, trying to make the best of the situation. Though constantly disturbed by their seemingly ceaseless interruptions, I, for my part, answer their calls and facilitate the meeting of their needs without comment. For this, they thank me. I am doing my best, and with a cheery attitude, I must add. Like them, I too never once complain. I am a good host as my coin belt's metallic melody fills the pristine country air with its merry tune.

"Mr. Christie, we'd like to go out on the balcony; however, the door to the balcony appears to be locked."

"Yes, it is locked. You'll need the key." Ka-Ching!

"There are no chairs on the balcony upon which to sit and enjoy the view."

"Not a problem." Ka-Ching, Ka-Ching.

"I see you've decided to take a walk through the garden." Ka-Ching.

"Might I add that there's a rustic bridge crossing the stream just ahead, that leads to a short nature walk and eventually to another bridge further downstream, emptying you at last onto the meadow below? It's quite interesting and a calming little jaunt." Ka-Ching, Ka-Ching, Ka-Ching.

"Can you suggest a restaurant?" Ka-Ching.

"Would you light the fire?" Ka-Ching.

"We'd like to use the hot tub." Ka-Ching.

"It seems we can't find a towel to dry off with." Ka-Ching. (They decided to share.)

They are really good sports and I have to admit, are nearly able to turn the tables on me a time or two.

Looking back, I recall one instance as they sat on the sun porch enjoying their morning coffee. From the look on their satisfied faces, the vibrating and heated sofa was obviously worth the expense. They seemed pleased with their breakfasts, as well, especially so when I encouraged them to take the remainder of the orange juice container with them. After all, they paid for it. I noticed the lady was reading one of the many books on Maine we have available.

"Now wasn't the pleasure and information you derived from perusing that book on Maine Lingo worth the trivial charge?" I asked her.

"Yes, it was quite nice," she replied and looked towards her husband who had a strange glint in his eye. "And," she continued as he nodded his head, "I assume you'll be deducting a dime off our tab for my solicited response?" They're getting good, I thought, slightly taken aback myself. I've got to be careful here. But I quickly regained my composure. I'd done my homework. "It goes with saying," I began, "that I would have made the deduction, certainly, had you merely noted the exchange and not asked in turn for a response from me." The glint in the husband's eye was gone. "We'll call that one even," I added. "And," I said in encouragement, "you're getting better at this. Perhaps you'll decide to extend your stay." There was no reply.

As it happened, our valued guests decided not to extend their stay, and in point of fact, decided to leave a day early. I like to think they were tired from all the pleasures they had enjoying the many amenities of our facility here at Ka-Ching-Grala. Of course, they forfeited the monies already paid for their next night's stay, but in their minds, I think they feel like they got off on the cheap. They were right. Still, I liked them and am going to miss them, whoever they were.

We have an open room for the night if you're interested. Think you know the game? Willing to take a chance on matching wits with a frugal New Englandah? You're most welcome to try. Besides, the Red Sox are on the left coast this weekend and I'm up for a challenge.

If you do decide to drop in for the night, just try to remember that I'm not proud of myself when I play the game, but I can't resist its allure. Like an old, tired fighter who drags himself through the ropes for one more round, one more beating, the spirit is ingrained in me. I can't shake it and yes, I'm ashamed to admit it. I don't know why (perhaps we live just too close to the "Granite State") but there's a little bit of the heart and soul of New Hampshire in all of us New Englanders. And I, for one, have a big heart. Ka-Ching is much more than a mere motto; it's a way of life up here. It's not the way life should be, but sometimes it's the way it is. We'll be watching for you, and if you call ahead, for a nominal fee, we'll leave the lights on for you so you don't trip on your way in. I wouldn't want to have to call the doc in town. That's a toll call you know. See ya!

P.S. We really do have a B&B, or soon will. Check us out. We have beautiful gardens, a stream, balconies, and a hot tub. And one more thing: there's no charge to peruse the "Hall of Hockey." All I ask is that you don't agree with my wife and say that it's hideous. If you do, I'll yank your jersey over your head and expose your suspenders, no charge.

Don't Think and Drive

Maine has approximately 1,256,763 people. That's approximately. If the number were exact, I wouldn't have rounded off to the nearest ... Okay, that's the exact number of people, or was when I wrote this. Population figures are never exactly exact. They're always in flux and yet, almanacs and census figures give us exact, to the digit head counts even though in the time it takes to write them down, they've changed. Why bother in the first place to claim to be exact? Why not just admit it's an estimate? For instance, in Maine's case, I personally am acquainted with several persons who have died, others who were born, and a select few who by virtue of medical experiments have been spread about, so to speak, so I can vouch that the exact number of Mainers noted above is approximately a reasonably correct guess, more or less, give or take few. I can also vouch that while it is reasonably correct, it also beyond a shadow of a doubt most certainly wrong. But still, having made my point, that's not the point I want to make.

The point I want to make is that Maine's population number is also approximately exactly one half the number of people living, if we can use that word—or more accurately, existing—in Afghanistan. Actually, I've never been to Afghanistan, but I hope never to go. I have seen enough photographs of the country to say without any hesitation that I believe we Mainers outweigh those "Afghanistanies," en masse, so to speak, even though they may be twice our number. How can that be? The answer is, "It be by way of fat, my good man, that's how that be." What I'm saying is that Mainers tend to favor rotundity. In other words, Mainers are by and large, and I do mean large, fat. It's a heavy burden to bear, for sure, but it's true. If all of us Mainers were condensed and crammed into a giant soup can and labeled for nutritional content, calories from fat would be the largest number on the can, without question. We are that fat. Not all of us, of course, just the really fat ones among us.

On what do I base this fact of assumption you ask? Why on personal experience I answer, what else? Sure it's only anecdotal evidence, but if a fat person sat on *you* and broke *your* ribs, that's the kind of anecdotal evidence that's going to catch your attention. It sure caught mine. But don't take my word for it; check it out for yourself. Travel to Maine and you'll soon see that this fat thing I'm talking about is for real.

Let's say you're on your yearly pilgrimage to Maine and you spy your typical Maine family. You want proof of what you've seen, so you want to sneak a candid shot with your digital camera just to prove to your neighbors back home that you don't lie about everything. You're gonna quickly realize you can't take that photo without a wide-angle lens. You're also gonna discover that if you move back far enough to fit everyone in the picture, and I'm talking a family of three, maybe four tops, you also gonna have to spring for a telephoto lens to be able to distinguish just who is who and not, say, the '85 Buick they are all leaning on.

(By the way, I once owned a '73 Buick that was not only a wonderful backdrop for family photos (it didn't reflect light), but with the headlamps off and weighing over two tons (slightly more than our family) it made an excellent hunting vehicle as well. Running the roads in the dark, smashing deer into oblivion and the cellar freezer all in one fell swoop, while listening to a hockey game, and all the while dressed in hunter orange (we must be legal) is something you just have to experience to fully appreciate.)

So, how did Mainers get to be such a large part of the countryside, you ask? My research points to one simple dietary supplement, a dietary supplement that quickly became, for Maine folk, a basic food staple. In fact, this food staple supports the entire nutritional pyramid of the state: forgive me Coke fans, but it's PEPSI! Yes, Pepsi Cola, in the common can or the ubiquitous two-liter bottle containing thirty tablespoons or so of useless, but tasty, white sugar just packed with the calories you need to face another warm summer's eve or cold winter's day. It's thirst quenching and tasty, but over time, say a week or less, it will also make you fat and rot your teeth. Don't care, don't care, don't care. Why not? Because we're addicted to the stuff, that's why. Contrary to what Ross Perot said, that giant sucking sound you hear is not American jobs heading south to Mexico, but the last frantic seconds of pure lust as another Pepsi bites the dust and is sucked bone dry, its plastic or metal skin distorted into a shriveled, crumpled shell by another fat Mainer armed only with a straw and his or her addiction. And in the time it took you to read that last line, Maine just expanded another cubic foot by volume. By the way, don't fat people have the smoothest skin?

Don't be confused by Pepsi, though. In Maine, Pepsi doesn't count as a soda or a carbonated beverage. In Maine, Pepsi is considered as basically elemental as water. You know, as in your basic "air, land, and Pepsi." But don't blame us for our addiction. As Jesus said, "Forgive them Father, for they know not what they do and do and do." We just don't understand and here's proof positive. We actually wash down our diet pills with Pepsi. We brush our teeth with it and rinse our mouths with it. Hell, we boil our potatoes in the stuff. It's everywhere, but surprisingly, it's not the state drink of Maine. What is? Well there are two as far as I can tell, and which is yours depends upon your age.

If you're under eighteen, and yes the "legal" age to consume alcohol is twenty-one, the state drink is without a doubt Mountain Dew! No, don't believe what you read. It's not Moxie. Moxie is the Official State Drink. Mountain Dew is the *real* State Drink. "The Dew" is Pepsi with an edge and it's now dyed in both green and red so you can celebrate Christmas all year long (and we all know how us Mainers love our Christmas and holiday season). But no matter what the color, Mountain Dew is some kind of serious soda. It packs the same wallop the kids are looking for in the slightly-harder-to-get Crystal Meth or Oxycontin you hear so much about. Imagine, "Mountain Dew: it has all the sugar your parents' Pepsi has, with a hell of a lot more caffeine to boot." Now you cannot only pack on the pounds just like mom and dad, but you get a rush as well! All this, while your eyes dilate along with your waistline and your pupils spread as dark and wide as your big fat ass. A sugar high and a caffeine rush—is there anything better?

Well, yes, yes there is. That is, if you're over eighteen, and by that I mean twenty-one. And what can this wonder drink of the older generation be? Is it a health drink? In Maine? Are you kidding? Is it a fine wine? Again, I ask you, in Maine? Are you kidding? Is it Maine's much publicized and lauded spring water or its wholesome, organic milk? Now I know you're kidding.

No, it's none of the above. You're not even close. No sir, the preferred drink of ninety-two percent of all true Mainers is none other than ... Old Milwaukee or more specifically, Old Milwaukee Light! (I determined the accuracy of the number myself, observing sales at our local variety store. The variety comes from your choice between regular and light.) Oh sure, we have our Shipyard Brewery, our Sea Dog, and our Carrabassett brands, but those are primarily for sophisticated consumers from away or those locals of us taking a "cation." Those "from away" include recent immigrants like myself who came to live in Maine, only thirty or thirty-five years ago or more, but are not yet considered "true Mainers." We've left our houses in the lower 47; we just haven't arrived home in Maine, so to speak. That doesn't officially happen until you're dead for a good ten years. But getting back to drinking, for day-in and lights-out consumption, Old Milwaukee Light is the only choice for the discriminating native Maine consumer.

Now, you can imbibe a Red Rust Twin Sail Ale while your spouse sips a Chateaubriande (that's a wine isn't it?) as you witness the sunset on beautiful Penobscot Bay if you want, but for that long ride home in the old Ford F150 after a hard day's work there's nothing better than slamming back a six-pack or two of Old Milwaukee to settle your nerves and help you transition into that mellow stupor that you've passed off as your personality. If you don't believe me, try it yourself. Stop off at your own local quickie stop. No, don't think of that hamburg pizza or that hoagie there in the tin foil, those will have to wait for "suppah." Head straight to the cooler and latch onto that classy red or blue carton. Or gather up those singles, left no doubt by those less fortunate than you, those who couldn't afford to fork over all of five bucks for a whole twelve-pack.

Now you're set to go; after all, you've got a "twelvah" or there about setting on your lap. Take a quick scan; no blue-lighted bastards in sight? No. Grab ahold of a cold one, pop back the tab and let her breathe for, oh, I'd suggest you give it a good three seconds, and then suck her dry. Now smash that can on your forehead. There, wasn't that refreshing? What? Didn't taste like much and your head feels a bit "achish"? Well there's more where that baby came from and miles to go before you pull in the dooryard. But be careful, though. You're driving, remember? Take the precaution to line up the center of the steering wheel with the space between the two yellow lines and you're pretty much good to go. And remember this too, for God's sake, don't talk on your cell while you're driving, that can be hazardous. Those electromagnetic waves can wreak havoc on what remains of your brain cell. In fact, why don't you do what I do: don't even think, just drive. Somehow or other I always end up somewhere.

P.S. (Closed course with expert driver.) Do not attempt the above. The author in no way, shape or form endorses the above-detailed behaviors. Driving and drinking is against the law. Drinking Old Milwaukee Light should be against the law in and of itself. This depiction is purely for entertainment purposes only and should not be attempted by any living soul either living or dead. Any resemblance to any person either living or dead or both as in "The Living Zombies of Milo," is purely coincidental.

Postlogue, or Post Log, or Log Post

Well, that's it, that's my book on Maine. I hope you enjoyed reading it half as much as I enjoyed writing it. I like to see other people suffer too. And speaking of suffering, why don't you drop me a line? I'd love to hear from you. Yeah, right. As for the book, it's all true, like I told you in the beginning. It's all true except for the facts, or at least some of them. The facts, or at least some of them, have been changed to protect the innocent, namely me. I am not liable for what I have written. I take medication. Besides, you can't sue me. Please don't sue me.

As for Maine and where I found all these facts, well, they're everywhere (not Maine, that is, but the facts). Maine is found only in Maine, you idiot. The facts are mostly on the Internet. You can find them too. Just "Google" it, whatever it is that you're interested in learning more about. You'll be amazed at what you will discover. I could have done all the work for you, of course, and listed all the web sites, but hey, that's work, right? Why should I work for you? I don't even know you. I don't even want to know you. You want to find out more about Maine, go for it, and be my guest. Check it out on the Internet like I said. It's all there and what isn't, well, take my lead and make it up. It worked for me, so it might just work for you too.

One last item for your information: I found that I have enough material for another book, so watch out. The next one is going to be chock full of even more facts than this one was. Some of those facts will be true facts, too. Some of them, but certainly not all of them. Not all of them, by any means, but most of them. Actually, not most of them but a few of them, a damn few of them. Okay, they're lies, all lies. It's all a lie. I'm a liar and a fraud. I admit it. I admit it and yes, yes, I'm proud of it. I don't care what you think of me. Whatever you think of me it's more than I think of myself. You can't think any less of me than I do. It's not possible. I think so little of myself that I don't even think of myself. How's that? Top that! You can't. I don't even think of myself so I can't even write about myself, I can't. See? And that's a fact.

The End

About the Author

George D. Christie is an curmudgeonly, aging reprobate who hides away in a cedar shingled hole he cobbled together with his own hands when he was young and naive enough to think he could build his family a home and a life in the western mountains of Maine. (Lip readers take a deep breath.) Of course he was wrong on both counts, but the house is still standing after all these years, so what are you going to do? It is what it is. What it isnt' is the proverbial large white mansion on the top of a mountain overlooking town. That is what it's not. On the contrary, it's a smallish, brown hovel at the bottom of a hill and there is no real town to speak of. Needless to say, it's on a dusty, dead end, dirt road as well. It's all too appropriate and as it should be.

Be that as it may, he passes time there with his wife Jean, black lab Diesel and three despised cats, all of whom are available for the asking. The last is purposefully misleading, but then again, make an offer. Anything's possible. After all, he managed to scribble what passes for a book didn't he? Maybe not, but either way, what you've read is the result of too much time, and not enough thought; the stuff of his life. Now, it's been rumored that idle time is the devil's playground. You've read his book: you've seen the proof of that statment. You've gone for a romp and took a gander at what passes for literature these days. It wasn't a pretty sight was it? Well, neither is he, but like his hovel, it's reflective of the man he pretends to be.

And last, but least, be forewarned; he's retiring soon. His hands will be filled with nothing but idle time to play with and no doubt there will be hell to pay as a result. Scuttlebutt has it that he's contemplating at least two more insults to the reading public tentatively entitled "Back With a Vengeance." and "Making the Bisque of a Bad Situation."

It sad isn't it? Let's just hope it's not true.